the

WITCH

of

WILLOW

HALL

the

WITCH

of

WILLOW

HALL

HESTER FOX

GRAYDON
HOUSE

GRAYDON HOUSE

ISBN-13: 978-1-525-83301-4

Recycling programs
for this product may
not exist in your area.

The Witch of Willow Hall

BookClubbish.com
GraydonHouseBooks.com

Printed in U.S.A.

For Donna

(and Roland, too)

Not lost, but gone before.

the

WITCH

of

WILLOW

HALL

❧ *1* ❧

1811

IT WAS THE Bishop boy who started it all.

He lived one house over, with his snub nose and dusting of freckles, and had a fondness for pelting stones at passing carriages. We were the same age and might have been friends, but he showed no interest in books, exploring the marshy fens of Boston, or taking paper kites to the Commons—unless of course it was the rare occasion of a public hanging. Catherine would sit in the window, watching him flee from angry coachmen, shaking her head. "That Bishop boy," she would say. "It's a wonder his pa doesn't put a belt to him, the vicious little imp."

I'd follow her gaze from the safety of the drapes, ducking back if I thought he might catch me looking at him. In my small, sheltered world the Bishop boy came to symbolize the murky edge of a larger evil of which I had no understanding. When Father lamented British aggression toward American ships, I imagined a fleet of freckled boys with sandy hair, identical in their blue coats as they drew their swords in unison. If there was news of a killer in the city, then he took on a slight frame, a shadowy figure with a snub nose protruding from his hood. The Bishop boy lurked around every dark corner, responsible for every terrible thing in the world that my young mind could not comprehend.

One day, Father—this was before he had made his fortune and he was still our "Pa"—found a little black cat under the steps at his office, and brought it home as a pet for Catherine and me with the stipulation that it wouldn't come in the house. Catherine said she was too old to play nursemaid to a kitten, though sometimes when she thought I wasn't looking I saw her sneak out to the stable with a bit of bread soaked in milk. This was before our little sister, Emeline, came along, so I was hungry for a companion, as Catherine and our brother, Charles, were practically joined at the hip. Every morning as soon as I could be excused from the breakfast table, I would rush out to the stable with a precariously balanced saucer of milk and a tattered hair ribbon that I had appropriated as an amusement for the cat.

It must have been spring, because I remember the heady scent of wet earth and lilacs as I emerged from the house into the garden, my heart light and happy to be free. To this day I can't smell lilac without a pit hardening in my stomach. And it must have been a Thursday, because Mrs. Tucker who came on that day to teach us French was there; I remember later the way her severe black eyebrows shot upward, her thin lips that never did anything except press into a tight frown, thrown open forming a perfect O, emitting that awful scream.

So it was a Thursday in spring. Usually Bartholomew—I thought myself very clever for this name until Catherine pointed out that Bartholomew was, in fact, a she—squeaked in greeting before I even got to the straw-filled crate that Mother had made for her. The only sounds that greeted me that day were the gossiping swallows and soft whickering of the horses. I slowed my step, not wanting to wake Bartholomew if she was sleeping. I rounded the corner to the empty stall and peeked over into the crate.

I think I knew what I would find there before I even saw it. There was something heavy and terrible about the silence, a disturbance in the air, quivering with secrets. I shouldn't have been surprised when I saw the blood-flecked straw. Something pure and loving made base, a pile of inert organs and tufts of black fur.

I don't know how long I stood there, unable to comprehend what lay in front of me, and after this it gets hazy.

I found myself outside, storming into the street with pounding ears and a film of red behind my eyes. It's funny, because for all the racing of my heart and the tightness of my throat, I have the recollection that I was remarkably calm. I had a sense of purpose, of what needed to be done. But for all that, I still didn't know how I was going to do it.

The Bishop boy was there. He blinked when he saw me coming, the slow, lazy blink of someone who either doesn't know what they've done, or else doesn't care. Why, he didn't even try to hide the fact that there was fur on his cuffs, that his brown shoe was damp with splattered blood. He just gave me that infuriating blink and then turned back to the stash of pebbles he was collecting.

There must have been at least a dozen people gathered around on the cobblestones by the time Tommy Bishop lay whimpering and crying out for his mother. That was when I came back to myself, when I realized just how many eyes were on me and what I had done. From somewhere behind the crowd Mother was calling to be let through, elbowing her way past a fainted Mrs. Tucker and snatching me up before a mob could form.

More than anything else I was frightened of what would happen to me. Would she tell Father? Would I be sent away? Catherine had told me that bad children were often sent to Australia, a desert land where they were forced to build their own prisons out of sunbaked mud bricks. The only food was rats roasted on spits, and there wasn't a book on the whole island.

Mother installed me on a bench in the garden and I drew my knees up to my chest, willing myself to disappear. A tear welled up as I thought about the little body in the stable. Would they at least let me give her a proper burial before shipping me off to Australia? I hastily wiped the tear away and braced myself for my sentencing.

But it never came. Mother took my hand in her own, her soft brown eyes studying my face, the lines around her mouth tight with worry.

"So," she said at last, "that answers that."

I had no idea what the question was, or even what exactly had been resolved, but something in her tone told me I wasn't going to be punished, and in my young mind that was all that really mattered.

She went on to tell me that I must never speak of what happened in the street again. If anyone were to ask about it, we would say only that it was a scuffle. Children get into scrapes all the time and sometimes they get out of hand.

"And Lydia," she added before I could dart away back to the stable, "you must never show the world what it is that you have inside of you."

So I carry it like a little locket, tucked deep down beneath my breast, never taking it out to open, but knowing that it will always be there should I choose to peep inside. We would never speak of it again after that day, but Mother made it clear that should it come bubbling out of me again, that we could find ourselves turned out of our home, or worse.

No, I never considered that we might be turned out for other reasons, and certainly not for the rumors that surround us now—which are just that: rumors.

2

1821

"IT MIGHT AS well be the edge of the world," Catherine says with disgust. "As if being banished weren't humiliation enough." She huffs and throws herself back against the padded carriage seat.

Mother assures us that it is neither banishment, nor the edge of the world, and that if it hadn't been for the horse that went lame outside Concord it would be a three-day journey from Boston. It might only be a matter of a few days, but as our new house looms into view, all I can think of is how isolated it is, how utterly cut adrift we are from everything familiar. No more rows of neat brick houses, no more cobblestone roads filled with the traffic of a bustling city, no more safe and sheltered existence.

"You'll be real country girls now." Mother follows my gaze out the carriage window to the jutting silhouette of our new home. Ever since that spring day ten years ago, there's been a pooling of sadness behind Mother's dark eyes, a heaviness to her once pretty face that has only worsened with the events of the recent months. "There's a ballroom on the third floor, and we'll hold parties and dinners. You'll be surrounded by fresh air and good, simple people." Desperation tinges her words, and Emeline stirs in my lap, looking up at me to confirm that this is something good, something that we sought out rather than were forced into. I force a thin smile for her sake.

"A ballroom?" Catherine perks up a little, craning her head to get a better look as the carriage lurches up the drive.

Willow Hall is fine, I will give Father that. Three stories of pristine white clapboard, and windows flanked with crisp green shutters. A carriage house abuts it on one side, a barn on the other. It stands in defiant contrast to the forested, sloping hill behind it. I try to imagine the windows glowing yellow in welcome, a stream of merry visitors jostling and laughing their way up the winding drive and I fail. It may be a handsome house, but this place will never be home. Yet at the same time I want to untether my heart, toss it up into the sky and let it take wing. There's a wildness here that, if nothing else, holds promise, possibility. Who needs society? What has it ever done for us?

A cloud passes over Catherine's face and she must be thinking the same thing, though for different reasons. She slides the little curtain closed. "There won't be any parties though, will there? No one will come. Fifty miles from Boston is still too close. We could be in Egypt and still it would be too close. We should have at least gone to London," she says with a wistful sigh. "If we were going to run out of town with our tail between our legs we might have at least gone there."

Everything is London with her these days, a faraway Mecca or Xanadu where the world is bright and polished, gleaming with possibilities.

Mother doesn't say anything, just wipes at her perspiring

brow and twists the handkerchief through her hands over and over. Her ideas for painting our situation in a rosy light ended with the balls, and now she has given up. Poor Mother, who has sacrificed her prized garden and the house she called home for near on two decades. Catherine, Emeline and I are young and adaptable, but she is like an uprooted oak, and I fear she will wither and fade. And Charles...well, I'm sure Charles is fine, wherever he is.

It's nearly dusk when the carriage comes to a stop. Apricot and coral streak the country sky, and fireflies flit across the broad lawn, blinking at us from the surrounding trees. My neck prickles under the scrutiny of a thousand eyes.

Emeline is the first to alight, throwing the door open before Joe even has a chance to come around. She's running ahead, up to the imposing white house. I follow her, slowly, stretching my aching back and wiping the sweat from my lip.

We put our feet on the hard ground, take in the night air and look around as if this whole place has sprung up for us and us alone. Not just the house, but the ancient trees, the watching insects, the stars and even the moon. But they have all lived without us for lifetimes that make our own look like the blink of the eye. The house, with its strict walls and severe lines, is shamefully out of place, something modern dropped down somewhere as soft as feathers, as twisty and spreading as willow roots. How do the trees and the insects and the stars and the moon like it, I wonder? How do they like to have to share their secret lives with us now?

Catherine unfolds herself, complaining of a headache. It was fatigue earlier in the day, and before that nausea. She calls out to Emeline to slow down, but Emeline is already running around the side of the house, free as a colt feeling grass under its hooves for the first time, her little spaniel Snip chasing at her heels. I haven't seen her so happy and carefree for months. Mother gives directions for the trunks to be unloaded and brought in, then sweeps up to where Catherine and I are standing. She catches Catherine's grimace.

"Our nearest neighbor isn't for some distance and she won't bother anyone." All the same Mother yells after Emeline to mind her dress.

Catherine grumbles something, and then picks up her skirts and stalks off to the front door where Father has finally emerged. He stands aside as the trunks are loaded in, and gives Mother a cursory peck on the cheek in greeting. When Catherine passes he affords her a chilly "Hello," and then looks away.

"How lucky for us that your father had this house built as a summer home," Mother had said last month when it became clear that the rumors were not going to abate, that Father was not going to be able to continue with his business in Boston anymore.

Luck doesn't have much to do with our new circumstances, but it calmed her to speak of it in such terms. Father had come out to New Oldbury the week before to meet with his new business partner here and tour the mill in which he was investing. It was a mercy that he was able to furnish the house and make it all ready for Mother; I don't think her nerves could have taken the prospect of starting over in an empty house.

Once the trunks are all inside, Father bids us good-night and disappears back into his study, leaving us to explore our new home.

"New Oldbury," Catherine says with a grimace. "Whoever heard of such a ridiculous name?" She's inspecting the rooms, running a gloved finger over the white mantel in the parlor. The house is more opulent, grander than I ever could have imagined. There's even a room for the sole purpose of dining. It's papered in a panoramic scene of people enjoying a French garden, some in boats drifting past marble ruins, others lounging on grassy banks with parasols and baskets. I imagine myself slipping into that static glimpse of paradise. Could I row the little boat out past the horizon? Or would I find that the world ends where the artist's brush had painted a thin blue line?

Everything is the best, the newest. Father has spared no expense, and yet my heart only drops deeper as I wander through each room. All the silk drapes and woodblock wallpaper in the world can't mask the fact that we're here as outcasts. All this wealth, and to what purpose?

I move to the library. A stern ancestor of Mother's on the Hale side glowers down at the finery from beneath her starched white cap. When I was little Catherine told me that the woman was hanged as a witch in Salem, and tried to frighten me by saying the eyes of the painting could see everything I did. I was never scared of the woman herself, but of her fate. Her face, to me, always held more of a grim warning than anger. "Do not make the mistakes I made," she seemed to say. What those mistakes were, I have no idea. To this day I can't pass under her portrait without a shiver running down my spine.

Mother hardly notices the decorations and furnishings, and bids us good-night and retreats to find her bedchamber. Dark rings hang under her eyes and her color is poor. It's hardly surprising; the house is stifling in the July heat. Father hasn't aired the rooms and it feels as though the gray, paneled wallpaper and golden drapes are closing in on me. I'm just about to step outside for some air when Emeline comes bounding back in, cheeks flushed, Snip bouncing at her side.

"There's a tiny house up the hill behind the house! It doesn't have any walls but there are benches and a little steeple. And a pond! Lydia," she says, taking my hand in hers, "a *pond*. Do you think there's mermaids in it? Can we go back and look for them?"

I've been reading to her from a book of poems, and one of them mentioned the mythical creatures. All she can think about since then is finding a mermaid and then no doubt exhausting it with a list of questions about life beneath the water.

"Why don't we take a look tomorrow in the daylight? It must be well past your bedtime now. Let's find your trunk and get you into bed."

Catherine has thrown herself down onto one of the plush, upholstered chairs, her hand resting on her stomach. "Let Ada do it, that's what she's for."

Emeline is on the floor playing with Snip, the mermaids apparently forgotten already. I lower my voice so that she can't hear. "Do you have to be so harsh? Everything she ever knew was in Boston. I can make it easier by tending to her myself."

Catherine rolls her eyes. "Oh, please. It's a grand house in the country, she'll be fine. Soon she'll completely forget what it was like to live in the city anyway."

A headache is coming on, and perspiration drips down my neck. All I want to do is get out of my dress and into a bed with cool, clean sheets, not argue with impossible Catherine. But I can't help myself. "So you'll be happy here then? In your grand house in the country?"

She bristles. "Boston was becoming tiresome. I—"

"It was tiresome because of the situation *you* put us in," I snap.

There's a tug at my skirt, Emeline is staring up at me. Catherine presses her lips and looks away. I sigh. "I'm taking her to bed. Good night, Catherine."

Catherine nods, her shoulders slumping forward. She looks so tired, and for a moment I almost feel sorry for her. But then I remember why we're here in the first place, and my sympathy evaporates.

★ ★ ★

The eerie stillness of this new place makes falling asleep almost impossible. I don't know how long I lay in my new bed, my body tensed, flinching at every faraway hoot of an owl that punctuates the night like a gunshot. It feels like hours later when the owl finally grows weary of its endless mourning and takes wing. My eyes are just starting to grow heavy when a terrible sound cuts through the silence.

Sitting bolt upright, I hold my breath as it comes again. It's a slow moan, a keening wail. The sound is so wretched that it's the culmination of every lost soul and groan of cold wind that has ever swept the earth.

My blood goes cold despite the stifling heat. I don't know where my parents' bedchamber is, and although the wail comes again and sounds as if it were in every plank of wood and every pane of glass, it must be Mother. She hasn't cried like this since Charles left, but the stress of the move must have taken its toll. I slump back into my pillows, guilty that I can't gather the strength to go to Mother and comfort her.

Kicking off the sticky sheets, I lie back down and close my eyes, trying to block out the awful noise. At last the wail builds and crescendos, trailing off into nothing more than an echoing sob.

The first dim light of morning is breaking when I finally drift off to a fitful sleep, unsure that the cries were anything more than a dream.

3

FATHER IS OUT on business, so it's just Catherine, Emeline, Mother and me around the breakfast table the next morning. Some of the color has returned to Mother's face, and she's smiling as she butters her toast, listening to Emeline chatter on about the pond and all the merpeople that are just waiting to make her acquaintance. Perhaps Mother's crying last night was what she needed, a cathartic release of all the stress and sadness that has led up to this move. Catherine is looking less well, her face pale and drawn as she sips her tea. I'm sure I don't look much better after my waking night.

I give Emeline's head a light pat before slipping into my seat and reaching for the teapot.

"...and Lydia is going to take me to the pond today so I'll probably be late for dinner if the mermaids are out and we get to talking," Emeline finishes triumphantly.

Before I can tell her that it looks like rain, Ada inches her way to the table, clutching a letter in her trembling hands. I catch Mother's eye. We used to have a bustling household that included five servants, a cook, a gardener, a host of rotating tutors, and drawing, painting, and dancing instructors. It was hard enough to hold on to the tutors before, but then the rumors started and one by one they all resigned. Now, we only have Joe and Ada, and I have taken Emeline's education into my own hands.

"Ada, what do you have there?" Mother puts down her napkin and holds out her hand for the letter.

Ada is a slip of a thing, and her perpetual nervousness has only intensified since all the trouble began. Only a couple of years older than me, she's been with us since I was Emeline's age, and sometimes feels more like a sister than a servant. She hesitates before surrendering the envelope. "Letter from Mr. Charles, ma'am."

Catherine's knife clatters to her plate.

Mother's face freezes, and she drops her hand like a lead weight. She gives a little sniff, and turns away, folding and smoothing her napkin over and over. This has been Mother's way of dealing with everything lately; if she pretends there's no problem then it simply doesn't exist.

"Give it to me," Catherine whispers.

Mother gives Ada a tight nod, and Ada slowly extends the envelope; she jumps as Catherine snatches it and runs back up to her bedchamber.

Emeline narrows her eyes. "Charlie did a bad thing," she says.

Mother doesn't say anything, but begins peeling an orange as if it's responsible for all our family's woes, juice squirting onto the tablecloth. I will her to explain everything to Emeline, to take some control. Her head is bent low, fingers digging into the pulpy flesh. I wait. But as usual she says nothing.

"Charlie didn't do anything bad," I say. "Those stories weren't true. Look." I point out the window at the gathering clouds. "It might not be the best day for the pond, but we

could take the carriage into town and take a peek at the shops."
What kind of shops there are in a little village like New Oldbury I have no idea, but I want to get out of the house. We've
been here only a day, but it already feels too full of ghosts of
a happy family that might have been.

The town center proves to be that in name only. A run-
down dry goods store with peeling letters advertises coffee,
and a little white church sits at one end of the town green.
That's it. No theaters, no gardens and, worse yet, no bookshops. Yet there's something charming about the simplicity
of the square and the dirt roads that wind up and around it;
there's no stink of fish wafting off nearby docks, nor cobblestones caked with horse droppings. I take a deep breath and
smile encouragingly to Emeline. Here's our fresh start, not in
the suffocating walls of Willow Hall with all its pretensions,
but in the blue sky above it, the little town surrounding it.

It doesn't take long for our fresh start to lose its rosy glow.

Two middle-aged women walk arm in arm, stopping to
watch us unload from the carriage, Snip nipping at our dresses.
They share a whispered word or two, and then creep a little
closer to get a better look.

The first woman lowers her voice and leans in toward her
companion. "Those are the Montrose girls, you know. The
family just came from Boston."

"Oh?" The other throws a glance back at us over her shoulder, greedily drinking us in. She remarks that Catherine is a
true beauty with her auburn hair and green cat eyes. "Wasn't
there some unpleasantness, some scandal involving her?"

The first woman puffs at the chance to explain, to be the
one who knows all the sordid details. "Well," she says, "the
whole business makes my stomach turn, I can hardly speak
of it." But that's a lie, she's thrilling at the taboo of it, revel-

ing in the currency of a juicy story. "The middle one had to break off her engagement because of it, poor thing. She's so plain and it was such a good match too. Not likely she'll find anything better, not likely she'll find anything at all now."

My heart drops at the oblique mention of Cyrus. I've hardly thought about him these past weeks, except in passing flashes of anger. I don't miss him. I don't care what he thinks. But their words sting because they're true; the only reason we were engaged was because our fathers were business partners. I'm not like Catherine who could have her choice of suitors.

"Yes," the other commiserates, impatient, "but is what everyone's saying true? It can't possibly be."

They're too far away now, their voices too low for me to hear anymore, but I understand enough to know what she's saying. She will embroider it a bit of course, make Catherine younger, more wanton. When she's done they'll both go home, feeling very well about themselves indeed.

My eyes bore into their backs as they walk away until Emeline tugs at my sleeve. Thunder rumbles in the distance and I put on a brave face for her, taking her by the hand. If Catherine noticed the two women and their sharp eyes, she doesn't say anything, instead she fans herself with her gloves and looks around at the little town. "I can't fathom why on God's green earth Father had to choose this forsaken place over all others. There isn't even a dress seller."

He chose it because of the river that runs through the town, powering the mills. Father doesn't know the first thing about milling—he made his fortune on a series of brilliant speculations—but he has a keen nose for business and knows a good investment when he sees it. The river towns up this way weren't affected the way the city was during the war in 1812, and a quick profit can still be turned. Knowing this, he had planned to build a small office, and Willow Hall as our seasonal residence. I doubt Catherine would care, let alone understand any of this, so I just point to the little shop across the street. "Maybe they sell ribbons there. Shall we look?"

Mother had wanted to make calls on some of our new neighbors, so I give orders to Joe to return with the carriage in an hour. Joe grumbles something about rain, but there's nothing to be done for it so I lead Emeline across the street, Snip tugging at his leash, Catherine trailing us.

Inside the shop it's musty, a comfortable smell of old leather and dried tea leaves. Emeline leaves Snip tied up outside, and he whines as the heavy glass door swings shut, his claws scratching at the window.

"He'll be fine," I say, directing her attention elsewhere. "Look there." Behind the counter a variety of silk and lace ribbons hang from spools. They're pretty, if not a little faded, but Emeline doesn't notice and is already running over to look for a pink one.

Catherine, who tried to feign indifference at first, is beside Emeline, unable to resist the prospect of a new trifle. I watch her running the silk through her fingers, holding different colors against her auburn hair.

The shopkeeper, an affable enough looking man with thinning brown hair, leans over the counter and gives Emeline a smile, the kind adults give children when they aren't quite sure how to interact with them. "It's not often I have ladies of such quality in my humble little shop," he tells her. "I'm very flattered indeed that you and your lovely sisters have chosen to patronize me on this gray day."

Emeline looks up at him with unmasked curiosity, studying him. I can see the wheels in her head turning as she tries to decide what he means by this. Before she can say anything, I hurry to her rescue. The shopkeeper can laud his insincere platitudes on me or Catherine, but he shouldn't direct them to a little child.

I give him a tight smile. "We're newly arrived in New Oldbury, and thought to explore the town today."

Even though my tone should make it clear that I'm not looking for a conversation, he turns his smile on me. "Is that so?" He couldn't care less if we had just dropped out of the sky, but his eyes are trained on the pearl earrings on Catherine's earlobes, the fine weave of her shawl. "And how do you find New Oldbury? Where in town are you living?"

"Willow Hall," I say shortly with another tight smile, trying to make it clear that the conversation is over.

He's watching Emeline running her finger over a pink velvet ribbon, but at this he looks sharply back at me. "Is that so? Hadn't thought that anyone was going to live there. I'd heard something about it being a summer house." He bends over again to Emeline and dramatically raises his brows. "There are stories around here that the place is haunted. All manners of ghosties and goblins."

I could slap him for trying to scare her. But Emeline just returns his patronizing gaze with wide, unblinking eyes. "Ghosts? What kinds of ghosts?"

"It seems that every town has its local ghost stories," I hurry to interject, but I already know that Emeline will be demanding ghost stories now in addition to the mermaids. "It's so very quaint." This time I firmly turn my back on him and confer with Emeline on the different merits of the ribbons while Catherine joins in to agree or disagree with me.

Rain begins to patter on the roof, first soft and indecisive, then a steady drumming. For a moment everything is normal and right; I'm shopping for hair ribbons with my sisters. It's cozy, and I can almost forget the two women in the street and their greedy eyes, the overly eager shopkeeper.

Emeline drops her ribbon and frowns. "We can't leave Snip out there, he's going to get drenched."

Mother won't be pleased to have a wet, smelly dog in the house so I pay for Emeline's ribbon and we plunge out into the sticky July rain, only to find that he's gone.

"He probably just went in search of somewhere dry. He can't be far." But as I look up and down the deserted street, I'm not quite sure where that would be.

Catherine frowns, pulling her fine Indian shawl—a gift from Charles before he left—up over her head to keep her hair dry. I think she's going to say something snide about just letting him go, but instead she points to the town green where a flash of white cuts through the downpour. Without waiting for us, Emeline hitches up her skirt and takes off.

Snip thinks it's a game. As soon as Emeline draws near, he freezes, wags his tail and then bounds off again. Catherine and I struggle to keep up with Emeline who has the speed of a gazelle, our dresses longer and heavier in the rain.

As if on cue, thunder cracks in a long, grumbling roll. A moment later the sky flashes yellow. We're well out of the center of town now, and Catherine is breathing heavily trying to keep up. "We can't stay out here, we have to get inside," she says, panting.

I have no idea where we are, Snip has taken several sharp turns on his merry romp. We're on a narrow road—really more of a dirt track—crowded with angry trees that threaten to crack in the heavy rain. Joe may be back with the carriage soon, but he won't know where we've gone.

"There!" Catherine points to a little footpath that cuts through the trees and brush. I can just make out a shingled roof through the clearing.

"Emmy!" I call out after Emeline, who has lost some of

her stamina and is suddenly looking overwhelmed in the unfamiliar surroundings. "Leave him for now."

Reluctantly, she follows as we run toward the building, some kind of old factory or mill. Overgrown with ivy and weeds, the mortar is crumbling around the foundation and the door lintel sags with rotting wood. At the very least it doesn't look as though we'll be bothering anyone.

My feet are cold and slippery inside my shoes and my dress is completely plastered to my body. Catherine and Emeline haven't fared much better, their hair undone and straggling down their necks. So much for our diverting trip to town.

We huddle under a little overhang on the side of the building, empty barrels and upturned crates with old straw the only furniture. Outside the rain comes down in sheets.

"Poor Snip," Emeline says. "He's probably so frightened. And how will he find his way home? We've only been here a day. He doesn't know the way back."

Seeing the way Snip was enjoying himself, I doubt he is afraid and tell Emeline as much. "He has a keen nose, I'm sure he can sniff his way back."

"The rain will have washed all the scents away though," Catherine unhelpfully volunteers, and I give her a sharp look over the top of Emeline's head.

We watch in silence as the trees thrash and bow, and jump when a particularly large branch snaps to the ground. The thunder eventually rolls off into the distance, the lightning following in its wake.

"Look!"

Emeline jumps off her seat and points out into the woods, where I can just make out the outline of Snip before he disappears into the trees. "We have to go get him!"

"I'm done chasing that stupid dog. My feet are wet and blistering, and there's no telling how much farther he'll go."

Catherine looks to me for agreement. "Let's wait for the rain to stop and then try to find Joe."

The lightning and thunder might have moved off, but the rain is still drumming down fast and steady. I look between Emeline's expectant face and Catherine, already steeling myself for what I know I have to do. "You stay here. I'll go follow him, but if I can't catch him right away then I'm coming back."

Emeline pipes up to say something, but I stop her with a stern look. "Mother won't be happy if you come back even dirtier and with a cold. Catherine, stay with her, and give me your shawl."

4

WHY COULDN'T MOTHER have gotten her a cat, I think as I set off into the thicket behind the old building, wiping rain from my eyes. Cats don't go romping about in downpours. Cats stay warm and dry in front of a fire, just like I wish I was right now.

Plunging farther into the woods, I give a half-hearted yell for Snip, followed by an indelicate word as my shoe catches against a slick root. There's no time to stop myself as I go sprawling headfirst into the wet leaves and mud. A rock breaks my fall. My hand smarts, and when I struggle to my knees to inspect the damage, there's an angry cut running down my palm. It's no use trying to wipe the dirt from it on my soaking dress, so I gingerly heave myself up the rest of the way, only to step on my hem in the process. There's a loud tearing noise. Just my luck. I curse again as I stumble forward, reaching for tree trunks to steady myself as I go.

The rain isn't as heavy here under the thick canopy of trees, but each severe plop still snakes its way down my clothes, vanquishing the last few dry spots on my body.

More than once I stop in my tracks, frozen by the snap of a branch or a clump of leaves falling to the ground. My neck prickles, just like last night when we arrived to an audience of fireflies and forest creatures. I'm a city girl, an intruder, unused to the thousand little sounds of a close woods.

"You're lucky you have such a sweet little master," I grumble to Snip, wherever he is. If it weren't for the fact that Emeline will be heartbroken if I come back empty-handed, I'd be tempted to leave Snip out here to fend for himself.

Something white flashes in the corner of my eye, but when I turn and look closer it's gone. A shudder runs through my body. "Snip?"

A moment later there's a rustle behind me and I close my eyes, letting out a sigh of relief. Maybe the end of this unpleasant day is finally in sight. "Well, you certainly took your sweet time. I hope you're happy with your—"

I freeze at the sound of a heavier tread, my words dying in my throat. The hairs on the back of my neck stand on end, and I don't have to turn around to know that it's not Snip behind me.

Do they have bears out here? Or maybe it's a moose. I once saw a picture of a moose in a book. They're taller than a man and they can toss you up into the air with their great antlers. But even as I curl my fingers into my skirts, preparing to turn around, I know that it's not an animal.

I take a deep breath and spin around.

It doesn't matter that I knew there would be someone there when I looked, I still almost jump out of my skin when my eyes land on the young man that has seemingly appeared out of thin air behind me.

"I'm sorry," he says quickly, taking a tentative step forward. "I didn't mean to startle you." He must see my heart pound-

ing in my throat, because he stops, and his lips twitch up at
the corner. "I think I failed on that account."

My breath comes out in a hiss. "Yes, well, in the state I
was in I think anything would have startled me." I lean back
against the wet bark of a tree and close my eyes, waiting for
my heart to slow.

I open my eyes. He doesn't look dangerous. Despite the
rain having its way with him, his clothes are fine, and there's
something warm and familiar about his face. I probably look
a good deal more suspicious in my torn and muddy dress and
bedraggled hair.

He takes his hat off and rakes his fingers through his wet
hair, brushing it out of his eyes. "Are you all right, miss? Are
you lost?"

"Quite all right," I lie. I'm not used to anyone—let alone
a handsome young man—talking to me as if I weren't part of
the most reviled family in Boston, or an unchaperoned woman
wandering the woods in a torn and muddy dress for that matter. "And it's my dog—or rather my sister's dog—who is lost.
I'm trying to find him."

"Ah." He rocks back on his heels, hands in pockets. "A
noble reason to be out in such conditions. Mine are much
more foolish."

He doesn't give me a chance to ask what his reasons might
be, and he doesn't elaborate before asking, "Perhaps I could
be some assistance in your search? I'm quite familiar with
these woods."

I should thank him and tell him that it's not necessary. I
should say good-day, turn around, and go find Catherine and
Emeline. There is no good and proper reason for me to accept the company of a strange man I found wandering in the
woods, even if the man in question looks like he just stumbled
out of one of my novels with his fair good looks, a Lancelot.

Yet when I open my mouth, the only words that come out are, "I think he went up that way."

I gesture up the bank and the man's gaze fixes on my hand. "You're hurt."

It isn't a question so much as an accusation, as if I should have told this stranger the moment I set eyes on him that I had a small scrape on my palm. I open my mouth to protest, but he closes the small distance between us in three long strides.

"May I?" Before I know what's happening, he's taking my hand in his gloves, gently wiping away the dirt from the cut. His movements are deft and quick. "You'll have to wash it when you get home, but this will at least keep any more dirt from it." He takes his cravat off and I watch him wind the white linen round and round my hand until I can barely flex my fingers.

"There now, that's better," he says with a smile as fast and brilliant as the lightning. When he's done he ties it off neatly. My hand lingers in his for a moment, relishing the warmth, before I remember myself and pull away.

"Thank you," I mumble.

Perhaps realizing just how close we're standing, the man steps back with a brisk nod. "If we're going to find your dog we should do it now while we have a break in the rain."

I'd hardly noticed that the rain has lightened to nothing more than a misty drizzle while his strong fingers held my hand. "Do you think you can manage...?" He trails off, looking discreetly at the ground. The cool breeze on my ankles reminds me that between my dress and the cut on my hand, I probably look like I've been mauled by wolves.

I tug at my bodice and adjust Catherine's shawl in a vain attempt at modesty. "Perfectly fine," I assure him, and, as if accepting a challenge, add, "I love a good walk in the woods."

He inclines his head, a glimmer of amusement in his eyes, and we set off.

We crest the little embankment, the man shortening his strides so that I don't have to run to keep up with his long legs. I chance a sidelong glance at my knight, wondering what on earth brought him to the woods in a storm at the same time as me.

"He can't have gotten far. The river cuts through over there, and if he has any sense he'll have stayed put on this side."

"I'm not sure sensibility is Snip's strong point. Chasing his tail, maybe. Or barking at shadows."

The man's eyes—arresting eyes, which are somehow blue and green at the same time—settle on me and he flashes me a grin before putting a light hand on my elbow and guiding me up the bank.

I've nearly forgotten about my sodden shoes and the stinging from my cut. The fresh, resinous smell of the woods fills me with renewed energy. We're Lancelot and Guinevere, fleeing through the forest from a jealous King Arthur. Any moment we'll come upon a white steed and Lancelot will swing me up upon its jeweled saddle and we'll gallop off together.

"There!"

My dream comes to a halt as I follow Lancelot's pointing finger down to the edge of the water. It's not a white steed, but a muddy Snip. He's gnawing on something, a piece of rotted wood it looks like, as we slowly approach.

Snip eyes the man suspiciously as he slowly advances with one outstretched arm, but doesn't make any move, just pants contentedly with his tongue lolling out. "I suppose he's had enough adventure for one day," Lancelot says as he scoops up the unprotesting Snip and hands him to me.

I almost wish Snip did have some chase left in him so that I could prolong my adventure with this handsome stranger.

But he just wriggles around in my arms and plants me with a sloppy kiss, and we head back to the old building.

"There you are! I was just about to..." Catherine's words trail off as the man steps into the little porch behind me. Her mouth falls open as her gaze swings up to him, then narrows suspiciously on me.

"Snip!" Emeline is up in a flash, arms outstretched, receiving her wayward pet among a tangle of dirty paws and frantic licks.

"Remember your manners," I say as I try to brush off Snip's dirt from my already ruined dress. "Thank Mr...." I flush. The man bandaged up my hand, helped me find our dog, and escorted me back to my sisters and I never even thought to ask his name.

"Barrett," he says with a small inclination of the head. "John Barrett."

The name is familiar, but I can't place it. Before I can ask him why I might know it, Catherine is sliding off her crate, her gaze fixed on Mr. Barrett. She's regained her composure and is twirling a damp lock of hair around her finger. "Catherine," she says with an unnecessarily deep curtsy. "We're indebted to you for returning Lydia to us in one piece." The sharp look she throws my way and tight tone suggest otherwise.

For some reason I color deeper when Catherine tells him my name. "And the young lady who's so busy playing with her dog is Emeline," I hastily pipe up to divert attention away from my flaming cheeks.

Emeline looks up from scratching Snip's muddy belly. "We got stuck in the storm."

"Well, I can't say you've chosen the most hospitable of places to seek shelter." He gestures to the little porch, hat in hand.

"This was my father's mill, and as you can see it's fallen into disrepair some time ago."

"A mill!" Catherine exclaims. "How very exciting. We've just come from Boston and I don't think I've ever seen a proper mill before."

Mr. Barrett raises a brow at Catherine's enthusiasm for mills. "And what brings you to New Oldbury?"

Catherine clamps her mouth shut, so I answer. "Our father has just invested in the cotton mill here." It's not a lie, I'm just omitting the other reason. All the same I feel a little stab of guilt.

"You don't mean…" His smile fades. "You're Samuel Montrose's daughters? And he's brought you here?" He isn't asking me, he's talking to himself. "Mr. Montrose never told me that he was planning on bringing a family with him," he says, his voice roughening at the edges.

He knows. Despite my best efforts at hemming the truth, he already knows who we are and about the scandal.

"Willow Hall was just to be a summer home," Catherine chimes in, "but we'll be living here permanently now." Her voice is light and she's twirling that damp lock of hair between her fingers like an idiot again.

"You're to live at Willow Hall permanently," he echoes, as if hardly processing the words.

"If you're going to tell us it's haunted, you're too late," Catherine says with a little laugh. "We quite got all the gossip on that score from the shopkeeper."

Mr. Barrett gives her a sharp look. "What did he say?"

Before Catherine has a chance to answer, something clicks into place in my mind and I know where I've heard his name before. "You're our father's new business partner."

He gives a tight nod. "I am." The mood has shifted in the little porch, and the only one among us oblivious to the tension in the air is Emeline who is singing to Snip while she tries to clean the mud from his ears.

"Ghosts live in our house," Emeline says, pausing from her ministrations to look up at Mr. Barrett with solemn eyes. "The whole place is full of ghosts. And goblins. You can't throw a rock but hit a ghost there."

"Emeline! He never said that." I give Mr. Barrett an apologetic look. "She likes to embroider the truth." Emeline starts to protest but I hush her.

But he hardly hears me anyway, and I dare not say anything else. He stands awkwardly in the silence, taking out a soaked handkerchief from his pocket and then putting it back in again. He runs a hand through his thick hair, shaking out some of the lingering wetness. It's the same color as the golden fields of shimmering hay, which we passed yesterday on our journey.

"Well, I must go, but you're welcome to stay and dry off as long as you need. Good day."

"Wait!" Mr. Barrett stops at my cry, looking at me expectantly. "Your cravat," I say, raising my bandaged hand as if he would possibly want it back, dirty and bloody as it is now.

He opens his mouth, hesitates and then says shortly, "Keep it." He gives a brief dip of the head, and then he's gone.

Catherine and I sit in stunned silence. "John Barrett," she murmurs. "Why wouldn't Father have mentioned bringing his family to New Oldbury?"

Why indeed? Father was never much for home life, and that was before the scandal. Now he probably wishes he weren't burdened with us. No, what's stranger to me is that Mr. Barrett should look so troubled at our arrival. It would be one thing if it had to do with the scandal, but the more I think about it, the more I'm convinced it's not that. He was surprised to learn that our father had a family at all, and that he brought us here. If he had already known about us, then it would follow that he knew about the scandal.

"Well," says Catherine standing and briskly shaking out her damp skirts, "I can't believe Father could be so shortsighted. He might have mentioned that his new business partner was young. And handsome."

I roll my eyes, and the little chill that had settled in my spine dissipates. The sun is inexplicably burning through the clouds, and the air is heavy with humidity. Steam rises from the road and the prospect of walking back in the stickiness is even more daunting than walking back in the rain. Despite that, there's a nagging tug in my chest, a rough edge that won't be smoothed down.

5

CATHERINE BOLTS UPSTAIRS to change, and I send Emeline up after her. I hardly care that my dress is torn, that my hand needs to be cleaned; I'm still back at the old mill, lost in the unsettling gaze of Mr. Barrett. I wander through the house, over the wood floors gleaming amber in the afternoon sun, the oriental carpets still crisp in color and soft beneath my feet. Everything is new and expectant, waiting for memories to be made, for stories to be layered down like dust.

When I come to the back hall, I find Mother on hands and knees, a soapy bucket of water beside her. She's scrubbing the tiles over and over in vicious circles. "Snip had a romp through the house with muddy paws," she says without looking up.

"Ada will get it." I help her to her feet. There isn't a trace of mud remaining, but she casts a remorseful look at the white tiles. Her hands are raw.

I install her in the parlor and fetch her workbasket and she finally notices my dress and hand. "Where on earth have you been? I was worried sick when Joe was gone so long with the carriage."

Catherine breezes into the room, Emeline behind her, just as I'm explaining our misadventure in town and chance meeting with John Barrett.

"Mother," I say slowly, not quite sure what I'm asking, "do you know any reason why Father's new business partner should be unhappy to learn that he had a family, or that he had brought us here?"

"Unhappy?" Mother echoes the question, picking up her embroidery. "What makes you say that?"

"We really must invite Mr. Barrett over for dinner," Catherine cuts in, throwing herself down on the yellow-and-pink settee. "Especially if he and Father are business partners."

Mother watches her with wary eyes over the rim of her embroidery hoop, stabbing the needle through the linen.

"I like him. He helped bring back Snip," Emeline adds solemnly.

I hold my breath, waiting for Mother's answer. We used to entertain all the time in Boston. That was one of the hardest parts of the scandal, the way everyone stopped coming around. Cyrus was the last of them. I try not to think about that awful meeting with the man who would have been my husband in the front parlor of our trim brick house. The way time stood still despite the persistent ticking of the clock, him standing not more than a few feet in front of me, but separated by miles. The way he raked his fingers through his dark curls and couldn't meet my eye. "I'm sorry, Lydia," he said. "You know that I am. But you have to see it from my perspective, from my family's." All the blood rushing up to my head, my knees weak and insides hollow. "I... I wish you the best." And then he was gone, the coward, striding out the door without so much as a backward glance. Good riddance.

"Well, yes, I suppose Mr. Barrett must come over for dinner," Mother says.

Something like relief washes over Catherine, and I can't figure her out. I don't know why it bothers me so much that she should have an eye for Mr. Barrett; after all, it would be a good sign for our family if she were to become interested in someone. And her inner character notwithstanding, she's beautiful. The man would be a fool not to notice her.

It's agreed that an invitation will be sent out to Mr. Barrett for next week, and Mother sends for Joe to deliver it. Just as Joe is leaving, Catherine takes something from her pocket and slips it into his hand with a finger to her lips. Mother is bent over her embroidery, and Emeline is busy giving Snip a stern lecture on running away. It all happens in the space of a second, and then Catherine demurely folds her hands, smiling out the window at nothing in particular.

It's a rare evening that Father joins us for dinner, but since we're entertaining his business partner he's made an exception from taking his meal in his office. In Boston we all dined together, but that was when Charles was still there, and we women outnumbered the men only four to two. Now that Charles is gone, Father doesn't find much to draw him to our table anymore, preferring to lose himself in the safety of his ledgers where everything adds up in tidy little columns.

Ada has already helped Emeline dress, leaving Catherine and me alone to finish our toilettes together.

"Move over, Lydia. You've been fussing with your hair for almost an hour and I need the mirror."

I scooch the little stool over so Catherine can lean down to see herself. "What's gotten into you anyway? You never do anything with your hair besides the same old drab bun."

I frown, trying to get my fine hair to hold some semblance of a curl. "That's not true."

When it's clear that the limp strands won't cooperate, I give up and sweep them up and back under a simple band. Catherine expertly puts hers in a neat row of tight little curls. Her hair is a luminous shade of auburn, alive with gold and copper. My hair by comparison is mousy brown. A warm, light shade, but brown all the same. And of course my Emmy has the prettiest hair of all of us, even more golden and vibrant than Catherine's.

I watch as Catherine rubs color over her lips, then plucks a stray hair from her brow. She practices different expressions, first one of surprise, her mouth open in an inviting O, her brows arched, then one of wide-eyed innocence. She could have anyone—any man wrapped around her finger. I can't help but be a little in awe of her, even if she is the vainest creature I've ever met. I always knew that she was different from me, above me somehow. As a child she shone so brightly, stealing the room with her perfect manners and charming smile while I struggled to keep up. She scowls when she catches me studying her.

"Oh, don't look at me like that, Lyd."

"Like what?"

She rolls her eyes. "With the disapproving, sanctimonious glower you always have." She stands up, giving one last glance into the mirror and patting at her coif.

"You're up to something."

With a shrug, she grabs her shawl from the bed and heads for the door. "I know you're up to something, Catherine!" I call after her. And I'm going to find out what it is, I add silently. This family has had enough of secrets.

Ada announces Mr. Barrett. He strides into the room, his face serious, looking like he's come more on business than pleasure. He gives Mother a kiss on the cheek though, like an old friend, and Father a hearty handshake. He's shined his boots, and his cravat is fresh and white, crisp. When we saw him in the rain the other day I didn't appreciate what a fine figure he cuts, what quiet power he exudes with his serious eyes and strong jaw. Not at all the kind of person I thought we would find out here in the country. He turns to me and gives a short bow, and I mumble something inconsequential.

"I'm glad to see that you've recovered from your soaking the other day," he says. His tone isn't cold exactly, but it's formal and doesn't invite anything more than a polite reply.

I hardly notice the dark-haired young man in the doorway until Mr. Barrett turns to him and takes him by the shoulder. "Where are my manners? This is my good friend August Pierce. August is a bachelor too and I hope you don't mind, but I thought he could do with a good home-cooked meal as well."

"Of course, of course. Glad to meet you, Mr. Pierce." Father pumps his hand, grateful for more men with whom he can talk business.

"I hope I'm not being a terrible intruder," Mr. Pierce says with a crooked smile. Catherine all but jumps at the chance to assure him that he is no such thing, relinquishing her position next to Mr. Barrett, which she had only just taken up. I catch Mother's eye.

With lank chestnut hair, full lips quirked at the corners and penetrating hazel eyes, he's the antithesis of serious Mr. Barrett. He turns his smile to Catherine, and Mr. Barrett is forgotten completely. What a fool she is.

I take up Catherine's abandoned position. "Have you lived in New Oldbury long?" I ask Mr. Barrett just as Ada creeps in to announce dinner is ready.

"I'm sorry?" He doesn't catch what I was saying, and then everyone is moving into the dining room. Before I can repeat myself, Emeline runs up and takes his hand, leading him to sit next to her.

Catherine slips into the seat on his other side, and an extra chair is brought for Mr. Pierce. I'm between him and Mother on the opposite side of the table, Father at the head. I might as well be in the next town over.

"Mr. Pierce," Father says, sawing away at his loin roast, "are you in the milling business too, then? I don't believe I've heard your name mentioned in that circuit."

"I'm afraid not. Barrett here is the man with a mind for business," he says. "I'm rather useless at the moment. I finished at Harvard last spring, and now I'm something of a boat without an anchor, drifting about looking for some occupation."

"I've been showing August the ropes at the mill, but I'm not sure it's exciting enough for him," Mr. Barrett says with a smile.

They're so comfortable together. I can't help but be jealous of their companionship. It's Mr. Pierce I'm jealous of, really, to be able to talk with Mr. Barrett like that. I imagine them together, sitting relaxed in an office, Pierce with his boots up on the desk, fiddling with a pen and recounting some funny story. John—I can call him John, it's my castle in the air after all—standing by the window, running his hand absently through that thick wave of amber-gold hair as he cracks a smile.

Mr. Pierce grins, lopsided and boyish. "Nonsense. If excitement was what I was after, I wouldn't be in New Oldbury."

"And what did you study at Harvard, Mr. Pierce?" Catherine is still playing her ridiculous role of gentle lady, speaking with downcast lashes and a demure tone that is anything but natural for her.

"Law. It's the family business. My father passed away some years ago and my uncle runs the firm now. It only took me a month to know that it wasn't for me. Too many documents and days spent in a stuffy office. Not for me," he repeats with a wink in Catherine's direction. "In any case, there wasn't much to keep me in Boston. My mother is bedridden since a fever took the use of her legs some years ago."

If Mr. Pierce is from Boston I wonder that he hasn't heard the rumors. But he's good-humored and warm, and doesn't seem to have any inkling that he's seated among the most notorious family in Boston. Perhaps Harvard kept him too occupied to engage in gossip.

Mother puts down her fork and tries to offer her sympathy, but he stops her with a casual wave of his knife. "Don't fret on her account. Mother has thrown herself into the occupation of invalid with her characteristic vigor and dedication. She has the whole household on pins and needles. It quite suits her. So you see, when John mentioned he might show me the mill business, I jumped at the opportunity."

"Well," Catherine says with a coquettish smile, "how lucky for us that you did."

Father, ever late to pick up on the social cues around him, is finally catching on to Catherine's game. He colors slightly and hurries to steer the conversation to safer ground. Standing to pour more wine he adds, "Well, there's value in a good lawyer, I would say."

Mr. Barrett raises his glass in a toast, graciously saying that the law has lost a fine son in August. Catherine hangs on their every word, laughing a little too loudly when someone makes a light remark, smiling a little too eagerly when Mr. Pierce's hazel eyes flicker in her direction.

Emeline, who had begged Mother not to make her eat with Ada in the kitchen tonight, looks as if she's regretting winning that fight. Her eyes are heavy and she's in danger of falling asleep in her plate. I give her a nudge under the table and she jerks back up.

"I think we'll start seeing more mills sprouting up along the river now that the power looms have proved such a success in Waltham," Mr. Barrett says. He cuts his meat briskly into even pieces. "As we speak, Chelmsford is expanding and breaking ground on a new venture. I see no reason why New Oldbury shouldn't be any different. We have the unique advantage of a river unspoiled by nearby cities after all."

Father leans back in his chair, hands resting comfortably on his paunch. "Do you see?" he asks of no one in particular. "That war with the Brits had some benefits. They blocked up our coast and inhibited the cotton trade, so by God we got to work and made our own cotton. Necessity is the mother of all invention, and nothing breeds necessity like the trials of war. It's bright young minds like Barrett's here that are going to ensure we continue industrialization and become a power to be reckoned with."

Mr. Barrett colors slightly, but reaches for his wineglass and raises a brow in acknowledgment of Father's words. Otherwise the praise rolls off his back.

"Hear, hear," agrees Mr. Pierce.

"I'll tell you one thing," Father says, plowing on. "We're going to have to buy out some of those farmers with parcels that abut the river. Take Ezra Clarke for example. He's got the fastest cut of river running through his land, and he's squandering it, letting that sickly handful of cattle nibble away at the field. A man ought to put his land to best use or give it up, that's what I think."

Mr. Barrett makes a polite noise of demurral, but adds nothing else.

I think of the dilapidated mill where we met Mr. Barrett, and seize my opportunity to join in the conversation, grasping at the only thing I know about him. "Is that why your father's mill isn't active any longer? He started fresh with the new technology and built the new mill upriver?"

Mr. Barrett pauses, his wineglass half raised to his lips. His face darkens. "No," he says shortly. "My father went bankrupt, and the wool mill was forced to close."

Catherine shoots me daggers, and Mother gives me a warning look. Undeterred, I blunder on. "Well," I say, "he's lucky to have a son who knows so much about the cotton industry. I daresay he must be happy with your new venture."

An unmistakable tension thickens the air and I realize I've somehow misstepped, said the wrong thing. Father is boiling up the color of lobster and Mr. Pierce opens his mouth to say something, but Mr. Barrett quickly silences them both.

"My father is dead, Miss Montrose," he says without meeting my eye. "I'd like to think the advancements I've put in place would have made him proud though."

"I'm sure they would," coos Catherine. She says something about how he must take us on a tour of the mill sometime, and then moves the conversation to the subject of printed cotton in fashion this year. I don't hear what they say as I push my food around on my plate. Mr. Barrett is equally silent. The rest of dinner drags on for an eternity, and I can't even begrudge Catherine her winning the night; after all, she saved me from further embarrassment.

After dinner, we retire to the parlor where Ada brings in coffee and little bowls of frothy syllabub, Emeline's favorite dessert. It's so unbearably hot, and it's all I can do to sit still without wiping at my brow constantly. Even Emeline, usually full of energy, is subdued, hanging over the arm of her chair, looking as if she's about to melt away into the carpet.

Myself, I try to disappear into the corner. Everyone seems to have overlooked, or at least forgotten, my blunder at dinner. I'm making too much out of it. How was I to know that his father was dead? I couldn't have, yet my stomach is still in knots over the way his eyes clouded when I mentioned his father, the change that passed over his face. I wish I could take it back, not for me, but to save him from any heartache and discomfort.

Catherine brushes by me and whispers, "His mother is dead too, you ought to know. Mr. Pierce told me."

I start to say something but clamp my mouth back shut. What's the use? I sit in penitent silence as Catherine takes up with Mr. Pierce across the room. My coffee grows tepid and undrinkable. When I look up I find that Mr. Barrett's studying me out of the corner of his eye. I color and quickly look away. He must be wondering what to make of me, how one sister can be so charming and polite, and the other such an utter dolt.

"It's too hot for coffee," Emeline announces suddenly, even though she's not allowed to have a sip of the beverage. "It's too hot for dresses and shoes and hair and fingernails. It's too hot for stockings and feathers and fur."

Mr. Barrett and Father break off their conversation, and silence falls over the parlor. Mother shoots our guests an apologetic look and then a pleading one at Emeline. "I'm so sorry. It's past her bedtime and she's getting tired."

But Emeline isn't done. She's goes over to Mr. Barrett and looks up at him. "It's too hot," she repeats. "And I'm not tired at all. There's a pond behind the house, did you know? I want to go to the pond and see the mermaids."

I should take her upstairs to bed, but I don't move. Mr. Barrett is looking down at her with a queer expression, a crease between his brows. She takes his hand in hers. His aren't tapered and elegant like Cyrus's; Mr. Barrett's hands are capable, strong, and Emeline's hand completely disappears in his.

"Please, let's go to the pond where it's cool and we can swim with the mermaids. I want to go play with the little boy at the pond."

"What little boy? What on earth are you talking about, Emmy?" But Emeline ignores Mother's question and her lip begins to tremble when it becomes clear that she isn't going to get her way.

By this time even Catherine and Mr. Pierce have paused in their giggles and whispers and both are staring. Crimson spreads over Catherine's face. "Really, Emeline. Leave poor Mr. Barrett alone."

Mother gets up slowly, and I can tell she doesn't have the energy for this. "It's dark out, Emmy. And Mr. Pierce and Mr. Barrett have business to discuss with your father." She reaches out to take her hand, but Emeline dives out of her grasp.

I'm mortified. I understand Emeline, but Mr. Barrett will never return to our house if she behaves like this. I try to catch her attention, but she misses the cautioning look.

"I don't *want* to go to bed!" I've never seen Emeline in such a pout before. She must be tired beyond reason, and the heat certainly isn't helping. Hands clenched at her sides, she looks as if she's on the verge of bursting into tears. But instead she just stomps her little foot.

But just as her foot comes down on the carpet, the doors slam shut with a great bang.

Mother jumps, Catherine lets out a little cry and Father's eyebrows look as if they are about to fly off his face. The room goes silent, the only movement the residual wobbling of a vase on the table.

We all look at each other. Even Emeline looks surprised, because if we didn't know better, it was almost as if she caused the doors to fly shut with her foot.

Father is the first to speak. He clears his throat and glances around. "Must be the wind," he mumbles. "You think you have a house built new and it wouldn't be full of drafts and loose doors, but I suppose there's no such thing as peace of mind in New England construction."

Mother is quick to agree with him, and Mr. Pierce gives a dubious nod. But we all know that there was no breeze, that it's been so still that a feather would have hardly quivered, let alone two doors slamming. No one wants to say so though at the risk of frightening Emeline.

Then, without warning, Mr. Barrett goes to Emeline and, dropping to his knee, puts his hands on her shoulders. He peers at her curiously, and when he speaks, it's slow and gentle, so soft that I have to strain to hear him. "Your mother's right, Miss Montrose. It's late and I'm sure that it's almost my bedtime as well. But perhaps you'll be so kind to invite August and myself back soon, and then we could have the pleasure of being escorted around the grounds by yourself. And your sisters," he adds, glancing at me. His blue-green eyes still hold a note of sadness, but there's no trace of anger or bitterness. With Emeline's outburst, my blunder must have been forgotten, or at the very least, forgiven.

I catch my breath. Emeline looks unsure, her bottom lip trembling. But ultimately she nods, even going so far as to brush his cheek with a kiss. He gives her a faint smile in return before standing and passing her off to Mother, who ushers her out of the parlor to Ada.

Despite Father's assurance that it must have been the breeze, an uncomfortable pall hangs over the rest of the evening. There are a few false starts in conversation as we struggle to fill the void, but it's eventually Father, who has looked exceedingly uncomfortable throughout this whole exchange, who picks up the conversation with Mr. Barrett again as if nothing happened. He has found a great friend in Mr. Barrett, who can rattle off figures and calculate the profit in a spool of wool or a cord of lumber just as easily as he. They're engrossed in a debate about the merits of some new kind of waterwheel, so neither notices the very friendly *tête-à-tête* that has resumed in the corner.

The lamplight illuminates Catherine's hair, giving her something of a halo. She's laughing behind her hand, eyes sparkling. She hangs on Mr. Pierce's every word as if he's the most interesting person she's ever met. I suppose it doesn't matter if it's Mr. Barrett or Mr. Pierce that's paying her attention, so long as someone is.

And August Pierce is very handsome, I'll give Catherine that. He must know he is too, judging by the way he's always smiling, almost smirking, at nothing in particular. I doubt he takes anything very seriously in life, including himself.

I'm not the only one watching Catherine. Mother is feigning interest in her syllabub, pushing it around with her spoon, but I see her studying her eldest daughter. Why doesn't she say something? Catherine's behavior is bordering on the improper, and the last thing we need is more fuel for rumors and gossip. But then Mother catches my eye. I've never seen that expression on her before, one of trepidation, cautious optimism and, most of all, relief. Then it dawns on me: Mother thinks that perhaps Catherine might be married after all.

And if Catherine could be married, then I could as well.

6

IT MIGHT BE the heat, or that I can't get the image of Mr. Barrett's sad eyes gazing at me unstuck from my head, but I can't sleep that night. When I can't stand the scratchy feel of my eyelids anymore or the sheets sticking to the backs of my thighs, I get up from bed and pour myself a glass of water from the ewer in the corner. Opening the window, I slowly drink my water, hoping for a scrap of a breeze blowing in from the yard. But the night is still and unyielding.

I'm just about to turn from the window and go back to bed, when a movement in the yard below catches the corner of my eye.

At first it looks like a bird taking wing into the night, a pale splash of movement. But when I look harder I see that's not a bird, but a person. A woman. I'm still drowsy, so it doesn't seem so ridiculous that perhaps it's Ada out in the garden, though doing what I can't imagine. But then the clock in the hall strikes three. What on earth would she be doing out there at this time of the morning?

I put down my glass and press myself against the edge of

the window frame, peering out from the side so that I can't be seen from below. Maybe it's a vagrant, hungry and in search of food. But the garden is barren, and they'll find no food there. Or perhaps it's someone with more sinister motives, here to rob us.

But the woman seems no more interested in the house than the contents of the garden. She's wearing a billowy, pale dress, which floats about her as she slowly moves one way, then turns and moves the next. Up and down the length of the garden she goes, but every time she turns, it's with her face away from me so that I can't tell if she's young or old, a stranger or someone I might know.

The longer I study her, standing there with a hand curled around the windowsill, the more something doesn't seem right about the way she's moving. It takes me a few more moments to place it, and when I do, I catch my breath.

She's gliding.

She moves as if she were walking on air. It's not a natural movement, and my skin prickles. The shopkeeper's sensational warning about ghosts suddenly doesn't seem so silly or impossible.

I watch her another few moments, holding my breath. That's all she does, glides back and forth, back and forth, the pale silk of her dress billowing out behind her despite the lack of breeze.

My legs are jelly and my heart pounding, but I won't be able to go back to bed and sleep a wink so long as I know she's out there. I have to go out and set my mind at ease.

Silently, I tiptoe through the house and to the back door. I take a deep breath before pushing the door open. Tentatively, I step outside and peer into the thick night air.

There's nothing there. The garden, just visible in the moonlight, with its thirsty shrubs and prickly flower stalks sits benignly in the yard, returning my vacant stare in equal measure. But there's no woman.

My knees go weak with relief and I have to brace myself against the door. I could laugh. It was someone snooping about, and they heard me coming and fled. In the morning I'll have to let Joe know that we might need a guard dog, or at the very least, a fence. I go back upstairs, climb into my bed and, with a body made weary with relief, drift off to sleep.

I don't know who's more excited to hear Mr. Barrett's light knock at the door the next day. Snip howls in delight and skids through the hall, circling Ada's heels as she tries to open the door, Emeline trotting close behind with her half-braided hair falling out of its ribbon.

Catherine lays aside the limp roses and lilies she's been arranging and passes a light hand over her curls. Sitting up a little straighter, I put my book down. I wish Mother had asked me to do the flowers. I always make a mess of them, but at least it would be me looking flushed and pretty when Mr. Barrett is shown in, a white rose stem in my hand. As it is, I'm bone tired from my bad dream last night. Because that's what it was, I've decided—a dream. Somewhere in that hazy margin between sleep and wakefulness, I must have thought I saw something. In the light of day and now that Mr. Barrett is here, it all seems faraway and unimportant.

He's not hugely tall, but when Mr. Barrett walks in it feels as if the walls and ceiling fall away around him. He fills the room with his quiet force, as electrifying and still as the moment before a storm breaks. Even Snip feels it, for he stops his nervous circling and sits patiently beside Mr. Barrett's leg, looking up and waiting to be petted.

Emeline is already prattling on about the pond and mermaids and even faeries, which are a new interest. He nods down at her politely, not saying anything.

"Emeline, for goodness sake, take a breath. Didn't Mother ask you to help her with the blackberries in the kitchen?"

This morning I had wanted to talk to Emeline about her tantrum the night before with the slamming doors, but when it came down to it I couldn't figure out what I was trying to say. So I settled with, "Emeline, have you been feeling quite all right lately? You like it here?"

She had looked at me as if I was asking her if the sky was blue. "Yes. I love it here, don't you?"

I had agreed that I did, and let the subject drop. No one else has brought it up, and so even though it makes me feel uneasy every time I think of the doors slamming shut in unison with her stomping foot, I've pushed it to the back of my mind. Like my bad dream, it melts away in my excitement to see Mr. Barrett.

But now, at the prospect of being sent away from Mr. Barrett, Emeline pouts, looking like she might break into tears, and that's when I realize that all of us Montrose girls are smitten with John Barrett. For a moment I'm even afraid that we might have a repeat of the other night. But the tears hold, and she shoots Catherine a reproachful look before dragging her feet back out of the parlor. Usually I would tell Catherine not to talk to her like that, except Mr. Barrett is right there, and I'm inwardly grateful that Emeline can't monopolize his attention now.

"I'm sorry to barge in here like this," Mr. Barrett says, "but I had a meeting with your father and it seems he's not quite ready for me yet."

"Oh, you aren't barging—"

"Mr. Barrett, you are doing no such thing." Catherine

sweeps to her feet and links her arm in his. "Please, sit down and do us the favor of entertaining us while you wait."

As he obediently seats himself Catherine arches a triumphant brow at me. The battle lines have been drawn. Let her play her game. And that's all it is to her. She can't possibly be interested in Mr. Barrett, not seriously. Not after the way she dropped him like a hot coal last night when she saw Mr. Pierce.

They chat a little, Catherine commenting on the weather and Mr. Barrett agreeing that the heat has been unbearable lately. If he's suffering he doesn't look it; his collar is crisp and his clothes pristine. I feel rumpled and stale in my dress, the straggling hair at my neck damp and unpleasant. A couple of times he directs a comment in my direction, but Catherine is quick, reeling him back in to her with a little laugh or foolish question. I arrange my book in my lap so that I can sneak a few sentences at a time; if I'm not to be included in their conversation then what's the harm in doing a little reading?

"Miss Montrose?"

When I look up, Mr. Barrett is crouching beside my chair and I nearly drop my book in surprise. I hadn't meant to get lost in the story and lose track of time. I dart a glance at Catherine who is scowling, but also making a great show of drawing her needle in long pulls through her embroidery.

"I didn't mean to startle you," he says. "That must be quite the book."

"Oh, yes." I don't know where to look. Certainly not directly in his eyes because then I wouldn't be able to think straight.

Unperturbed by my ghastly manners, Mr. Barrett tips his head to see the title. *The Monk.*

The book is well-worn with little slivers of paper marking some of my favorite passages, and the spine is as creased as a bellows. "Yes," I say again, even though he wasn't asking anything.

"I'm not familiar with it."

A loud sigh escapes Catherine from the other side of the room.

"You've really never heard of it?"

"I confess I haven't," he says, rocking back on his heels. "Will you enlighten me?"

There's a warmth in his eyes that I haven't seen before, bolstering my confidence, and I'm relieved to have the opportunity to smooth over my careless comments from dinner last night. Before I know what I'm doing, I'm giving him a detailed summary in a breathless rush, going back when I forget certain parts, and miming the best scenes. When I finally realize how long I've been talking I clamp my mouth shut, the blood rushing to my face.

I think he's going to laugh—I'm certain I heard Catherine snickering once or twice—and my cheeks burn as I study the gilded cover. But when Mr. Barrett speaks there's no hint of ridicule in his voice, and to his credit he looks only slightly overwhelmed.

"Well," he says at last, "I can see why it has so captured your attention."

I want to insist that he borrow it. How it would thrill me to know that his eyes passed over the same lines of text as me, to know that his soul is stirred as mine is by the passionate love of Alphonso and Agnes.

"Are you a reader, Mr. Barrett?"

"I'm confess I'm not much for books," he says.

Catherine seizes her chance. "Of course not, you're much too busy running the mill, I expect."

"Business does have a large claim on my time, yes."

"Oh," I say, disappointed that I've lost a chance to make a

connection with him, my imaginings of shared stories quickly destroyed. "Of course."

"In my spare time I do rather enjoy birds though," he adds.

"Ah," says Catherine, pleased. "You shoot then."

"I enjoy the study of birds, I mean." He turns his attention back to me. "I'm afraid most of the books you would find in my library would be on that subject."

A naturalist at heart! And I've just had the nerve to think him a bore. We could take walks through the woods, Mr. Barrett guiding Emmy and me, pointing out the different songbirds of New Oldbury. Emeline would love that. Afterward he would take us back to his house, spreading out his volumes of richly illustrated books, quizzing Emmy on the birds we'd just seen. He would smile at me over her head while she puzzled out the answers, a secret smile just between him and me.

"I think," he says, his voice low, hesitant, "I think that, Miss Montrose, you are something of a lover of nature too? I seem to recall you mentioning the day we met that you enjoyed a good stroll through the woods."

It's the first time he's referenced that day, and I can't believe he remembered so small a detail that I had all but forgotten myself. My heart beats faster as I think of the way he smiled at me then, an unguarded, genuine smile. Perhaps he isn't so disgusted with our family. Perhaps there's a chance he'll smile at me again like that.

But before I can say anything, Father wanders into the room, spectacles jammed up to his eyes, a stack of ledgers in his arms.

"Ah, John, my boy. Forgive me for keeping you waiting." He looks up long enough to glance at Catherine and then me. "I hope my daughters weren't being a bother."

Mr. Barrett unfolds himself and stands up, disturbing the

air next to me with his clean scent of soap and something deeper, something woodsy. "No. On the contrary, I was intruding upon their time and they graciously thought to keep me occupied."

Father doesn't look convinced, narrowing his eyes at my burning cheeks, but business is calling and he hasn't the fortitude to get involved in our womanly affairs.

Before Mr. Barrett disappears through the door, he turns and gives us a nod. Father would have to be blind not to see the way Catherine looks at Mr. Barrett now. "Thank you, ladies, and again, I hope I haven't taken up too much of your time."

I'm too flustered to say anything, but Catherine has no problem assuring him again that it wasn't the case. She gives him a breezy smile, and as he turns to leave, that's when I see it. I don't know why a sour lump in my throat rises, or why I suddenly want to flee the room, but when I see the single white rose bloom tucked into his buttonhole, I feel sick.

"I hate baths."

Emeline is standing wrapped in a towel, glaring at the tub that Ada has filled with steaming water. She's still mad at me about being sent away this morning when Mr. Barrett was here.

"I know you do," I say, "but you're filthy and haven't had a proper bath in too long." The longer she stalls, the cooler it will become, and by the time it's my turn I'll be bathing in tepid water.

Emeline is unmoved, refusing even to look at the tub.

"You can pretend you're a mermaid," I offer, my voice rising in desperation.

She considers this, and, finding it acceptable, puts out her hand so that I may help her in. She's just settling into the water and complaining that it's too hot when Catherine pauses at the doorway to frown in at us.

I've successfully avoided Catherine since Mr. Barrett left, unable to look her in the eye after her triumph. But as the day has worn on, the effort at being mad at her has become too much, and I'm willing to extend an olive branch. "Do you want a bath? If you go change, you can go after me." Good graces or not, I'm not giving up position as second in line for the hot water.

Catherine crosses her arms. "I'm not sharing water with you two. If I want a bath I'll have Ada draw one for me later."

I give her a dubious look. With this unbearably hot and humid weather, we would all benefit from a bath, her included. Catherine is usually the first among us to whine that Mother doesn't let us have enough water for hot baths, and demand that a tub be filled whenever the whim strikes her.

"You'd make Ada heat more water and carry it all the way upstairs again? Don't be silly, just wait a few minutes and have one now."

Something like fear flickers across Catherine's face. But in the time it takes me to blink, she's scowling again, and turning on her heel back to her room.

I don't have the energy or the inclination to persuade her, so after Emeline is done with her bath and tucked upstairs in bed, I slip into the tub and luxuriate, taking as much time as I want.

I close my eyes, letting the warm water loosen my knotted muscles and wash away my tension from the past few days.

But just as my shoulders are starting to sink beneath the surface, the air around me turns frigid. I shiver, my teeth chattering despite the warm bath. The lamp gutters as a gusty breeze kicks through the window.

Cursing the sudden change in the weather, I hoist myself

out of the tub and reach for the towel I left draped on my vanity. That's when I see it.

My heart stops in my chest and my arms break into gooseflesh.

"Catherine?" I yell over my shoulder, unable to tear my gaze from the mirror on my vanity. "Catherine, get in here!"

Catherine appears in the doorway, brow puckered and lips in a pout. "What do you want? You can't just call me from across the house like a dog and—"

I don't let her finish. "Did you do this?" My voice is shaking.

She heaves a sigh, but comes into the room and looks around. "Did I do what? What are you talking about?"

I gesture to the mirror, my throat too narrow to choke out even a word.

Catherine cranes her neck past me to see the mirror and gives an impatient huff. "Is this some sort of game? Don't you think I have better things to do than drop everything and come look at your mirror for some whim of yours?"

Angry, I spin around and point at the mirror, ready to chastise Catherine for being willfully obtuse. But I drop my hand. The words that were just there, written as clear as day in the steam, are gone.

My mouth opens and closes, unable to produce any words while my mind sluggishly works to comprehend what I'm seeing. Then, "No! I don't understand. I... There was writing on the fog on the mirror. It was just here..."

Catherine flicks her glance to the tub. "The water isn't even steaming...how on earth could the mirror be fogged?" She shakes her head. "You need to get some sleep. You're seeing things."

But I know what I saw. The only thing I don't know is what it meant.

With one last suspicious look at me, Catherine leaves me dripping there, the image of the fogged words burned into my mind.

You attract them. Some mean you harm. Prepare for what lies ahead.

7

MY HANDS ARE stained and scratched, my back aching, but when I stand to stretch from weeding I feel better than I have in a long time about our new life in the middle of nowhere. The garden at Willow Hall is small, a scorched vegetable patch that hasn't yielded much except a handful of misshapen tomatoes and some resilient squashes, but I'm determined to see it productive and beautiful. I wonder if my dream about the pale lady the other night wasn't my mind's way of telling me that I ought to pay more attention to the garden. I haven't dared breathe a word about it to Emeline because I don't want to scare her, or to Catherine because she would just laugh at me. It's bad enough that Catherine saw me flustered and in a panic about the words in the mirror. The more I thought about it as I lay in bed last night, the more I'm convinced that, like the pale lady who has not reappeared, the words were nothing more than a figment of my imagination. Otherwise, how do I explain it?

Our flower garden with the lilacs used to be Mother's pride and joy, but here she hasn't shown any interest in the plot behind the house. When I told her I wanted to clean it up and start an herb garden—something she had forbidden in Boston—she had looked pained and told me she didn't think it was a good idea, but in the end, she had not fought it.

I never understood Mother's aversion to having a nice herb garden. I have vague memories of my grandmother's house in Cambridge with an ambling garden behind it, full of every herb and healing plant imaginable. When I was little I used to love to rub my fingers into the bergamot flowers, releasing their spicy scent, and chewing on the leaves of lemon balm. But one day when I had brought Mother a remedy I'd concocted from some of the herbs for her chronic headaches, she had blanched and recoiled from me, telling me that I must never dabble with herbs. Apparently it wasn't ladylike, or proper for young girls. I can't remember now.

But now Mother has given up on that, I suppose, not having the energy or inclination to ensure that I'm a proper lady. My hands move automatically, pruning back the plants like mint and chamomile that like to spread, and encouraging the shier plants like hyssop and parsley. For all that I am lousy at arranging flowers and don't know the first thing about wildlife, it's almost as if herbs speak to me, telling me what they need. I wipe the sweat from my eyes and survey my progress with pride. Despite the scorching weather, the plot is lush and already teeming with eager plants. It's miraculous really, like they sprang up overnight. I wonder that the vegetable patch and the flower garden are so withered and decayed, while my little herbs have grown and thrived so quickly.

The back door bangs open, shattering the peace. Emeline cuts directly toward me, little fists balled at her side, brow furrowed in distress. Snip bounds at her heels, wagging his tail furiously as she barrels on.

"It's not fair!" she shouts before she's even halfway to the garden.

I quickly wipe off the dirt on my apron and crouch down to receive her, but she stops short and glares at me.

"What's not fair?"

Before she has a chance to enlighten me, Catherine comes out, throwing up her hands when she sees us. "Get back inside this instant, Emeline!"

"I will not! Lydia, tell her that it's not fair."

"Someone is going to have to tell me what's going on, because—"

They start talking over each other, both acting like eight-year-old children, even though only one of them is, and the other a young woman of twenty-two.

Emeline gets her words out first in a triumphant rush. "Mr. Barrett sent a note along saying he and Mr. Pierce are coming over for a picnic and Cath says that I can't come because it will be an uneven number and it has to be two men and two ladies but I don't think it's fair because I don't know any other—"

"Mr. Barrett is coming today?"

Emeline stops, and they both look at me as if I have two heads.

"It doesn't matter anyway, you're too young," Catherine says. Turning to me, she lowers her voice. "She'll say something dreadful, I just know she will."

She means that Emeline will say something about Boston, and then all the trouble Catherine has gone to with both Mr. Pierce and Mr. Barrett will be lost. "Emeline knows what's appropriate conversation for company and what's not. Don't you, Emmy?"

Emeline glowers at us and then looks down, scuffing her shoe in the dirt. "Yes, I know."

"There," I say brightly. I'm already taking off my apron

and trying to remember if Ada was able to get the stain out of my favorite cream silk dress. "When will they be here?"

"After lunch," Catherine says. Crossing her arms, she juts her chin over my shoulder. "What are you doing out here anyway? I don't remember there being plants there."

I follow her gaze, having already forgotten the gardening in which just moments ago I was so absorbed. "Just doing a little weeding."

Emeline is hopping from foot to foot, her patience quickly running out. "So can I come?"

"Oh, just come, what do I care." Catherine turns to leave. "But it's your job, Lydia, to keep her out of trouble."

I'm pulled from the dark romance of *Mathilda* by the sound of men's voices carrying down the road. I put my book down and close my eyes. My stomach has felt light and fluttery all day, and now that Mr. Barrett is here I'm afraid I won't even be able to sit still or have a level conversation. Mother is sleeping upstairs with a headache, and Father is who knows where on business. It will just be us today. A delicious shiver runs down my spine.

Taking a moment in front of the big gilded mirror in the hall, I smooth out my dress and cast a critical eye over my reflection. I wish I had Catherine's clear eyes, playful and bright, that make men love her. Mine are dark and serious, just as she always accuses me of being. I test my smile the way she always does in the mirror, but the result is strained, and instead of looking pretty and lighthearted, I look like a bee just flew up my skirt.

Emeline is the first to the door, pulling on it with all her weight. It finally creaks open, swollen in the humidity. I feel the same—sluggish and heavy. Catherine sweeps down the stairs, and though her dress is still crisp and white, there's a pallor to her complexion, and I know she's suffering just as the rest of us are in this awful heat. But that's not what gives me pause. "Catherine, you can't possibly be wearing that."

She stops, hand on the railing, and snorts. "And you can't possibly think I'm about to take fashion advice from you of all people." Nevertheless, doubt flickers across her face and she rolls her eyes. "Go on then. What's wrong with it?"

I glance at the door where Emeline is standing, waiting for Mr. Barrett and Mr. Pierce to come up the drive, and lower my voice. "You're all but spilling out the top." She's always been more endowed than me in that area, but this is immodest even by her standards. I imagine her sitting upstairs, plumping and padding, just another feather in her hook to snare Mr. Barrett. Or Pierce. Whoever it is that she feels like playing with today. "That button is near bursting off."

She gives me a look of utter disdain, and then breezes past to welcome Mr. Barrett and Mr. Pierce.

Emeline is already chattering excitedly, leading Mr. Barrett by the hand straight through the hall and to the back door. I intercept them.

"Let's offer our guests something to drink first, shall we? I'm sure they're parched."

Mr. Pierce's waistcoat is partially unbuttoned and his lank hair rakishly slicked forward. He barely bobs his head at me before his eyes alight on Catherine, taking her hand with a wolfish grin. I send Emeline with instructions for Ada to bring refreshments to the parlor, and then fall into step beside Mr. Barrett.

He's watching Catherine and Mr. Pierce with a little frown, his eyes melancholy. I want to say something to him, to have him say something back. I want him to turn those blue-green eyes on me and look at me the same way Mr. Pierce is looking at my sister right now. But all my words get tangled up in my head and the only thing I can think to say is, "They make a handsome couple, don't they?"

Honestly, of all the things to say. I burn as Mr. Barrett glances down at me, but the look is fleeting and he returns his attention back to them. He's standing very close and, despite the heat, a little flutter runs through me when his sleeve brushes my arm.

"Yes," he says. "They do."

We sit in the parlor, Mr. Pierce and Catherine whispering to one another. Mr. Pierce leans in close to her, and Catherine sweeps her lashes down, occasionally tilting her head back and laughing. Her color is high; she must be feeling better. Emeline monopolizes Mr. Barrett, lecturing him on the habits of mermaids and asking if he thinks there might be one in the pond.

"There might be, I'm not sure."

He's distracted. Emeline doesn't notice, but he keeps glancing up at Mr. Pierce and Catherine, and he doesn't look pleased. His fair brow is clouded, his jaw tense. How is it that Catherine can have not one, but two men vying for her attention? I might as well be invisible.

Ada presses a glass of something cold into my hand and I sip it automatically as I study him. He has the face of a classical statue, all strong angles rendered soft and beautiful as if by a practiced sculptor. His eyes are the misty green of shipwreck glass, and indeed I fear they could lure me to a stormy fate. Because if I'm understanding the look he keeps throwing in Mr. Pierce's direction, he's jealous of his friend. The light fluttery feeling in my stomach hardens and sours.

Damn Catherine. Damn her and her beauty and her cunning and the way she always comes out on top. And damn John Barrett too. I hardly know him, yet I would have thought someone so grounded, so sober, would be impervious to her charms.

The drinks are finished and Emeline is near to bouncing out of her skin. I clear my throat, bringing Mr. Barrett out of his reverie, and Catherine and Mr. Pierce out of their private conversation. "Should we go for a walk?"

Outside, the thickness of the air hits me like a wall, and I immediately wish I had finished that drink. Emeline skips ahead. Where does she get that endless energy? It's a labor just to breathe in this heat and humidity. We're barely out of the yard when Catherine stops in her tracks, her arm laced through Mr. Pierce's.

"Mr. Pierce wishes to see..." She trails off, giggling into his shoulder. "What was it you wanted to see, Mr. Pierce?"

"Rumor has it you have the finest...roses...in New Old-bury," Mr. Pierce declares with good humor, "and your sister has graciously offered to show me."

They head off in the opposite direction.

"Your sister is rather fond of roses," Mr. Barrett observes.

I look up at him, surprised. But then, of course he would remember that she was arranging roses the other day, and he probably saved the one she gave him as a keepsake.

"I suppose so." I don't care what flowers Catherine likes. I don't care what little tricks and pretty things she says to get her way.

"And you, what's your favorite flower?"

He's either trying to be polite, or mask the fact that he's interested in Catherine's preferences. I shrug, hardly attempting to keep the irritation from my voice. "Foxglove, I suppose," I say offhandedly. "Or poppies."

Emeline is growing restless. "We can look at flowers on the way," she says, before Mr. Barrett can respond. Then she's dragging him by the hand down the path.

"In the poem the mermaids ride dolphins and wear crowns

of seaweed and pearls. Catherine says they aren't real but she's never looked so how can she know for sure?"

Mr. Barrett slowly brings his attention back to us and looks down at her. "Well, she may be right. You probably won't find any mermaids in the pond."

Emeline's face falls. I'm torn between scooping her up and hugging her or giving Mr. Barrett a harsh word.

But before I can do either, he's crouching down and squinting off in the direction of the pond. Then he shakes his head. "No, this isn't the right weather for mermaids," he says solemnly.

Emeline studies his face, not sure if he's putting her on or not. "What do you mean?"

"Well," he says, frowning as if in deep thought, "mermaids usually keep to the ocean. That's where all the dolphins and pearls are after all. No, I shouldn't think the mermaids would trouble themselves with a little pond." Seeing her face, he quickly amends, "Unless perhaps they are at the deepest part, where humans can't find them. Quite shy, are mermaids."

She stares at him, enraptured. Then she turns to me, hands on hips. "We just *came* from the ocean and I never thought to look for a mermaid in the harbor." Exasperated, she heaves a sigh and tramps on ahead of us.

I can't help smiling, and I almost forgive Mr. Barrett his weakness for falling under Catherine's sway. Almost.

8

I'M WALKING A few steps behind them. Mr. Barrett has
stripped down to his waistcoat, his riding coat slung over his
arm, white sleeves rolled up revealing tanned arms taut with
lean muscles. Perhaps there are some benefits to this heat
after all.

Snip bounces at Emeline's and Mr. Barrett's ankles, then
doubles back to make sure I'm coming before bounding off
again. I can't help but think of the day I met Mr. Barrett in
the woods and how different he had been then, smiling and
warm and eager. And then he had found out who we were
and the door slammed shut.

We climb the little hill behind the house, past the summerhouse and back down into the woods. Sunlight filters in
through the glass-green canopy above. It's cooler here, but
only just, and the air is thicker with moisture. I wipe the sweat
from my brow and wish I hadn't done my laces so tightly this
morning.

The air is quiet and still, charged with an uneasy energy. It's
an alive thing, prickly and filled with restless spirits. Cicadas

and crickets grind away, and bullfrogs hold their breath until we pass, then join the chorus. If I stand still and listen closely it almost sounds like whispers. Yet for all the oppressive heat, the farther away from the house we get, the lighter I feel, as if a weight is gradually being lifted from my shoulders. I run to catch up with Emeline and Mr. Barrett.

A bird calls out above us, and a moment later a streak of yellow flashes between the branches. "Oh! That looks like a golden thrush, doesn't it, Mr. Barrett? A male, I believe."

"Hmm? Oh, yes. A golden thrush," he agrees. For a moment he doesn't say anything else and I wonder if he's even paying attention. But then he slants a glance down at me, the corner of his lips quirking up ever so slightly. "You know your birds, Miss Montrose."

I quickly look away, trying to keep my smile from growing too broad under his gaze. "Some. I'm sure I would love to learn more about them, if only I had a teacher."

Where did *that* come from? I sound like Catherine. I hazard a quick peek up at him but he's already looking away, scanning the trees for other birds, presumably.

The truth is, I don't really know anything about any species of birds, aside from the most common ones. We had gulls and sparrows in Boston, some doves I think. Here, I might be able to point out a cardinal or jay, but that's where my knowledge ends. That might not even have been a golden thrush for all I know. As soon as I had learned Mr. Barrett was coming over today, I pulled out all the volumes of *Histoire Naturelle* in our library and pored over the colorful plates, trying to memorize as much as I could. After hours of study all I had to show for it was an aching back and dried-out eyes. Who would have thought there were so many species of the creatures?

Mr. Barrett and Emeline are a little way ahead. His hand is light at Emeline's elbow as he helps her navigate a tangle of roots, the graceful line of his broad shoulders bent endearingly close to her. For a moment I consider pretending to stumble so that he'll come back and take my elbow, but as soon as the thought forms, I dismiss it. I won't stoop to Catherine's level of tricks and deceits.

When the trees clear I catch my breath. The little patch of shimmering green gives way to a full view of the pond. It's beautiful, and I can see why it has captured Emeline's imagination. Rocks edge the water, green and slick, and a weeping willow's tendrils dip into the glassy surface. It would be the perfect place for a mermaid to emerge and lounge in the sun.

"Be careful, Emmy," I call to her as she bolts ahead, stick in hand, eager to stir at the water and find her aquatic friends. Snip yelps happily as he tries to steal her stick away.

"I *am* being careful!" she yells back, her voice equal measures of irritation at being parented and excitement to finally be here. "After the mermaids I'm going to find the boy and we'll all play together."

I shrug; it's impossible to keep up with all her fancies and play stories. "Just don't go so close to the edge."

Mr. Barrett stands rigid as he watches her go, squinting against the sun. He looks uncomfortable, as if he wants to say something.

"She'll be fine," I say. "I'll make sure she minds herself." It's sweet that he's concerned for her, but with Emeline busy she won't be able to let anything slip like Catherine was so worried she would.

With a wary eye still trained on her, he lays his coat beneath the willow and extends his hand. I press my own into his and he guides me down. It's the first time we've touched like that, skin to skin, our fingers twined. That day in the woods when we met he had been wearing gloves, and I've been waiting since then to feel his touch again. A tingle runs through my arm and blooms in my stomach. I catch my breath and carefully look out the corner of my eye to see if he felt it too. But his face betrays nothing as he settles down beside me.

I make sure that Emeline is still in my line of sight before I allow myself to enjoy his company. He's so close that I can see the fine lines at the corners of his eyes, the way the sun catches and filters through his thick, golden lashes. Maybe he wishes that it was him inspecting Catherine's roses right now instead of Mr. Pierce, but he's here all the same, with me. I don't know what it is exactly, but I feel safe when he's nearby. Not that there's any reason I should be afraid. It's more like finding something you never knew you were missing. The bad dreams, the unsettling occurrences of the past weeks all melt away when I'm with him. Even if he doesn't feel the same way, sitting here beside him watching the pond is enough. This moment is enough.

"How do you like your new home of Willow Hall, Miss Montrose?" He's not looking at me, and his question startles me out of my thoughts.

"Well enough," I say. I don't tell him that I abhor the house with its heavy, watching walls, nor that I can feel the displeasure of the woods for having been felled for such a creation. I don't tell him that since coming I haven't had a full night's sleep, and what sleep I've had is filled with disturbing dreams. I certainly don't tell him about Mother's wails or the woman in the garden, the writing in the mirror.

"I'm glad to hear it." His voice is distant, almost wistful. I want to ask him why he was so surprised, so unsettled when we first met him and he learned that we were his business partner's daughters. Why do his beautiful eyes hold so much sadness? Why does he never smile in my presence like he did that first day?

He has his knees drawn up, arms casually crossed over them

as he squints off across the pond. "See that line of pine trees there? No, a bit to the right." He points. "There. That's where my property edges yours."

"Oh," I say, a bit taken aback. "I didn't know we were neighbors."

"Yes," he says. "Though when I sold this parcel to your father, I was under the impression it would be used only for a small office, perhaps a summer home." He lapses back into silence before adding, "I know you like to explore, but you should have a care when wandering around the woods by yourself."

Maybe that's why he was so surprised to meet us, why he's so reserved around us still. He had sold his land under one pretense, only to see it used for another. And now he's afraid that I'll trespass on his property.

"I hope I don't come to regret it," he says. It's not clear if he's speaking to me; he's still watching Emeline, tensing when she gets too close to the water. She's having a time of it, dancing under the feathery willow boughs, making a little crown for herself out of daisy stems. I'm too taken aback at his frankness to return her smile.

He stops when he realizes that I'm watching him. Seeing my expression he hastily adds, "It's only that the land is so wild, it's not a comfortable place for a family."

It's a lie. He doesn't want us here. Our conversation trails off, I have no clue what to say next and Mr. Barrett won't even look at me. I'm not upset, not really. It's so beautiful here, wild woods or not, yet I can't help but feel uncomfortable, as if there's an undefinable wrongness about the place. The trees and creatures here have no need of my family, and they watch us with wary, slightly accusatory eyes, the way Mr. Barrett must.

There's something comforting about knowing that Mr. Barrett lives nearby though, just out of sight. I want to make him glad that he did sell the land and that we're neighbors now. I want to say that whatever he heard about Boston, the things that happened there weren't true.

But he's distracted, peering off into the woods and fiddling with a loose button on his discarded coat. The heat prickles and I'm having trouble concentrating because I know he's thinking about Catherine with Mr. Pierce. Is that what today was supposed to be? Some sort of wager laid down between the two men to see who could win Catherine? Suddenly sitting here beside him is not enough. The empty place that I didn't even know I contained is aching with want, trembling with fear that it may never be filled.

Abruptly, Mr. Barrett springs up, disrupting the still air and peering off into the woods behind us.

"What is it? Is everything all right?"

"Er...yes." He drops his gaze from the woods, a hint of color creeping up from his collar. "I thought I saw something," he mumbles as he sits back down. "It was nothing."

We sit in silence. Is he looking for Catherine and Mr. Pierce? Did he think he saw them, and was eager to join them after all? If sitting here beside him is not enough for me, it seems it is certainly not enough for him either.

Cyrus taught me that no man would ever want me for anything other than my family's money, and this was something that I always accepted about myself. But with Mr. Barrett I saw a brief glimmer of hope, that maybe, just maybe, there was more for me. A heaviness presses against my chest.

"Miss Montrose, are you all right?" His gaze has been darting about, ever watchful, as if at any moment he expects someone to materialize from the trees. But now it lands on me.

"What?" His eyes have lost some of their distance. I color, sure that he could read my thoughts as I stared at him. "Oh, yes. Fine. I'm fine." But I'm not. There's something wrong, I can feel it. I've been jealous before, angry, but this is more than just a passing melancholy mood. It's as if a dark mist is creeping at the edge of my mind, curling gnarled fingers around me, fogging my thoughts with terrible and ugly feelings. I take a shaky breath, trying to ignore the sensation.

He doesn't look convinced. "You're very pale. Are you sure?"

"Am I?" I attempt a careless laugh but it comes out in a choke. "It's just the heat. I think maybe I need to lie down."

Mr. Barrett is already on his feet offering me his arm, and I shakily accept it. "Let me walk you back," he says, peering down into my face. "I'm afraid that I've said something to upset you." He looks genuinely remorseful.

The dark mist curls further into my mind—I can't think straight. My temple throbs. I must get away from this place, this man. I don't like the dark turn my thoughts have taken sitting out here with him. I don't like the jealousy and anger that's simmering beneath my breast. My heart beats hard, every palpitation a threatening command of *Just go. Just go. Just go.* Deep within me I know that if I don't leave, all of that anger and frustration will come erupting out of me in a way I can't control. *Just like that day with Tommy Bishop*, a singsong voice says in my mind. *Just go. Just go.*

But what do I have to be so angry about? I try to shake the fog from my mind, to remember what we were speaking about even a few moments ago. All I know is that I can't be here right now. I have to leave.

"No, no. Please, stay with Emeline." I wave off his polite concern. "I just need to get out of this heat and rest."

Mr. Barrett takes a sharp breath, and I follow his line of sight. Emeline. Emeline is gone.

In the midst of my jealousy and anger, I forgot to watch her, to make sure she was all right. The dark thoughts dissipate, a hundred snakes slithering back from whence they came, as a knot of unease settles in my chest.

She must have gotten bored while Mr. Barrett and I were talking, ignoring her. "She can't have gotten far," I say, though my voice trembles, belying my misgivings.

Mr. Barrett is already snatching up his coat, his jaw clenched tight and eyes scanning the surrounding trees. He heads off back into the woods, and I have to jog just to catch up with him. His tense silence compounds my uneasiness and I start to feel real panic. What if she got lost in the woods going back to the house? What if someone, some malicious vagabond wandering through our property stole her away? My blood goes cold. What if those words in the mirror weren't my imagination at all, but some sort of warning? I hike my skirts to my knees, running as Mr. Barrett increases his pace.

We are just coming up the hill toward the summerhouse, when a crashing in the trees stops us. My heart leaps to my throat and Mr. Barrett comes to an abrupt halt, putting out a hand to keep me back.

The brush rustles with movement, and then a moment later out tumbles a giggling Catherine, Mr. Pierce on her heels.

I let out a deflated breath, relieved that it wasn't something malevolent, but irritated that we're losing time looking for Emeline when it's only Catherine making a spectacle out of herself.

Mr. Barrett parts his lips as if he wants to ask his friend what they were doing, but one look between them tells the whole story; Catherine's hair is unkempt, her color high and Mr. Pierce's collar is undone. But there's no time to chastise her for her careless, lewd, behavior.

"Lydia!" Catherine looks up at me in surprise, a tipsy smile lingering at her lips. "What are you doing here?"

"Emeline is missing," I snap at her.

The smile fades as Catherine's gaze flicks between Mr. Barrett and me. She looks more annoyed than worried. "I thought you said you were going to watch her."

I bite my tongue and resist the urge to take her by the shoulders and shake her. She's right, but there's no time to bicker about it.

Mr. Barrett takes charge. "August and I will go back out to the road. Miss Montrose, you and your sister go back to Willow Hall. Send word if you find her before us, and we'll do likewise." His tone is commanding, and I'm too sick with worry to do anything other than obey.

9

MY KNEES GO weak with relief when we come back down the hill and around the front of the house to see Snip dozing in the sun on the lawn. A little ways away a horse has been carelessly hitched to the fence; Mother must have a caller, and Emeline has joined them. My heart rate slows. All that worry was for nothing after all. Emeline is safe and sound.

"There," says Catherine in a grumble. "She just went back to the house. You needn't have made such a fuss and driven Mr. Pierce away."

I grit my teeth. "Why don't you go find Mr. Barrett and Mr. Pierce and let them know that Emeline is safe? They can't have gotten far."

Catherine looks as if she wants to argue, but then clamps her mouth shut. An opportunity to have both Mr. Pierce and Mr. Barrett to herself is simply too good for her to pass up, so she turns on her heel and stalks off to the road.

I take a deep breath, watching her go before I square my shoulders and go inside. I hate having to be the one to discipline Emeline, but someday she'll get herself into real trouble if she doesn't learn to listen, and God knows Mother won't be the one to do it. I only hope that Emeline isn't pestering Mother's caller.

But when I step into the parlor, it's not one of Mother's callers that Emeline is bombarding with questions.

"Cyrus?" At the sound of my voice the young man that had been lounging by the window with a bored expression springs up. What on earth is he doing in New Oldbury, in our parlor? It's almost as outlandish as if Napoleon had stormed in for a cup of tea. But here he is standing before me in his fine double-breasted coat, his short black hair usually so trim and precise, sticking up at odd angles.

"Lydia," he says, with his honey-smooth voice. "Forgive me for intruding, but Miss Emeline was kind enough to invite me inside." He runs a hand through his ruffled hair and flashes me an apologetic smile. "I've just arrived from Boston and haven't even gone to my inn yet. I wanted to see you first."

I don't even know how to respond to him. Is this the same Cyrus Thompson who said he could never see me again? The same Cyrus Thompson who sealed my family's fate in society when he severed our engagement? I take a deep breath. One thing at a time. Turning to Emeline, I try to plaster a stern expression on my face. "You gave us an awful fright running off like that without a word," I say, conscious that Cyrus is watching us with his sharp brown eyes. "Go up to your room to clean up and we'll talk later."

Emeline shrugs, giving me a sly look. "If you hadn't been so busy with Mr. Barrett you'd have heard me say I was going back to the house."

My gaze involuntarily flickers to Cyrus at this, and one of his dark brows rises in interest.

"We'll discuss this later," I hiss at her, and with a reproachful "hmph" she leaves me alone in the parlor with my ex-fiancé.

"She's gotten so tall," Cyrus muses, his gaze following her to the door. When it shuts, his eyes land back on me. "You two used to have such adventures together, I remember. Always coming home muddy from tramping all over Boston, full of fantastic stories."

I'm surprised he remembers anything about our time in Boston. I've hardly spared a thought for Cyrus these past months, and I figured he would have done the same with me. We might have been engaged once, but we rarely saw each other, and after he broke it off I was more upset for my family's sake than any idea that he might have loved me. When he showed up in Boston to let me know the engagement was off, I was taken aback that he delivered the news in person rather than with a note. Now here he is in our parlor on the other side of the state, fondly remembering little details about our old life.

But I'm in no mood for small talk and I gloss over his pleasantries. "What brings you to New Oldbury?" I ask coolly.

He gestures that I should sit, but when I remain standing he shrugs and seats himself on one of the chairs. "I'm in town on business for my father."

"You came to New Oldbury on business?" My disbelief must show on my face, because he cocks his head and breaks into one of his dazzling smiles.

"Your father isn't the only one who sees that New Oldbury is a ripe plum for the picking when it comes to mills. Or that mills are where the real money is to be made these days."

I open and close my mouth a few times, trying to find the words to address him. Cyrus is a relic of a terrible time in our lives, and he belongs in Boston, in the past. "And you came to find me to tell me this?"

In an instant he's up out of the chair, dark gaze locked on me. He moves a step closer, his expression fervent and amused. "Business isn't the only reason I came, Lydia."

I take an awkward step back. He's not saying what I think he's saying, is he? "I...what? You can't be serious."

Ignoring my incredulous tone, he launches into his appeal. "I had to see you. I..." He places his hat on the chair and closes the distance between us, taking my hands in his. He's looking right into me with his dark eyes. "Everything that happened in Boston, it was a mistake. I told my father that I don't care about the scandal. I made him understand that I'll have you or nobody. I want you as my wife, Lydia."

The wind goes out of me, and I reach back to steady myself against a chair. Closing my eyes, I rock back on my heels, letting the implication of what he's telling me sink in. I can feel him looking down at me, the firm set of his lips softened with my name still lingering on them.

Ours was an engagement settled by our parents years ago, a business partnership between our fathers that would benefit our entire family. Even at the age of fourteen I knew that I would never be a beauty like Catherine. It didn't hurt that Cyrus was tall with dark good looks, and he was always polite. But I never made the mistake of thinking that he loved me, or even that I might love him. Love would come later, Mother had said with forced cheeriness. That was often the way with these kinds of matches. Knowing that I would probably never have the kind of chances Catherine would have— and that Catherine would never allow herself to be used as currency in a business transaction—I agreed. Besides, it made Mother happy to know that I'd be settled and taken care of, and after a few years I'd grown more comfortable with the idea—and with Cyrus. Until I met Mr. Barrett, I had thought that I could be happy with a life like that.

From somewhere in the house I hear the back door open and then close; Catherine must have taken the back stairs to avoid who she thinks is a caller of Mother's in the front parlor. Thank God she doesn't realize that it's Cyrus, or she would never let me hear the end of it.

"Why now?"

His hands are around my waist. How many times did I lie awake at night, imagining what this would feel like? Not with Cyrus, but some adoring man, his features obscured by darkness, fingertips warm with love as he trailed them down my body. But the reality is nothing like my naive fantasies and I feel uncomfortable, not enraptured.

"Because I can't stop thinking about you." He's nuzzling my neck, the tender spot behind my ear. "I've missed you every day since you left."

I stiffen as he combs his fingers up through my hair at the nape of my neck, and when he searches for my lips with his, I evade him.

"Stop, Cyrus." I push myself back and he looks at me from under his refined brows, his dark eyes making a show of hurt feelings. "Why are you really here?"

"I just told you. I—"

"Please, don't lie to me."

His expression loses some of its vulnerability and he drops his hand. "I was going to come anyway."

I don't say anything. My heart rate slows, and the flush of confusion dies.

Then the ridiculous happens. He drops to one knee, my hand in his as he looks up at me, pleading. "Don't be this way. Lydia—"

"Get up this instant!" I hiss, darting a glance over my shoulder, sure that I heard a footstep in the hall. I yank back my hand, throwing his balance. Cursing, he lands hard on his backside, crumpling his carefully pressed coattails.

This seems to snap him out of it. "Oh, all right. Just don't look at me like that, would you?" He huffs to his feet, brushing off the crumbs of indignity. "The business has not survived since your father left. We...we're in a very bad way, Lyd," he says in a hoarse whisper. "My father asked me to call on you and see if you would be amenable to renewing our engagement, but I wanted to see you anyway," he adds hastily. "You have to believe me on that score."

I'm not inclined to believe him about anything at the moment. My expression must say as much, because he's pacing about the room, loosening his cravat and running his hand through his hair.

I bite the inside of my mouth, trying not to smile. So there is some justice in the world after all. I speak as levelly as I can. "Your father was the one who demanded that mine leave. He said he wouldn't be in business with a man whose children's names were always in the papers. If the business is failing, then it's your fault. Not ours."

He stops short, running a finger over one of the green bottles on the table, mementos of our fathers' shared glass venture in Boston, now used as vases for wildflowers. He glowers at me, those dark eyes no longer beautiful and soft, but calculating and angry. "We were going to be married anyway. What do you care why I came back? What other chances do you think you'll have? I can save you from the cloud of scandal and a life of loneliness, and you can save me from poverty."

The smile fades inside my mouth. He thinks I'm a puppet. I don't know why I thought that someday maybe he would have looked at me the way other men look at Catherine. The way Mr. Barrett and Mr. Pierce look at Catherine. I feel cheap, used at his words. He's right, which makes it hurt all the more.

"You came all the way here with the intention of charming your way into my good graces, into my family's money. Go home, Cyrus."

I didn't realize I was holding my breath, but I let it out now as he snatches his hat up. He stalks to the door, turning around and thrusting an accusing finger in my direction. "You're a fool, Lydia. As if I would want anything to do with you or your sick family." His look drips with contempt, but there's a break in his voice, and I know that for the right price, he would change his tone in a heartbeat.

I can't sleep that night. If I fall asleep the bad dreams will come again. Even when I'm awake there are footsteps, cold stares from invisible eyes, figures in the woods and in the garden. I've even hung a linen over the mirror, lest new words appear and stare back at me. I kick off the blankets and turn over trying to find a comfortable position, but no matter what I do my dry eyelids won't stay shut. My skin is still crawling from where Cyrus touched me, and I can't get his words out of my head. *What other chances do you think you'll have?*

I punch my pillow down to make it fluffier, but punching it feels good so I do it a few more times. I imagine that it's Cyrus's smug face, his aquiline nose crooked and bloody. Shameless little opportunist. But suddenly the dark hair shifts to amber, the sharp chin broadens and the face becomes John Barrett, his melancholy, clear eyes looking at me from beneath gold lashes. I stop my fist in the air and slump back. Unlike Cyrus, he's a good person. I saw it in the way he spoke to Emeline as if she were an adult, his equal. I saw it when he crouched down beside me and took an interest in what I was reading, even though Catherine was right there, watching him. But most of all, it's just a feeling I get, a warmth he exudes despite his serious, sad demeanor. And if he notices

Catherine's beauty and sparkle, well, I can hardly fault him for that, can I?

When sleep finally comes, it's hot and fitful. I drift between shallow dreams. An owl's echoing question hangs on the night air. The footsteps and laughter of a child. Not Emeline's carefree laugh, but that of a boy. The way Tommy Bishop used to laugh when he was pulling the wings off flies, mirthless and unsettling. I'm running, the laughter inescapable, following me at every turn. A chorus of *You attract them! Are you ready? Prepare! Prepare!* rings out. And then the willow from the pond comes, with its rustle of papery leaves, growing and growing until it's a hurricane of swirling branches grabbing at me, pulling me down. I have no choice but to succumb to the blackness of its deafening roar.

❧ *10* ❧

"WHAT'S THE POINT of having a ballroom if we never use it?"

Catherine is sprawled on the settee in dramatic repose, studying a chipped fingernail with a frown. I watch her from over the top of my book as I try to read. Emeline is cutting paper dolls out on the floor, and is still refusing to talk to me after the other day when I reprimanded her in front of Cyrus.

"We've been here long enough now and people will be expecting some sort of formal introduction."

Emeline perks up. "A ball? Really? Oh, I've always wanted to go to a ball!"

My mouth goes dry. A ball would mean opening up our home to strangers, opening *ourselves* up to their curious eyes and all their gossip. Mother will be too tired, too ambivalent to carry it off, and Father will think it a frivolous waste of time. Which means that it would fall to Catherine to plan, and me to help her. "You can't be serious."

Catherine scowls at me. "Oh, yes I am. I think I'll ask Mother."

"Cath, don't. You know she doesn't want to entertain and

we're barely settled as it is, never mind inviting dozens of people to tramp through the place."

"Mother isn't some fragile bird to be kept cooped up." She gives me a pitying look as if I had never even considered what was best for our mother. "A ball would be just the thing to keep her spirits up, give her something to be excited about."

A ball would also mean Cyrus, who presumably is still lurking about New Oldbury on his father's behalf, would no doubt come. He might have given up in his half-hearted pursuit of my hand, but I doubt he would give up so easily on his father's business interests and recouping his family's fortune the honest way; a ball at Willow Hall would be too tempting with all its local businessmen in attendance.

Catherine's expression is one of carefully studied boredom, a favorite she uses to antagonize me. "If you weren't so selfish you would see that it would be doing Mother a favor."

I scramble to reason with her, trying to keep the desperation from my voice. "You said it yourself, the first night we were here…we could hold all the balls we wanted and no one would come! Don't you think people already know who we are here? Don't you think it would just be drawing more attention to ourselves?"

"That was before we met Mr. Barrett and Mr. Pierce," she counters. "There might not be much polite society in New Oldbury, but what little there is we have a duty to keep up with."

"I thought you said this was for Mother's benefit. Which is it, for Mother, or for keeping up with society?"

"As if there can't be more than one reason why it's a good idea!"

Emeline watches us volley insults and arguments. I know I should stop; more than likely Catherine will lose interest and forget about her scheme in a few days. But I'm hot and irritable after my poor night's sleep, and the prospect of formally entertaining has me on edge. "And there are more reasons why it's a bad idea!"

"Don't you ever get tired of being such a bore?"

"Don't *you* ever get tired of all your pompous conceit?"

She's losing her patience. Pushing herself up from her seat, Catherine crosses her arms and stares daggers at me. "Well if we just sit in this house like a bunch of invalids, afraid to step foot outside, then I'll die of boredom."

"I wish you would!"

No sooner so my words slip out than I regret them with a biting intensity. I cut too hard and too deep. "Cath, I'm sorry. I didn't mean…"

Before I can apologize, Catherine shoots me a barbed look and slips out of the room.

As soon as Catherine leaves, Mother comes in with her basket and seats herself by the window, so it's some time before I can escape upstairs to follow her.

I pause in the hall outside Catherine's room and tap at the door. "Catherine?"

When there's no answer, I gently turn the knob and open the door a crack. The curtains are drawn. Catherine is lying on her side in her shift, the silhouette of her body softened by the evening glow. She could be sleeping, but then I see the uneven rise and fall of her shoulders. A muffled sound comes from the depths of her pillows.

I shouldn't be here. Quietly, I close the door, hoping that she doesn't hear the click of the latch. I've never seen Catherine cry before and it strikes me that I don't know how to be a good sister to anyone besides Emeline.

Breakfast the next day is a subdued affair, even for us. Mother is tired and withdrawn, and Father hasn't made his appearance yet. I slip into my chair and help myself to a plate of eggs and bacon, which promptly grows cold in front of me. Unsurprisingly, I didn't sleep well last night again.

Catherine watches with disinterest. She doesn't look much better, her face puffy and green. A piece of cold toast lies untouched on her plate. We haven't spoken since our fight, and I get the impression that she's feeling just as bad as me.

Emeline is oblivious to the tension, playing with paper dolls in her lap, making them ask each other to dance and then tossing them up in the air and watching them flutter back down. She hasn't stopped talking about dances and balls since yesterday, trailing behind me everywhere I go, listing off all the dresses she would wear and the dance steps she would debut in our ballroom.

Just as I'm pondering how I might make amends with Catherine, Father barrels through the door in a search of some breakfast to take back to his study. He drops a distracted kiss on the top of Mother's head before taking a plate and piling it with toast and bacon.

"I'll be late at the mill today," he says, surprising exactly nobody. "That Ezra Clarke still won't be reasonable about the price for his land. Barrett suggested a town meeting where we can address his concerns and hopefully get some more of the townspeople on our side, but of course the church is still undergoing repairs from all the water damage." He adds an angry spoonful of eggs to his plate with a grunt. "I want this deal done soon," he says more to himself than to us.

It comes to me in a flash. I clear my throat delicately, putting aside my plate. "Why don't we hold it here, in the ballroom?"

Father looks up sharply, glancing between Mother and me like he accidentally wandered into the wrong room with the wrong family in it. He opens his mouth but before he can say anything I hurry on.

"It's criminal that we have such a beautiful ballroom and never use it." Looking at his blank face I realize I need to appeal to his business sense, so I add, "And the sooner the meeting is held, the sooner the mill can be built and that's good for business, isn't it?"

"Well, yes, but..." Father absently stuffs a piece of toast into his mouth and chews slowly. He's still standing by the sideboard, plate in hand. When he swallows he looks thoughtful. "It's not a terrible idea."

I steal a sidelong look at Catherine who is staring listlessly off into space. "And afterward there could be refreshments and maybe even dancing."

Mother stares at me, mouth ajar as the egg slides off her knife. Catherine looks up sharply to see if I'm joking. I plunge on.

"Isn't that the way these country functions usually go? There's always cider and entertainment afterward. All the townspeople will come to hear what you have to say if they know there will be dancing. Besides, it will give us something to look forward to."

This last point is a lie. I will dread this meeting and all the small talk and dancing and smiling faces that go along with it, but I know that Catherine will not, and I owe it to her to at least try to be a good sister; otherwise, I have no one to blame but myself for our relationship. It won't be as formal as a ball, but it will be a compromise, something Mother can handle, and, God willing, me as well.

Emeline's gaze darts between Father, Mother and me, her eyes shining with hope. At the very least, I can take comfort in the fact that I'll be making Emeline happy.

Father turns to Mother. "What do you say, Martha? Do you think you can shine up the ballroom and act the hostess?"

"Yes, of course," she says without enthusiasm. "We should hold the meeting here."

"Excellent." Father licks some jam off his finger and gathers up his newspaper. "I'll leave you ladies to the planning then."

By now, Catherine is sitting up straight, face bright and eyes shining. "I'll plan it all," she quickly offers. "You won't need to lift a finger, Mother. We'll have to invite Mr. Pierce. And of course Mr. Barrett will be coming," she adds, catching my eye.

My body tightens. Of course Mr. Barrett will come. I hadn't even considered that when I was hatching my plan to make amends with Catherine. Just his name makes my heart pump harder. I'd be lying if I said I didn't think of the way our hands touched at the pond at least several times a day, the jolt of warmth we shared playing over and over again in my mind. But what could I possibly say to him?

Emeline is practically vibrating out of her seat. "A ball! Here!" she squeals as she pushes her chair from the table, too excited to sit a moment longer.

I give her a weak smile, my thoughts racing. And what about Cyrus? In a small town like this, he's bound to catch wind of the meeting and invite himself. Maybe this was a bad idea after all. What was I thinking?

"Are you all right?" Catherine stands up, pushing in her chair. "You went as pale as a sheet."

"Yes," I say, with forced cheeriness. I muster up a smile for her, but she's already tripping out of the room, humming a little tune under her breath.

11

"MOTHER, WHAT ON earth are you doing?"

I find her in the ballroom on hands and knees, scrubbing away at the shiny hardwood floor. Despite Catherine's pledge to take care of all the preparations, the past two weeks have seen Mother in a flurry of activity, doing everything from beating out already clean carpets to polishing silver while Ada helplessly looks on.

She doesn't look up. "We can't have a filthy house when everyone arrives tonight. Everything must be clean."

The ballroom is pristine. I crouch beside Mother, putting a light hand on her shoulder. She gives me a quick, anxious glance, but doesn't stop what she's doing. With a sigh, I stand back up. "Where's Catherine?"

Mother's face darkens. "In her room, trying on gowns."

I watch her narrow back, stretching and shrinking as she throws herself into the long, jerking motion of the rag. What happened to my rosy mother who used to sing while she floated around the house, always so quick to smile, so generous with her kisses?

"Please don't strain yourself," I say uselessly to her back.

My footsteps and Mother's scrubbing fill the echoing space. I try to imagine it filled instead with dancing, sweaty bodies tonight and my stomach plummets at the thought. Devoid of any furniture save the pianoforte and some chairs, I've rarely found reason to come up to this room before. Mother occasionally uses it for a large quilting project, and more than once we've had to make Emeline stop playing boisterous games of chase with Snip. Other than that it's a sad room. I can't imagine it ever being one of grandeur.

I'm turning to leave when Mother's voice stops me. "We're expecting nearly forty guests," she says without pausing in her scrubbing. "I don't want Emeline getting underfoot or causing a scene like..." She trails off, but I know she's thinking of the night in the parlor with the slamming doors. "Besides, the dancing won't start 'til well after her bedtime."

"But she's been looking forward to this for weeks," I tell her. "She'll be crestfallen."

"She can watch the guests arrive, but then it's into bed for her."

I'm ready to argue with her, but she's wound tight as a coil, and with Mr. Barrett and even maybe even Cyrus coming, perhaps it is for the best if Emeline isn't there.

With a sigh, I leave Mother to her cleaning, hoping that she'll stop before exhaustion takes over. I make sure I knock extra loudly on Catherine's door before entering.

"Oh, Ada, thank goodness. I—" Catherine stops when she sees me. "Oh. It's you."

"Yes, it's me."

She hesitates a moment and then pulls me into the room. "I needed Ada to help with my laces, but I suppose you can do it."

"What an honor."

Catherine gives me a cool look but turns around all the

same and lifts her long hair out of the way. I tug at the laces and she winces.

"Do you want them tight or not?"

"I do," she whines. "Just don't be such a beast about it."

When I'm done I sit on the bed and watch her ease into her dress. Despite the tight laces she struggles to get it on, and she's in peril of spilling out the top again. I don't say anything but she gives me a sidelong glance and huffs. "It's the food here. Ada has gotten in the habit of cooking like a country house-wife. All that lard and beef."

I don't point out that the rest of us haven't suffered for Ada's cooking. Our relationship is a strained bridge, both of us making an effort, but one careless word and the whole thing will crumble down.

"Have you picked out what you're going to wear?" she asks me without turning around.

"I was going to wear the white one."

She turns, looking at me blankly. "Which white one?"

My wardrobe is a rainbow of dresses with shades starting at ivory and ending with beige. "I don't know...it has the darts in the bodice and the little lacy things at the sleeves and hem."

"You're hopeless, but I know which one you're talking about. Good choice," she adds grudgingly.

We lull into silence as she tries on more dresses, a mountain of silk and calico growing on the bed. I wonder if Mr. Barrett will come, and if he does, what he will wear. Even though he's not interested in me, I can't help the mounting sense of excitement as the hour for the dance draws near.

Catherine clears her throat and I snap out of my thoughts. "What?"

"I asked you to pass me those pins over there."

I follow her pointing finger and hand her the jar full of pearl pins.

"I'll help you do something with that hopeless hair of yours, if you want." She gives a practiced flick of her wrist, jabbing a pin into her tight swirl of curls.

I don't really want or need her help. I don't care how I look tonight since I'll just be watching from the side. I can't imagine anyone will ask me to dance. But she's watching me impatiently from the mirror and it's not worth a fight. I give in and let her dress me up and fuss me until I pass for decent in her book.

"You want to look nice for Mr. Barrett, don't you?" she demands with a small smile as she gives my hairpin a final, wrenching twist.

I wince. "Why should I care what he thinks?"

"Oh, please. You turn wide-eyed and trembling whenever he's nearby." She shrugs, as if it's no concern of hers. "I can see why you like him…he's just as quiet and sullen as you are."

"Well, you're wrong."

"Oh?"

I know this game. She pretends to be interested and I inadvertently let something slip, and confide in her, give her something she can use against me later. I've fallen prey to it more times than I care to admit. And while we might be on better terms right now, I don't for a moment believe she has my best interest at heart. I won't make the mistake of giving her ammunition she can use against me later.

"Mr. Barrett is Father's business partner," I say, stating the obvious. "He's very nice but he doesn't mean anything to me."

Catherine arches a brow at my reflection in the mirror. "If you say so."

"Yes," I say, making a show of inspecting my fingernails. "I do."

She shrugs again, taking out a little pot of something red and, opening the lid, she dips her finger inside. It smells waxy, with an artificial tang of roses. I watch her with wary eyes, and jump back when she thrusts her finger toward my lips. "What is *that*?"

"Have you honestly never seen lip rouge before? It gives your lips color." She gives me a look that is a mixture of impatience and pity. "Really, Lydia, don't you think it's time you grew up?"

I hesitate. What if Cyrus comes? For some reason the idea of him seeing me dressed up and painted makes me feel ashamed, as if he could see right through my charade and to the plain girl I am at my core.

"Oh, don't be such a bore," Catherine says as she liberally applies some to her own lips. She blots off the excess color with a handkerchief, studying her reflection as she dabs. "You can pretend you don't want to impress Mr. Barrett all you want, but I know deep down you care."

I hate that she's right. "Oh, fine, do what you wish." I let her smear the color over my lips. When I look in the mirror, I hardly recognize the girl with the wide dark eyes and the softly parted pink lips.

"All you need now is a smile," she says. "Looking miserable isn't doing your complexion any favors."

Emeline intercepts me coming down the stairs. She's dressed in her best muslin, with an old silk sash of Catherine's. But she didn't know how to tie it, and it hangs down past her ankles, threatening to trip her. In lieu of ostrich feathers, she's arranged two tattered bird feathers in her hair that she must have found outside.

I had been hoping that Mother would inform her of her curfew, and I wince as I realize I have to break her heart. Crouching down beside her, I touch my fingers to her cheek. "I'm so sorry, sweetheart. You know that by the time the dancing starts it will be well past your bedtime. Mother wants you in bed after the guests arrive."

I brace myself for tears or desperate pleading, but Emeline doesn't move. She stands stock-still, glaring at me from suddenly hostile eyes. "You're mean, Lydia. You're supposed to be the nice sister, but you're just as mean as Cath."

Standing up, I carefully turn my face away so that she can't see how much her words hurt me. What has gotten into her? She never used to throw tantrums like this in Boston, but since coming here she seems as on edge as I am, her moods souring in the blink of an eye.

"If you're going to be willfully contrary, then you had better go to bed right now, and forget about watching the guests arrive. Ada has made up the spare chamber for you, and will help you get undressed."

Emeline gives me a look of lingering reproach. But at last she turns, and she stomps her way up to the spare bedchamber.

I close my eyes and rub at my temple. I hate having to speak to her like that. If only Mother could find it within herself to gently discipline Emeline. But as I duck into the kitchen to sneak a bit of punch, my heart feels suspiciously light, my stomach free of anxiety. It's hard not to get caught up in the energy that thrums through the house, filling the expectant rooms and for a moment the scandal, the unsettling dreams and occurrences, are in the past. Maybe this is what the house has been waiting for. All those silent accusations, that cold watchfulness, the restless spirits…it was just the house waiting to be filled with love and happiness. Soon I've completely forgotten about Emeline's spat in my excitement.

In a freshly starched cravat and a waistcoat with shiny buttons fit to burst, Father thumbs through his list of local businessmen attending tonight, oblivious to the flurry of preparations around him. Mother, with some help from Catherine, has had her apron taken away and is in a clean, if not somber, dress. Despite Catherine's best efforts it still hangs off her slender shoulders, and Mother looks lost and tired. But even she manages a smile. "The house looks clean, doesn't it? No one can say we live in a dirty house now."

The first guests arrive by foot, and soon a carriage is rumbling up the gravel drive, discharging its passengers. The door was sticking so badly today that Joe had to go and find a big rock to keep it propped open. Mother worried that people would trip over it, so she's taken it upon herself to stand post by the door and make sure that there are no stubbed toes.

"Do you see them?"

I'm on the second-floor landing, leaning out the window. Catherine comes up behind me and cranes her neck to catch a glimpse of the arriving guests. "Who?"

"Oh, don't be dense, you know who."

At the thought of Mr. Barrett, the bottom of my stomach drops out and the little vein in my neck starts pulsing. Even the possibility of Cyrus showing his face here tonight can't dampen my spirits.

"Look! There's Mr. Barrett." Catherine points down the road. He's walking briskly, his dark coat flapping behind him. His hat obscures his face, but the broad shoulders and determined gait give him away. She frowns. "He's alone."

"Maybe Mr. Pierce is coming separately." But we both know that he has no occupation, and that he's been staying with Mr. Barrett. If he's not with him now chances are he's not coming at all.

Catherine slams her fist down on the windowsill, rattling the glass panes and I jump. "He has to come! He has to!" Color rises to her cheeks, and are those tears pricking at my sister's steely eyes?

"Catherine, I'm sure we'll be seeing him again soon. I—"

"Shut up! Just please shut up! You don't understand. He needs to be here. I can't wait any longer!"

Before I can ask what she's talking about, she's running to her room, hand to her eyes. I could go after her, but something tells me Catherine has no interest in confiding in me and it will only make matters worse.

From downstairs Mr. Barrett's baritone floats up as he greets Mother and asks after her health. She thanks him and then their words are lost because more people are coming in and clomping up the stairs.

The meeting takes all of about twenty minutes, Father's booming voice convincing Mr. Clarke and the others with land abutting rivers that he and Mr. Barrett have grand plans to put New Oldbury on the map as an industrial center to rival Manchester and Waltham. The end is marked by a polite round of applause.

I go to Catherine's door and knock. "The dancing is about to start. Are you coming?" There's no response.

Well, let Catherine sulk in her room. One of us needs to make an appearance, so I take a deep breath and grit my teeth.

The ballroom has transformed from the lonely, echoing sun-filled room into a space bubbling over with the rustle of gowns, chatter and the scent of women's perfume. As I take up a corner on the far side of the room, I can't help but feel angry that this was all for Catherine in the first place, and she won't even show her face.

"Miss Montrose."

A warm tingle runs through my body at the sound of his voice. He's standing right behind me and I don't have time to prepare myself. I had wanted to be across the room, to watch him first before deciding what I'd say. I had crafted a few neutral sentences but now that he's right here they all fly from my head.

"You look…" His clear eyes are burning through me and I feel as naked as a rose in January, and every bit as exposed. I know how I must look to him in my lip rouge, the dress showing too much of my skin thanks to Catherine's adjustments. He clears his throat, as if coming back to himself. "You look much recovered."

It takes me a moment to realize he's referring to the day at the pond when I nearly fainted from a mixture of heat, anger and jealousy. Has it really been weeks since I saw him last? "Yes, thank you." I struggle to keep my voice impassive, reserved. It comes out muddled and fast, half my mind determined to snub him because of his preference for Catherine, but the other half of me is shamefully excited by the prospect of being close to him. Just his familiar scent unearths that comfortable, safe feeling deep inside me again. I tighten my grip on my glass, willing myself to keep my guard up.

"I'm glad to see it. I've been worried about you since that day at the pond. And of course I was glad when Catherine let us know that Emeline had been found safe."

The punch glass sweats in my hand and I don't know where to look. He's being polite, but he's already looking around the room, gesturing with cup in hand and making strained small talk about the various guests. He says something about Mr. Pierce and I snap back to attention.

"Pity he couldn't come, but his mother took a turn for the worse so he's gone back to Boston to attend her."

"Oh, how sad." I stare at the amber liquid in my glass, swirling it gently side to side.

"I understand these scares are something of a regular occurrence when it comes to his mother," he says. "All the same, August thought it best not to leave it to chance." He glances around the ballroom, now filled with guests itching for the music to start. "He asked me to send Catherine his particular regards, but…is your sister unwell, Miss Montrose?"

"Er, yes," I say, scrambling to think something up. "She has a headache." It's a flimsy excuse, but I can't tell him that she's throwing a tantrum because Mr. Pierce didn't come.

Perhaps Mr. Barrett was relieved when he found out his friend wasn't coming, knowing that Catherine would turn her attention back to him. I haven't forgotten the notes I've seen Catherine passing to Joe to deliver, and I haven't forgotten the white rose in Mr. Barrett's buttonhole.

My ears are pounding and I don't want to be here. No, that's not true. I want to be near him. I'm painfully aware of him, the dark fabric of his waistcoat, of his gestures, the way his eyes wander over the room before settling deeply on mine. I wonder what his hands would feel like, wrapped around my waist the way Cyrus's were, and I sway ever so slightly. I need to get away. There's no use torturing myself with what will never be mine.

He must have read my mind. "Well, I've monopolized your time long enough. No doubt you must welcome all your guests." His voice is clipped and I know I'm being terribly rude, standing there mute and staring just past his shoulder.

"Yes, of course." But I don't move away. I don't know any of the people gathered here save for a couple of familiar faces from Mother's calls. They might as well be miles away; the only other person in the room is him.

Mr. Barrett doesn't move either. People flow around us, a lady's hair feather brushing my bare shoulder, sending a shiver down my spine. "Miss Montrose…" He looks uncomfortable, turning his glass in his fingers over and over, looking everywhere but at me. "I feel I must explain about—"

Just then a matronly woman glides up and puts a doughy gloved arm through Mr. Barrett's and the little bubble around us shatters. Her mouth is already moving before she's even come to rest.

"Mr. Barrett! You wicked man." She's dripping in jewels, her face plastered with makeup. She looks like one of those actors who perform Shakespeare at the Federal Street Theatre in Boston, and speaks just as loudly. "We've hardly seen anything of you at Oakridge these past months and the girls have been asking after you, especially Abigail." She gestures to a tall, slender girl across the room watching the exchange from beneath heavy lashes, which she drops with a shy smile when Mr. Barrett looks at her. "I remember how you loved our Abby's boiled mutton last time, and you announced that you would take up residence at our house indefinitely if only to have her mutton every day. Now don't tell me you don't remember that! Abby certainly does and she will hardly leave me alone asking when you'll be by."

Color rises to Mr. Barrett's cheek but he takes the woman's hand and lifts it to his lips in a polite gesture. "Mrs. Tidewell, nothing would give me more pleasure."

I shift my gaze swiftly away, having been caught in that unpleasant role of unintentional eavesdropper. Now would be my chance to escape, but the ample Mrs. Tidewell is blocking my exit.

"You must join us for supper one of these nights. Now I won't take no for an answer," Mrs. Tidewell scolds with a playful rap of her closed fan upon his arm.

Mr. Barrett catches my eye and quickly looks away, embarrassed. His jaw tightens, but Mrs. Tidewell is blissfully unaware of his discomfort. "Yes, of course. Time has gotten away from me lately what with the mill and—"

"Oh, you men and your work." Mrs. Tidewell leans in toward me conspiratorially, for some reason deciding to include me in the conversation. Her breath smells like onions, and I wonder if it's from Abby's boiled mutton. "Whenever you want something from them it's work work work, but put a pretty girl in front of them and they forget about it all soon enough, eh? And my Abby's the prettiest in New Oldbury." She turns back to him. "Wouldn't you agree, Mr. Barrett?"

I don't know if she's staking a claim, or merely clueless as to the effect of her words. Mortified, I open my mouth, but Mr. Barrett swoops in before I can say something I'll regret.

"Certainly, madam. New Oldbury is lucky to boast so many lovely young ladies, Miss Montrose of course being the latest arrival."

When my eyes fly to meet his, there's a glint of amusement in them, but also something questioning. My body flushes hot. He's just being polite, gentlemanly. His words mean no more than the kiss he gave Mrs. Tidewell's hand.

Mrs. Tidewell lets her gaze run over me, making little effort to mask her thoughts. "Yes, I'm sure," she says, her tone frosty.

She's moved out of my way, her grip tightening on Mr. Barrett's arm, and I seize my chance. "I should go...greet the other guests," I mumble.

"Miss Montrose..." He moves to catch my arm, but Mrs. Tidewell holds him fast and I slip by him.

The fiddle is tuning up and couples begin taking the floor. Father has some local businessman cornered as he talks his ear off about the rising price of cotton, the poor man looking longingly at the dance floor. Mother nurses a cup of punch amid a clump of women chattering on about some provincial scandal involving a runaway farmhand.

A wave of melancholy washes over me and takes root in the pit of my stomach. It doesn't matter that I knew that Mr. Barrett wasn't interested in me and was hoping that Catherine would be here, I had still built up fantasies of us swirling together on the dance floor. And even if he wasn't in love with my sister there are still a bevy of country girls who would love to be Mrs. Barrett, not least among them the lovely Miss Tidewell. I hope he chokes on her stupid mutton. I sigh. No, I don't really hope that. For a moment Cyrus's proposition doesn't seem so ridiculous, so insulting.

And as if I had summoned him with my mind, that's when I see him.

Cyrus has come after all. He's dressed impeccably, scanning the room with one disdainful brow arched. My stomach tightens. Of course he would have heard about the meeting if he's been in town nosing around about a mill site, but I had held out hope that he wouldn't have the audacity to show his face after his bungled proposal.

I duck behind two women engrossed in conversation, waiting for Cyrus to move away from the door. He sees Mother, and pasting a disarming smile on his face, bows over her hand, murmuring some comment that's too low for me to hear. Quick as lightning, I dart into the hall.

I had thought that this night couldn't get any worse, after Catherine abandoning me and Mr. Barrett's polite but stilted conversation, but how wrong I was. With heavy feet, I drag myself down to the second floor. I'm in front of Catherine's door and before I know what I'm doing, I knock. Nothing feels right. I'm restless, unable to settle. I try not to think about Cyrus and Mr. Barrett being in the same room together, of their paths crossing and Cyrus somehow divulging our history. I knock again before Catherine throws the door open and glowers at me, eyes red and puffy.

"I'm not coming up, Lydia, so spare me a lecture about how this night was supposed to be for me."

"Can I come in?"

She stares at me for a moment, then moves aside. The room is stuffy, the faint smell of sickness filling the air. Damp handkerchiefs cover the bed, and aborted letters, splotchy with ink, litter her desk. She hastily pushes them into a drawer as I sit on the bed. "What do you want?"

"There were too many people up there," I say. I can't tell her that my jealousy drove me away, nor that Cyrus is on the prowl for me, with who knows what intentions.

She just stands there, looking at me as if I didn't say anything.

"John says that Mr. Pierce went back to Boston to attend his mother." I don't know why I use his first name, but it just slips out. "Apparently she's not doing well. That's why he didn't come, not because he had some other engagement." At the very least I can rest her mind on this matter.

"John said that, did he?" Catherine crosses her arms. Her look is all venom. "I wasn't aware you were calling each other by your Christian names now. Does Cyrus know? Don't think I didn't see him here the other week, sniffing around. I swear, Lydia, for a girl who spends so much time in her books, you can be quite the little minx when you put your mind to it. Can we expect a wedding soon? But who will be the groom? So many choices! Perhaps it will be Mr. Pierce when all is said and done!"

She's pacing up and down, one hand on her stomach, the other fanning herself. Her face is ghastly white and I've never seen such malice, such despair in her pretty green eyes before.

"What are you talking about?" I grope for words, I don't even know where to start. "Mr. Pierce? You don't think that I—"

"I don't know what to think with you sometimes!" She leans against the wall, massaging her brow and staring at me accusingly. "Why are you here anyway? Why aren't you upstairs with your precious John?"

"He's not mine, you know that." I burn just saying the

words. "What's this all about? I was willing to put Charles, Boston, all of it behind us and start fresh with you. I thought earlier this evening that we might be friends…why can't we be friends?"

"Friends?" She laughs, a joyless sound. "We can never be friends."

Something isn't right. Her hand is clutching her stomach, and her face is pulled tight with pain.

I move toward her but she shrinks against the wall like a cornered animal. "Catherine? What's wrong?"

"Do you really want to know what's wrong? You say that you want to be friends, but if I told you what's wrong you would be sick, like you and Mother and Father and the whole world is already sick at me. How come I never hear a word about Charles? Why is no one as sick with him as they seem to be with me?"

"The rumors? Catherine, we all know that they weren't true. No one is sick at you."

She's raving, not even looking at me as she paces, talking to the walls, the ceiling. The little gold *C* necklace around her neck glints in the lamplight. She compulsively twists the chain round her finger. "Well it doesn't matter, does it? Soon everyone will know and if you thought we were pariahs now, just wait until I hold the squalling truth in my arms in five months."

My blood goes cold. "Catherine," I whisper, afraid that I already know the answer. "What are you talking about?"

She finally stops and levels her gaze at me, as if seeing me for the first time since I came in. "I wonder how you can be so blind, Lydia." She smooths down the front of her dress, framing the small round of her stomach with her hands. "I'm with child."

12

I SIT DOWN on the bed, hard. Catherine is laughing or sobbing—I can't tell which—and my head has gone light and fuzzy.

"Now do you see? Now do you see why Mr. Pierce must come?"

Oh God, I do. The baby needs a father and she needs a husband.

She's still going on between sobbing gasps, the awful truth cold and obvious in light of her revelation. I've been living under a veil, seeing only shapes and movement. Now the veil has fallen away and everything comes into focus. Her moods, her changed figure, her desperate attention to Mr. Pierce, to Mr. Barrett, to anyone.

I try to reassure her, calm her ruffled feathers. "He's only gone to Boston, he'll be back. Catherine—"

Her look is so caustic that I let the rest of my words die in my throat. "Please, just stop. I'm not a fool. I know the kind of man August Pierce is, and it'll take a miracle to get him to the altar. I don't have long before it's harder to hide, and then there won't be any chance for me, for us."

I don't know what to say to her. The ceiling creaks under dozens of dancing feet above us. We stand there in charged silence until Catherine snaps, "Leave me, Lydia. I can't stand the sight of you slender and unspoiled in your ball gown, with your choice of dance partners upstairs. Just go!"

I can't go back upstairs to the dancing.

Emeline should be in bed by now, but all I want to do is hold my little sister, the last vestige of purity and innocence in this family.

Still shaking as I close Catherine's door behind me, I make my way to the spare chamber. It's dark and still as I slip inside. As quietly as I can, I take off my shoes and slide into the bed. But when I reach out to lace my arms around Emeline, all I encounter are empty sheets.

"Emeline?" I whisper into the darkness. "Are you there?"

No answer. I reach for the lamp and light it, casting the room into jagged shadows. It's empty.

Swallowing down my alarm, I slide back out of bed and put my shoes on. The last time she disappeared she was fine; she'd just gotten bored and gone back to the house without me. There's no reason to think tonight is any different. She probably snuck back up to the third floor to watch the dancing from some secret spot. But the sense of unease I had when I left the ballroom intensifies and my stomach begins to churn.

Back upstairs the dancing is in full tilt. I try not to notice that Mr. Barrett is engaged in conversation with Mrs. Tidewell's pretty daughter, and to my relief, it appears that Cyrus has gone.

I catch Joe bringing up a fresh batch of punch. "Have you seen Emeline?"

He furrows his brow in thought. "Not since dinner. She's not in bed?"

I shake my head, already turning back into the ballroom. I don't want to make Mother needlessly anxious, but I have to ask her. "Mother," I say, making my voice light, "have you seen Emeline?"

She frowns, darting a glance around the ballroom. "No. Isn't she in bed?"

"I... I don't know. Probably." I can't tell her my suspicions, not yet. I force a smile. "She must have snuck back into the nursery. Don't worry." But the lines around Mother's mouth are already tightening, her eyes dilating in alarm.

Mr. Barrett catches my eye as I turn from Mother, but I duck into the nursery. It's empty, just as I knew it would be.

Ignoring the curious glances from our guests, I run down the stairs, my pulse racing. "Emeline? Emeline, where are you?" My voice hitches higher as I move room to room on the second floor, calling her name.

"What are you doing?"

I spin around to find Catherine, watching me from her doorway. "I can't find Emeline."

"She's not in the spare room?"

"I wouldn't be searching high and low for her if she was," I snap.

I think Catherine is going to give me a sharp retort, but she falls into step behind me as I run to the first floor, uselessly calling Emeline's name.

A cluster of people have gathered behind us, and I'm vaguely aware of their whispers and craning necks. But it's Mr. Barrett who breaks from the crowd and takes me by the elbow, asking what's wrong.

"Emeline, Emeline is missing," I say, trying to keep the trembling panic from my voice.

I expect him to smile off my concern—after all, I had been equally alarmed that day she disappeared from the pond, and it turned out she had been fine then—but Mr. Barrett's brow darkens, and he looks down at me, his clear eyes boring into mine. "Are you sure?" he asks, his voice full of urgency.

My throat tight, I nod.

Glancing away, he mutters a light curse under his breath, and then asks, "Do you have any idea of where she might have gone?"

I start to shake my head, but then it comes to in a flash. I know where she is.

Mr. Barrett has long legs and he moves sure-footed and fast through the woods. Even Joe struggles to keep up. Father, red faced and panting, quickly falls behind. My heart is pounding in my ears as I run, my lungs threatening to burst. *Be there, Emeline. Be there safe and laughing under the willow. Wait for me.*

How did no one notice her slipping out of the house? I imagine her teetering on the edge of one of the mossy rocks and falling in, no one to hear her shouts for help. No, I push the thought away. She'll be there, under the tree, looking up in surprise as she sees us burst out of the woods. I'll swing her up in my arms and bury my face in her hair and she'll laugh at me for being so worried. Whatever she wants for supper tomorrow I'll make sure she has, even if it's strawberry ice or roasted peacock. Whatever she wants.

We plunge farther into the gathering twilight. Snip's shrill barks ring out as we near the pond. Mr. Barrett stops first, eyes rapidly scanning the water. "Emeline?" he bellows. "Emeline?"

I pick up the call. "Emeline! This is no time for games. If you can hear me come out at once!"

Catherine is panting, having just caught up. She doesn't say anything, but I can feel her nervous energy pulsing from behind me. Joe adds a few shouts but it's useless.

Mr. Barrett swings around to face me, hands on my shoulders. "Could she have gone somewhere else?"

"I don't know, I don't think so…not without Snip!"

We lock eyes and in one horrible moment the truth dawns on both of us.

It all happens so fast. Joe is running to the water, peeling off his shirt and kicking his boots aside. Mr. Barrett just stands there, his eyes still held fast on to mine. He hesitates. It might not even be a second, but he hesitates all the same, something like fear flickering across his face. Then, as if a spell has been broken, he's running after Joe.

Hold on, Emeline. Hold on. They crash into the water, disrupting lily pads and causing birds to take wing. Snip stops barking, wagging his tail ferociously now that help is on the way.

Please, I beg some unknown force, *please, I'll do anything. Please let her be all right.*

There is nothing else in the world, no summer dusk settling around us, no crickets, no Catherine beside me clutching my arm, no silent willow. There is only the pounding of my heart and a desperate, violent hope that refuses to be squelched.

Joe surfaces, spluttering and empty-handed. A rippling ring is the only indication of where Mr. Barrett went under. Just as Joe prepares to plunge back under there is a terrible gasp and Mr. Barrett comes up.

I wrench myself free of Catherine and run. Everything is far away and bright. My chest collapses in on itself when I see her, hanging limp as a rag doll from his arms. Her auburn hair, long and wet, tangled through his fingers.

Mr. Barrett sloshes through the scum and lily pads and I meet them at the edge. *Please be all right.* The smell of mud, of algae, of tepid sun-warmed water radiates from him as he lays her down on the grass. She's so cold, too cold.

We take her clothes off, her pretty muslin dress and the too-long sash. "Emmy," I pant as I frantically try to pat her face awake. "Emmy!"

Someone says that she needs to be warmed, but both Mr. Barrett's and Joe's clothes are dripping wet, so it's Catherine who surrenders her shawl.

"Emeline! Wake up!" She'll be all right, she has to be. People go under water all the time and wake up minutes later—maybe longer—gasping and spitting. She'll wake up.

Mr. Barrett is pressing on her chest while Joe tilts her head up. But no water comes out and she doesn't open her eyes. Her head lolls to the side.

Joe puts his ear to her mouth and shakes his head.

"Emmy!" I try again. Her skin is clammy cold. It's so hot out, why can't she get warm?

If only I could breathe my life into her, my breath coursing through her body, making her heart quicken and beat again. I open my mouth as if there are words that could call such a thing forth, but nothing comes out. What would I say? What would I do? Yet something inside me sings for the chance, taunting me and my impotence.

Someone is pulling me from behind and all the sounds that I blocked out come roaring back. Catherine is crying. Father. Father has caught up and is cursing and yelling. The cicadas grind louder as dusk falls. Snip has nosed his way under Emeline's limp hand and is whimpering.

"Christ," Joe says softly.

Mr. Barrett grips me by my arms, my back against his chest. He doesn't say anything.

That's when the truth sinks down into my bones. It rides through my blood and takes root in the pit of my chest, a terrible bleak thing that grips its cold fingers around my heart. "No." At first it's a whisper, a plea, but then it grows. "No! *NO!*"

The tips of my fingers burn, my eyes blur. It's as if a dark fire has been lit in my heart, and its scorching tendrils are winding to every corner of my body. The flame begs for release, and I know that if I surrender to it I could hurt Mr. Barrett the way I hurt Tommy Bishop.

I spin around, pounding my fists against Mr. Barrett's chest, and he just stands there, letting me. I want to scream. It builds up inside of me, a lifetime's worth of pain that has changed the course of my world in only a matter of moments.

I open my mouth, but the noise that comes out of me is not my own voice. It's otherworldly, a terrible thing, that reverberates off the trees, the rocks and the pond. It echoes back a mockery of my pain and anger, and churns the water as if a tempest brewed above it. Clouds gather and the temperature drops. Still my screams ring out.

Do the others see it too? Catherine clamps her hands over her ears, and Joe and Father take a few hasty steps back, but no one seems to see the swelling of the water or notice the descending clouds. Mr. Barrett alone stands his ground, holding me tightly by the shoulders as if my scream threatened to tear me away like a leaf in the wind.

From somewhere deep within me comes the realization that I could go on screaming and the water would work itself into a frenzy and the storm would grow. It could crash into waves, pulling us all under.

But what's the point? Hurting Mr. Barrett won't change anything. Screaming until I'm mute won't change anything. I stop pounding at his chest, my fists aching. The darkness recedes. The scream that is not my own dies in my throat, the churning water of the pond calming once more. *Emmy is dead.* I repeat the words to myself, but they aren't real. "Emmy is dead." My voice comes out in a broken sob. "My little sister is dead."

13

I CAN'T BREATHE. Thorny roses, twisting and winding, giant white lilies smothering me with their heady scent, pulling me deep within a blanket of rotting petals. I claw at the tightening vines, fighting for air as the thorns draw blood. Somewhere far away just beyond my senses, a child laughs.

"Emeline!"

I awaken with a gasp. It's just the floral canopy over my bed, fluttering in the afternoon breeze coming through the open window. Exhaling, I lie back down. A dark haze clouds my mind, and I know that as soon as it clears I'm going to remember that something has happened. Something awful. I close my eyes and will myself to fall back asleep. But it's too late, and in patches and fits it all comes back. The pond, the scream, the darkness roiling inside of me. All because Emeline is dead. Emeline is dead and it's my fault. We argued about her curfew, and my last words to her were harsh. How can I ever forgive myself?

My chest aches and my limbs are heavy, too heavy to get up. When I test my voice it's hoarse and barely comes out in a squeak. Ada moves around the room on tiptoe, clearing away dishes and gathering up crumpled linens. She jumps when I speak again, louder this time.

"What time is it?"

Darting a glance at the window, she shifts her weight uncomfortably and hesitates before answering. "It's ten in the morning, miss."

I slept all night and right through the morning. I vaguely remember bringing Emeline home, Mr. Barrett laying her on the yellow-and-pink settee, her countenance pale and ghastly by comparison. Mother hovering in the doorway, her face a white smudge like an apparition, her eyes and mouth three black holes. The shocked murmurs and greedy eyes of the guests craning their heads to get a better look from the hall. Mr. Barrett's hand heavy on my shoulder until I violently shook it off. Curling myself around Emeline, cold and damp, tracing the soft contours of her face with my finger. After that, there's only darkness and nightmares.

"What? What is it, Ada?"

She won't meet my eye. "It's ten in the morning on Saturday, miss. You've been abed for nearly three days."

This jolts me out of my stupor. "Why didn't anyone wake me!" My stomach clenches in dread. "The burial...when are they burying her?"

Ada wrings her hands and looks like she wishes she could dissolve into thin air. "They're dressing now... No, miss, please! You mustn't try to get up, you've had a terrible fever and—"

Her warning comes too late. I'm pushing the blankets off and swinging my legs out of bed. All the blood rushes from my head and I see spots behind my eyes. When my feet touch the ground I pitch forward.

Ada drops her pile of linens and dashes over, catching me

under the arms. "You've had a fever," she says again. "Dr. Jameson said to call for him when you woke up."

"I'm fine, Ada. I'm fine." I attempt a smile, but she blanches, recoiling. I must look like walking death after not eating or bathing for days. It's probably not so different than if I were awake anyway; I can't fathom finding the will to wash and eat and do all the little actions that fill a meaningless life. I want to be with Emeline. Wherever she is, I want to be with her.

Despite her protests, Ada helps me dress. I should be in full mourning—we all should be—but the last time there was a death in the family and we buried my grandmother, I was only twelve, and that dress won't fit me anymore. I go through the motions of dressing, raising my arms above my head so Ada can relieve me of my old shift, and step into the darkest dress I own, a deep dove gray.

"Miss Catherine is already dressed," Ada says. "I made sure to tie some black crepe about her bonnet, and a little more around her sleeve."

I squeeze Ada's hand in thanks, knowing that Catherine wouldn't think of these things on her own.

"And…and Emeline?" My eyes water up and I catch myself, taking a deep breath before I completely let the tears take over. "How is Emeline dressed?" I force myself to ask.

She'll still be lying in her coffin downstairs in the parlor. I should have sat with her these past days. She's always been afraid of the dark. I can only hope that Mother or Father thought of this, and left a lamp lit for her. What a sorry excuse for an older sister I am, all this time in my bed while I could have done this one last little thing for her.

Ada sniffs back her own tears. "Like a little doll. Her blue silk dress. I brushed out her hair myself 'til it shone."

Pale, delicate silk. Her favorite dress. She looked like a child of the moon in that dress, a little water sprite. Oh God.

I grit my teeth. Knowing that I won't be able to thank her in words, I give Ada a nod and another squeeze.

Her brushed hair makes me think of something, and once it's in my mind I can't shake the idea. I force my throat to clear. "Is the coffin already sealed up?"

Ada stops fiddling with my hem. "I don't know. I would think so."

"Quick, can you go downstairs?" I retrieve a little pair of sewing scissors from the basket on my table. "Take these, and if you can..." I can't finish my question, but Ada takes the scissors and nods her understanding.

When she leaves, I stand very still and listen to the sounds of the house. It holds its breath, trying to outlast me. No creak of a little foot playing hide-and-seek, no Snip giving chase to his young master. Outside Joe is hitching up the carriage, the horses jingling their bridles as he leads them out. I think of Emeline's little body being borne away, the horses trotting briskly along as if it was any other day.

Ada comes back a few moments later with a thick lock of auburn hair. I reach out my hand and take it from her, gripping it like a lifeline.

"It wasn't...that is, they're almost ready and it wasn't closed yet." She bites her lip, unable to meet my eye. "Would you like to go down, to see her before they do?"

I should, but my feet stay planted where they are, Emeline's hair twisted around my white knuckles. The last image I have of her is on the settee, wet and muddy and surrounded by chaos. Ada puts a tentative hand on my arm. "Go on," she says quietly.

I tiptoe downstairs, slow because I'm still weak, but also because I'm desperate to put off what will be the last time I ever see her little face again.

Joe is just lifting the coffin lid when I hesitantly come into the parlor. When he sees me he puts it back. "Just come out and get me, miss, when you're ready."

He leaves me alone, but it's a long time before I can bring myself to approach her.

Snip lies under the table, barely lifting his head to acknowledge me, his eyes accusing. I vaguely wonder if he's been here the whole time. It's been hot these past days, and there's a sickeningly sweet, pungent aroma hanging heavy around the coffin. I put my handkerchief to my mouth, not sure what to expect when I peek over the edge.

She looks at peace, at least. Not in the way that a sleeping person looks peaceful, but in the way that someone does who has been relieved of all their worldly burdens, including their spirit. There's no sign of the pond on her, no weeds or mud, and I think it a cruel trick that such violence could come and pass, taking with it her life and not leaving so much as a mark.

Her pale little hands are spread out across her stomach; someone has placed a silver cross on a chain in one of them. Something seizes me, and I run to Mother's sewing basket and paw through it until I find her scissors. I tilt my head and take a few ragged cuts until a lock falls loose from the rest of my hair. I have something of her, and now she will have something of me. Carefully, I wind the hair around my finger, tying it with a bit of red ribbon from the sewing basket, and then take it back to the coffin. It's a small gesture, but it feels like a tangible link that will connect us long past this moment. "Now you will be with me, and I shall be with you, forever," I whisper.

As I place the curl beside the cross, my hand brushes her. I recoil. Her skin's not cold like I thought it would be, but it's not warm either. It's nothing. My stomach churns and I wish I hadn't come after all. The lifeless form in the coffin isn't my sister, because all the spirit and laughs and songs and smiles that made up my sister are gone, like dust scattered to the wind, never to return.

I run from the room without a backward glance.

I didn't think it could sink any lower, but my heart plummets as we pull up to the burial ground. Crumbling, lichen-specked stones dot the scorched grass. Trees edge the balding hill, but cast no shadow, provide no dappled shade. And this is where my Emeline will lie. In Boston she would have been buried in one of the lush burying grounds among the old churches and blooming gardens.

The minister's scripted words flow over me. I block him out. I don't know any of the people here except for Mr. Barrett and Mr. Pierce, who is apparently back from Boston. I wish they hadn't come. What must Mr. Barrett think of me, of what happened at the pond? I had no right to lash out at him the way I did. When I remember the way the water roiled and the clouds that gathered, I grow cold all over again. Surely it was just coincidence, Mother Nature's morbid sense of humor, the weather blowing up a gale to mirror the despair that I felt in that moment. Surely Mr. Barrett didn't notice, or if he did, he thinks it a coincidence as well. The more that I dwell on it, the more uncomfortable it makes me, and so I push the thoughts away. I choose a patch of wilted asters to focus on so that my eye won't accidentally meet his.

Most of the other people probably work at the mill, or are the women on whom Mother makes calls. A few I recognize from the meeting and dance. I suppose it was kind of them to come, but I wish we were alone. I feel numb and inside out, and I can't stand their eyes on me, privy to every tear, every choked-back cry.

Dirt cascades down on the coffin and something primal reaches into my insides, making me want to throw myself down into the hole, to feel the cool, grainy earth cover me completely with her. But I just stand there, numb and unmoving, watching as the little wood coffin gradually disappears. People are starting to come up to us, offering us condolences, shaking Father's hand and kissing Mother's wet cheek.

"Lydia, I came as soon as I heard."

I freeze, my stomach sliding at the familiar voice.

"Cyrus," I manage around a thick tongue.

I just gape at him and I think I'm laughing. People are staring at me. But I don't care, I don't know what else to do. Of course he would come. Of course on this day of all days, the person I want to see least in the world would make it his business to come. The ex-fiancé who won't leave me alone. It could almost be a scene out of one of my books, except that this is real life and there's nothing romantic about it at all.

Catherine swoops in, taking me by the arm. "You have some nerve, Cyrus," she hisses.

Unperturbed, he gives her the smallest bow of his head. "Miss Montrose."

I don't know what's more absurd, the fact that Catherine is playing my protector, or that Cyrus has come thinking I would want to see him on this day. "It's all right," I tell her. "Go be with Mother."

She passes a look between us, tight-lipped like she wants to say something else. But I give her a nudge and she turns away with one last withering look at Cyrus.

In his deep blue frock coat, an emerald cravat pin glinting on the breast, Cyrus looks terribly out of place on the scorched hill amid the dowdy townspeople. He always was something of a dandy. Save for our family and Mr. Barrett and Mr. Pierce, most of the mourners wear clothes at least five years out of fashion, the men in patched trousers and faded waistcoats, some of the older ones even still in breeches. Casting his gaze over them, Cyrus's distaste is written plainly on his face. But then he turns back toward me, and his dark eyes soften and fill with concern.

"Are you all right? Lydia," he says taking my hand and leaning in like he's never cared about anything so much in his life, "I know we didn't leave on good terms, but I had to see you again. I stayed in New Oldbury, hoping that you would send for me. I even came to Willow Hall for the town meeting, but you weren't there. As soon as I heard about Emeline though, I knew I had to see you."

The sun beats down through my bonnet and I don't want to be here anymore. Whatever illness I fell into over the last few days still has me tight in its clasp, making my legs shake, my head dizzy.

"Thank you, Cyrus. It was very kind of you to think of my family." The words are cold and meaningless, said only so that he'll go away. He's stealing my last moments with Emeline, depriving me of standing near her while the earth hasn't completely covered her yet.

He leans in closer, the tang of sweat and his expensive pomade making my stomach turn. "It wasn't your family I was thinking of, Lydia," he says with unmistakable meaning.

I take a shaky step back. Is he really trying to declare his love to me, here among the graves where Emeline has only just been lowered into the ground? Didn't I make myself more than clear the last time? "You broke our engagement off." I pull my hand back from his grasp and look for somewhere safe to direct my gaze. "Then you came crawling back, and when I refused you, you leveled insults at me and my family."

"I never wanted to, Lydia, you know that. It was…the unpleasantness with your family. My father made me call it off." He rubs at the back of his neck before regaining his composure. "And I feel terrible about the other week. I didn't mean what I said, I only…well, I was so sure you would say yes. You hurt me, Lyd."

"Cyrus, not now. Please." The ground is swirling under my feet and I'm not sure how much longer I can stand upright. Through the small crowd I catch a glimpse of Mr. Barrett's back as he speaks with Father. "Please, go."

I turn, but Cyrus catches my hand again. "I have to return to Boston, but one word from you will bring me back. Please, tell me that I can see you again." There's a desperation in his eyes that I've never seen before.

"Fine." Anything to get him away from me. "Please, just go."

He bows, and looks at me from under dark lashes as he presses a kiss onto my hand. My breath escapes in a hiss of relief as he stands to leave. Just as he does, Mr. Barrett turns from Father, and before I can yank myself away, I lock eyes with Mr. Barrett, my hand still hanging in the air from the kiss. For a moment everything stops, and I'm back by the pond, light and giddy from being the object of Mr. Barrett's attention. But this time it's a deep sense of shame, as if a part of me, a rotten, bad part, has been peeled back and exposed.

Hesitating, Mr. Barrett gives me a short nod and says something in Mr. Pierce's ear, and then they're turning to leave. Although he already left a heaping bouquet of white lilies near the grave, Mr. Barrett's carrying a handful of flowers. When they reach the gate, he pauses, looks around and then tosses them on the ground.

I'm hot. I'm dizzy. And I'm tired in a way I've never known before. I don't care what Mr. Barrett thinks or what those stupid flowers were for. I just want to be home, even if that home is an empty, haunted place.

I jump at the touch of a hand on my arm. "What did that bastard want?"

"I don't know," I tell Catherine, and it's the truth. I don't believe for a minute that Cyrus came only out of some delayed sense of chivalry.

She bristles. "Well, he has some nerve showing his face here, and today of all days. I hope you told him to clear off and not come back."

A lump is rising in my throat, so I give her a wordless nod. I don't have the heart to tell her what a coward I am.

Mother can barely stand. She looks as if all the life has been drained out of her, and she stares around the burying ground with glassy eyes.

"We should get her back home," Catherine murmurs to me.

As we're passing under the iron arches of the gate, something colorful against the dead grass catches my eye. It's the flowers Mr. Barrett tossed aside as he was leaving. Crouching, I pick up the mangled bouquet.

Poppies and foxgloves.

❧ 14 ❧

TIME SLOWS DOWN to a nearly stagnant trickle of minutes and hours, and yet one morning I awaken and realize it's been almost a week since that awful day. I want to throw my body against the uncaring hands of the clock. I'm afraid that with every stroke of the hour that my memories of her will fade, and that I will acclimate to the numbness, as if it was always such and she was nothing more than golden-tinged dream.

I wander the house, uneasy and restless. We've barely lived here two months but every room holds some memory of Emeline. There was never any need for her to have a room of her own; we always shared a bed in Boston. But Father built Willow Hall with five bedchambers—including a nursery on the third floor—anticipating that we would each have our own bed with room to spare for overnight guests. Many nights Emeline would come tiptoeing down and slip into my bed, where I would tell her stories until she fell asleep, curled around my arm.

Snip pads behind me as I stumble into the nursery. I never spent much time in here, and I assumed Emeline didn't either. We were always so busy exploring or sprawled out in the library surrounded by stacks of books. She was such an old soul, I forget sometimes that she was just a child of eight. But as I stand enveloped by the heavy silence of the nursery, it dawns on me that she did still spend time here, that she did leave her mark.

Bottle flies hurl themselves at the windows. Joe has been setting out jars of vinegar to trap them, but they don't seem to be helping much, and I have to bat a few of the more aggressive flies away. I move slowly, running my hands over all the things that used to be hers. A dollhouse complete with a miniature family has been emptied out, the rooms filled with twig dolls and carpets of moss. I crouch down to open her little leather trunk and Snip throws himself down beside me in a sunbeam, watching me with subdued interest through the lazy dust motes.

I run my finger over the lid, Emeline's initials spelled out in smooth, silver studs. How many times she must have opened this trunk, putting in some new treasure, taking out the others, all of them special because she chose them, imbued them with her own meanings. I close my eyes and inhale, desperate for some lingering scent of her. What did she smell like? Pressing my eyes until they water, I reach for some sliver of memory, but come up empty.

There's the gold necklace that Mother gave her on her fifth birthday, but Emeline had taken off the pearl pendant and replaced it with an acorn. Mother used to call Emeline her "little pearl," a rare surprise, found later in life when Mother had thought herself past the age for such miracles. There are some scraps of paper with her childish scrawl from when I was teaching her how to write her name. An embroidery sampler with a crooked alphabet and numbers up to ten. A little farther down I find the pearl strung on a cotton thread and wrapped around a smooth stone. We used to collect stones like that in the harbor. Running my finger over it brings back the sharp, salty air filled with woodsmoke, the gulls wheeling overhead as we ran down the beach with wet hems and sandy shoes. Emeline was always faster, even though she was so much smaller. Sometimes I would whisper a secret word into the wind, and she would try to catch it down the beach. It was almost as if we could read each other's thoughts, because she always knew the word, even if she was much too far to hear it. I wince with guilt that I didn't know she was in trouble the evening of the dance when so many other times I could sense what she was thinking, doing.

I'm just about to close the lid when something stops me. A glimmer in the depth of the trunk catches my eye, peeking out from beneath the embroidery. My breath catches in my throat. It can't be... With shaking fingers, I reach down and pluck it out.

It's hair. Soft, mousy brown hair, tied in a red ribbon.

I drop it like a hot coal.

How did my hair get into Emeline's trunk? I don't remember ever giving her a lock of my hair. That is, not until I placed one in her coffin.

My head goes light and my mouth dry. Well, I must have given her one. Or perhaps she took it upon herself to cut one while I was sleeping. It would have been daring for her, even if she had been in a naughty mood, but I suppose it's possible. It has to be possible.

I haven't heard voices or seen cryptic messages in weeks, but now that Emeline has died, all the stress has come back tenfold and my mind is playing tricks on me. I put the hair back, tucking it under the embroidery and covering both with the beach stone. I can't let my desperate imagination get the better of me.

Closing the lid, I rock back on my heels. There will never be any more runs by the oceans. There will never be any more stones or acorns or little treasures added to this trunk. I will never be an older sister again. All that I have are my memories, and I won't let them wither and fade with time.

I sit paralyzed like that until my ears buzz with silence and my legs fill with pins and needles. I'll never be an older sister again, but I am still a sister.

Mother settles gingerly into her seat at breakfast the next day. She looks thin and brittle, dark smudges in the hollows under her eyes. She helps herself to an egg with shaking fingers, and when she almost knocks over the teapot reaching for it, I swoop in to pour it for her. Since Emeline's death she's receded into herself more and more, until it feels like she's nothing but a ghost, a living shadow. Most days she claims it's headaches, though anyone can see it's her spirits, dampened to the point of being extinguished.

"We ought to invite Mr. Barrett and Mr. Pierce for dinner again sometime," Catherine says lightly.

Mother stares blankly at her and even I'm not sure I heard her right.

When no one says anything she raises her brows and looks at us. "What? We ought to thank them for coming to the burial, and for the flowers."

"A note would suffice, I'm sure," Mother says coolly.

She brushes off Mother's suggestion. "Well, I think it's the correct thing to do. Besides, goodness knows we could use a bit of distraction around here."

I butter my toast without taking my gaze from Catherine. She's doing a good job of pretending to be her breezy self, but there are little lines of worry around her mouth, and a tinge of desperation in her eyes.

The last time that I tried to do something nice for Catherine, we had the town meeting and dance. I try not to let myself dwell on the aftermath, but I haven't forgotten her revelation to me that night. Catherine needs a husband, and soon.

There is nothing more I would like in the world—short of it never having happened in the first place—than for Catherine to clean up her own mess. But that won't happen.

Even though it makes my stomach curdle, I force myself to give a tight smile. "That's a good idea, Cath."

She snaps her gaze to me in surprise, but then her expression softens, and a flicker of gratitude lights her eyes.

Mother's shoulders slump a little. I'm taking advantage of her weakness, knowing she won't fight. But I also know that if Catherine isn't married safely soon that an entirely fresh scandal will be laid at our doorstep, one that Mother does not have the strength to handle.

Mother sends an invitation to Mr. Barrett requesting his presence and that of Mr. Pierce at dinner the next week. I had thought that my heart was dead, that it would never beat fast and excited again, but to my surprise—and shame—as I dress with Catherine that evening I can't help the nervous flutter in my chest at the thought of seeing Mr. Barrett.

Catherine is in a rare good mood, rooting through her gowns and pulling out different options, even going so far as to insist that I borrow her best silk shawl, a creamy buttermilk-colored one that I've always coveted.

Emeline would have made a game of it. We would have pretended that we were spies, dressing up as genteel ladies to infiltrate some sort of military ball where powerful men would fall over themselves to tell us secrets in the hopes of securing a dance with us. I blink back the hot tears that seem to linger so close to the surface every day now that she's gone.

If Catherine notices, she doesn't say anything, instead handing me her lip rouge.

I hesitate. It feels wrong to be dressing up like this when we should still be in mourning. A clean dress and neatly done hair is one thing, but painting my face feels like something else entirely. I give her a weak smile, and dab my finger in the pot.

The hours have flown by, and evening is settling in around the house. "Catherine," I say. She's rooting around in her desk for a necklace. I look down at my lap. "Do you...that is, do you ever think about that night?"

Her back is toward me, and her intake of breath is so small I almost miss it, but it's sharp, quick.

"What night?" She continues opening drawers.

"You know what night. After the dance... Do you ever think about it? Think what would have happened if we hadn't left Emeline alone?"

Now she does pause, slowly retrieving her necklace and shutting the drawer. "Why should I think about that? What's done is done."

Seeing my face, she softens a bit. "Hand me those earrings, would you?"

I hand them to her. Her hand bobbles ever so slightly as she guides the pearl drops in, but her voice is light and even. "You think it's your fault, don't you?"

I don't say anything.

She sighs. "The way I see it, you can always trace it back to something. Did you leave her alone? Yes, but we all thought she had gone to bed like she was supposed to. Should she have had more sense than to run off to the pond by herself? Of course she should have, she knew better than that. Maybe it's

Father's fault for moving us here. Maybe it's Mother's for never taking an interest in us anymore. Maybe it's mine for causing all the rumors in the first place, driving us from Boston."

I'm behind her, fastening the clasp of the necklace. It's the gold one with the little *C* charm. When she says this last part the auburn curl at the nape of her neck quivers. I stay my hand. I'm not sure what I was expecting, but it wasn't this flash of honesty. I'm suddenly awash with loneliness, so close to Catherine yet so far away. I want to put my chin on her shoulder and cry with her. I want to ask her so many questions and try to understand. But she's already standing up and giving herself a last look over in the mirror.

"Anyway," she says brightly, "as I said, what's done is done and it's no use wallowing in guilt. Now," she says, straightening and turning to me, "are you ready to go down?"

How I wish I could feel as light and blithe about it as her. But there is one question I must ask her, something that has been clawing away at the back of my mind since her revelation the night of the dance.

"Catherine," I say evenly, "who's the baby's father?"

She goes completely still, and then stands up abruptly, moving to the window.

"Catherine?"

"Oh, what do you care?" she snaps without turning around.

I care because something is very wrong and in a few moments two young men will be in our dining room, each completely besotted with her and at her mercy. When she first told me of her condition I had assumed that it was Mr. Pierce, and that it had happened that day we went to the pond. But she's already starting to show—just a little—and that was barely over a month ago.

The curtains are closed, but she's staring at the window, her eyes misty. For the first time in my life my older sister looks lost, and it's unnerving. "Catherine?"

She's playing with the *C* necklace again, her face etched with misery. "If I told you," she says, her voice low, "you would be sick."

It's the way she says it. The necklace runs through her fingers and something heavy sinks within me. I know. My first impulse is to tear the necklace from her neck, to hurl it out the window. It's only a little thing, filigree gold, but I imagine it smashing through the window, landing in a pile of shattered glass on the lawn outside.

"They weren't rumors," I whisper. It was true, true all along. My head spins as another piece of my world crumbles beneath my feet. "Did he...did he force himself?"

"No!" She launches herself at me, taking me by the shoulders and shaking. "Never! Those vile things everyone said about me, about us...those self-righteous gossips, clucking like hens, they had no idea what really went on. They said that I seduced him, and that he was so depraved that he..." She spits. "None of them understand what we share, how it's always been him and me. How ever since we were children he was there for me, my protector, my friend."

Her fingers dig into my collarbone, sending ribbons of pain through my body. "You're hurting me."

Catherine looks at me blankly and then pushes me away, turning and standing with her back to me. "You don't understand," she says. "No one understands."

I don't want to understand. How did I never see it? Was it right there in front of me all along? All the times they walked arm in arm, laughing together at some private joke, was it as lovers? All the times that they shut me out, said that I would just get in the way... Maybe deep down I knew, but just didn't want to admit that it could be possible.

My body is heavy and the room is too small. She's still talking, looking at his miniature on her desk and stroking the little gilded frame with loving fingers.

"Do you know how hard it's been? It's like having half my being torn from me and hidden away where I can never find it. Everything, every part of me aches for him. And there's nothing I can do about it! All I can do is sit here, growing big with his child. The most I can hope for is a marriage, a loveless one, but one that will at least save me—us—from further scandal. And even then, I'll grow old without him. Oh." She lets out a long sigh, her white shoulders falling like the broken wings of a bird.

She's sick. There's something inside of her, something damaged. That's the only explanation. For all her vanity and all her games, her bright smiles...they just mask what lies beneath.

Her lips curl into a bitter smile. "You might have told Cyrus that there was a sister willing to overlook his character and lack of fortune in return for a husband. If I don't get a proposal out of Mr. Pierce soon then, well..."

Swallowing hard, I force out the question I'm afraid to know the answer to. "Or Mr. Barrett?"

She can throw herself at Cyrus for all I care, but Mr. Barrett... I press my palms against my eyes, desperately trying not to envision them standing hand in hand at the altar, of Mr. Barrett taking her to bed in his house just beyond the trees. She would be sentencing him to a life without love, using him for nothing more than his name and protection.

Her expression loses some of its venom, and she looks faraway, thoughtful. "Yes," she says, "perhaps there's still hope with Mr. Barrett."

Just then there is a knock at the door downstairs. Catherine and I look at each other. "Ah! Speak of the devil." She takes a deep breath, pastes a bright smile on her face and trips out of the room, humming as if she hadn't a care in the world.

I linger in the doorway, my chest tight, as I watch my sister walk away, swollen with our brother's child.

15

AS SOON AS I set foot downstairs, I know this was a mistake. Mother is withdrawn, barely noticing as Catherine flits around her, placing fresh flowers in the vases. Even Father is subdued; he hasn't pulled out any papers to show our guests, and he sits in his chair, swirling a glass of Madeira side to side without drinking. It's too soon for entertaining, even if it's only Mr. Barrett and Mr. Pierce. It's too soon to make polite conversation and sit down together and eat and laugh as if nothing has happened. Catherine's revelation rests on my shoulders heavy and constricting as a noose. When Ada shows Mr. Barrett and Mr. Pierce in, it's all I can do to lift my head and murmur a greeting from dry lips.

Catherine and Mr. Pierce move off immediately together to their corner in the parlor, and I watch them with a queasy stomach. For as little thought as I usually give to Mr. Pierce, I can't help the pang of pity for him that runs through me; he has no idea the breadth and consequence of the snare Catherine is setting for him.

"Miss Montrose."

Mr. Barrett moves out of the shadowed doorway and gives me a stiff bow of his head. "I confess I was surprised to receive an invitation so soon after..." He trails off, frowning into the corner where Catherine is speaking in soft tones to Mr. Pierce.

"Yes, well, we wanted to...thank you." I never would have agreed to this dinner, championed Catherine's cause, if I had known then what I know now about her condition.

The conversation is stilted, painful, both of us going through the motions of saying the right things. What happened at the pond hangs between us, heavy and unspoken just as I knew it would. I can't look at Mr. Barrett without seeing him emerging from the water, face white and jaw set, Emeline hanging from his arms. And he must look at me and see a foolish girl, jealous and petty, someone who would entertain a suitor at her own sister's burial.

We sit down to an informal meal of roast beef and potatoes. Catherine and Mr. Pierce are the only ones who are oblivious to the mantle of gloom that sits over the rest of us, though even Mr. Pierce has the good sense to keep his voice low, his look deferential when speaking to Mother.

Ada has barely cleared the first plates away when Mr. Pierce pushes back his chair and stands up. "I'm so sorry, but I'm afraid I have an engagement in town and must say good night."

"Oh, that is too bad," Mother says, but the relief in her eyes at having one fewer person to entertain is palpable.

Catherine's face falls. She forces a bright smile, but there's no hiding the tight lines around her mouth. "But it's so early yet!" she protests with a nervous little laugh. "Surely you won't leave us so soon."

I give her a swift kick under the table. The sooner this torturous dinner ends, the better. But she only glares at me and squares her shoulders in defiance.

Mr. Pierce bows and assures her that if his engagement

weren't of the most pressing variety he would stay for hours yet, but unfortunately it is. If Catherine was hoping for a proposal tonight, then her hopes are quickly dashed.

"Mr. Barrett, you aren't leaving us so soon too, are you?" she asks, turning her gaze sweetly on him.

He should go, leave us to our grief. But my eyes are greedy for him, my skin alive at the knowledge of him so close by. I don't know what would be more unbearable: for him to leave, or for him to stay.

Mr. Barrett looks up, pausing his glass midair. He flickers the swiftest of glances at me before clearing his throat. "It's growing late. I think perhaps I should accompany August."

"Oh, nonsense," Mr. Pierce says with an easy smile. "I'm more than capable of navigating these country roads. Stay, stay."

Catherine nods eagerly in agreement. "At least stay for coffee," she says with a wheedling pout.

Mr. Barrett looks uncomfortable, but to his credit his voice is gracious and genuine. "Yes, of course. Coffee would be lovely."

Mr. Pierce takes his leave, and we move back into the parlor. No sooner does the front door click shut than Catherine has angled her chair in Mr. Barrett's direction, leaning in low to him to offer to pour his coffee.

Mother announces that she has a headache and must retire, but that she hopes Mr. Barrett will stay and enjoy the coffee and cake that Ada has brought in. Father acts as reluctant chaperone, but within a few minutes he's nodding over his newspaper and soon after is snoring with abandon on the settee.

Mr. Barrett sits with his back straight, coffee in hand while Catherine asks him shy questions and blushes at his answers. She knows just what will work on him as opposed to Mr. Pierce, how to use his quiet, dignified personality to her advantage. I watch with increasing agony, helpless to do anything but sit mute as a statue while Catherine charms and flirts her way into Mr. Barrett's heart.

Picking up a book, I pretend to be absorbed in the story, though it might not even be in English for all I know. I steal glances over the top of the pages, my face burning, my mouth dry. I'm just about to tear my gaze away and force myself to read, when Mr. Barrett catches me staring at him.

Before I can drop my eyes, Catherine intercepts the look. "Lydia," she says in a pointed tone, "weren't you saying before dinner how tired you were?"

Her voice is sweet, but there's a flinty determination in her eyes.

"I…" I open my mouth, ready to deny saying anything of the sort. She's made her intentions more than clear, and do I really have the spirit to battle Catherine tonight? Can I find in myself the will to laugh and smile and bat my eyelashes alongside of her, all in the vain hope of catching Mr. Barrett's fancy?

"Yes," I say, standing. "I am tired. If you'll excuse me, I'll say good night as well now."

The heat has finally broken, but I need air, I need to clear my head of the image of Catherine's awful secret growing beneath her gown, the image of my other sister pale and lifeless in Mr. Barrett's arms. Instead of returning to my room, I head outside. Cursing, I trip over the rock propping open the door and stumble into the night. My clothes are too tight on my body, it's hard to breathe. Yanking off my gloves, I leave them wrinkled in the drive as I start walking toward the road.

We're ruined and I don't even care. Catherine has driven the final nail into our coffin. Every time she spoke longingly of London it was because *he* was there. Every time poor Mother wrung her hands because a friend turned their face from us in the street it was because of her. Every time Father reproached her for how she let herself be portrayed in the papers, why, she knew all along that those columns spoke the truth. How could she do this to us? What if the baby is born damaged, proof of its unnatural beginning? How will Mother bear it?

I double back away from the road and up behind the house. The windows glow yellow and warm, and inside Mr. Barrett and Catherine are sitting *tête-à-tête* as Father, oblivious, snores softly in the corner. If I was heartsick at the thought of Mr. Barrett's hands on Catherine before, I'm seething now that I know the truth behind her motives. And this is the family that I mourned? This is the family that I would have done anything to keep together?

The woods have grown thick and unfamiliar, and I stumble blindly with outstretched hands. The lace at the hem of my dress snags and unravels. I can't believe I let Catherine primp me up. I feel dirty, and I smear off the lip paint with the back of my hand. She's right, it was her fault. If it weren't for her and Charles we never would have come here. But Catherine was also right about another thing: what's done is done. And if Emeline can't be here, then I will go to her.

The weeping willow greets me, swaying despite the lack of breeze. *Come, Lydia. Come to me and spill your troubled soul. I won't judge.* When the stonemason is finished with Emeline's gravestone it will bear a weeping willow bent over an urn, that tree sacred to Persephone, to the underworld. That tree that the Greeks believed bestows the gift of poetry and understanding, of transcendence, but only to those willing to descend into the darkness. For Emeline it's either a beautiful tribute or a cruel irony.

I carefully take off my shoes, lining them up at the rocky edge of the water. My stockings are next. I peel them off and neatly fold them, placing them next to the shoes. Out come my earrings, off with the pearl hairpin that Catherine stuck in so deep. I shake my hair out so that it spills down my neck and back, my scalp tingling. Lighter and lighter. I can't take my dress off myself, so I hike it up, tying the torn lace and silk in a knot at my thigh.

Everything is so clear now. My body is light, my mind free of the tangled thoughts that have plagued me for weeks. No more sick Catherine and Charles, no more Cyrus, no more Mr. Barrett, no more spirits forever lurking at the periphery, no more aching loneliness.

The water is smooth and tepid and I barely feel it swallowing first my ankles, then my calves, the back of my knees.

I want to know. I have to know. What did it feel like? What filled the last moments of my sister's life? Was it quick and peaceful, like slipping into the embrace of a pleasant dream? Or did she panic, fighting for air as the water stole her breath away? The willow watches me, nodding. *I know. Come, Lydia. Come and I will show you.*

The bottom is slippery and rotten; my toes curl around the slick rocks as I move farther out into the black. Water laps at my chin. I open my mouth. Putrid, stale. Oh, Emmy. I close my eyes. Stifling silence closes in around me, the steady chorus of peepers and owls far away and muffled as I slip below the surface. The only sound is the beating of my own heart, steady and unafraid.

It's peaceful, but in an awful, greedy sort of way. The night, the water, they want to take me. They want to swallow me up until I'm nothing more than a sigh, a forgotten secret. And I want to let them. *Come, Lydia. There is nothing for you above, but down here you can have her again. You can be with your sister, forever.*

Slip away. How easy it is. Why is the darkness so feared in favor of light? In the day everything is laid bare, the truth naked and ugly for what it is. But in the darkness everything is possible. It is pure, forgiving. I can forget.

Let go, Lydia.

I let my fingers float out in front of me. The water softens everything. My vision blurs, my need for air replaced with my need to be with her. I'm so close. Only a little farther, a little longer, and everything will be all right.

A jolt. Something grabbing around my arms, hard. The silence gives way to a deafening roar as the force pulls me backward, upward, water rushing around me. I was so close. Just a little farther and I could have reached out and touched her, her auburn hair swirling around her pale face like a halo.

I gasp, water and slime choking out of me as my body betrays me and fights for air. Darkness explodes with light. Arms tighten around me, lifting me despite my wet dress weighing me down.

My body is lead and my lungs ache, but I'm not ready to come back. Blind panic takes over and I thrash out. My only thought is that I must get free. I must get free and find Emeline at any cost.

"Lydia! For Christ's sake, stop!"

Mr. Barrett. My ears are clogged but his voice comes through sharp and familiar. I stop struggling, hoping that I still might be able to slip from his grasp and into the depths of the pond.

But he locks his arms tighter around my waist, pulling me back to the shore, half swimming, half trudging in the thick water. Pondweeds wind around my ankles, loath to let me go. Every step back to shore is like a broken promise to Emeline.

When we reach solid ground we collapse in a heaving tangle of limbs. As soon as I feel the damp earth beneath me, all my strength, all my fight, dissolves from my body. I'm deflated, empty. I failed in the one thing I thought I could control.

The willow holds its tongue, and the night becomes ordinary again. Mr. Barrett lets go, rolling over onto his back, his breathing heavy and ragged, a limp arm draped over my stomach. To think of all the times I imagined his closeness, his touch, and this is how it has happened. I could almost laugh. I turn my head, the dirt cool against my cheek as I struggle to bring the world back into focus. Moonlight streaks pale and fleeting through breaks in the clouds, softening the edges of Mr. Barrett's profile in the darkness. There's a dark stain under his nose—blood?—and his hair is matted down to his cheeks. A pang of guilt runs through me.

My throat is burning and I don't think I'll ever get the taste of slime out of my mouth. Rolling over, I retch. It's not just the taste I am frantic to rid myself of, but the failure, the realization that I'm still here.

When he's regained his breath, Mr. Barrett sits up and rakes his hair back with shaking hands. "Christ," he says, softly. He turns to me, peering through the dark, and I'm sure the moonlight is betraying the shame written all over my face. Why did he have to come? Why do I have to suffer this embarrassment on top of everything else? It could have all been over by now. I turn my face away, wishing the pond was an ocean like the day when I screamed and screamed, that it would lap up the small bank and pull me back in its receding tide. But the placid water just shimmers, dark and still.

"You're shaking," he says, more to himself than me. I can't feel anything, but there's a warm, metallic taste in my mouth. I must have bitten my tongue from chattering. His coat lays crumpled on a rock, as if thrown off in a hurry and forgotten. He slowly hefts himself up, grunting at some injury, and stumbles over to retrieve it.

He steps over my shoes and stockings, arranged so neatly, smug that they would never be worn again. Seeing them like that, empty and still needed, cracks open something deep inside of me. Despite my hoarse throat and lingering breathlessness, a broken wail cracks out of me, followed by a torrent of tears. It's nothing like the scream the evening Emeline died; this wail is mine and mine alone. It doesn't churn the water or send clouds scudding across the sky. It is my misery and grief distilled into a single, plaintive note.

Mr. Barrett doesn't say anything as my sobs gradually subside into miserable hiccups, he simply sits me up and wraps the coat around my shoulders. When I'm snugged tighter than a mummy, he stays crouched beside me, cupping my face in his hands and brushing a stray tear away with his thumb.

"I know, I know. There now, you'll be all right," he says with unbearable tenderness. "Everything will be all right."

How I wish I could believe him. How I wish I could lean into his warm, capable hands and let all my problems fall away from me. But he can't know that everything will be all right, and his words promising otherwise are the kind that a parent offers to a child with a scraped knee—meant to comfort, but without any real meaning behind them. If only he hadn't come.

Crying has left me hoarse and it's hard to form my words, but I can't stop myself. He leans down to hear me, so close that my lips nearly graze his ear.

"You saved the wrong sister."

Slowly, he pulls back. His face contorts in something like pain, a spreading realization of betrayal as if he were Caesar and I Brutus. I want him to reproach me for saying such a terrible thing, or to rush to assure me otherwise even if it's not true. Anything. But he just levels a long, unreadable look at me. When he does speak it's softly, with words so heavy with pity and disappointment that I think I will die of shame.

"Oh, Lydia."

He stands up, and I suppose he's finally had enough of me. It must be time to go home. I close my eyes, curling my fingers into the loamy dirt. At home there will be questions, more hurt looks.

He doesn't say anything else as he scoops me up, draping my arm behind his neck, his trembling hands digging into my flesh. His shirt is cold and wet, but underneath his chest is warm. I'm exhausted, my body inside out and spent, but still he clutches me as if I might try to escape back into the pond.

The breeze sighs with regret. I crane my neck back, watching as the water recedes into the night, indistinct and black. It might not have claimed my life in the end, but as I let my head fall against Mr. Barrett's chest, his heartbeat strong and fast against my ear, I know that nothing will ever be the same again.

My eyes are heavy and tired, but just before they close, I catch a glimmer of movement. Emeline.

She stands beside the water, still as a little statue. This isn't the mirage of a desperate mind, or imaginings, delusions, visions. She's there, as real as anything. The whispered promises that drew me to the pond were not hollow.

I open my mouth to call out to her, to beg her to give me some sign that she sees me, but my throat is too hoarse, too dry. When Mr. Barrett feels me renewing my struggles, he tightens his grip, his fingers curling into my wet clothes. It's no use. I'm spent of energy, and so I watch Emeline grow smaller and smaller until the night swallows her whole.

❧ *16* ❧

EMELINE. EMELINE IS DEAD, but she is not gone. It was her, I know in my heart of hearts that it was. The pale lady, the writing in the mirror, the voices on the wind…if they are all real, then why not the vision of my dear sister? My mind swirls with questions, my heart swells with hope. Will I see her again? Why has she come back?

The pile of books I keep by my bed has nearly doubled over the past few days. I can't seem to read anything cover to cover, growing distracted with thoughts of Emeline and abandoning the stories I used to love after only a few pages. I run my fingers across the softened paper, the black letters jumbled and meaningless, but the musty book smell is comforting. When I think that I might never have held a book again…

I chuck aside the German ballad *Lenore* with a sigh. The first time I read it, the heroine's midnight horseback ride with her lover sent delicious chills down my spine. But now I know that the man she thinks is her William returned from war is nothing more than Death in disguise, and he's bearing her away not to their wedding bed, but to her grave.

Something wet presses against my arm and I jump. Snip stares back up at me with imploring eyes, giving me another nudge with his nose and then looking under the bed. His little wood ball is stuck. With a sigh, I heave myself out of bed and get it for him, watching him scamper over the clutter, upending my sewing basket and a pile of books as he goes.

It's been three days since Mr. Barrett carried me back in silence from the pond, and I haven't left my room since. Ada helped me into bed that night. Mr. Barrett explained to Mother that he'd been cutting through the woods back to his house when he found me walking. He said that I must not have seen the water in the dark and accidentally stumbled in. Mother didn't say anything, but I caught the long, meaningful look that passed between them.

The next morning, Mother had come by to ask me how I was feeling, her tone cold, skirting what she knew to be the truth. I waited for her to come sit on the bed with me, brush the hair from my forehead as she used to do when I was little. But she just stood in the doorway, hands clasped in front of her tiny waist, staring in at me as if I were a stranger in her daughter's room. "What were you thinking, Lydia? How could you?"

It had all seemed so clear at the time, like it was the only natural thing to do. I haven't let myself think too much about my rescue, but now as I remember the way that Mr. Barrett looked at me in the moonlight, the way I fought him in the water, I let out a little whimper that becomes a groan. How many times will he have to bear the marks of my anger? How can I ever repay him? How can I erase the terrible way I acted? And that's to say nothing of what I saw—*who*—I saw standing beside the water as Mr. Barrett carried me away.

A knock at the door pulls me out of my thoughts. I want to

tell them to go away, but before I can say anything, the door opens and in glides Catherine.

She stops short at the foot of the bed, a look of surprise when she sees me. "Oh," she says. "You're awake." Snip stops chewing his ball to cast a reproachful eye at her. "I… I thought you would be sleeping. I just came to bring you these." She holds out a little bouquet of parched flowers.

I give her a short nod of thanks, feeling as on guard as Snip.

"You look awful," she says casually, the way one might comment on the weather, but she catches my expression and tries again. "Are you feeling better?"

"Yes, a little." I could say she doesn't look so wonderful herself, but it wouldn't be true. She's fresh and radiant this morning, dewy skinned and bright eyed. The clean, sweet smell of lavender in the bouquet makes her seem even more out of place in my messy, stale room. When I don't say anything, she sighs and sits down, arranging herself amid the folds of her crisp, white morning dress.

A smile tugs at the corner of my sister's lips as she stares out the window, her eyes unseeing as a light rain begins to fall. Here I thought I was going to get a lecture or a few cold words, not silence. We haven't spoken since the other night, and it's been a welcome stay of execution. What could we possibly say to each other after her revelation, and her behavior toward Mr. Barrett?

"Yes?"

Catherine comes to her senses with a little jolt, as if forgetting she was the one who came to me, and the bouquet slips from her hand. She bends down to retrieve the flowers and puts them in a vase by the window. "I cut these from your garden. It's been cold the last few nights and I wasn't sure how much longer they would last out there." She slants me a curious look. "It seems a little late for plants to be growing, but what do I know."

My poor garden. I've neglected it for weeks, long before I took refuge in my room, and the lavender and coneflowers stare back at me accusingly from the window. Weeding and cutting things back for the coming frosts should be a good reason to start getting out of the house—out of bed, for that matter—yet every day when it comes down to it I just can't find the will.

When the flowers are arranged to her satisfaction she sits back down, hands fidgeting in her lap now that she doesn't have anything to hold. "I... How are you feeling, really?"

"What do you care?" I say coldly.

The smile vanishes and Catherine's face darkens. She seems to struggle with what she's about to say, opening and closing her mouth several times and staring into her lap. "I was wrong. I'm sorry, Lyd. Really. I shouldn't have said those things the other night. I..." She looks up, and must see my skepticism because her bottom lip comes out in a pout, reminiscent of Emeline. She doesn't mention her behavior toward Mr. Barrett, how she all but threw herself at him. "Look, you're not making this easy for me."

Of course I'm not going to make this easy for her. I've been living with a deviant this whole time. The Catherine I thought I knew was bad enough, but that was nothing compared to what I know her to be now. Catherine's condition and what it means might make me sick, but finding a solution to it is the only way to save our family further humiliation. I will never, ever be able to truly forgive her, but I will act the part for the sake of what's left of our family. I take a deep breath. "You're right. I'm sorry." I force myself to say the words.

Catherine looks up sharply, mouth parted, as if she was already prepared to argue. But then she nods and goes on, her voice dropping as she wrings her hands in her lap. I try not to stare at her stomach. "When I saw Mr. Barrett coming back with you the other night and you were... You looked like Emeline that day, all wet and limp. And you didn't even care. You looked like you wish he hadn't found you, and I couldn't bear it. I couldn't bear it if you died, Lyd. Maybe we'll never be friends, but that doesn't mean I want you dead."

"We may never be friends, but you don't want me dead," I echo, amused.

She pouts. "Look, I—"

I wave off her objections with a tired hand. "I know. Thank you." I have a hard time believing this revelation of hers will last long, but I'm too weary to spar with her. "Is that what you're smiling about?"

"Was I?" She looks down and compulsively smooths a hand over her stomach. "I had a note from Mr. Pierce come by messenger." She looks up conspiratorially, her green eyes dancing with excitement. "He not only sent his regrets about having to leave early *and* missing the dance, but also some very pretty lines about...well..." She trails off with a dreamy look.

"I'm glad, Catherine."

"Really?"

"Really." It will give Mother a reason to be happy, or at least, to save her from further heartache. It's at least one fewer thing to worry about, and perhaps now Catherine can leave Mr. Barrett alone.

Catherine takes out a piece of paper worn with folding and unfolding. "He says he has to go to Boston but he'll be back in one or two weeks' time. Apparently, his mother has rallied and is expected to live after all." She puts down the letter and frowns. "The woman sounds awful. I hope she doesn't try to talk him out of a proposal. But if all goes well I think we could be married within the month. Just think, a wedding to plan!"

I'll never understand her. How can she claim to feel such a passionate love for one man and still sound so honestly excited about a marriage proposal from another? But I suppose the pressure of her situation is stronger than anything else at the moment, and if I know one thing about Catherine, it's that her vanity runs deep. Flattering, pretty words, no matter whom they're from, are as necessary to her as water and sunlight are to a growing plant.

She rises to leave, smoothing her skirts, the corners of her mouth lifting as she continues scanning the letter, and I watch her float out of the room in a cloud of dreams and grand plans for the future.

It's cooled considerably in the past few days, summer gracefully bowing out as autumn claims her throne. After Catherine leaves I feel a bit lighter, like I've made a first step in the right direction. Getting some fresh air in the room would be another good step, so I force myself out of bed and throw my shoulder against the protesting window.

No sooner does the window gasp open than the sound of footsteps and voices float up from the drive. I can't see him from this angle, but I instantly know who's speaking. A moment later Ada is knocking at my door, peeping her head inside.

"It's Mr. Barrett, miss. Your mother is trying to send him away, but he's insistent, saying he must see you." She casts a glance at the messy room, my disheveled hair, and looks at me expectantly. "I thought you might want to know."

I'm up in a flash, wrapping a clean shawl over the dress I've been wearing for three days straight, and sweeping my greasy hair up into a loose bun. "Thank you, Ada."

She's already gone, and then the sound of brisk footsteps clipping down the hall grows closer, accompanied by frantic murmurs. A moment later Mr. Barrett is striding through the door, Mother hot on his heels. Snip gives a joyful yelp and forgets his ball when he sees his favorite person.

"Mr. Barrett, please. She hasn't been well. I—"

Mr. Barrett stops abruptly, nearly tripping as Snip weaves between his legs. I stiffen when I see the dried cut on his lip and the bluish red bruise on his cheekbone, realizing that both were my doing. He's vibrating with silent energy like a violin string long after the note has died, and I can hardly blame him. Now that I'm out of immediate danger he must be furious with me.

I swallow hard. "It's fine, Mother."

She casts an apprehensive glance between us. "I'll have Ada make up the parlor and bring some tea."

It's taken me three days just to work up the nerve to open the window, and seeing Mr. Barrett so suddenly has thrown my new little world into chaos. I'm not sure I have the energy to make my way downstairs. Anyway, he's already seen me in all my desolation. "I'd just as soon stay here."

For the first time since barging into my room, Mr. Barrett looks a little less self-assured, finally noticing the precarious stacks of books on every surface, the dirty linens piled in the corner, the plate of untouched ham and toast that Ada left this morning. "This is a bad time..." he says, dipping his head and rubbing the back of his neck.

"No," I say quickly. Seeing Catherine has given me some courage, and I must face Mr. Barrett sometime. It might as well be now. "No, it's not a bad time."

Mother tightens her lips and I know that I'm toeing the line of decency. But she doesn't press the matter, just crosses the room to draw the curtains closed around the bed as if to eliminate any possible temptations. If circumstances were different I might laugh that she's even concerned of the possibility of seduction. Then she takes a blanket out of the trunk and leaves it on the settee Joe optimistically brought in so that I could entertain visitors in my room while I recovered. Mr. Barrett and I both follow her with our eyes until she's made up a proper seating arrangement. Normally I might be embarrassed by all of this, but I suppose it's a promising sign that she's taking an interest in me at all.

"I'll be right down the hall if you need anything," she says with a lingering look of doubt.

Mr. Barrett nods, a little flustered at finding himself granted an audience after all, and in my bedchamber no less. I should be too, but I'm too on edge, wary of what he might be here to say. Mother leaves the door conspicuously open when she leaves.

He takes a tentative step farther into the room. "I... Would you have a seat?" His body is so still, only a slight tremor in his voice belying that he isn't in full possession of himself either.

It's ridiculous, him in my bedroom inviting me to have a seat, but I don't know what else to do except nod and tuck myself up under the quilt. At least this way he won't see how crumpled and dingy my dress is. Self-consciously I run a hand over my hair, wishing that I'd done just a little bit more to try to look presentable.

Mr. Barrett scrapes up a chair beside me and sits with folded hands. Snip has all but forgotten about me, curling up by Mr. Barrett's feet, promptly falling asleep and snoring softly. Besides that and the faint patter of rain outside, the room is as silent as a tomb. The familiar muscle in Mr. Barrett's jaw is twitching, something that I would usually take to mean that he wishes he were elsewhere, but that I now get the impression might be a levee holding back a flood of words.

I try to look anywhere but the injuries on his face, studying instead the slightly scuffed toe of his left boot, the light feathering of golden hairs on his wrist. His clothes always look as if they were made for his body, elegant without being fussy, stylish without looking belabored. Not at all like Cyrus. Mr. Barrett leans forward slightly and I close my eyes, steeling myself against the things he has every right to say.

But he doesn't say anything, he simply reaches past me for *Lenore*, picking up the tented book and flipping through the pages. The slim volume looks small and fragile in his hands, his reverent fingers tracing over the gilded title. "Is this one as good *The Monk*?"

It takes me a moment to find my tongue. "You...you remember that?"

The little lines around the corners of his eyes crinkle ever so slightly. "It's not every day that I get such an animated book recommendation. Or any, for that matter."

I hold out my hand for the book, his fingers brushing mine as he hands it back. "No, it's not as good," I say. "I like happy endings and this one doesn't have one. The heroine dies."

The lines around his eyes smooth out and there's an almost imperceptible shift of the light in them. I can't help but feel I've said the wrong thing, and we fall into an immediate, strained silence.

We begin to speak at the same time.

"Lydia, I need to—"

"Mr. Barrett, I feel that I've acted—"

I give a strained half laugh, and Mr. Barrett relaxes a little in the chair, disrupting Snip as he leans back and crosses his boots. "Please," he says, lacing his hands casually across his stomach. "We're friends, aren't we? Call me John."

I hesitate, wishing that I'd let him go first. "Yes," I say faintly. "Of course. Friends."

He gives me an encouraging nod. His posture may be relaxed, but his gaze is as intense as ever and I have to look away lest I lose my nerve.

"John," I say slowly, unused to speaking out loud what has come to feel like my secret, special word. "I'm so sorry."

He looks surprised, his brows rising slightly. "Good God, for what?"

I gesture to my face, touching my lip where his is split, my cheek where his is bruised. Saying sorry doesn't even come close to expressing how terrible I feel. "I didn't mean to hurt you."

A tiny smile quirks at the edge of his lips. "I would hate to see what you were capable of if you were trying, then."

I blanch, and his smile evaporates. He awkwardly clears his throat. "You needn't apologize for that," he says quickly. "Only hurts a bit to shave."

This doesn't make me feel any better, and now I'm also picturing him at home with his shirt open and beautiful, high cheekbones lathered in soap. I take a deep breath. "Still, I'm sorry."

"I'm the one who should be apologizing," he says. "That's why I came. And to see how you were doing," he adds.

Blood creeps up my neck and I bite the inside of my cheek. I thought he would ask me what I was doing at the pond, or admonish me for being careless with my life. An apology is the last thing I was expecting.

He looks down at Snip, rubbing under the dog's ears and eliciting a sleepy whimper of contentment. "There are things I should have told you before now, and maybe if I hadn't been so cold and shut you out, maybe you wouldn't have tried to... I can't help but feel responsible."

"Mr. Barrett, I mean John, you—"

He stops me with a shake of his head. "No, I haven't acted well. I told you that this wasn't a good place for a family, and

I only meant... There have been tragedies here in the past and..." He trails off, struggling to finish his thoughts. "Well, it doesn't matter now." I don't dare ask him what sort of tragedies; if he wanted to tell me, he would. "I expect you're angry at me," he says quietly, "and you have every right to be. I acted badly at the dance, and again at Emeline's burial." His voice drops so low that it's little more than a murmur. "And... I think about that night a hundred times a day, wishing I could have saved her."

My heart stops in my chest. I have to look away, inspecting where the wallpaper seams meet, the gaudy chrysanthemums overlapping in the wrong places. How desperate I was to hear those words before, and now that I have heard them, I realize how little they actually change anything. I hastily wipe a stray tear away before turning my attention back to him.

He stares at his hands as he knits them together, watching each knuckle whiten and relax in turn. "There's something else." He takes a breath. "I know about Boston," he says, his tone soft and apologetic.

"Oh," I say, as if he was telling me that he knew my hair is brown, or that the sun rises in the east. I should be ashamed, wary, defensive, *something*, but instead I just feel vaguely relieved. He's known this whole time and he's still Father's business partner, he still visits our house. He's still here. "Why are you telling me this now?" I ask in a whisper.

"Because I want to be honest with you. I don't want you taking unfounded notions into your head and making rash decisions based on them."

What would he think of us if he knew that they weren't rumors? But I nod. I can't tell him that, and I can't tell him that Catherine's attention to him and his friend are because of the testament of the truth she carries in her belly.

"Are you angry? For not telling you that I knew, for what

happened at the pond?" His voice is soft, barely a whisper, but there's a hard, urgent edge and when I look up to meet his gaze, his eyes are searching.

I let out a breath. "Of course not."

Mr. Barrett slumps back in his chair, his eyes closing for a moment. When he opens them again his face is washed in relief, his blue-green eyes clearer than I've ever seen them. "Good," he finally says. "I'm glad."

Outside dark clouds are rolling in and the breeze picks up. The lace curtains swell and billow into the room, knocking over the vase of flowers. The rain comes down harder, but Mr. Barrett is lost in some private thought and makes no movement to close the window. Silence fills the room.

"May I ask you something?"

"Of course," he says, coming back to himself. "Anything."

"The other night… What were you doing there?"

The chair creaks as Mr. Barrett shifts his weight, measuring his words before he answers. A daring bird trills and calls despite the steady rain. "I was walking."

"Were you following me?"

It's a moment before he responds, his answer dropping heavy and defiant into the stillness of the room. "Yes, I was."

"Why?"

A hint of exasperation creeps into his voice. "Why do you think?"

I shake my head, unable to explain the quick, almost painful racing of my heartbeat. My body flushes with heat.

Mr. Barrett holds my gaze a little longer, as if there are two paths in front of him, and my face alone can tell him which to go down. He nods, more to himself than me, having apparently decided.

"I felt bad for how Catherine was acting. I wanted to make sure you hadn't taken it to heart. I couldn't find you, but when

I went outside, I found these instead." He produces my gloves from his waistcoat. They're neatly folded and he handles them as if they were made out of spun-gold silk.

I hold out a shaking hand, jealous of the soiled and crumpled gloves. I wish he would keep them forever. As soon as he gives them back a little link that I didn't even know existed between us will be broken.

There's so much I want to say to him. It's like he's pushed a door open a crack, and now I want to throw it the rest of the way open, spilling out everything that's inside of me. *Thank you for caring enough to come looking for me. Thank you for following me and being a good, decent person. Thank you for ignoring what I thought I knew was best for me.*

But I don't. It's the same as with Catherine; just because he wants me safe doesn't mean that he wants anything beyond that. I carefully close the door again, tired of being the only one who seems to want so much more from the other. "Thank you," I say, accepting the gloves.

Thunder rolls in the distance and the rain pelts into the room at a slant. My books will get wet if the windows aren't closed. I'm about to push off the quilt and shut the window, but when I see Mr. Barrett, I freeze. He's cradling his forehead in his hands, elbows on his knees. For a moment I think he might be crying, but his back is still. Taking a slow, ragged breath, he draws his hand down his face and sits back up. It's a weary gesture, as if he has lost a fight and is gathering the energy to go on. When he sees me, he follows my gaze to the books, and slowly crosses the room to shut the window. The rain throws itself angrily against the glass.

Mr. Barrett stands immobile, hands jammed into his coat pockets, gaze focused on the runny landscape. His voice is hoarse and low when he speaks.

"I won't ask you why, because I know all too well what

drew you there. But I will ask, no, I will *demand* that you not do it again. I can't..." He trails off, choking on his words. "Do not do it again."

My own voice is small and tight. "I... I won't," I say, and I mean it with every fiber of my being.

He nods absently, not looking at me. The moment stretches out between us. Then he takes a deep breath that shudders through his shoulders to his chest. I'm still frozen, afraid that he has more to say, that he's come to his senses and decided to have it out at me after all. But he only takes out his pocket watch, and says lightly, with apology, "I'm afraid I must be off."

"Yes, of course," I say a little too eagerly, loath to let him know how desperately I wish he could stay.

He turns to leave, then hesitates with his hand on the door frame. "By the by, I spoke to your sister on the way in."

Good lord, Catherine is fast. "Oh?"

"She says that you haven't left your room in three days."

I don't say anything.

He nods, taking my silence as affirmation, and frowning into the messy room. "Well," he says, "I'd like to visit you again. That is, if it would be all right with you."

Even though I'm sitting down my legs go wobbly, and I have to bite my cheek from smiling too much. "I'd like that."

Mr. Barrett doesn't have any such inhibitions, and his smile is slow and dazzling. "Good." His eyes hold mine. "Good," he says again, this time briskly, returning to his old, businesslike self. "I expect that the next time I see you it will be in the library, or the parlor, or the garden—anywhere else but your room—and that you will have a new book recommendation for me. Hopefully something with a happy ending this time."

❧ *17* ❧

I'M DRIFTING BETWEEN wakefulness and sleep, my head hopelessly full of Mr. Barrett's smile, of the willow tree, of Catherine's rounded stomach, when Emeline comes to me.

I sit up slowly, blinking away the haze of sleep, hardly daring to breathe.

She pads through the darkness to my bed, leaving little puddles of water in her wake. She moves with purpose, though there's something sluggish, something halting in her gait, as if with every step she's pulling away from some invisible force dragging at her ankles. Her face is as pale and glowing as the moon and there's a sunken darkness around her eyes, but as sure as the wind blows, it's my little sister.

I let out a long, shaky breath. How I have dreamed of this moment, desperately willing the universe to bend its laws and allow me to see her just one more time. I knew that my eyes had not deceived me at the pond, knew it as surely as I know the beat of my own heart.

Emeline stops when she reaches the bed. Her face is bloated, her lips blue and her lovely auburn hair is tangled with pondweeds. She doesn't just look like she did when Mr. Barrett pulled her from the pond, but worse. As she studies me from solemn eyes so like hers in life yet so different, I shiver, trying not to inhale the wet smell of decay.

"Emeline," I whisper through the darkness. Is she like the pale lady who will disappear as soon as she senses I'm watching her? It doesn't matter. I am not scared of her. How could I fear my own sister?

"Hello, Lydia." She comes right up to the edge of the bed, her intentions unmistakable.

Before I can move over to make room for her, she climbs up beside me as she has done so many times in the past when she came seeking refuge from the dark.

"Oh, Emmy," I whisper. I'm too relieved to be frightened, too desperate for her touch to recoil. "Oh, sweetheart, what are you doing here?"

She snuggles in beside me. She's so cold. Colder than after Mr. Barrett pulled her out of the water, colder even than the last time I touched her lying in her coffin. I put my arm around her tiny, translucent shoulders, breathlessly wondering how it is that she can really be here next to me after so many aching days and weeks of unanswered prayers. Is she just one of so many other spirits who seem to haunt Willow Hall now?

It's unnatural, I know that. But, as if she were a small, skittish bird, I don't want to frighten her by letting my apprehension show, so I pull her closer, relishing the familiar yet somehow different feel of her against my body.

"I'm so glad you're here," I tell her. "I've missed you more than you can know."

"I don't like that hill," she says. "It's cold and dark, and I would rather be with you." Her voice is watery, and though she has the same high, light tone that she always did, there's something harder around the edges of it now. Something adult and knowing.

I hesitate. "But how, Emeline? How did you come here?"

"Didn't you want me to come? Isn't that why you gave me this?"

She holds something out in her damp little palm. I reach out, and then catch my breath. It's the lock of hair, tied in a faded red ribbon.

"Where did you get that?" I ask in a whisper.

She gives me a queer look. "You gave it to me."

"I..." I did give it to her, when she died. "I saw it in your trunk."

"Sometimes I keep things there." She regards the hair gravely. "But sometimes I like to take them out and carry them."

How long has she been lingering at Willow Hall? How long has she shared the same halls, the same rooms as me since she died and I haven't known?

The candle flickers across her pale little face, her skin dewy as a rose petal. The air is suddenly thick with all the things I have wanted to tell her, to ask her, since she left. I measure my words, cautious that saying the wrong thing might make her disappear as suddenly as she came.

"Why did you go away? Why did you leave me here? You knew that it was always supposed to be you and me, together."

My arms are wrapped around her, but rather than making her warmer, she's making me colder, and I let out an involuntary shiver. A hurt look comes over her face.

"You would have left me someday though. You would have gotten married and gone away and left me all alone."

"Oh, Emmy, I would never do that." Though as soon as I say it I think of Mr. Barrett and shame flushes through me. "Besides," I say, "one day you might have met a nice man and you wouldn't want your older sister hanging about as you tried to kiss him, would you?"

She screws up her face at the thought of kissing a boy and laughs. I smile too, though it's difficult, knowing that she will never fall in love, never start a family of her own.

"You don't need to worry about me."

"But I do," I say. Tears are welling up faster than I can blink them away. And then I finally ask the question that has tortured me, "Oh, Emmy, *why* did you do it? You must have known better. How could you have been so careless?"

She regards me for a moment with her bottomless gray eyes, and then shrugs in my arms. "It was the little boy," she says. "The little boy told me he would show me the mermaids."

I suck in a breath. "What little boy?"

"The one in the water. He said he wanted a friend and that he would show me the mermaids if I was his friend."

She says it so matter-of-factly. A shiver runs down my spine. "Is the little boy like Wicked George? Can only you see him?"

When Emeline was very young she had an imaginary friend who was always getting into trouble. George—or Wicked George, as he came to be known by Mother—was responsible for all sorts of things that were suspiciously like the kind of trouble little girls might get into. Could she have dreamed up a new imaginary friend that she never told me about?

"How should I know if you can see him or not?" This line of questioning is obviously tiresome to her and she gives a little yawn, her chilly breath scented with pond water.

I hesitate, wanting to hear more about this little boy, but I know better than to press Emeline on something she doesn't want to talk about and risk her shutting down completely.

She shrugs. "I thought I could get back out, that the boy would help me, but he didn't. I didn't mean to."

I can hardly breathe. "Oh, Emeline."

"You tried to find me, didn't you? You came into the pond to try to find me."

"Yes," I say. "I did."

"But I wasn't there."

"No, you weren't. Not until I was leaving."

She thinks on this for a moment. "John had to come pull you out."

"That's right."

"I like John. He tried to help me."

"Yes, he did." My breath catches as I wipe my eyes. "I like John too."

Emeline touches my cheek with her cold little finger. "He'll try to take you away someday," she says forlornly. "The little boy told me he will."

I catch her hand in my own and squeeze it. I want to tell her that a little hope has flared in my heart that maybe Mr. Barrett might see me the way I see him, that perhaps I won't always be the younger, plainer version of the woman he actually admires. But even if he does return my feelings, there is no love worth more than the one I have for my little sister.

"No," I say fiercely, pulling her closer to me. "No, I'll never leave you. Not again."

I'm afraid to go to sleep, to lose her again. We lie in silence for hours, one heartbeat shared between us, until finally I drift off. The next morning, sun streams in through the windows in piercing golden shafts. I roll over to an empty bed, the pillow damp, and the air smelling of stale pond water and weeds.

The next few days pass in a fog. I move automatically, dressing and eating, and occasionally finding my way into the library. More than once Catherine suspiciously asks me what I'm smiling about, but I just tell her it's nothing. She wouldn't understand how seeing Emeline, how holding her again, has left me dazed and with a renewed sense of hope. I hold my secret close, Emeline came to me, and me alone. I've wound her hair into a little braid, and coiled it inside a locket. I finger it constantly throughout the day, the metal warm and comforting against my chest.

At night I lie awake, tensed for the sound of approaching footsteps, sitting up every time a log shifts in the fire. But aside from Snip, I have no visitors, and after four nights of fitful sleep and increasingly tiring days, I begin to wonder if it was no more than a dream.

But on the fifth night, after having just resigned myself to falling asleep, a horrible sound wrenches me back awake. Heart racing, I bolt upright.

It's not Emeline, but Mother again, that terrible wail in which she indulged our first night at Willow Hall. Just like that night, it starts low and plaintive, building into an unnatural keening. I'm about to put my head under my pillow to muffle the sound when I chastise myself. Here is my chance to comfort Mother, to make amends for my lack of judgment in going into the pond. I throw on my dressing gown and pad out into the hallway. The wailing is louder here, each sob clear and ringing; it's a wonder that no one else has been awakened by it. When I reach Mother and Father's bedchamber, I give a hesitant knock. There's no answer, and the wailing continues. I'm just about to try a second time when my hand freezes in the air.

It's not coming from behind their bedchamber door. It's coming from the third floor.

My rational mind tells me to go back to bed, that Mother is probably upstairs in the nursery, mourning Emeline and in need of privacy. But something irrational and morbidly curious tells me that it's not Mother, and that I ought to go upstairs and investigate.

Convincing my feet to obey me is another matter entirely. I move with small, hesitating steps, all the while the groaning sobs filling my ears, chilling me down to my bones. They grow louder as I near the stairs, and by the time I'm at the top I can almost make out distinct words.

Wiping my sweating palms on the sides of my dressing gown, I freeze again, teetering on the top step outside the ballroom. Cold seeps from the floor through the soles of my unslippered feet, but I'm knocked backward by the overwhelming smell of smoke. I don't see any signs of a fire, but I press my mouth into my elbow to keep from choking, and move closer.

The voice, low and mournful, is not Mother's.

"My boy," groans the female voice. "Oh, my boy." The timbre is achingly hopeless, and fills me with sadness as much as it does horror.

It can't possibly be her, but I can't stop myself from calling in a whisper, "Emeline, is that you?"

The cries continue as if I hadn't said anything. The thick smell of smoke winds around me like an embrace, but the air is clear as ever.

Just as suddenly as it started, it stops. The words drop away, the cries evaporate, the smell of smoke recedes and a heaviness I hadn't realized was pressing down on me lifts. I'm left alone with my thudding heart and dry mouth, and an uneasy sense that until this moment, I shared the company of something not quite of this world.

Slowly and quietly, my legs shaking, I make my way back downstairs and to my bed. No doors open, no one peers out to ask me what all the commotion was. The house is silent and everyone else sleeps on undisturbed.

When I awake dazed and tired to the light of day, it seems impossible that the hellish cries of last night had been anything

more than a dream, a figment of my imagination. When I ask
Catherine if she heard anything, she gives me a peevish look
and informs me that the only thing making sleep difficult for
her are the lumpy mattresses here. Even though I don't think
Mother would admit to such an outburst, I ask her anyway if
she's had bad nights recently. She just gives a weary sigh, and
I drop the matter.

Over the course of the next few days I gradually I ease into
a routine, tucking away the memories of my secret visit from
Emeline, as well as the moans that apparently I alone heard
in the night.

Mr. Barrett hasn't come back since the day in my room, but
if Father's schedule is any indication, they're both busy trying to tie up the land deal with Ezra Clarke to get the rights
to the river that runs through his farm. I'm almost glad that
Mr. Barrett hasn't been round yet, as it gives me more time
to emerge from my fog, more time to decide upon a book to
recommend to him.

I'm happily curled up in the library with Snip at my feet and
a quilt round my shoulders as I pull out every book I think
he might like and sort them into piles. I've just moved *The
Castle of Wolfenbach* out of the Maybe pile for the third time
when Catherine flounces in.

"I need to go to town and buy cloth for my wedding dress,
and Mother says you have to come with me."

A wedding dress seems like something of a leap to make
from the one letter that Mr. Pierce sent her after the failed
dinner. More likely she's looking for an excuse to buy a dress
to flatter her quickly changing body.

I look at the organized chaos of my book piles, at the cozy
fire licking and snapping in the hearth. "I'm busy."

I've been relishing the prospect of reliving my favorite stories as I sorted my books, trying to see them as if through

Mr. Barrett's eyes for the first time. But apparently even after everything that's happened I'm still the responsible one, and Mother thinks that I'm somehow capable of keeping Catherine in check.

"Please? Your books will be here when you get back." Catherine's tone is wheedling, artificially high, the kind of voice she used to use when she wanted a bigger allowance from Father. When she sees that I'm still unmoved, she adds, "You look like you just stumbled out of a crypt. Getting some fresh air will put some color into your cheeks for when you see Mr. Barrett."

I try not to care, but she's touched upon my little spark of vanity that ignites whenever I hear Mr. Barrett's name. So not even an hour after I'd resolved to spend the day with my books and memories of Emeline's visit, I'm in a fresh dress with my hair pinned up off my neck and trundling toward town with Catherine.

❧ *18* ❧

THE WEEK'S RAIN has left everything clean and fresh, lacquering the world with bright, glistening autumn colors. As we pass along the edge of the woods and over the bridge into town, I realize just how much I've missed the world outside the walls of Willow Hall. Not the people and their dramas, but the steady, faithful rhythms of nature and all her secrets. High above us the lonely cry of a hawk rings out as if echoing my sentiment. How small we must look to him down here.

Much to Catherine's annoyance I open the carriage window and lean out, closing my eyes against the cool breeze. I've never seen a season transition with such fierce determination, and I'm inwardly grateful for the return of chilly nights, for a world tipped on the precipice of a great change. Summer felt like it would never end, stretching from the sticky days in Boston before we had to flee, to Emeline's passing, and then to the swampy heat the night I sank into the water to follow her. I take a moment, letting the cool, damp air fill my lungs and course through my body with the promise of better things to come.

"For heaven's sake." Catherine pulls me back in. "You've been shut up for days complaining of a cold, do you want to catch another?"

I let her close the window, but as we approach town we begin to encounter other carriages, pedestrians, men on horseback, and I can't help but catch my breath and look to see if one of them might be Mr. Barrett, half hoping that it is, half hoping that it isn't.

"I already told you that Mr. Barrett is at the Clarke farm signing papers with Father today, so I don't know what makes you think we might run into him here."

I flush, more annoyed at myself that I'm so transparent than at Catherine's keen perception. I give a little shrug. Her words don't even merit a response, and I lean back and pretend to be absorbed in the book I brought along with me.

When we arrive, Catherine waltzes into the little shop as if she were Marie Antoinette. "I'm looking for a satin or a silk. Something special, something that no one else has," she says, breezing over the shopkeeper's greetings and peeling off her gloves, making herself right at home.

The man's eyes glint in appreciation. We haven't been back here since our first day in town when he tried to scare Emeline with stories of hauntings and ghosts. He had probably thought he'd lost our business forever. "Yes, of course, madam. Would you be so kind as to follow me? I have just the thing."

I roll my eyes and leave Catherine to her shopping and the shopkeeper to his bowing and groveling. As I wander around the small shop, I play a game of pretending what I would buy if it were me shopping for my wedding gown. I run my fingers over a soft bolt of mossy green satin, then put it back and let my gaze wander down the stacks of bolts. It's not a bad selection, but I'm surprised that Catherine didn't want to go somewhere with a bigger and finer stock.

The shopkeeper is draping a length of silk over his arm, eagerly trying to gauge Catherine's reaction. It's an indecisive shade of yellow—almost green—and Catherine is oohing and ahhing over it like it's the most beautiful thing she's ever seen.

I've found the cloth that I would buy, and I can't help but wonder if it was made in Mr. Barrett's mill. Of course he wouldn't have woven it himself, but he might have felt it just the way I am now, checking the quality, making sure it met his standards before sending it off to be sold.

As the shopkeeper brings out more and more fabric bolts, instead of becoming more excited, Catherine grows distracted, glancing out the window every few seconds.

"What about this one?" I lift the corner of my chosen cloth, a pink silk so pale and soft that it's almost white.

The shopkeeper sets aside what he was showing Catherine and nods his vigorous agreement. "It's been reported that Mrs. Griegson of Boston was seen wearing this very shade of pink at the opera last month," he says in reverent tones. "Very hard to find, but I got my hands on this bolt straight from Waltham and you won't find it anywhere else."

So it didn't come from Mr. Barrett's mill then. The pink suddenly looks drab and ordinary, and I remember that it's cotton that he produces, not silk.

"Yes," Catherine says without looking at it. "Very pretty."

He ignores her distant tone, running a solicitous hand over a bolt of striped satin that even I recognize as being several years out of style.

"The sleeves are to be fuller this season. Just imagine this puffed up at both shoulders, a dipped neckline, the colors setting off your lovely hair to its full advantage. Why," he says, wetting his bottom lip with his tongue, "you won't have a fellow in town who will be able to keep his hands off you."

Normally Catherine would give him a sharp word for his

boldness and threaten to withhold her patronage, but she only murmurs distractedly, "Yes, I heard as much about fuller sleeves."

I ask the shopkeeper to excuse us for a minute and take Catherine by the arm to the corner of the store among the large barrels of sugar and salt.

"You were the one who begged me to come with you, and you're hardly even looking at anything," I chide.

She jerks her arm back, rubbing it as if I hurt her. "Oh, I don't know," she says irritably. She throws a glance over my shoulder at the counter covered in a rainbow of silks and satins. "The lavender one I guess."

I'm about to tell her that she is perfectly capable of asking for the lavender to be cut herself, when she takes a sharp breath, her eyes fixing on something beyond the window. I follow her gaze, but it takes me a moment to place the swaggering gait of the man she's watching across the town green.

"Catherine!"

"Keep your voice down, will you?" She glances at the shopkeeper who's pretending not to be interested in our conversation in the corner.

When she sees my color rise, she hurries back to the counter and gives the shopkeeper instructions to cut her off a length of the lavender silk and be quick about it.

"Catherine," I say again, catching her by the hand. "Did you know that he would be here?"

Pretending not to hear, she counts out her money and makes a show of being absorbed in getting the right change. When I don't let go she gives me a sharp look that says I had better wait until we're outside.

The shopkeeper takes an unbearably long time cutting the silk, all the while darting curious glances between us. I give him a hasty thanks and then drag Catherine out by the arm.

Outside, Catherine whirls to face me. "That was rude."

"Is that why we came here today, really? Were you planning on meeting him all along?"

By now Mr. Pierce has seen us, and he raises his hat in acknowledgment as he ambles across the green.

Catherine throws a hurried smile at him, and then gives me an impatient little shrug, confirming my suspicions.

"Mother told me to keep you out of trouble. I hardly think she would be grateful if she heard you went off with Mr. Pierce for the whole town to see."

"Oh, Lydia, don't be such a sop. I'm already pregnant," she says with a breezy wave of her hand. "What other trouble can I get into? Just find something to do with the carriage for an hour and I'll meet you back here. Mother will be none the wiser. And besides..." She lifts the lavender silk in her arms to show me. "I can't very well use this until there's a proper engagement."

I open my mouth but then close it again, pressing my lips tight. The sooner she's engaged the better, but why can't she go about it in a proper sort of way? Mr. Pierce should have already made his intentions clear with Father, and he should be coming by the house where our parents can chaperone. I don't like all this sneaking about.

By the time I've started explaining this to her, Mr. Pierce has caught up to us. Catherine's annoyance with me evaporates as she fixes a gracious smile on her face.

"Mr. Pierce," she says, a bit coyly. "What a pleasant surprise."

"The pleasure is all mine." He presses his smiling lips to her hand, and then gives me a cursory nod.

"A surprise indeed," I say with thinly veneered scorn. "Tell me, Mr. Pierce, are you still a guest of Mr. Barrett's?"

He raises a brow, glancing at Catherine before answering. "I am," he says, humoring me.

"Ah," I say. "You must be quite the expert on milling by now. I wonder that you're still in New Oldbury if you've learned so much that you don't even need to accompany Mr. Barrett to Clarke farm today. Tell me again, what is your position in Mr. Barrett's employ?"

"Lydia!" Even Catherine is blushing scarlet now.

Color rises to Mr. Pierce's face. "I'm sure I don't know what you mean."

"It's only that you seem to come and go as you please. I thought perhaps you have been acting in a traveling supervisor role. What *does* bring you back to town?" I ask with an innocent furrow of my brow.

"You're mistaken, Miss Montrose," he says. "John doesn't employ me, you'll remember that he's merely been showing me the ins and outs of the milling business."

"Ah! Of course. So kind of you to remind me of the particulars. Mr. Barrett is lucky in any case to have a friend that he can count on to take his mentorship so seriously."

Mr. Pierce's perennial smile fades. He narrows his eyes, giving me an appraising look, as if really seeing me for the first time and realizing just how little he cares for what he sees. Catherine pinches my waist.

"John is the best sort of friend a fellow could ask for," Mr. Pierce says briskly. "I'm sure I'm the lucky one." He clears his throat and holds out his arm to Catherine, careful not to meet my eye again. "Shall we?"

Catherine thrusts the bolt of silk into my arms with a hiss. "I'll be back in an hour."

They head off, arm in arm, Catherine leaning in close to him and laughing loudly in response to something whispered in her ear. Some jab at me, no doubt.

With a huff, I turn to carry the silk back to the carriage. But the bundle is heavier than it looks, and as I shift the weight into my other arm it becomes tangled, slipping from my grasp and cascading to the ground.

I consider leaving it on the wet ground and letting it soak up the brown puddle water. That would serve Catherine right.

"Let me get that for you, miss," Joe says coming up behind me.

I stand there stupidly, staring as he whisks the bolt away into the carriage before it can stain.

How can Catherine be so careless with her reputation after all that we've been through? A fresh wave of anger washes through me and I give the wooden hitching post a good kick, and then another and another.

"Miss Montrose? I thought that was you! Heavens, what are you doing to that post?"

I take a deep breath before turning around, sending up a silent prayer for strength.

"Mrs. Tidewell," I say, mustering a polite smile. "How lovely to see you."

She gives me a lingering glance of concern. The daughter— whose name I can't remember—is hanging shyly behind her, looking, if I'm not mistaken, a little relieved not to be the object of her mother's attention for once.

"Well, Abigail and I were just taking some air and I thought I saw you and your sister, but I wasn't sure because a young man was blocking my view. I said to Abigail, 'Why, that must be the Montrose girls,' and then of course she said that it was and I knew that we must come over and say hello and thank you for the lovely dance at Willow Hall last month. And of course to pass along our deepest condolences on your family's loss. Didn't I say that, Abigail?"

Abigail opens her mouth to reply, but Mrs. Tidewell is already turning back to me and giving me a detailed account of all the minutiae of her daily existence from the past few weeks.

The last time I saw her in our ballroom I had the general impression that she was a woman of means, but in the daylight the jewels jammed onto her stubby fingers and hanging from her ears are a dull, cloudy paste, and some of the gold plate has worn off, exposing the metal underneath. Her cheek rouge is applied too heavily, giving the appearance of two red apples bobbing up and down every time she laughs. The lace at the cuffs of her emerald green dress is yellowing, and even as she goes on about how accomplished her Abby is with a needle and thread, I can't help but feel a little sorry for her.

She catches my eyes taking in these details and quickly says, "The weather took such a sharp change the last few days, didn't it? It's all I can do to pull out last winter's clothes until I can have something new made up."

This must remind her of why they're here in the first place, because she acknowledges her daughter again by saying, "Abby, go in and ask Mr. Anderson about a wool delivery."

Abigail hesitates, darting her glance between Mrs. Tidewell and me before saying, "But Mamma, remember last time we were here Mr. Anderson said we had to pay the last sugar bill before we placed any more orders."

I feel rather than see Mrs. Tidewell stiffening, heat rising to her cheeks. She turns back to me, forcing a light laugh. "Tradesmen are always so eager to shake you down for one more penny, when they know quite well that all the best sort of people live off credit." She gives a disdainful sniff. "It's vulgar really. When my husband was alive Mr. Anderson wouldn't dream of harassing me for money, but I suppose a widow makes for easy pickings."

I can't help but feel bad for her, and give her an encouraging smile. "What was it that your husband did?"

Her eyes briefly flash with gratitude before resuming their usual haughty squint, and she settles into her favorite subject of herself again.

"Mr. Tidewell? He was a cooper by trade, but made a fair bit of money on cattle." She gives a little sigh as if to say that if Mr. Tidewell were considerate he might have done a good deal better before dying. "I might not be so grand as some of the ladies in Boston, but I can hold my head high knowing that my daughters have immaculate reputations and will make good matches."

I let her meaning go by without fight, and Mrs. Tidewell for her part seems content to ramble on about the shortcomings of all the other citizens of New Oldbury.

My head snaps up and I stop her midsentence. "What did you say?"

She looks a little taken aback. "Mrs. Barrett. I said she was the only other lady in New Oldbury that was really of any quality."

I take a dry swallow. "Mrs. Barrett? John Barrett is a... widower?"

She laughs, an unpleasant sort of gurgling sound. "Mercy! Mr. Barrett a widower! No, his mother, God rest her soul. Very kind lady, she was, though with such a cold air about her. She often would send a basket round to our house when I was nursing the girls. Of course, these days I would never accept that kind of charity," she hastily adds. "We keep our own cook now, though of course her mutton is so dry that Abby has too—"

"I'm sorry," I interrupt. "But...Mrs. Barrett. When did she die? Was Mr. Barrett very young?"

I suppose it's all the same to Mrs. Tidewell whether she talks of the personal lives of her neighbors or her cook's shortcomings. She transitions easily back to the former, positively glowing that someone has recognized in her the mark of an expert.

"Well now, let's see. The fire was in what, '02? '03? No, that can't be right. Ginny was colicky that winter, which means that it couldn't have been more than—"

"Mrs. Tidewell," I say trying not to let my irritation creep into my voice. "What fire?"

She looks at me as if I just asked in what country we're standing. "Why, the old house. Surely you knew that your property used to belong to the Barretts?"

"Well, yes." That day at the pond Mr. Barrett said something about that. "But what do you mean, the old house?"

Linking her arm in mine like we're old friends, she begins walking toward the green where stone benches are arranged around a plaque commemorating the town's first settlers.

"The first Barrett house used to stand right where yours does now," she says, vaguely gesturing to the road that leads to our house. "But after the fire Mr. Barrett—that is, the senior Mr. Barrett—had a new house constructed on the other side of their property. That's the house that stands there today. Just as well, if you ask me. The old thing was a shabby little affair. Not nearly as grand as Willow Hall," she reluctantly concedes with a sniff.

"But what about the fire? Is that how Mr. Barrett's mother died?"

"It was a terrible thing," she says with a look of genuine remorse. "Mrs. Barrett was such a queer sort of woman. Very kind as I said, and yet so cold. She was like a phantom almost with her pearly white skin and faraway blue eyes. You would be speaking to her and after a time realize that she wasn't there."

This is something I hardly think would be singular to Mrs.

Barrett when listening to the long-winded Mrs. Tidewell, but I let her continue.

"The only time you felt she was really present was when she was with her little boy. Oh, how she doted on him! There was nothing too good for him, no suit of clothes too fine, no little pet too exotic. Apple of her eye, he was."

I try to imagine Mr. Barrett growing up coddled, in suits of crushed blue velvet with a little squirrel on a chain. "He must have been heartbroken when she died."

Mrs. Tidewell's brow furrows quizzically. "I'm sure he would have been, only he died alongside of her."

We've just about reached the benches when I stop suddenly. My stomach drops and cold spreads over me. "But John...you can't mean...?"

"Oh!" She lets out her wet laugh again. "Oh dear, you didn't think Mr. Barrett was a ghost all this time!"

Her face grows serious and I let out my breath not sure *what* I had thought she was talking about. "No, it was his little brother, Moses, the poor mite. Moses was the favored son, and it was he who died alongside his poor mother in that fire."

I lower myself slowly to the cold, slightly damp bench and Mrs. Tidewell settles beside me with a grunt and heavy rustle of silk.

Poor, poor John. What was it like to grow up in the shadow of his mother's favorite, and then for them to both die? How heavy the guilt must weigh on him. Is that why he always has such a look of sadness about him? He may be a grown man now, but I wish I could sweep him up into my arms and hold him, stroking away the bad memories.

"For all her beauty, Theodosia Barrett was not a happy woman." Mrs. Tidewell beckons me to move closer and looks around as if the grass itself is listening. I humor her and lean in, trying not to inhale her cloying perfume.

"I saw the marks on her myself. Such white skin as that and there'd be a terrible angry bruise at her wrist or near her neck. She tried to hide them, but not well enough, poor thing. Such a cruel man, was her husband."

My mind races and breathless, I ask, "And what of the fire?"

"Well, there was— Why, is that Mrs. Wheeler?" Mrs. Tidewell half sits up from the bench, squinting across the green and then waving her handkerchief frantically at a pair of strolling women. "Oh, Mrs. Wheeler! Mrs. Hopkins!"

The women pause, and I can only imagine that there's a tense dialogue taking place in hurried whispers debating whether or not they should acknowledge her. *Please, please keep walking*, I silently beg them.

But I'm to have no such luck, and I have to wait to hear more about the fire while the three women engage in a conversation devoid of anything of importance save pleasantries about the weather.

When they've exhausted all the different ways to comment on the recent rain, the women take their leave. With a bit of a tipsy smile still lingering on her lips, Mrs. Tidewell whispers to me, "You would never know it from looking at her now, but that Mrs. Hopkins once worked as a tavern girl in Manchester. Can you imagine? Ever since she married that lawyer she acts like she's some sort of society woman through and through. Shameful, really."

"Yes," I hastily agree. "Very shameful. But you were saying something about a fire?"

"A fire? Oh, right. Mrs. Barrett had some great row with her husband. I never knew the particulars of it, but they were easy enough to guess. He tried to turn his hand to the boy— Moses, that is—and she barricaded herself with him in the house. Made Mr. Barrett mad with rage. Took a match and put the whole house aflame, her and the boy in it. I don't think it was ever his intention to kill them, nor to make a ruin of his house. Just wanted to put a fright into her, get her to come out. But the fire took over faster than he thought, and there it is."

I can hardly breathe. "And John?"

She looks surprised. "He was only a little thing at the time. He must have been off with his nurse somewhere." She pauses, thinking. "I do remember him at the burial though, so solemn in his little mourning suit. Didn't shed a tear the whole time, brave little fellow that he was."

I can envision him perfectly, his jaw set, golden hair falling across his eyes as he watched his mother's and brother's coffins lowered into the ground. His father, an equally solemn man but with a vein of anger running through him as hot as lava, gripping his son's shoulder. He would have leaned down and whispered in his son's ear with breath full of brandy, "Now don't you make a sound, boy, lest you want a taste of my belt on your back later." And young Mr. Barrett would have been silent as the tomb.

"Oh, that burial." She puts a hand to her heart in a gesture of being overcome, rolling her eyes up toward the heavens. "They never recovered Moses's body, so they buried an empty coffin for him. Horrid, horrid business."

"Horrid," I echo back in a whisper. Willow Hall stands where the old house burned down, and they never found Moses's body. My mouth turns to cotton as realization dawns. My God, his remains must still be under our house.

"The whole town turned against Mr. Barrett after that, wouldn't do business with him. It took John Barrett years to pay off his father's debts."

I remember the dinner we had what now feels like years ago where I spoke out of turn, forcing Mr. Barrett to confess that his father died bankrupt. I feel even more terrible now that I know the story of what led to that bankruptcy.

"Miss Montrose?"

I start. "Yes?"

"I asked if you knew anything of an engagement between Mr. Barrett and a young lady of the town."

I barely register her words, thoughts of fire, of Moses, of Mr. Barrett, racing like clouds through my mind. "No, I don't think so," I say, trying to make my tone light and inconsequential and, to my ears at least, failing miserably.

Mrs. Tidewell lets out a sigh of relief. "I figured it was nonsense when I heard as much. Still hope for Abby then."

I get the sense that whatever little friendship we just shared on the bench is already slipping away, and I'm once again an object of contempt. That's more than fine with me. I need to get away from this gossipy woman and her insincerity. I stand quickly, the blood rushing from my head.

"Yes," I say faintly. "Mrs. Tidewell, you must excuse me. I'm afraid I've just had a terrible headache come on. I think I must go home at once."

19

I CAN'T GO home right away though, because Catherine isn't back yet. With my mind faraway and my legs shaking, I nearly miss the step as I climb in the carriage, and Joe has to catch me by the elbow to help me inside. I sit there, frozen, wrapped in thoughts as constricting and tangled as a spider's web.

Why didn't Mr. Barrett tell me? That night when he pulled me from the pond, he saw the trembling, smoldering wick of my soul, the truest, most vulnerable part of me. And whether I shared it willingly or not, it doesn't matter, because I am at a disadvantage for being so transparent while he remains opaque and unknowable. Sometimes I feel as if we are standing on opposites sides of a great chasm, and I must watch helplessly as the gaping space between us widens.

I don't know how long I sit like that biting my lips and letting my thoughts run away from me. I nearly jump out of my skin when the door opens again and Catherine appears, plopping herself unceremoniously across from me without a word. I take a deep breath.

As Joe closes the door behind her I catch his eye, silently trying to convey just how important it is that he doesn't say anything to Mother. Good, dependable Joe who has been with us so long and must himself understand the importance of keeping Catherine out of trouble. He holds my gaze and gives me a short nod before gently latching the door and climbing up to the driver's seat.

Catherine doesn't say anything, just slowly peels off her gloves and folds her hands in her lap as she gazes out the window.

"Well," I say crossly, "should I be congratulating you?" If she was going to act so brazenly and put our family's reputation at risk again then she better at least have gotten a proposal out of him.

Catherine's cool gaze slides away from the window and lands on me. She shifts a little in her seat, the faintest pink rising along her neck and at the tip of her ears. "He didn't propose."

I swallow back my disappointment and my urge to take her by the shoulders and shake the details out of her. Keeping my voice as level as I can, I ask, "Do you think he will soon?"

She heaves a sigh as if I had her chained up in a dungeon and was interrogating her for a crime she didn't commit. "If you *must* know, he was rather detached. After I made it clear that we wouldn't be doing anything besides talking he became disagreeable and left. If only I weren't starting to show already," she adds, more to herself than me. As if in chorus to this lament, the carriage jostles over a rut in the road, the wheels groaning and her hand instinctively flies to her stomach.

Catherine ignores my silence, though she must feel the angry charge in the air. Instead she takes up the bolt of fabric and runs her hand over it, frowning as if she had completely forgotten about the original purpose of the trip. "Was that Mrs. Tidewell I saw talking to you? What did she want?"

So she did see Mrs. Tidewell, and still went off with Mr. Pierce right in front of her eyes. I take a deep breath, willing myself not to lose my temper. "Nothing. It was nothing important. Just some passing gossip." Not completely untrue, but Catherine immediately catches the hesitation in my voice.

"You're a terrible liar," she says. The pink has all but faded from her neck and she gives a little shrug. "You don't have to tell me if you don't want to."

I don't think I've ever missed Emeline more than I have in this moment. I want to pull her up into my lap and forget my worries as I braid her hair and listen to her tell stories. She was always my shoulder to cry on, even if she didn't know or understand what I was crying about. It's not the day at the pond that makes me miss her the most, with its confusion, anger and helplessness. No, it's these tiny, empty slivers of life, pockets of time, into which she had fit so perfectly and is now so conspicuously absent that leave me rattled and aching.

The words slip out against my better judgment. "She was telling me about how Mr. Barrett lost his mother and little brother. And to think, this whole time we've known him he's never said a word about it." I can't stop the heavy, shuddering sigh that runs through me. "Poor John."

Catherine unrolls the satin, her eye instantly locking on the minuscule stain from when I dropped it in the street. "Hmm? Oh, yes, the fire. I heard about that."

My skin prickles hot. "You did? When?"

Her gaze sharpens as she realizes she has my attention now. "Mr. Barrett told me, though I can't for the life of me remember when exactly."

Mr. Barrett confided in Catherine, not me. Just the other day he sat in my bedroom and told me how sorry he was about Emeline, and never mentioned that he knew what it was like to lose a beloved sibling. What is it about me that he feels he can't place his trust in me? What makes Catherine such a good confidante?

Catherine is still watching me with interest. "What, are you upset that he didn't tell you? Don't be small about it, Lydia. He lost his whole family and all you care about is that he told me instead of you."

"No," I say stubbornly. "I don't care that he told you."

"Mmm." She shrugs and continues working her fingernail over the spot of mud.

She's right of course. He lost his mother and brother in the most gruesome way possible, grew up destitute with a hard father, and then had to struggle and scrape to pay off debts that were not his own. How can I grudge him such a trivial matter as whom he decides to tell about his past?

But I still can't shake the image of Catherine and Mr. Barrett standing close together at the far end of the hall, speaking in whispers, stealing a few moments together while I lay convalescing in my room. It's the only time he could have told her.

God, how I wish Mr. Pierce had proposed. Because now, the next time Catherine and Mr. Barrett run into each other in the hall, what's to keep her from throwing herself completely at him again?

The next day Catherine informs us—with a pointed look at me—that she must go back to town, because the fabric she bought is too stained to use. Mother, who still doesn't know the purpose of the fabric, has calls to make, and Ada needs supplies in town as well, so it's agreed that an afternoon will be made of it. I beg off coming along, saying that I have a headache, but really I just can't stand the idea of spending another afternoon with Catherine and her deceitful schemes. Father is at the mill, and Joe is driving everyone else so I have the house to myself. I'm enjoying a plate of cold pie on the floor in the library. Snip, my accomplice in crime, gobbles up the spilled crumbs so that Mother will never know I was eating on the carpet.

I've finally finished *Mathilda* and am just cracking open *The Romance of the Forest*—an old favorite—when a clatter from somewhere in the house cuts the silence. I sit up, putting a hand on Snip's back to keep him quiet. "Hello? Is someone there?"

I wait, listening for an answer. If they've come back through the kitchen, then maybe they don't hear me. "Mother? Catherine? Is that you?"

Silence is the only answer. I sit perfectly still, straining my ear, but nothing else comes. Despite that, I have the prickling feeling that whoever—or whatever—made that noise, came from the dining room, and is still in there.

Gingerly, I get up, my legs full of pins and needles from sitting on the floor so long. Just like the night of the woman in the garden, I can't stay in the library knowing that someone might be there. I must go and look for myself.

Even with the sun coming through the windows, illuminating the wood floors and catching the light of the crystal lamps, I feel as if I'm making my way through a dark, murky passage. My feet are heavy, as if they know something that my mind does not.

The door to the dining room is closed. It beckons me, yet repels me, exuding a sense of silent occupation. My ears buzz. A singsong chorus of whispers grows as I approach.

Are you ready?

I am here.

You attract them.

Are you ready?

Prepare for what lies ahead.

Prepare.

Prepare.

They mount and mount into a dizzying jumble of sound and I run the rest of the way to the door, my heart in my chest, my eyes squeezed shut. Grasping the knob, I fling open the door. The voices die away.

I knew it would be there. But it doesn't stop me from gasping as every part of me curls back in on itself in horror. My blood turns to ice.

Seated at the table is a woman, or what used to be a woman. She sits as if she has every right to be there, as if she has always been there. A veil covers her face, but it is gauzy and threadbare, and I can see the contours of the features beneath. Her dress is old, black as night yet opalescent as the moon through a cobweb. Paralyzed with fear, I watch as it moves about her of its own accord, a soft undulation as if she were underwater. And though I can see her as clear as day, the veiled woman in our dining room, there's a translucence to her, and the panoramic wallpaper is just visible behind her. She is like nothing and no one I have ever seen before, and yet she is familiar, as if I have always known her.

"Come, child." Her voice comes from everywhere and nowhere, and when her words are finished, I have the unnerving feeling that they weren't spoken aloud at all, but came from within my head.

She beckons me with a knobby finger, more bone than flesh.

I can't drag my gaze away from her face, the sunken holes where there ought to be eyes, the lipless mouth, all teeth and blackness. The cold pie that I just enjoyed churns in my stomach and threatens to come up. She beckons me again, and I imagine those long, terrible fingers closing around my neck and choking the life out of me. I imagine them raking me across the face until ribbons of skin flutter from my skull. I stand my ground, unwilling to deliver myself up to her. She is the stuff of my novels, a grotesque horror that titillates on the page, but sends terror into my heart when in the same room as me.

She gives something like a grunt, and as if able to read my thoughts, says, "One hundred and thirty years of death is not gentle on a body. Come, do not gawk." I dare not disobey her, so I force my leaden feet to move a few steps closer.

The smell of decay and death fills the room, sickly sweet and putrid at the same time. My stomach clenches at the memories the odor brings back of Emeline in her coffin. My throat is tight, my mouth cotton, but somehow I'm able to gasp out, "W-who are you?"

She makes a noise, something between a snort and a laugh, a scraping, rattling sound, though it's devoid of humor. "Do you not know your own forebear?"

The blackness of her dress curls around her like a snake, but she sits as motionless as if she were carved of stone. Her stillness is suffocating, it dares the house to be silent, and punishes the sunlight for filtering in through the window.

Warily, I come to a halt at the edge of the dining room table. I don't know what she's talking about. "Forebear?"

"Have you not looked upon me since you were a babe? Do you not recognize in me what flows through you?"

"I..." But then it comes to me. The lace collar, though tattered and black as her dress, is unmistakable around her neck. "You're the woman in the painting. Mother's ancestor."

The inclination of her head is small, barely perceptible.

"I saw you in the garden, when we first moved here. What do you want?"

That noise again that might be an impatient snort or a laugh. "It was not me you saw. You attract them. This is a haunted place and you attract the unhappy spirits that call it home.

They know what you are. Haven't I been telling you that for these two months past?"

You attract them. My eyes widen at the familiar refrain, the words that I had convinced myself were nothing more than a figment of my imagination, though I saw them written in my mirror, and heard them on the whispers of the breeze.

I can't tear my gaze away from her, yet I'm terrified that the veil will fall away, revealing her face in more horrible detail. Before I can ask her what she thinks I am, the voice comes again.

"You've been asking questions. Your mother would do well to educate you."

"Educate me?"

"Tch, ignorant and incendiary. A dangerous combination. You might ask her for the book. It was my mother's. Yet look at the good it did me," she says. At this, she lifts the veil to her chin, revealing a crooked neck, one of the bones snapped clean through. My hand flies to my mouth and I stifle a cry. She drops the veil back into place. "That is what I got for my trouble."

Despite the pounding of my heart and the coiling of my stomach, her roundabout way of speaking is wearing on my taut nerves. "Why are you here? Did you come just to berate me? Are you a spirit come to try to frighten me away? Because that's what you are, isn't it? A spirit?" As soon as my questions tumble out I brace myself. What if I anger her?

But my barrage of questions has no effect. "I have watched you since you were a little girl. I have watched and waited, wondering when you would begin to open your eyes to the world around you."

The thought of this creature watching me from the shadows makes me feel sick. "If you've been watching me for so long, then why did you come now?"

She gives a sigh that lifts the curtains and wilts the flowers on the table. "I will not waste my breath on words you're not ready to hear. I thought that this place would open your eyes, but I see that I've come too soon."

Frustration overtakes fear. "But I *am* ready! Something is happening here, to me. There's something inside of me. You must have come for a reason. I've heard your voice in the woods, seen your words on my mirror! If you've come to say something to me, then just say it!"

She holds up a single finger, silencing me. "Take this as a warning. If you are not able or willing to control yourself, it will not only be you who suffers the consequences, but those around you as well. If your mother will not educate you, then you must seek out your own answers. You cannot protect yourself if you do not know that of which you are capable. Already you have consigned your sister to a living death. Your ignorance has consequences, can you not see that?"

I didn't think my blood could go any colder, but at her words, my veins turn to ice. "Wait, what do you mean? My sister Emeline?"

From somewhere far away in the house, a door opens and the sound of Mother and Catherine talking floats down the hallway as if from another world. Yet I can't break my gaze from the decayed visage of my ancestor.

"You hanged for witchcraft. My mother told me that much. Have you put some sort of curse on me, on us?" If Emeline has returned it must be because of this grotesque spirit. How could it be because of me?

She gives another sigh. "Do not mistake death and decay for evil. Both are the legacy of all of us, the good and the bad alike. I was not a perfect woman in life, but I was not evil either, and I am no different now. I have done nothing to your sister. As I said, you are not ready to hear what I have to say."

"But I am ready!" I must be ready, for whatever it is. If I'm somehow responsible for Emeline's return then I have to know. I wanted her back so badly I did not stop to consider that she doesn't belong here, that it might cost her dearly to stay in this world.

"Who are you talking to?"

I jump at the sound of Catherine's voice and spin around. "What? No one."

She gives me a hard look and cranes her neck over my shoulder to see into the dining room. I catch my breath, but when she doesn't say anything I turn back around. The apparition is gone. If Catherine notices the oppressive stillness that our ancestor left in her wake, she doesn't say anything.

With a swallow, and legs that aren't quite ready to move again, I follow Catherine back into the library where she spreads out several parcels, the fruits of their errands. I watch her as she unwraps a paper package containing embroidery threads and a card of new needles. Is this the same day as it was five minutes ago in the dining room standing before the spirit of my ancestor? Is this the same house, the same world, watching Catherine go about her business as if the most extraordinary thing I've ever seen in my life had not just occurred?

"What are you staring at?"

I force an inconsequential shrug. "Nothing. Just looking to see what you bought."

She scowls. "That mean little shopkeeper wouldn't take back the damaged silk, so now I'm stuck with it, stain and all." She's removed her bonnet and is pulling out her workbasket. I perch on the chair next to her, desperate to draw her into what I just experienced. How can it be real if no one else sees what I see?

But there's no way to come at it directly, so I just ask, "Do you ever have trouble sleeping here?"

Catherine looks up. "What do you mean?"

I try to sound casual. "Oh, I don't know. The house makes such strange noises at night, I can't fall asleep."

She gives me another scowl and goes back to her sewing. She's taken one of her best gowns and is embroidering a border of delicate white flowers around the neck with her new thread. It's a charming addition, and I wonder that I never think of such things. "I sleep just as well here as I did in Boston," she says. "I already told you the only difference is the sorry excuses for mattresses."

I open my mouth a few times. *I can't sleep because I have the most awful dreams. But in my waking hours my mind plays tricks on me. I see the strangest things. Not a moment ago I was conversing with the skeleton of our ancestor who was hanged as a witch over a hundred years ago. I feel as though I'm going mad, not knowing what is real and what is not.* But I can't find the right words. It all sounds so ridiculous, and besides, would Catherine even believe me? So I close my mouth, and we sit in silence as she works.

❧ *20* ❧

THE NEXT EVENING Mother makes a rare appearance in the library where I'm immersed in the final pages of *The Romance of the Forest.*

Though the last thing I want to do is drag myself away from the safe, romantic world of my book, there are too many questions burning the tip of my tongue since my visit from my ancestor. I can no longer pretend that what happened was a figment of my imagination or a bad dream. And if what the spirit said was true, then Mother has some secrets of her own.

Yet I must be careful with Mother; she has yet to emerge from the cocoon of despair she has woven for herself over the past weeks, and I'm starting to worry about her. Sometimes she looks so small and unassuming that I imagine her gradually fading into the woodblock wallpaper and heavy drapes, consumed by the grandness of Willow Hall. I won't let that happen.

I glance over her shoulder at the fabric she's unfolding from her basket. It's an embroidered coverlet. I smile, heartened at the vibrant flowers and fanciful pattern of birds and blackberry vines. "That's beautiful. I didn't know that you'd started a new project."

She doesn't look up. "Blackberries were Emeline's favorite. It's for her bed in the nursery."

My smile fades as I watch her sort through her thread box looking for the vermillion. We should be going through Emeline's things, putting them away or giving them to some other child in need. It worries me that Mother has taken it upon herself to start a new project, one that Emeline will never use.

I turn back to my book, unable to give her any encouragement. The Hale ancestor glowers down on us as I read and Mother works. Today the portrait's expression is one of grim commiseration, as if she understands and pities Mother and me our plight. Now that I have seen her in the flesh, so to speak, I wonder if that is indeed the case.

I choose my words carefully. "You know, I don't think I even know the name of our old friend up there," I say, nodding at the painting. I make my tone cheery and inviting, hoping to draw Mother away from her introspection.

Mother's gaze flickers up to the portrait and she gives a faint frown. "That would be Mary Preston."

When she doesn't offer any more information I try again. "I thought she was a Hale. How is she related to us?"

This time Mother doesn't look up from her embroidering when she answers. "Mehitable Hale was our ancestor. She fled from persecution in England. She married a Barnabas Preston. Mary was their daughter."

"Ah," I say, and we lull into silence again. A thousand questions whirl through my head: *What do you really know of her? What is the book she spoke of? Has her spirit ever visited you as it has me?* But they all sound ridiculous, and I can't bring myself to come at it directly. The last thing I want to do is upset Mother further.

"Is it really true that she was hanged during the witch hunts in Salem? I always supposed it a fancy of Catherine's."

Mother's needle stops, and there's a flicker of something like uncertainty in her eye. When she draws the thread through again, it's a long, deliberate motion. "It's the truth," she says at last.

"Goodness," I say. If I hadn't met her ghost, seen her snapped neck for myself, I might have been surprised. "What did she do to draw that kind of attention to herself?" I've heard stories of the people of Salem, envious of their neighbors' lands, casting accusations at people whom it would benefit them to see removed. Or perhaps she had simply been a woman who lived outside of convention in some way, earning herself the suspicions and animosity of her fellow townspeople.

Mother looks at me, her weary features taking on an expression of mild surprise. "What did she do?"

"Well, yes…what did she do to be found guilty of witchcraft?"

Mother presses her lips together. If I had thought asking Mother outright would have been hard, coming at my questions in this roundabout way is proving just as difficult. I'm about to try again, when something stops me.

A sound, coming from somewhere above us.

"Lydia? Lydia, what is it?"

I don't tear my eyes away from the ceiling, where the faint thuds are coming from upstairs. "Do you hear that?" I ask in a whisper.

Mother glances between me and my line of sight, shaking her head. "I don't hear anything."

It's an unnatural sort of sound. A quick succession of pattering feet, a lurching halt and then…is that laughter? My skin pimples with gooseflesh and I have to force myself to swallow. I put down my book and stand up.

"Emeline," I whisper.

Mother's face goes white. "What did you say?"

I ignore her, transfixed by the sound as I slowly make my way to the hallway. I mount the stairs to the second floor, pause and then continue to the third. The evening sun casts broody shadows across the long ballroom floor, obscuring the pianoforte and the doorway to the nursery.

There are no more footsteps, no more laughter, yet I can't help feeling as if I'm not alone. It's the same sensation that I used to have when I would play hide-and-seek with Emeline, and could feel her watching me from her hiding place. The air goes cold.

"Emeline?" I wait for her to appear, just like she did that night beside my bed.

How I want to see her again, just one more time. Yet something prickles uneasily inside of me as I recall Mary Preston's words: *You have consigned your sister to a living death.* If that were really true, wouldn't I have seen Emeline again by now?

But my held breath is in vain. The light softens, and the air warms again. If it was Emeline, then she is gone.

Three letters arrive the next day. Mother, Catherine and I are all in the library, various mending projects and embroidery hoops spread between us. I've been half-heartedly darning stockings, my hands working automatically while I think of different books to lend to Mr. Barrett. Too many of my favorites feature houses that burn down, heroines trapped behind heavy doors while smoke curls around the hero trying to reach her. Everything is different since Mrs. Tidewell told me about his past and the fire that shaped it; the world I thought I understood has shifted slightly, casting everything in a new light. I'm overcome with the urge to protect him in any small way possible from the specter of his past. There's also a little niggling of worry in my stomach. What was it Mrs. Tidewell said? That she heard he was engaged already? Maybe he was only visiting out of pity after all. Is there someone else? But Catherine hasn't mentioned anything about that, and she makes it her business to know everything.

Father wanders in, letters in hand, and passes an envelope to Mother. "I suppose the one from my sister is for you, my dear."

Aunt Phillips is Father's older sister and only sibling. She lives in Boston with her husband where they're well-to-do society types thanks to a generous loan Father gave Uncle Phillips in the early days of his printing business. With no children of her own, Aunt Phillips always took an active interest in us girls, and many a visit to their neat brick house on Acorn Street was spent getting our cheeks pinched and our dresses fawned over. That is, until the rumors started swirling and the invitations dried up. Maybe now that we've been out of Boston awhile and things have quieted down we're finally back in her good graces.

Father frowns, squinting at the next in the stack. "Can't make out the hand on this one, and it's only addressed to Miss Montrose."

He looks between Catherine and me, but it's Catherine who springs up to take it before retreating to the corner to tear it open. Mother had forbidden Catherine from corresponding with Charles, not wanting even the appearance of scandal, but of course as with all things, Catherine got her way. Now I realize that all those notes I saw her slipping Joe when we first came must have been to Charles. And as with all things too, Mother doesn't have the energy to enforce her own rule.

Father raises a brow in surprise at the last latter. "Lydia," he says, passing it to me.

With a frown, I take it from his hand. My shoulders slump when I see the handwriting. Cyrus.

This isn't the first letter that Cyrus has sent me since he returned to Boston, and if the previous letters are any indication, this one will be full of clumsy declarations of love, followed by disdainful accounts of his reduced circumstances. I crumple it up and press it into the side of my skirts.

With a heavy grunt, Father lowers himself to the settee beside Mother and takes her small hand in his while he reads his paper. He's in a rare good mood now that the land deal with Ezra Clarke has gone through and he can start construction on the new mill.

"Oh," says Mother, her temple creasing in a little frown. "Aunt Phillips has had an accident."

Father raises a brow but doesn't say anything, already absorbed in his newspaper.

"It seems she took a tumble getting out of the carriage. The doctor thinks her ankle might be broken, and she's confined to bed while it heals. Uncle Phillips is in New York, but they have that hired girl now who's helping tend to her and see that she's comfortable while she recovers."

"Grace always was clumsy like that," Father says, shaking his head. He goes back to his paper and Mother silently reads the rest of her letter.

Aunt Phillips always was a martyr to her gout, and I suspect that it wasn't a tumble from a carriage so much as an eruption of her old condition that has left her bedridden.

It's suspiciously quiet on the other side of the room where Catherine is hovering, her knuckles white as she clasps the back of a chair. Her eyes are feverishly scanning the lines, but as she does her smile fades and her face goes colorless. For a second I think she is going burst into tears, but then she hastily folds the letter back up and composes her face into a cool mask.

Mother sighs, folding up her own letter again. "What's wrong, dear? Not more bad news I hope?"

"No, it's nothing. Just a letter from an old friend." Catherine hastily slips it into her pocket. "I think I'll go read the rest of it in my room. Lydia?"

It takes me a moment to understand that she expects me to come with her. I don't want to leave the library. It's so nice for once to all be in the same room, Father, Mother, Catherine and me. It's like having a normal family again, almost, and even if we're all in our own worlds, I can pretend.

But there's a desperate, pleading note in her voice, so with a sigh, I put aside my darning and leave the cozy fantasy behind.

No sooner does the door click behind us than Catherine thrusts the letter in my face. "How dare he! I knew him to be selfish and false but I still can't believe he would have the nerve!"

I quickly take in the contents of the letter while Catherine paces about the room ranting. It's not from Charles, but Mr. Pierce. *My mother has informed me of an unfortunate story circulating in Boston... Can't attach myself to a family with such a reputation... Feel that you've misled me... Regret that I will no longer be able to...*

I look up. "Oh, Catherine. I'm so—"

"It was his miserable mother who put the idea into his head, I just know it was!"

The letter says as much, and I'm only surprised that it took him so long to hear about the scandal. I bite my lip, trying to mask my own disappointment. What is there to say? "I'm sure he didn't want to leave you, Cath. I'm really sorry."

Ignoring my attempts at consolation, Catherine throws herself facedown on the bed, only coming up for air occasionally to curse her would-be groom and mother-in-law. So far "miserable" is the tamest description she has come up with.

"The old bat, pretending like she's on the verge of death, and all the while her ears are open and her mouth is flapping that tired story all over Boston. I could wring her old neck.

And August! Playing the dutiful son, all the while using his mother as an excuse to get away from me every chance he could."

The way she says it I don't doubt for a second that Catherine could indeed wring Mrs. Pierce's old neck. I run a meaningless hand down her back, soothing and shushing, but my heart isn't in it. It's over. Catherine's best chance for finding a husband and avoiding calamity have come to naught.

Suddenly Catherine sits up and wipes a careless sleeve under her red nose. "Maybe it really is all his mother, and not August at all." Her face brightens and she sniffles back her slowing tears. "She probably made him write that letter and kept him in Boston, forbidding him from coming back to marry me. He could be trying to make his way back to me for all I know."

"Catherine..." It's false hope and I think even she must know that. A bedridden woman couldn't keep her strapping young son hostage in the house, though she could cut off his inheritance, and for a dandy like Mr. Pierce that would be even worse.

"But why not?" The tears have dried and she's pushing me aside, stumbling to her writing desk. "You could ask Mr. Barrett for me. You could give him a note to give to Mr. Pierce." She's already scribbling away, ink still wet as she thrusts the missive at me. "Please, Lydia."

I sigh and take it from her expectant hand. Why would Mr. Barrett want anything to do with this? As much as it pains me to think about, he's probably relieved that his friend has stepped aside. And Mr. Barrett's a gentleman, a true one, not like Mr. Pierce. Our checkered past won't deter him from pursuing Catherine.

"I don't think we should be dragging Mr. Barrett into this or that he'll want to help. He—"

"Of course he will. I've seen the way he looks at you. He'll answer you anything, and he'll straighten this whole mess out with August. Besides, he confided in me before, remember?" She gives me a sly look out of the corner of her eye. "He'll want to help me."

I could ask Joe to take me in the carriage to Barrett House, but hitching up the horses and then being jostled about for such a short trip hardly seems worth it. Besides, Mother might want to make calls and would need the carriage for that. I go find Ada, who's in the kitchen, sleeves pushed up to her elbows as she rolls out a piecrust. She looks up when I come in.

"Yes, miss?"

"I need go to Barrett House to deliver something, but you're busy. It can wait."

She wipes her floured hands on her apron. "Is Joe not about? I'm sure he would deliver it for you. No need to trouble yourself."

"No," I say quickly. "That is, I have to deliver it."

She gives me a queer look, no doubt wondering why I don't go with Mother as a chaperone if I'm bent on making a trip there. But she doesn't question me and just says, "If you wait a few minutes until I tidy up I can go with you."

I hate to trouble her when she's busy, and while she's brushing the flour off the table I start to wonder what would happen if I went on my own. Maybe I don't need a chaperone at all. I could just slip the letter for Mr. Pierce under the door and be on my way. And if Mr. Barrett is home and happens to come out to see who's at the door, why, I could hardly be blamed for that, could I?

My mind fixes on the idea. Why should Catherine be able to buck convention whenever she pleases? Why shouldn't I be able to see Mr. Barrett during an innocent errand? I feel reckless and excited.

Ada is taking off her apron and rolling her sleeves back down. "On second thought, I think I'll just go for a walk. I'll have Joe deliver it later."

I can hardly meet her eye as she frowns, studying the flush of color at my neck. "All right, miss. If you say so."

Feeling more than a little guilty about lying to Ada, yet at the same time breathless and eager to be out on my own, I set off for Barrett House.

❧ *21* ❧

BEFORE I LEAVE, I tuck my weathered copy of *The Italian* under my arm. It's one of my favorites, with lots of twists and turns, a dashing hero and luscious Italian scenery. It positively drips with romance. Most important, it has a happy ending.

I've never been to Barrett House before, and rather than taking the shorter, more direct route through the woods and around the pond, I set off down the looping, winding road. I don't think I could stand to pass so close to the willow tree today, nor to see the flat rocks littered in freshly fallen leaves, a reminder that the world moves on from that fateful summer day.

Twice I nearly turn back, talking myself out of it. I'm supposed to be the good one, the dutiful daughter. What am I doing walking alone to meet a man at his house? What if Father found out? And what if I get there, showing up alone and unannounced and Mr. Barrett is put off by my forwardness?

He hasn't come by since that day in my room. I pause on the dirt road. He's probably busy, with the land deal and drafting plans for the new mill. Again I think of Mrs. Tidewell

and what she said about an engagement, and I can't squash
the little niggling voice in my head that says, *He was just being
nice. He pitied you, that's all.*

But whatever my excuse for making my way to him, the
promise of seeing him is too great, and as I start walking again
a thousand little thoughts of him send tremors through my
body. Like the place where his starched white collar meets the
narrow, tender strip of lightly tanned skin of his neck. Him
absently caressing Snip's ears in my room. The calmness that
surrounds him, belied only by the smallest fidget in his fingers
when he is deep in thought. All those little things that make
my heart beat faster and my stomach fluttery are just around
the next bend of the road. I walk a little faster.

When I finally come upon the house, I stop in my tracks.
This can't be the right place. The neat little white home tucked
under the generous shade of an elm tree is nothing like the
shabby house that Mrs. Tidewell described. An equally neat
white fence hems the property, broken only by an arbor arch-
ing over the front path. In the spring it must be beautiful, with
trailing roses and clematis, and even in the drab, late days of
autumn it's cozy and welcoming.

So this was the home that Mr. Barrett's father built after
the tragedy where Willow Hall stands. I was expecting peeling paint and broken shutters, signs of the senior Mr. Barrett's
anger and hatred imprinted in the house. But there's nothing
sinister about the curl of smoke coming from the chimney,
nor the late-blooming asters that cluster around the path. The
tightness in my jaw softens, and I relax. John lives here, how
could I have thought it anything but completely charming?

I climb the steps to knock on the front door, but it's already
pushed halfway open.

"Hello?" I call softly into the front hall, hoping that a maid will intercept me and tell me that Mr. Barrett is out and that I better just go home after all. I call again and no one comes.

With equal parts relief and disappointment, I turn to go, when the low murmur of a voice stops me. I freeze, my hand on the open door. It's too quiet to hear the words, but it's a man's voice. Maybe Mr. Pierce is still here. The thought of confronting him on Catherine's behalf makes my stomach drop. But I promised her, and I have a vested interest in the answer, so against my better judgment I slip into the hall.

The voice grows louder, carrying through the first door on the left, which is just cracked open. I should knock loudly, make myself known. Instead I creep up to the door, putting my ear against the crack.

It's Mr. Barrett, but he's not talking to another man, certainly not Mr. Pierce. He's speaking softly, lovingly. The way a man speaks to a woman.

I shouldn't be here. Mr. Barrett is with a woman and it's none of my business. But just as I'm turning to go, the floor under my foot lets out a long, protesting creak. His voice breaks off. My elbow brushes the door the rest of the way open and I have no choice but to stand my ground like the spy that I am.

But when I look up, it's not a woman in Mr. Barrett's arms.

He's holding a big, sleek white cat, cradling it like a baby. His head snaps up, and he looks every bit as guilty as if I had just caught him in an amorous embrace. The cat impatiently flicks its tail, glaring at me with drowsy yellow eyes.

Seeing him standing there, his big arms enfolding the cat, his head bent low whispering the silly things one says to a pet, compiled with a deep, overwhelming sense of relief that he wasn't with a woman after all, leaves me light-headed and tipsy. I take a few deep breaths, but it's no use. Laughter starts to bubble up deep in my throat.

It's the kind of laugh that makes your eyes water and your whole body shake. The cat, stoic dignity insulted, twists its way violently out of Mr. Barrett's arm, tearing his shirtsleeve down the middle in the process.

Mr. Barrett lets out a yelp. "Goddamn it! The devil take you and those wretched claws!" Humiliated, the cat streaks past my legs and out of the room.

Pink creeps up his neck past his cravat, his eyebrows stitching closer together into an angry frown. I brace myself for a stern reprimand on trespassing.

"I'm sorry..." I can't get my words out through my gasps. The longer he stands there, hair disheveled, sleeve torn, with that bewildered look on his face, the harder I laugh.

His lips twitch and I do my best to pull myself together and not further injure his dignity. But instead of yelling, demanding to know just what I think I'm doing barging in unannounced, he smiles.

He smiles with his whole soul. It's the most beautiful thing I've ever seen, John Barrett's face all lit up, his eyes crinkling at the edges.

"What?" he asks helplessly. "What is it?"

I couldn't even answer him if I wanted to. He blinks slowly, and then he starts laughing too, soft at first, then rich and throaty, every bit as beautiful as his smile.

"You..." I start again. "The cat's face..." This sends me into a fresh riot of laughter for no reason.

When we finally come to our senses, there's a stitch in my side and Mr. Barrett is wiping his brow. His face is still pink, though whether it's from the exertion of laughing or embarrassment that I caught him sharing a tender moment with his kitty, I can't tell.

He clears his throat, trying to regain his composure. "Well, Miss Montrose," he says, trying his best to assume a grave expression, "that's my favorite shirt ruined. I hope you're happy with yourself."

"I am," I say, wiping away the last of my tears, meaning it.

He flashes me a grin and then unwinds his cravat and starts unbuttoning the torn shirt. "I'll be sure to tell my housekeeper just whose fault it was that she has to mend it."

I swallow, my mouth suddenly dry and my face growing hot as I realize he means to change his shirt. Desperate not to look like I'm watching, I lean to inspect a framed print on the wall, nearly knocking a vase off the table behind me in the process.

Mr. Barrett looks around the room as if expecting a spare shirt to be sitting there. Despite my best efforts, he catches my eye before glancing into the hall behind me. "Did you come alone?" His tone is light, but I can't help but notice the carefully inflected note of hope.

My mouth still too dry to say anything, I nod. I struggle to keep my eyes trained on his, pretending that I don't notice the open V of his shirt, showing glimpses of smooth, defined chest muscles, and a light feathering of golden hair that trails down his stomach.

He holds my gaze for a drawn-out moment, as if not sure how to respond. If he thinks me rash or uncouth for coming unannounced and unescorted, he doesn't let it show. Besides, he is the one standing in the middle of the room in partial undress. Coming back to himself, he asks, "Will you have a seat? I'll be right back."

I seat myself and watch him leave; he shrugs his shirt the rest of the way off as soon as he's through the door, and then his footsteps pound up the stairs. I imagine him crossing bare-chested to his wardrobe, pulling out a fresh shirt and sliding it over his broad, muscled shoulders. I can almost feel the cool linen as if it were brushing against my bare flesh. Then, as if he might be able to read my thoughts through the floor, I quickly push the image from my mind.

I take the opportunity to drink in everything in the room. Did he furnish it himself, picking out the expansive mahogany desk? Father's desk is always buried under stacks of papers and loose receipts, but Mr. Barrett's is neat and clean, only a writing set, a slim stack of papers and a couple of books on the polished surface.

Over the desk hangs a portrait of a beautiful woman wearing the fashion of decades gone by. There's no mistaking her identity. She has stormy blue eyes, and instead of the fanciful powdered wigs popular in her day, she wears her own abundance of dark blond hair romantically pinned up on her head. With her faraway gaze and a backdrop of clouds rolling across a hilly landscape, the woman cuts an arresting figure, much different than any Puritan Montrose ancestor hanging in our house. Beside her, looking up at his beautiful mama is a wispy little child in white. He bears a striking resemblance to Mr. Barrett, with his blue-green eyes and amber hair. Maybe it's because I know about his past that I see a sadness in Mr. Barrett's eyes that his little brother lacks. Moses instead looks self-assured in his status as favorite child, possessive of their mother.

Mr. Barrett returns buttoning his cuffs, humming under his breath, his hair still sticking up slightly from when he pulled his shirt off. He looks up to see me standing under the painting, studying it, and his face darkens.

"Is that your mother?" I already know the answer, but maybe if I take the first step, if I show him that I understand, then he'll open up to me.

"Yes," he says shortly, wrestling with the last button without looking up.

"She was very beautiful."

"Yes, she was."

A chill settles in the room. Quickly, I turn away and my eyes alight on an engraving of a bird. "And this one," I say lightly, "this must be one of your collection?"

"Mmm, a wood duck." His cuffs are buttoned, his hair smoothed back down, and he looks as composed and unruffled as ever. The chill in the room recedes. "Now," he says, rubbing his hands together and brightening, "would you like some tea? Coffee? Hannah is just in the back and I'm sure—"

I quickly wave off his offer, though I'm somewhat relieved that his maid is about, that if Catherine asks later I can say I wasn't completely alone with him. "Oh, no, please don't put yourself to any trouble. I won't be staying long."

Mr. Barrett raises a brow, and I instantly hear the rudeness in my own words.

"Well then," he says, putting his hands in his pockets and rocking back on his heels. "I'd ask you what's brought you here, but of course I already know the answer."

I let out my breath, surprised, but relieved that I won't have to explain the particulars of Catherine's errand. "You do?"

He gestures to the book in my hand. "I said I'd come by for a book, and I've been so busy that I've completely broken my word."

"Oh, no. I—" I stop myself. My side is still sore from laughing. There's something about Mr. Barrett's house, something so different than Willow Hall. A lightness. At home I always feel on edge, as if I were holding my breath, waiting for something to happen, and that's to say nothing of the torturous nights with their evil dreams and the footsteps and wailing. Here I can just *be*, and with Mr. Barrett no less. I want to bask in his attention for a little while without the shadow of Catherine's troubles looming over me.

"No," I say again, this time with confidence. "You mustn't apologize for not coming. Here." I hand him the book and his eyes run over the title. He gives me a smile before placing the book gently on his desk.

"I wanted to come," he says. "It's just this…" He gestures to the modest pile of papers behind him. "This land deal has been taking much longer than I anticipated. We've been working late into the evenings, and Mr. Clarke has been stubborn as an ox about signing anything."

"But Father says you've settled it now. You must be glad."

A paper has caught his attention and he frowns. "Mmm," he says without looking up. There it is again, his detachment that tears him away, as if he has more pressing matters on his mind. Then with a little "tch" of self-reproach he comes back to himself. "I'm sorry." He puts the paper away.

"Will you buy more farms along the river now? For more mills?"

"No. Well, yes, maybe. It depends."

I know he's trying to spare me the tedious business details, but to my surprise, I'm actually interested. I want to know how he spends his days, what kind of documents he signs, where he goes and whom he meets.

"It depends on the banks, you mean?"

He leans back against his desk, head tilted slightly. He's looking at me—or rather, through me—and I'm not sure he even heard my question. I'm about to try again when he suddenly asks, "Can I tell you something?"

"Oh, of course," I say breathlessly, not in the least curious as to this new direction in the conversation. "You can tell me anything."

He gives me an appraising look and nods. "Well, the thing is…" He trails off, rubbing his jaw and a small smile pulling at his lips as if he can't quite believe what he's about to admit.

I'm leaning in so far that I'm in danger of toppling over. I hold my breath, my mind forming scenario after scenario of what it could possibly be that he wants to tell me, and then dismissing them all just as quickly. He's pulling out of his partnership with Father. He's moving. He's engaged. Or just maybe—and I know this one is ridiculous—he's going to declare his feelings for me.

22

"WELL, THE FACT of the matter is that I find milling reprehensible."

My breath comes out in a slow, deflated hiss. "Oh," I say, trying to mask my disappointment. Then, seeing his earnest expression, his eyes seeking mine for some kind of reassurance, I say, "But you've such a good head for business, Father always says so. And you've been so successful."

"To be good at something isn't to necessarily enjoy it," he says. A hint of color touches his face. Embarrassed, he forces a smile. "I shouldn't complain. I don't know what made me say that, I—"

"No," I say quickly. "It's fine, really. What is it about milling that you don't like? What would you rather do?"

He considers the question. "I don't know," he says, frowning out the window. "Farming, perhaps." He hoists himself up on his desk, dangling his legs and bracing his elbows on his knees, like a little boy fishing on the edge of a stream.

"It's not so much the product itself. After all, cloth needs to be manufactured and it needs to be done so in the North. And there's no denying that the industry has made New Oldbury a prosperous outlier. It's just..." His words trail off. "Have you ever been to a mill, Lydia?"

A little ball of warmth forms in my stomach when he says my name. "No. Well, only that day that we met you."

He nods. "My father's old mill. I'm talking about a working one though, with a wheel that churns up water, looms that pump so loud that you can't hear yourself think. Shouts of men over the din and fiber choking the air. Mills are like hungry beasts, and they must be fed a constant diet of labor and wool or cotton or wood. And those in turn must be harvested from somewhere, which in America's case is in the South by the forced labor of slaves."

"It's a violent sort of business, isn't it?"

He had gotten up and was pacing around his desk, but now stops short, staring at me. "Yes," he says softly. "That's just it."

His gaze lingers on me for a moment and then he clears his throat and starts pacing again. "There's an ever increasing demand for goods, and as British products come back on the market people will expect a greater variety and at better prices. How many mills will there be in five years? Ten years? Will every river be clogged with competing wheels?"

I can't help feel a little ashamed that I ever grudged Catherine for holding Mr. Barrett's confidence. Surely he would never have spoken to her like this, like an equal. And if he had, she would have had to pretend that she was interested, politely nodding at the right times, demurring. I don't have to pretend. "And yet, you still do it. Why?"

"At first it was a way to pay off my father's debts. But they've long since been settled." He pauses, standing a couple of paces from me, and looking out at me from under shy lashes. When he speaks again his matter-of-fact tone has shifted into something almost eager, his words picking up speed. If I didn't know better I would say that John Barrett is nervous.

"I don't have extravagant needs and could live comfortably enough within my savings and investments. When your father wrote to me about backing a new milling venture in New Oldbury I decided that I would help see it off the ground and then bow out. But—" he gives me a nervous glance "—things have changed. I thought…" He makes a show of clearing his throat and compulsively straightens the stack of papers on his desk. "Well, if a man is to take a wife, he should have a way to provide for her. A bachelor can live well enough off less, but it isn't fair to ask a woman to live below the means to which she might be accustomed."

My body goes rigid. I don't know what to say. I don't even know what he means, except that he must be referring to the mystery fiancée Mrs. Tidewell asked me about. The silence grows very loud and I can hear my own heartbeat in my ears.

"Oh," I finally say. "I see." If I were better spoken, politer, I might comment that it's very gracious of him to anticipate the lady's needs and comforts, and that I'm sure any woman would be lucky to be his wife and mistress of his house. I can't bring myself to speak about her though, even if she is hypothetical.

He seems embarrassed and hastily shuffles the papers over and over, not meeting my eye. "Well," he says, "I've taken advantage of your kindness to listen to me ramble on long enough."

"You weren't taking advantage of anything," I assure him. But something in his expression closes, the animated look replaced with his usual cool mask. He's done sharing.

I can't put off my original errand any longer. "Actually, there was something else besides the book that brought me here."

"Oh?"

I hesitate. "It's Catherine. She... I was led to believe there was some sort of understanding between her and Mr. Pierce, and now it seems that he's gone. She's heartbroken, and I promised her I would try to find out anything I could. And that I would deliver this," I add, holding out her note.

I hate lying to Mr. Barrett—Catherine isn't heartbroken—but what choice do I have? I can't very well tell him the real reason that she's so desperate to get her would-be groom back.

"Did he tell you anything before he left? Give you any clue as to if he might come back?"

Mr. Barrett takes the letter and sighs. He doesn't look surprised in the least about the charges laid against his friend. "The thing about August... Well, he's incapable of taking responsibility for his actions. I'm sure he did feel for your sister, but he's just as beholden to money and social opinion as his heart. In the end it was his inheritance and the threat of being cast out of his social circle that mattered most. He shouldn't have been a clod about it though. I told him to let her know in person."

It's just as I expected, and I push aside all the unpleasant thoughts about what this means for Catherine and her child, as well as for the rest of the family. "Well, thank you anyway. I—"

There's a knock at the front door, and before I can say anything else Mr. Barrett excuses himself to answer it. I wait while there's a quick exchange in the hall and then the door closes and he comes back into the room, shrugging on his coat.

"Is everything all right?"

"Oh, yes, fine," Mr. Barrett says waving off my concern as he searches for his hat. "There's been some sort of fight at the mill between two of the boys. Something about a girl. It seems they nearly took down a loom in the process of establishing their manhood. I need to go make sure that everything is in order and the appropriate parties get a stern lecture."

"Of course," I say, disappointed that I have to leave the cozy study, but aware that I've probably stayed too long as it is.

Mr. Barrett accompanies me outside and looks around. "Did you come on foot?"

I hesitate, standing on the front steps behind him, desperately searching for some excuse to stay with him. But he's looking at me expectantly, so I nod.

"Let me walk back with you to Willow Hall. It looks like rain and I don't want you out here alone."

"Oh," I say, caught off guard. "I couldn't let you do that. Aren't you needed at the mill?"

"A few minutes won't make a difference. Let me at least accompany you back as far as the fork to town."

He saddles his horse, and then, leading it by the bridle, falls into step beside me.

I ought to be ashamed of myself, that I reprimanded Catherine for going off with Mr. Pierce unchaperoned and now am walking alone with Mr. Barrett. But this is different, I tell myself. Mr. Barrett isn't like Mr. Pierce, and besides, there's no one here to see us. My skin tingles at the thought.

After the conversation flowed so naturally in his study, now I find myself tongue-tied and slow-witted with Mr. Barrett walking so close beside me. I feel small next to him, coming just up to his shoulder, and the deep blue of his brushed wool coat fills my field of vision when I dare to glance sideways.

There's a smile pulling at the corner of his lips and he looks like he wants to say something.

"What? What's so funny?"

"No." He shakes his head, but the smile wins out. "It's nothing."

"What is it?" I ask, unable to stop my own smile from spreading. "Tell me!"

He slants a sidelong glance down at me. "You'll laugh."

Now I have to know. "I won't, I promise!"

"I'm supposed to believe you can keep that promise after seeing you in stitches this afternoon?"

I tilt my chin up defiantly, feigning insult. "I can't believe you would suggest such a thing," I say in my primmest voice. "I never break my promises."

He nods, matching my mock seriousness. "Well then, in that case." He clears his throat. "I don't know what made me think of this, but I was just remembering that the first time I came over to your house, I brought a little slice of ham with me."

"What? Why?"

"For Snip," he explains. "Damn if this isn't the most embarrassing thing I've ever admitted to. I brought it as a sort of bribe, so that he might like me, and in turn, his masters."

"Oh," I say, too surprised to laugh. "Well, it worked."

He doesn't ask if I mean on Snip or on his masters. "There," he says instead. "You've managed a confession out of me. Fair is fair, your turn."

"You want me to confess to something?"

"More than anything in the world."

His confession is endearing, a glimpse into the shy part of him I long to know more about. But what could I possibly say that wouldn't make me look silly or childish in his eyes? Should I tell him that I've never worn the glove that he brought back to me so that I wouldn't have to unfold what he had touched? That I still have his cravat from that first day we met, folded and kept under my pillow like a talisman? Or maybe that every night I look out my window toward his house behind the trees and try to imagine what he's doing at that moment?

But I don't want the game to end, not yet. I rack my mind, and then before I can talk myself out of it, I blurt out, "I don't know the first thing about birds."

He's quiet for a beat, and then gives me a long, sly look. "I know."

"You do?"

"That day when we were walking through the woods. You said you saw a golden thrush." He flashes a mischievous grin. "Golden thrushes are only found in Australia."

I should be mortified, but I can't help smiling. All those hours spent studying my natural history books and I've been found out anyway. "Why didn't you say anything then?"

"You looked so pleased with yourself. I hadn't the heart to correct you."

On the way to Mr. Barrett's the walk had seemed to take so long, but now it's going by quickly, far too quickly. We're almost at the bend that will take me back to Willow Hall and him to the mill. I would do anything to make the road stretch out for miles yet before we had to part.

Maybe it's the laughter we shared, or that he finally opened up to me. Or maybe it's the cool autumn breeze that winds through the small space between us, making him move a little closer so that I'm not too cold, but I finally have found some courage. "Can...can I ask you something?"

He looks down, a little surprised. "Of course, anything."

"Are you... That is, I heard you were engaged." My words hang in the air, and even I can hear the desperate tinge in them.

Mr. Barrett stops abruptly, the horse shaking the bridle in protest.

"Engaged? Well," he says with a frown, "that would certainly be news to me." His look softens. "Where did you hear that?"

"Mrs. Tidewell." I feel like a tattling child, though my shame is tempered with a deep sense of relief.

"Ah," he says, picking up the pace again. "I'm not sure I would put so much stock in what Mrs. Tidewell says when it comes to other people's business."

We walk a little farther in silence. There's a tension in Mr. Barrett's face like he wants to say something else but is battling himself. Finally he asks, "What else did Mrs. Tidewell tell you?"

"Nothing," I say a little too quickly. "Nothing at all. Just that."

We've reached the fork in the road. The horse swipes its tail at an invisible irritant and paws at the dirt, wondering why we've stopped. The air hangs heavy with expectancy, and I'm not ready to say goodbye yet. Still embarrassed and unable to meet Mr. Barrett's eyes, I stroke the horse's warm, downy nose, and direct my goodbyes to it instead.

"Such a sweet horse," I murmur. Our horses are carriage horses, not much interested in human company unless you have something sweet for them, and even then they merely offer a sideways glance while they munch away. Mr. Barrett's horse is as gentle and sweet as a puppy.

"Lydia," he says after a moment. "Before you go, there's something I'd like to ask you."

The horse bobs its head in blissful appreciation as I scratch behind its big, feathery ears. "Mmm?"

"Perhaps now isn't the right time."

Something in his tone snaps me back to attention, and for the first time since we stopped I realize that he hasn't taken his eyes off me.

"You can ask me now. You can ask me anything. What is it?" I say breathlessly.

He looks around the country road as if to make sure we are truly alone, his gaze flitting from the golden treetops to the darkening clouds above. Then, so quickly and so gently that I hardly have time to register what's happening, he takes my chin in his hand and tilts my face up, pressing his lips to mine. His body moves close to me and everything in me comes alive. I want to press myself against his chest, wrap my arms around him and feel the steady beat of his heart like I felt that night at the pond.

My body explodes with warmth, an exhilarating sensation starting where his lips meet mine, running like a fuse down my spine and blossoming between my legs. My knees are weak, but he's there, holding me upright to him like his life depended on it. It's a long, slow kiss, expertly administered. When we pull away, I can barely breathe. Drowsily, I open my eyes. He's flushed and sparkling. With one hand still cupped under my chin, he takes his other and gently as a breeze tucks a stray lock of hair behind my ear.

"No," he says more to himself than to me. "Not now, not like this."

Before I can even regain my balance, he's swinging up into the saddle, and asks, "Are you sure you can get home all right from here?"

Too breathless to speak, I nod.

"Good," he says, wheeling his horse around. "And if I call on Friday, will you be at home?"

I nod again.

He doesn't start riding away though, instead he brings the horse right up next to me. I crane my neck up to see him, feeling every inch like a young maiden in a fairy tale, looking upon her golden prince, desperate and grateful for any little favor he might bestow.

"I didn't come the last time I promised you I would," he says. He sits so well on the horse, so straight and composed, but his knuckles are white around the reins and when he swallows, it's hard and fast.

"Oh," I say, surprised. "I know you were busy." I think he could say anything in this moment and I would forgive him.

When he speaks again it's low and even. Determined. "It does matter. I'll be back for you, Lydia. I swear it."

And with that, he touches his heels to his horse, taking off at a canter down the road. I hardly dare to breathe as I stand there, watching his straight back and broad shoulders grow smaller and smaller until the trees swallow him up.

23

THE WIND TUGS at my dress, and rain is starting to spit when I finally drag myself away from the fork in the road. I clutch my cloak tighter, shivering despite the lingering warmth in my stomach. The woods that were sparkling and magical when Mr. Barrett was here press around me, and the rain comes down harder, staining the lichen-splotched stone walls a dark, unhappy black. But there might be a thousand spirits glaring at me from the woods today, following my every movement, and I wouldn't care. It doesn't matter that my clothes are soaked through or that my toes are cold and gritty with mud. A flood could rise up from the river and sweep me away, and in this moment I would still be the most content I've ever been in my entire life.

By the time Willow Hall rises before me the rain is coming down in heavy, unforgiving sheets. Ada and Joe are standing in the back doorway, Ada wiping floured hands on her apron and laughing at something Joe says as he smokes his pipe. When she sees me she breaks off midsentence and Joe turns around, silently running an eye up and down my sorry figure.

I duck between them, the warm, yeasty smell of baking bread greeting me like an embrace. "I was caught in the rain," I say, as if it weren't perfectly obvious.

They share a knowing look. Joe gives me a polite nod, taps out his pipe and leaves Ada to her fretting.

"What were you thinking? You'll catch your death of cold!" Taking me by the arm, she drags me away from the door, her eyes widening at the trail of muddy footprints in my wake.

"Your mother will have a fit," she says, wasting no time in fetching the mop and getting to work on my mess. "And you ought to take off those wet things and get in front of a fire."

There's a strange clattering noise, and it takes me a moment before I realize that it's coming from me. My teeth are chattering so hard that I'm in danger of biting through my tongue. Obediently, I peel off my cloak and wring out my stockings, letting the snug warmth of the kitchen envelop me. It might be the only room in Willow Hall that feels cozy, thanks to Ada's cooking and the fact that, unlike the rest of the house, it's a bit messy. With flour still smeared across the wood-block table, and upturned bowls and pots full of simmering broths, it looks like someone actually lives here.

"S-sorry," I stammer as I warm my purple fingers by the kitchen fire. I should probably be helping Ada clean up my mess, but mopping floors and being sensible about wet clothes are part of a faraway world in which I'm not part of the moment. I'm living in a dream, or a novel, where handsome princes ride all night, thundering down a country road to save their lady's honor. A place where my feet never touch the ground—let alone leave muddy tracks. A place where I'm wanted, needed, even loved.

Ada stands up, stretching her back and casting a critical eye over the tile floor. "Did you have a good walk then?"

"Hmm?" My fingers are finally starting to regain a more natural color as I stiffly flex them back into feeling.

"You're grinning like your head is fit to crack. It must have been a good walk."

"Oh," I say, doing my best to straighten my face. I take the blanket that Ada holds out to me and wrap it around my shoulders. "Yes, the best walk I've ever had."

Catherine puts down the ladies' journal she was reading when I slip into her room. "Well?"

She's recovered from her tantrum, her face cleaned of streaked tears and her hair neatly pulled back. Cool and calm, she's hardly the picture of a woman jilted by her lover. It seems like years ago that I left her crying on her bed to go to Barrett House, not a couple of hours.

I shake my head. "He's not coming back."

She doesn't move or say anything, just studies my face for a moment as if there might be something else written there that I'm not telling her. "I see," she says finally. "You were gone an awfully long time just to find out that he's not coming back."

"It's a long walk."

She turns back to her journal of colorfully dressed ladies with tiny waists, flipping the pages with studied nonchalance. "Well in that case, I guess it's no use moping about. August Pierce can rot in hell."

"I'm sorry, Catherine," I say with my hand on the door-knob. I want to go back to my room, cuddle up under my warm blankets and hibernate until Friday. If it weren't for the promise of seeing Mr. Barrett in five days and the memory of his hand warm against my cheek, thinking about Catherine's broken engagement and what it means for our family would chew me up from the inside.

I'm about to make my escape when she says, "I think I'll

call on Mr. Barrett soon. It seems ages since we last spoke, and I really ought to thank him for everything he did for August and me, even if it didn't work out as I'd hoped."

The door swings away from my grasp as I stop cold in my tracks. Swallowing, I quickly say, "I already thanked him on your behalf. I don't think you need to bother."

"Oh, it's not a bother." She puts down the journal and stretches her arms above her head in a lazy show of casual indifference. "I want to."

My mouth is dry, and before I can tell her that Mr. Barrett won't have anything to add to the subject, she asks, "Don't you ever get bored here, Lyd?"

"What do you mean?" I close the door and sit back down, my suspicion outweighing my desire to flee.

"I mean we used to entertain all the time in Boston, and here there's barely a handful of anyone you could call polite society. Now that Mr. Pierce is gone I would be hard-pressed to name another gentleman besides Mr. Barrett."

My stomach contracts into a hard pit. "Catherine, please don't," I whisper.

She shrugs her delicate shoulders, the pearly blue of her dress setting off her ivory skin. I vaguely wonder when exactly she'll start showing, when she'll get fat.

"I know you may find this hard to believe, but I consider Mr. Barrett a good friend, and we've enjoyed each other's confidences in the past. Well don't look so stricken," she says, raising a brow. "You've told me yourself you don't have any feelings for the man. I'm the eldest daughter of the wealthiest man in New Oldbury, and of Mr. Barrett's business partner. It's only natural that we should find ourselves thrown together."

"But you ignored him whenever Mr. Pierce was around!"

Catherine's face darkens and she snaps the journal shut. "Grow up, Lydia. You know the position I'm in. Do you really

want to destroy Mother? Besides, you're too young...too..."
She trails off, as if mentally cataloging all the possible ways in
which I'm lacking. She finally settles on, "Too serious. What
could Mr. Barrett possibly want with you?"

I don't know what it is about my sister, but she has the
power to cut me down like no one else. My insecurities
come rushing back, winding their way up my bones like ivy.
Maybe my memory is betraying me, making me think that
the warmth in Mr. Barrett's eyes was friendship and not admiration. Maybe his voice hadn't caught when he said there
was something he wanted to ask me. Maybe he came to his
senses, and his visit on Friday will just be to tell me that he
made a mistake in kissing me, that he didn't mean to give me
any ideas. Maybe Catherine is right.

I chew my nail, refusing to rise to her bait. What could I
say anyway that would convince her to leave him alone?

"I think I'll call on him Thursday," she says with a cutting
smile and returns to her journal as if I weren't even there.

A sharp prick of pain stabs at me, and looking down I realize I've bitten my nail down to the quick. There's only one
thing that I know for sure, and that is Catherine will stop at
nothing to get what she wants.

I don't fool myself into thinking that I could fall asleep even
if I wanted to that night. Instead, I sit by the window, replay-
ing every moment of my visit to Mr. Barrett's house, from
our laughter, to our kiss, and his promise to come on Friday
for me. And then I remember Catherine's veiled threats and
my heart sinks. How can I compete with my beautiful sister
if she chooses to throw herself at him?

I'm wondering what tricks Catherine might have up her
sleeve, when a movement catches my eye in the garden. The
pale lady hasn't made an appearance since that night in the

summer, but now that I've stared the fleshless face of Mary Preston in the eye, the lady that roams the garden holds no terror for me.

But then I peer closer out the window and catch my breath. It's not the pale lady. It's Emeline.

Without even pausing to put my shoes on, I fly down to the garden.

"Emeline!" I can't help the excitement that bubbles up in me to see her. But as I draw nearer, my pace slows. Her face is bloated and her eyes cloudy. Something is hanging from the corner of her mouth, and my stomach flips when I see it wriggle. A maggot. I push down my revulsion. *She's my sister*, I tell myself. But it's wrong. No matter how I long to see her, she shouldn't be here. And if what Mary Preston said was true, then it's my fault.

Coldness from the wet grass seeps up through my shoeless feet as I stop in front of her. The night is thick and murky, and Emeline is little more than a pale wisp in the darkness. She looks up at me, running her hand carelessly under her mouth and sending the maggot to the ground.

"I'm lonely," she says without preamble.

I crouch in front of her, and give her a hesitant touch on her cold cheek. "I'm here now. What would you like to do? Shall we play a game?"

She doesn't respond, and I'm about to ask again when she says, "I'm tired. Too tired to play."

"I know, sweetheart. I'm so sorry. I wish I knew what to do to make things right."

Wordlessly, she taps at the locket around my neck.

I hesitate, my fingers curling protectively around the locket. "If I give it to you, will you be able leave, to rest?" I don't want to give up my last link to her; even as wretched as she is, I don't want to think that I'll never set eyes on her again.

To my relief, she only gives a little shrug of her shoulders. "I don't know. But I want to go home." I know that she's not talking about Willow Hall.

She's begun pacing the perimeter of the garden, and I fall into step beside her. I watch her out of the side of my eye. "I thought you didn't want me to leave you. Are you sure that's what you want?"

Panic flashes across her face and her step falters. "I... I don't want to. But I'm tired."

She looks as if she's on the verge of tears, though whether a spirit can cry I have no idea. I have to remind myself that she's just a child, that she's scared and just as confused as I am about what's happening to her.

I stop beside her and stoop to drop a kiss on the top of her wet head. "I'll figure something out," I tell her. "I promise."

❧ *24* ❧

Sunday

I'M STANDING IN my little garden, trying to save what I can before the inevitable frost that will come creeping along any night now. Mother still doesn't approve of my herb garden, but this morning she had said that if I was going to insist on cultivating one, then I had better at least have the decency to keep the beds neat and weeded. Now that I'm surrounded by the mingling scents of plants and damp earth, I'm glad for the distraction. I need something to do to keep me busy while I wait until Friday, or Catherine and I kill each other, whichever comes first.

I look for some trace of Emeline's nocturnal visit, but she has come and gone without leaving so much as a footprint or a disturbed branch. I wince. How could I have made such a weighty promise to her when I haven't the slightest idea how I brought about her return in the first place?

As I saw away at some of the woody stems of the rosemary—

Ada makes a delectable stuffing with rosemary—I can't help but think back to that summer day when I was weeding and Emeline stormed out, demanding that I let her come to the pond with us. It's no more than the usual sort of regret that lurks around the corner of every memory every day since then, but that's not what makes me suck in a sharp breath.

The herb garden is every bit as lush and full as it was that day, over four months ago at the peak of summer.

The growing season in Boston would already be winding down by now, but in New Oldbury it's even shorter, given how close we are to the mountains. All but the hardiest of the plants should be shriveled and dead, burned by frost. Unease pricks at me, the little hairs on the back of my neck standing on end. Everything else, from the grass to the trees at the edge of the woods are gray, brown. Dead. Everything except the verdant patch of herbs at my feet. I try to remember last night, if it had been this way when I saw Emeline, but it was dark and I hadn't been paying attention to the plants.

Well, there are a thousand reasons why my herbs have done so well. Aren't there? But I grew lax about the weeding over the last couple of months, and despite an autumn of heavy rains, there hasn't been much in the way of sun. It's uncanny how well they've survived despite the unfavorable conditions. I don't know what it means and I don't want to know, so I push the thoughts from my mind.

I'm about to stand when my gaze lands on the silvery-blue petals of my rue plants. I stop, rocking back on my heels. Rue. It's one of my favorites with its rounded leaves that fan out into feathery, dipping branches. The last time I tried to introduce rue at the dinner table Father spat it out on his plate and asked if I was trying to kill him. I don't mind the bitterness, but it's not to everyone's taste. Sometimes I like to press it between the pages of a heavy book, and then paste it onto white paper with flowers to create a botanical piece of art.

An unbidden, terrible thought flits through my head: it also, when used correctly and taken at the right time, can be used to rid the womb of its unwanted fruit.

The leaves flicker in the breeze. The idea wraps around my mind like a snake, squeezing and making its presence known. It would be so easy to snip off a few slender stalks and take them back to the kitchen. There wouldn't be time for drying them. *But you could cut them into fine slivers, steep them with a tea.* As if far away from myself and not in control, I watch, helpless, as I poise my shears just under the flat plane of leaves and draw back to cut. *That's right, Lydia. See how easy it is?*

But I would never hurt Catherine's baby, even knowing its origins and what it might do to my family...would I?

I feel dizzy, my thoughts not my own, just like the day at the pond with Mr. Barrett. These words are not the gentle, persistent whispers of Mary Preston that come to me on the breeze or in my mirror, but the chiding of something older, something more sinister, the voice that led me to the water. And just like that night, I am helpless to disobey. *It is the only way, Lydia. How easy it is, how simple a solution to all your problems.* My hand falters. But then in one swift movement I cut them, the feathery branches falling to the ground. I hastily gather up my basket of rosemary and mint, thrusting the rue stems underneath as if someone might see them and make the connection. I run back to the house, my head pounding, my mouth dry. From far beyond my mind I see myself, as if I were watching another person. But I am like a dog with a command from its master, my vision narrowed only to completing my task.

In the kitchen I glance around for Ada, but it's empty. With shaking hands, I remove the mint and rosemary, placing them on the counter for Ada later. Then, with one more quick glance over my shoulder, I pull out the rue. I put some water on to boil, and then go about chopping the leaves up into tiny slivers, so thin that they are almost transparent. I don't know how much I need, but my hands work automatically, as if they know, and I follow them. To mask the bitter flavor, I add in a good amount of honey as well as regular tea leaves.

When the tea is made, I pour it into one of the dainty teacups with gilding around the edges and a delicate pattern of pink roses. My hands shake so hard that it spills down the side and I have to clean it up with the edge of my cloak. Then I carry it to Catherine's room and knock on the door.

She calls to come in, so I balance the cup in one hand and push the door open with my other. I don't think. I just follow the dark path my mind is telling me to take. She glances up from her writing desk. "Yes?"

"I brought you some tea."

Putting her pen down, she pushes her chair back and looks at me with a suspicious frown. "Why?"

I swallow, trying to look casual and pleasant. "Why not? I was just having a cup and figured you might want one as well. It's so chilly out and it's seeping inside today."

I'm sure that I'm sweating under her gaze despite just telling her how cold it was. But she just gives a shrug and goes back to her writing. "I suppose it might be nice. You can leave it on the table there."

The teacup clatters in its saucer as I slowly bring it to the table. I didn't think she would make it so easy.

Just as I'm about to place it on the cluttered surface of ladies' journals and old correspondences, a breeze blows in and with it whispers telling me: *This isn't you. You are a good person, Lydia.* The whispering breeze wars with the dark thoughts and then my mind unfogs in a brief flash of clarity. What am

I doing? How could I take this awful idea so far? The black snake that has been winding tight around my thoughts recoils and slithers away.

Catherine's back is to me, her head bent over her letters. In one swift movement I knock the cup from the table, spilling the vile tea and sending the gilded porcelain shattering.

Catherine snaps around and looks between the wet pile of shards on the floor and me standing there frozen with my hand still in the air. "For goodness sake, what happened?"

"I… It slipped from my hand. Sorry," I mumble.

She shakes her head. "Well I hope you're planning to clean it up! I swear, Lydia, I didn't even want tea and then you come barging in here and now you've made a mess. Mother is going to be cross as two sticks when she finds out you broke one of her rose cups."

"I'll get something to wipe it up with," I say weakly.

"I should hope so," she says, turning back to her letters.

When I'm out of her room I pause in the hallway and lean against the wall, closing my eyes. My breath comes in shallow spurts. What came over me? How could I even consider such a thing? What is it about this place that drives my thoughts in such appalling directions?

But I know that despite whatever darkness had me in its grip, that it was right. *You almost did it because so long as that baby exists you aren't safe. Mr. Barrett isn't safe from Catherine's plotting. Your family isn't safe.*

Monday

Mother comes into the parlor where Catherine and I are sitting on opposite sides of the room, Catherine at the little mahogany table and I in the chair near the fire with Snip dozing in my lap. A heavy, prickly tension has gathered around us since yesterday, like the calm before a storm. Even though Catherine doesn't know my true purpose in bringing her up that cup of tea—and she never will—she must sense the growing animosity from me. We both know that there's been a subtle shift between us, an understanding that there will be a winner and a loser. We want the same thing, and only one of us can have it. What Catherine seems to forget though is that it's not a toy we're quarreling over, but a grown man. A man with his own thoughts, motivations and desires.

"I'm going out to call on the widow Morton." Mother looks between Catherine and me, as if able to read the invisible words flying between us. "I thought one of you might like to come."

Mother always loved making calls on those less fortunate than us, packing up baskets of food and blankets for widows and families fallen on hard times. I think it makes her feel better about our lot, especially since Emeline died. Or maybe it's her way of feeling like she's in control of something, that she can make a difference. Dealing with someone else's problems is always easier than dealing with one's own, it seems. I know we should go with her, but I also know that Catherine is just waiting for her chance to get rid of me so that she can see Mr. Barrett.

Catherine folds the letter she was writing, and without looking up and says, "I *would* but I just have so much to do here. Lydia, maybe you'd like to?"

"No," I say, matching her tone in sweetness. "I have a bit of a headache. I think I'll stay here."

Mother narrows her eyes, but as usual she doesn't press the matter, and as her slender figure disappears down the hall, I have to swallow back a pang of guilt.

Not half an hour later Catherine is regretting staying behind. "If I don't get out of this house I'm going to die of boredom." She stands at the window looking out at the drive, as if willing someone to appear and whisk her away. "This house is dull, this town is dull, and if we ever had company they would be dull too."

"Maybe you should have gone out with Mother then."

Scowling, the glass fogs and Catherine wipes it with an impatient hand. "And leave you alone? Never."

I shrug, going back to my book. I have to stop reading every few pages because I can't stop wondering if Mr. Barrett has started *The Italian* yet, and if he has, what part he's up to and what he thinks of it.

Catherine doesn't say anything for a moment, and I assume she's gone back to her letters. But when I glance up, she's looking thoughtful. "Maybe I'll go for a walk."

"You hate walking."

But she's already up, pulling on her gloves and tucking her letters into her reticule. "That's not true." She pauses, as if considering something. "I've never walked all the way toward Barrett House, maybe I'll head in that direction."

I'm up quick as lightning, sending Snip tumbling to the floor. "I'll come with you."

Catherine is bundled up looking more like she's going on an arctic expedition than a walk down the road, but I only grab a light spencer and forgo a hat completely. I want to feel the cold air prick my skin, I want to invite the dampness to settle in my bones. Something, I just want to feel something more than the endless, stale hours of waiting for Friday to come.

I don't think we'll actually go to Barrett House, because what on earth could we say showing up there? Instead we play a game of mutual feigned disinterest, neither of us wanting to admit that we're here to keep an eye on the other.

The road is deserted save for a crow who eyes us suspiciously as he drags away some rancid piece of meat. The wind and rain of yesterday have left the trees bare, and the skeleton branches feather out across a colorless sky. Sometimes it feels as if my whole world has shrunk down to this place, this little town in the middle of nowhere, walled in by the hills on one side and the river on the other.

We've barely walked five minutes when Catherine complains of a stitch. I ignore her, setting a brisk pace, savoring the crisp air and the illusion of freedom.

"Do you have to walk so fast?" She struggles to keep up, her hand on her side.

"I'm not," I say, even though my breath is starting to come quicker. I'm tired of always accommodating Catherine and her sense of delicacy. "If you can't keep up I'll go on ahead and meet you back at the house."

She falters, her voice uncharacteristically small. "I... There's something about the woods here. Please, don't leave me alone."

I slow my pace a little and I can feel her relief as she falls into step beside me. Behind the trees the weak November sun is dipping lower, and my skin prickles as the temperature drops with it. Even with Catherine beside me I can't shake the sensation that we're being watched, that if I turned my head just fast enough I might catch a fleeting glimpse of someone in the brush. Knowing that Catherine feels the same way about the woods here doesn't help. I had hoped that it was a foolish fancy of mine, but she feels it too. I shiver.

Catherine moans, playing up the stitch in her side for effect. "Why did you come if all you're going to do is complain?" She stops, doubling over. "I have to go back."

"Well I'm not ready to go back yet," I say stubbornly. I don't want to go back home and sit there, listening to the clock tick away and dwelling on Catherine's schemes to steal Mr. Barrett.

"Please, Lydia," she says.

The quiet strain of her words stops me. "Catherine?"

Her face blanches white and I follow her horrified gaze down to her feet. I suck in my breath. Blood pools around her shoes, seeping through the front of her dress.

She lets out another moan, pain laced with fear.

"Catherine?" I ask again, panic rising in my throat. "What's happening?"

When she looks up at me, her eyes are wide and afraid. "The baby," she whispers.

I'll never know how we manage to get back home. The wind picks up out of nowhere, buffeting us against every step as Catherine leans into me, whimpering and gasping. I've never been so glad to see the large, gaping windows of Willow Hall as I am when we round the drive.

Catherine stops me, gripping my arm so hard that I'll probably have bruises come tomorrow. "The back door...we have to go round the back. Mother can't know."

I glance at the growing stain on her dress. "It's too far." Mother is probably still out anyway. As for Father, it doesn't matter if he's home or not. We could fall through the front door with the hounds of hell hot on our heels and he wouldn't even raise a brow from his papers.

I guide Catherine upstairs by the elbow, one hand at her waist. She's breathing hard. I don't look back but she must be leaving a trail of blood behind her and God knows Mother won't be able to miss it. But there's nothing for it, so I trundle her into bed and lock the door behind me.

"We have to stop the bleeding." I push Catherine's dress up past her knees despite her weak protests and force back the gag rising in my throat. I need something to stanch the blood flow but that Ada won't see in the laundry. Something that won't be missed. My gaze lands on the bolt of lavender silk, untouched and meant for her wedding gown.

I move with purpose, as if I'm watching myself from far away. I calmly fetch the silk and return to the bed where Catherine watches me with terrified, feral eyes.

From somewhere in the depths of her panic and half-formed moans, there's a disconcerting awareness. She knows as well as I do what this could mean for us: no more baby means no fresh rumors, no need for Catherine to dash off to the altar with the first willing man she finds. I'm tearing off a strip of silk and winding it into a thick pad when she grips my wrist with surprising strength.

I lean down so her lips are at my ear. "Please," she whispers hoarsely, "save my baby."

❧ *25* ❧

TIME SLOWS DOWN, and when it's over, Catherine lies drained and ashen on the bed, her lips parched but silent. The baby—if you can even call it that—lies wrapped in what would have been Catherine's wedding gown in the corner.

I pat a damp cloth over Catherine's brow, but her eyes never leave the pile of lavender silk. "What was it?" she whispers.

My hand wavers for a moment, then I start again, small, gentle motions with the cloth. "I don't know. I don't think that it was anything yet." I don't know exactly how far along Catherine was, and I don't want to know. But it was far enough to look like a macabre parody of a baby, with its bulbous head and fingers like tiny curls of paper. It will haunt me until the day I die.

"We have to bury it."

"Catherine, you—"

Suddenly she's animated, struggling to prop herself up and reaching out to grab my wrists. "We have to. My…my child needs to be buried. Besides, Mother can't know. She just can't. It would destroy her."

I wonder when Catherine became so concerned about our mother, but maybe she's right. By some miracle no one is home yet, but Catherine isn't in any state to go outside and do this unthinkable task. Which means it falls to me.

She slumps back down into her pillows. It's hard to read her expression in the thick darkness. My hand trembles as I touch her fingers. "Cath, it's too dark out. I can't."

How is this real? I get up and light the lamp, avoiding the far corner. "We'll just have to wait until tomorrow, and hope that Mother goes out."

"I'm not sleeping with that thing in my room... You have to do something with it!"

"And you need to calm down!" She's sitting up again, making as if she's going to jump out of bed.

"Stop yelling at me!"

"I'm not yelling," I say, taking a deep breath and lowering my voice. "But think, Catherine. Where? How? I don't even know where Joe keeps a shovel."

For some reason the shovel, this particular detail, sends a shiver down my spine. There's a little misshapen body in the corner next to the beautiful blue-and-white ewer and the yellow damask curtains, and we are going to bury it. *I'm* going to bury it.

The sound of wheels clattering cuts through the sharp stillness. Our eyes lock. "There's no time. Keep your door locked and I'll go down. I'll tell Mother that you're ill, that the blood is from... I don't know. I'll think of something, but you have to stay in here."

"You can't leave me in here with...with *it*!"

So much for "it" being her child. I hurriedly splash my hands with water from the basin, suppressing a shudder at the heap of cloth next to it.

Catherine fumes, cursing under her breath, but she gives

up, sinking back into her bloody sheets. Those will have to be taken care of too without Ada knowing. She's pale and for a moment I waver in my decision to leave her alone, wondering if she's in any danger from succumbing to her ordeal. Maybe I should fetch the doctor. Almost as if she's reading my mind she narrows her eyes. "Fine. But swear to God, Lydia, swear on Emeline's grave that you will not call the doctor."

I wince at her choice of words, but I swear.

The latch turns in the door downstairs. I force a few calming breaths, check my dress for any remaining streaks of blood and then go down to lie to my mother.

The moon hangs behind a hazy bank of clouds that night, as I wait until the last sounds of the house settle; Ada closing the grates, Father lumbering upstairs after dragging himself away from his study, and then the lighter, swifter steps of Mother following him.

Mother had been more concerned with the stains on the carpet than the lie I told her about Catherine having a bloody nose. She had asked if she should send for the doctor, but she'd already been looking around for something to clean the blood up with, frowning that Ada had run out of vinegar. I should have known that Mother wouldn't have noticed anything was amiss, that she wouldn't care enough to take me aside and make sure Catherine was really all right.

Catherine is fast asleep when I slip into her room, lightly snoring as if she were tired from a day of shopping or dancing at a ball. Anger surges through me. She's dragged me into another one of her messes and as usual I have to clean it up. I could wake her up, force her to be a party to what I must do now. But as I stand beside her peaceful figure, pale and faintly frowning in the dim moonlight, the anger fades, replaced with pity and guilt. It hasn't escaped me that the very thing I so longed for, that I was so near to making sure occurred myself, has happened of its own accord. What a horrible coincidence. It doesn't make me feel any better that I got what I wanted. I let out a weary sigh, and then leave my sister to her sleep.

The night is cold and still, the woods every bit as watchful as the last time I made this trip. My breath comes out in short, white puffs as I struggle up the hill, one arm wrapped around the lifeless bundle, the other clearing thorny brush and dead branches out of my path.

A sound behind me—or is it in front?—and I stop, holding my breath. The dry rustle of naked branches in the breeze, and the faraway echo of an owl fill the emptiness. I move faster, with purpose. What if someone is following me? Ada or Joe, or even Mr. Barrett? What would he think of me, out here alone with a dead baby in my arms?

"Emeline?" I whisper out into the darkness. "Emeline, is that you?"

The only answer is the sweep of breeze that lifts the hem of my skirt.

"What are you doing?"

I freeze. My blood goes cold as I slowly turn around. "You." My voice comes out in a choked whisper. "What do you want?"

The pale little boy laughs, the unsettling sound that has plagued my dreams and spilled over into my waking moments. He wears the same clothes as in the portrait that hangs over Mr. Barrett's desk, but they are ragged and sooty. The tip of his nose and fingers are singed black, and he looks at me from lidless eyes that never blink. "I asked you first," he says, sticking out a scorched tongue. How could I have not seen what has been in front of me all these months? The little boy laughing in my dreams, Emeline's mysterious friend and Mr. Barrett's dead little brother are all one and the same.

Something tells me he already knows what I'm doing. I shift the bundle to my other arm trying to maintain a steady composure. Every instinct in me makes me want to recoil and flee as far and as fast as I can. But I won't let this little spirit see my fear. "Why are you following me? What do you want?"

He regards me with eyes that are so like Mr. Barrett's that I find myself powerless to look away. My anger grows. "You took Emeline from me. You lured her to the pond to have a playmate. Isn't that enough for you? Why do you continue to plague me?"

He doesn't answer me, just launches into an intense fit of coughing. Blood and soot come up, which he spits on the ground. I flinch. Then he turns a terrible grin on me. "You should go away from here and leave John alone. You should go away and never come back."

"Why, Moses?" My voice is steady and even, but my heart is pounding against my ribs.

He laughs again. "Ask John. Ask John what he did and then you'll see."

Before I can ask him what he means, he's gone. He disappears in the time it takes me to blink. I stand there for another moment, the air around me heavy in its stillness.

I sprint the rest of the way to the pond, tripping once and clutching the bundle tighter, scraping my palms against an outcropping rock as I brace my fall. Ignoring the stinging, I hang on and keep going. I don't look back until I reach the clearing, my breath coming in painfully shallow gulps. Moses is nowhere to be seen, and again I almost wonder if it's just my imagination playing tricks on me, a product of my over-burdened mind. I never seem to sleep soundly anymore so it wouldn't be any wonder. But by now I know that it's not my imagination, that nothing that has happened to me at Willow Hall has been my imagination. The sooty boy with blistered burns and lidless eyes was as real as what I carry under my arm.

The pond is visible only by the smallest reflection of clouds on the glassy surface. Before I go any farther I poke around in the dark, and my hand closes around a small rock, then another. I plunge them into the silk folds of the bundle, praying that my hand doesn't touch what lies within.

One thing, I tell myself. *I just have to do this one thing and then this nightmare will be over. Mr. Barrett will come on Friday and Catherine won't have reason to interfere anymore. It will all be over.*

I take a deep breath and wade out into the blackness, the icy water nipping my ankles but somehow making me warm. There's no siren call from the willow this time, no Moses watching me, and when the water reaches my knees, I stop. The air is so thin, so devoid of life that you could hear a lone bird sigh a hundred miles away.

Carefully, I take the bundle out from under my arm and, closing my eyes, toss it out in front of me. The splash echoes off the trees and rocks, the blanket of clouds. When I open my eyes, only the faintest ripple on the inky black surface betrays that the water has accepted its offering.

Tuesday

By some miracle Catherine is already awake the next morning when I stagger downstairs to breakfast. Her face is drawn, her eyes vacant. Her dressing gown hangs limply from her shoulders, and with dawning horror I realize that she's still wearing her shift from yesterday under it, blood specks visible around the hem when she leans for the teapot.

I glance at Mother and Father to see if they notice, but Mother is listlessly studying the enamel grapevine border on her plate while she pushes her creamed wheat around with her spoon. Father is buried in his paper, blindly groping for his plate from behind it. If ever there was a day when I wish I could slip into the panoramic wallpaper and its world of gentle sloping banks, carefree ladies in rowboats and picnicking children, it's this morning.

"Look here," Father says without emerging from his newspaper fortress, "the Boston Manufacturing Company is buying up more land in the Merrimack Valley, and they're paying out dividends of over 27 percent to the investors. Twenty-seven!"

No one responds, and he goes on muttering to himself, exclaiming that he'll have to watch those slick Lowell city men in the future.

Mother catches my eye. "You look pale, Lydia. Did you sleep poorly?"

"Do I?" I make a bright show of smiling and taking an extra helping of bacon. It doesn't help that the crisp meat reminds me of Moses and his burned face. I force myself to swallow a tiny piece and almost gag.

"Catherine, your color is low too. There's a fever going round the town, widow Morton has it too. I wonder if I shouldn't call the doctor."

Catherine's head snaps up and we both exclaim in unison, "No!"

"Really, we're fine," I hurry to reassure Mother. "Just a touch of a sore throat from our walk yesterday. Catherine was saying she had one too, weren't you, Cath?"

Catherine raises her gaze slowly to mine, and I give her a weary smile. If nothing else we're in this together now.

But instead of understanding, or a silent look of thanks, her eyes meet mine with a malice so intense that my blood instantly goes cold.

I silently mouth "What?" but Catherine turns her nose up and looks away.

Mother sighs. "I hope it's not catching. I've been feeling rather tired lately."

Father finds her hand from behind his paper and gives it a pat. "You really ought to rest, my dear. No more of this calling on sick widows, it isn't good for your constitution. Why don't you go have a nice lie-down?"

Mother opens her mouth as if to say something, but closes it and nods. "Yes," she says, pushing her chair back. "Perhaps that's a good idea. Excuse me."

"I'll bring you up a cup of tea soon," I tell her, thinking of the mint I harvested and how that might be a nice addition to a hot drink. She gives me a thin smile before disappearing to her room.

Catherine glares at me from across the table. "You and your tea."

"What?"

She flickers a glance to Father who's still absorbed in land deals and dividends, then scrapes her chair back and stands. Her arms are wobbly and she has to brace her weight against the table. "Don't play stupid with me, Lydia," she hisses.

"What are you talking about?"

Then, without a word of explanation, she bolts out of the room.

❧ 26 ❧

"CATHERINE?"

I catch up to her in the front hall, where she's leaning against the stairs, face cradled in her hands. When she hears me coming she jerks her head up, hastily wiping away a tear.

I know I should leave well enough alone, but she looks so small, so pathetic with her uncombed hair and stained shift. She lost so much blood yesterday that I can't help but be worried for her, and that's to say nothing of what must be going through her head right now, the hollowness of her loss.

She glares at me from red-rimmed eyes. "What do you want?"

I ignore the razor-sharp hostility in her words. "I'm sorry about…about what happened yesterday. Really, I am." I reach out and touch her on the shoulder. She violently shrugs off my hand.

"You're sorry," she repeats tonelessly, studying the carpet. Then, lifting her eyes to mine, she takes a deep breath, raises her hand back and, with surprising strength, smacks me clean across my cheek.

Gasping, I stand there, too stunned to do anything except rub my stinging face. "What was that for?"

"You know exactly what it's for," she hisses.

I wince, vaguely wondering if it will leave a mark, and if it does, if it will dissolve by Friday. "No, I don't."

Glaring, she leans in so close that I can smell the lingering odor of blood, of sickness, of death that wreathes her. The front hall shrinks around us and grows quiet, the only sound the faint clinking of dishes as Ada clears the table in the dining room. Catherine's words fall into the silence like steaming coals.

"You murdered my child."

The accusation knocks me back, sucks the air right out of me. I reach for the sideboard behind me, steadying myself. "Catherine," I whisper. "How can you say that?"

"Admit it," she says, jabbing her finger into my chest, backing me farther up against the sideboard. "I saw you out poking around your herbs. You thought you could slip me something in my tea and I wouldn't know. You make me sick."

Blood rushes to my head. My face must be red as fire and it feels just as hot. I can't get my words out around my suddenly thick tongue. "N-no! I would never."

Her eyes narrow to slits. I shrink under her penetrating gaze, hopelessly aware that my guilt must be written on my face plain as day. It doesn't matter that I didn't go through with it; I thought about it, I prayed for the same outcome, and coincidence or not, the baby is dead.

I bite my lip, unable to meet her eye. "You never even drank the tea." I feel rather than see the bitter, triumphant tilt of her chin.

"I knew it! For all your downcast lashes and moral high ground, you're just as bad as the rest of us. Worse even, because you really believe you're a good person. All the while you're skulking around, plotting against me and my innocent baby."

"That's not fair. I don't—"

"Oh, shut up, just shut up! I know what you are even if you don't see it yourself. Did you know that I watched you that day with Tommy Bishop? I saw you from the window, the whole thing. You never laid a finger on that boy. Everyone else came running around after it was over and thought it was a street fight between two little brats, but I saw it all and you never touched him, not with your hands."

My skin prickles cold. "I don't know what you're talking about."

Her voice is low, deceptively steady. "Maybe you didn't put something in my tea, but there's something wrong with you, something different inside of you. You used whatever…" she searches for a word "…power you used on Tommy Bishop, on me to kill my baby. Have you forgotten that I was there at the pond? That sound that came out of you, it wasn't…human."

Snippets of memories, incomplete pictures from that long-ago day flash across my mind: matted fur and blood, the film of red behind my eyes as I found Tommy Bishop in the street, a pressure building and rising inside of me until my hands tingled and my body vibrated. The same sensations I felt when Emeline died and I wanted to strike out against Mr. Barrett and the pond churned with my rage. My stomach lurches and I push the memories away.

Catherine is watching me. "You're evil," she says with something between awe and disgust. "You're really evil and you don't even realize it."

My last vestiges of guilt fade as her accusations break against me like waves, one after the other. I draw myself up taller, moving away from the sideboard. "I don't know what you're talking about," I say, firmer this time.

Catherine stands her ground. "Yes, you do!" Her voice is rising, her words cracking with hysteria. "You wanted my baby dead. You thought it was an abomination and you're glad that it died!"

At one time I might have held back, but the words erupt out of me now, a swift torrent of bad feelings, barely suppressed grudges and untold truths held below the surface for too long.

"Of course I'm glad that it died! That thing would have ruined our lives. I saw it, and it wasn't even a baby, it was... grotesque! It was unnatural from the very moment of its conception. How can you possibly think it would have been born healthy and right?"

Her face drains of color and she takes a shaky step back, as if she had never even for a moment considered this. But then her eyes narrow and she regains her balance. When she speaks it's low and dangerous, like a snake in tall grass, ready to strike its prey. "You. Little. Bitch. My child was conceived in love. You think the world is black-and-white, that because Charles is my brother he couldn't possibly love me in any other way. You could never possibly understand what he and I shared, and now you've taken away the only thing I had left of him."

"You're disgusting. You—"

She lets out a shrill, piercing, laugh. "Oh, grow up. You're almost nineteen and you act like you're still in the nursery. Playing make-believe with Emeline was one thing, but she's gone and you can't seem to shake your fantasy world. Maybe someday you'll learn that in the real world happiness doesn't just fall into your lap, that you have to go out and take it for yourself, like me. But until then, by all means sit inside lost in your silly novels and pining away over the man you love and don't have a clue how to get."

"Maybe because I'm too busy trying to clean up *your* messes to be able to even think of anything besides keeping this family together. Do you have any idea how much I've done for you? The things I've sacrificed to make sure that your careless, disgusting behavior didn't ruin us completely?"

"And did I ask you to do anything, Lydia? Did I?"

"Of course not, you were too busy opening your legs at every chance you got and—"

Catherine laughs again. "Do you know what your problem is? You think you're some sort of martyr, that the world is broken and only *you* can fix it."

"Trust me, I *wish* someone else would take some responsibility. Like Charles. Where is he in all this? If you love each other so much, how come you aren't with him? He must know you hate it here, must know that you were carrying his child. Mother might turn a blind eye, but don't think I don't see you posting letters to London all the time. So why hasn't he sent for you? What's keeping you here?"

Catherine's face freezes, and then she turns away, curling her fingers around the balusters of the stairs. "That's none of your business," she murmurs.

Now it's my turn to laugh. "None of my business? How can you possibly say that after yesterday?"

She spins back to face me, emerald eyes flashing. "Because he abandoned me, that's why! Don't you think I'd rather be anywhere than stuck in this godforsaken place with you?"

She looks as if she instantly regrets divulging this. "Oh," I say, taken aback. "I didn't know."

"Oh, what do you care?" Catherine runs an impatient hand through her tangled hair. "I got a letter from him a couple of weeks ago. He's met some English whore, a dancer, and he's going to marry her. He told me before I had a chance to write about the baby."

"Catherine, I—"

"You're sorry? Spare me."

I'm not sorry, but I'm about to tell her that it's for the best no matter what it feels like right now, when the door flies open. Father thunders out of the dining room, brandishing his newspaper over his head like when he used to swat Snip for having an accident inside. His face is as red as a beet, a vein I never knew he had pulsing in his temple. Catherine and I exchange a look of horror.

"For God's sake, would you two be quiet?" he roars. "You would think we were at war with all the carrying-on out here."

Catherine and I don't say anything, our last words still simmering in silence between us. Father doesn't give a backward glance as he jams his hat on his head, grabs his cane and yanks open the front door. "I'm going to the mill," he mutters. "At least there the only noise to contend with is the looms."

The door slams shut behind him and Catherine's unflinching gaze slides back to me. When she speaks it's so cold and detached that a shiver runs up my spine. "Just know this, Lydia—I will do everything I can to ensure that you are miserable and alone for the rest of your pathetic life."

And just like that, the last tenuous strands of love, of family, of sisterhood strain and snap. Only yesterday her blood stained my hands, her laboring body vulnerable and helpless before me. I can't take it anymore. I pick up my hem and head for my room.

"That's right, go on, Lydia! Run away, you coward."

My eyes are hot, but the tears stubbornly absent as I take the stairs two by two. I'm halfway up when I come to a sudden stop, nearly teetering backward.

I don't know how long Mother has been standing there, one hand over her open mouth, the other clutching her shawl at her neck. Usually small and wispy among the imposing rooms of Willow Hall, she now towers above me, a queen of her castle. And the queen is not pleased.

I glance behind me to find Catherine has the decency to look ashamed, her gaze quickly settling back on the carpet. I can't stop staring at my mother though, transfixed by the fury on the face that is usually so vacant and withdrawn.

Mother's words are low and crisp. "That's enough." She sweeps down the rest of the stairs, her diminutive figure brushing me aside. "I won't have another minute of this in my house. I'm at my wit's end with all the bickering and animosity between you two."

I've never seen Mother so angry. It doesn't come naturally to her, it's almost as if she has to feel her way along, not quite sure of what she should say. But it takes her only a matter of seconds to find her footing.

"It's past time you were both married, but since you seem determined to spoil every opportunity, then I expect you'll at least behave civilly to each other so long as you are under this roof."

"Mother, that's not fair. I—"

Mother cuts Catherine off with a look so frigid that it could turn the ocean to ice. Catherine clamps her mouth back shut.

"Now," Mother says as she retrieves a letter from the sideboard. Catherine and I watch her in stunned silence. "This," she says, waving the envelope, "is another letter from your Aunt Phillips. She's lonely and doing poorly with her foot, and in need of a companion around the house."

I swallow, casting a sidelong glance at Catherine.

"I told her that one of my daughters would be happy to come and—"

Before I can protest, Catherine blurts out, "Lydia should go."

"Me? But I—"

"I don't think it would be right for me to go," Catherine hurries on. "I don't want to start any fresh rumors about running off to Boston after Mr. Pierce."

Mother doesn't see the look of smug exultance that Catherine flashes me, and my heart plummets into my stomach as I realize what she's doing.

"Catherine should go," I say obstinately. "She's the one that's always going on about New Oldbury not being grand enough for her. She's wanted to go back to Boston since the first day we arrived."

"Oh, and you don't? Just the other day you were complaining about how there are no bookshops here, and before that it was how much you missed the ocean."

I feel my footing start to slip out from under me. "But…" I protest feebly. "But Mr. Barrett is calling on Friday and—"

"If Mr. Barrett were going to call on you he would have by now," Catherine snaps, relishing the knife twist all the more because she knows it's true.

"ENOUGH!"

The single word slices through our bickering like a knife. Mother closes her eyes and massages her temple, her flush of outrage receding just as quickly as it came on. "Lydia, you'll go to Boston. Catherine, I don't know what's gotten into you but I agree, I want you home where I can keep my eye on you."

I open my mouth to tell her what Catherine's doing, that it's not fair, but Mother holds up her hand to silence me, shattering my last fragment of hope. "As for Mr. Barrett," she says with finality, "he can wait."

❧ *27* ❧

BOSTON GREETS ME with a sharp, gusty wind carrying the tang of woodsmoke and fresh-caught fish. The coach bumps and rumbles over cobblestone streets, past the market with pyramids of cabbage heads and silver cod where Emeline and I used to explore. Nothing has changed since we left; Boston has awakened and slumbered just the same without me. Even though the woods of Willow Hall are my home now, where Mr. Barrett lives just out of sight, where Emeline roams by night to find me, I can't help but feel a melancholy prick of betrayal that my old city has not missed me.

Mother hadn't cared when I pleaded with her to let me stay until Friday, that I would go anywhere she asked if I could only see Mr. Barrett first. "I think you would do well to get away from Willow Hall for a little while," she had said with a cryptic look that I didn't understand. Her eruption of anger had drained her, leaving her reclining by the fire and coughing into her handkerchief. When she raised her eyes to mine, they were so tired, so resigned that I had swallowed the rest of my argument and went upstairs to pack my trunk and write a letter to Mr. Barrett. I explained that a family emergency had arisen and I'd been called away to Boston, but that I would be back soon, and I was very much looking forward to his call. It was a pleasant, formal letter, the kind one writes when one regrets that she won't be able to call for tea. That was Tuesday night, and I've spent every minute of the two-day coach ride regretting my empty words to Mr. Barrett, Catherine's voice echoing in the back of my mind: *happiness doesn't just fall into your lap, you need to go out and take it.* And what about Emeline? My chest tightens when I think about her, searching Willow Hall only to find me gone. If I can somehow help her, it certainly won't be all the way from Boston.

Aunt Phillips is waiting outside the neat brick house on Acorn Street when I climb down weary and dusty from the coach. She's leaning heavily on a crutch, her foot bandaged up to comic proportions. Like Father, she's short and well built, and has an inordinate interest in everything that can be measured in currency, and what things cost. Unlike Father, she is perpetually talking and moving, a whirlwind of pleasantries and endless questions that catch me off guard after my long journey.

"Lydia, Lydia, Lydia," she says with both hands outstretched, the crutch clattering to the ground. "Come here, child." She kisses my cheeks with a force that almost knocks me over, and shouts for the butler, Blake, to come and take my case. Tall and crooked as he is ancient, Blake has been a fixture at Acorn Street since my earliest memories of visiting here as a child. He hefts my trunk up over his shoulder as if it were nothing, and with little more than a nod of recognition, leaves me to Aunt Phillips.

"You must be exhausted! Those coaches are terrible contraptions. So crowded and bumpy and they never stop at the good inns. Well never mind that now, you must come inside and have a cup of something hot to drink."

I'm installed in the parlor in front of a roaring fire, my head already throbbing from Aunt Phillips's steady stream of questions and chatter. She and Mrs. Tidewell would probably get on famously.

"Oh, but am I glad to see you. It's been so lonely here since your uncle has been in New York. Has it really only been five months?" Aunt Phillips shakes her head, tight curls bouncing out at the edges of her lace cap. "Tch, you've gotten too thin. It must be that horrible country food. I'll see if I can't get that good-for-nothing cook to put something together for you." She pours out two steaming cups of tea and hands one to me. "How is your poor mother doing?"

"Well enough," I lie.

"That's good to hear." She sounds a little disappointed. "To lose a child that age to such an accident..." She trails off, gesturing helplessly into the air. "Of course your uncle and I were never blessed with children of our own, but unfortunately one grows accustomed to hearing of infants dying as a matter of course. It's when they make it past a certain age only to be snatched back that you can't help but feel it unfair."

A lump forms in my throat, threatening to rise up and spill into tears. I push it back down. "Yes, of course it is. I'll tell Mother you asked after her. Thank you."

She sighs. "And this business with Catherine...well, I won't speak of it," she says with a distasteful little wave. "But it's enough to break any parent's heart what your family has had to go through."

If she only knew the half of it. I just nod, staring into the depths of my cooling tea.

"And what about you, my dear?"

"What about me?"

"Well," she says, putting her tea down and leaning across to my chair. "Has your mother said anything about getting you settled? Surely it's time, and I can't imagine she's willing to wait until Catherine is married. Do you have your eye on some young man?"

I jerk my head up, unable to mask my surprise at the question. It might be different if she was asking me a week from now, in a world where Mr. Barrett had already left me with some understanding. Even if I had just had a letter from him, anything so that I knew what he wanted to tell me last week in the road. "No," I say, hoping she doesn't catch the slight quaver in my voice. "There's no young man."

She arches a questioning brow at me and sits back. "No? What about...what was his name... He used to work with your father. Started with an *S*... Silas? Or maybe it was a *C*."

I nearly drop my cup. "What, Cyrus?"

"Cyrus! Thank you, my dear. That would've bothered me all day."

"The engagement was broken off when we moved," I hurry to explain. She doesn't need to know about Cyrus's unwelcome appearance in New Oldbury or his ridiculous proposal and letters. "I haven't seen him since then."

"No?" She furrows her gray brows, tilting her head in deep thought. "But didn't he go to Emeline's burial? I could have sworn your mother wrote something to that effect in one of her letters. That was kind of him, wasn't it?"

"Oh," I say weakly. "Yes, I had forgotten. Very kind. Aunt Phillips, do you think I might be shown to my room now? I'm afraid the journey here has quite worn me out."

Aunt Phillips looks startled. "Did I say something wrong? I was only asking because—"

"No, it's fine," I assure her with a thin smile. "I'm just tired, that's all."

★ ★ ★

As I lay in an unfamiliar bed that night, the sounds of Boston surround me like a long-forgotten lullaby. Carts rumble down the hill and the clatter of horse hooves echo through the narrow street. Somewhere two men are shouting over each other, then abruptly break off into laughter. It's a far cry from the nocturnal sounds of New Oldbury where the only traffic is that of the stealthy foxes and the beating of owls' wings. I strain my ear for the sound of ships in the harbor, canvas sails crumpling in the wind, bells alerting the sailors of curfew. I picture them returning drunk and sleepy to their swaying hammocks. On Washington Street my favorite bookshop is quiet and dark, books lined up in precise rows of thick, uncracked spines as Mr. Brown turns the lamps down for the night. The grocers down in Faneuil Hall will have long since taken in their wares, chucking any spoiled apples and onions to the barefoot beggar children. Aunt Phillips will be snoring away downstairs, foot propped up in front of the fire, no doubt dreaming of gossip and fresh scandals.

In New Oldbury I imagine Mr. Barrett sitting at his desk, running his hand through his hair, a frown catching at his lips as he reads my letter for the fourth or fifth time before crumpling it up and throwing it away.

And then there is Emeline. Lost, alone, scared, unable to rest.

The next morning as soon as I can reasonably be excused from helping Aunt Phillips dress her foot, I bolt to Mr. Brown's bookshop where I buy the first volume of a new book on his recommendation: *Ivanhoe*. He promises that it's full of knights, castles and "all those things that seem to so capture the imagination of young women in particular." He accepts my money with a wink and a promise from me that I'll be back for the next two volumes.

Just as I'm about to leave, I turn back and he looks up in surprise. "Is there something else I can help you with? Perhaps you'd like the second volume now?"

On an impulse, I ask, "Do you have any books on witchcraft? That is, specifically its history in Massachusetts? The Salem trials and such."

A bushy gray brow shoots up behind his round spectacles. "Witchcraft? Well now, let me see." He crosses his arms and leans back behind his desk, deep in thought.

My cheeks burn and I wish I hadn't asked, but now he's on the case and I know there's no stopping him.

Mr. Brown springs up and in a moment he's rifling through an overcrowded shelf, pulling off volumes, inspecting the titles and then discarding them.

"Aha!" He coaxes a slim little book off the back of the shelf and hands it to me. *"Tales of Witchcraft, Sorcery, & Other Macabre Happenings in Olde New England."* He looks at me and gives me a conspiratorial smile. "Doing a bit of research, are we?"

My cheeks burn hotter. "I... It's just a passing fancy," I stammer. "Really more of a fancy of Catherine's," I lie. "I promised her I would look for a book for her while I was in Boston." I certainly can't tell him the real reason I'm desperate for information is because of the black mark on my family's history, and that Mary Preston's visit and cryptic warnings have been churning in my mind for weeks now. There is something wrong with Willow Hall—or me—and I need answers.

But he hardly hears me as he makes his way back to his desk and begins to wrap it up in brown paper for me. "Not such a popular subject these days," he says without looking up. "Now it's all haunted castles and wicked highwaymen and the like."

When I realize he's making a joke about the books I usually come in looking for, I let out a little laugh and relax.

He hands me the package and I add it to my other book. "Let me know what you find with your research," he says.

I promise that I will, though now that I'm in Boston, far away from the spirits and strange happenings of Willow Hall, it doesn't seem so urgent anymore.

Once outside with a crisp ocean breeze at my neck and my new books under my arm, I can almost forget about my reason for being in Boston in the first place. Winding along the familiar streets and feeling the cobblestones through my leather soles it's like the past five months never happened. I pretend that we still live in our brick house with the ivy climbing up the front, and that when I go home Emeline will pull me into the library, demanding that I read to her from my new books. Mother will be smiling in the way she used to, her gentle brown eyes lighting up when she sees me and Emeline curled up together by the fire. Ada will bring in chocolate and...

I've just reached Acorn Street when I stop dead in my tracks. Oh no. No no no.

His back is to me as he leans down to kiss Aunt Phillips on the cheek, but I would recognize that neatly combed black hair and slender, trim figure anywhere. He hasn't come in a carriage—I suppose his father had to sell that—but he looks well enough in his double-breasted coat and polished Hessians. Aunt Phillips clasps his hand as she says something, and then smiling, ushers Cyrus inside.

I stand there, turning the books over in my hands and biting my lip. I could go somewhere else, wait for him to leave. Maybe back to Mr. Brown's and browse for an hour? Or to the docks and watch the ships come in?

As if in answer, a fat, icy raindrop falls onto my neck, worming its way down my back, followed by another and another. If I found out Cyrus could summon storm clouds at his whim I wouldn't be surprised. Grumbling, I shield my books under my arm and plunge inside to see what my ex-fiancé could possibly want now.

"Oh, Lydia, there you are! I saw the dark clouds rolling in and I was worried you'd be caught in the rain." Aunt Phillips hobbles over to greet me. "Well, don't just stand there in the door, come in, come in."

As I step inside, she leans in and whispers in my ear, "You don't have to say a word. I saw how heartbroken you were when you mentioned the engagement was off, so I sent for Mr. Thompson, telling him it was all a misunderstanding and now he's obliged us with his company."

My mouth falls open but I can't sort my thoughts into any coherent words. Aunt Phillips gives me a knowing look and smiles. "There'll be time to thank me later, now go on."

Cyrus is already lounging in the parlor, fingers tapping erratically on the arm of the big chair by the hearth, one boot propped up on Aunt Phillip's gout stool. I don't bother smiling or pretending I'm pleased to see him as I drag my feet inside.

"I'll go see how Blake is getting on with tea." Aunt Phillips gives me a ridiculous wink and before I can beg her to stay, she's backing out of the room, closing me in there with him. So much for propriety.

"Hello, Lydia," Cyrus says without getting up. "You're looking rather down about the mouth."

I peel off my gloves and throw them down on the table along with my books. "And you're looking well enough for someone who so bitterly claimed they were on the cusp of abject poverty."

"Abject poverty is a *poor* excuse to let one's self go, wouldn't you say?" He cocks his head at me to see if I noticed his stupid little pun.

"What do you want, Cyrus?"

"Want? Why, your lovely aunt invited me over. Am I not welcome?"

I glare at him in answer as I shake my cloak off. Then, even though I've never had the urge to take a drink in my life, I go over to the sideboard to pour myself something from one of Uncle Phillips's crystal decanters. Whatever it is, it smells awful and scalds down my throat like fire. I choke a little, aware that Cyrus is watching me with cool, unwavering eyes.

"I never knew you to take a drink, Lyd. Have things really gotten that bad?"

I don't say anything, just return his patronizing gaze from behind the rim of the glass with as much haughty composure as I can muster.

"I guess we're past mincing words, eh? Well then, that should make this infinitely easier on both of us." He's still sitting, cross-legged and elegant, looking as if he has every right in the world to be here. I don't like standing in front of him as if I'm at his beck and call, yet I can't bring myself to sit down, to concede that we're actually having a conversation.

"I was charmed to get your aunt's invitation, but I must admit I had reasons of my own for wanting to see you when I found out you were back in Boston. You never answered any of my letters." When I don't say anything he looks a little disappointed, but carries on. "I want to renew my offer. Your hand in marriage, bringing with it the Montrose money, and in return, my spotless name and a chance for you to reclaim your place in polite society."

The bark of laughter that escapes my lips is so loud that I make myself jump. I wait for him to crack a smile, but his face remains infuriatingly unreadable. "You...you can't be serious."

Slowly, and with the grace of a cat, he unfolds himself and

comes right up beside me, so close that I can't tell if the smell of alcohol is from his breath or mine.

"Would I waste your time if I wasn't serious?" His tone is gentle, wheedling, like our last meeting never happened. "Come on, Lyd. Don't you want to hear what I have to say?"

I turn to leave. "No, I don't." I would have read his letters if I wanted hear his empty declarations of love. This has gone on long enough, and I want to be upstairs writing a letter to Mr. Barrett, the letter I should have written the first time.

Cyrus reaches into his waistcoat and produces a folded piece of paper. "Oh," he says with grim satisfaction, "but I think you do."

The floor creaks outside the door. Aunt Phillips is listening.

Cyrus realizes this too. Just as I'm about to turn the knob, he raises his voice, calling out after me, "Who's the baby's father, Lydia?"

28

MY HEART FREEZES in my chest. In two strides I'm back over to him. "Shut up!" I hiss. "How did you know about that?"

A grin spreads over his face and I realize my mistake at once. I slump down into the chair.

"So there *is* a baby." Smug, he saunters to the sideboard and pours himself a glass. At least he's lowered his voice now, and there's a reluctant creak in the hall as Aunt Phillips tries to tiptoe quietly away.

He flops down into the chair opposite me. "I'll try to make it quick, but I have to say I rather have a mind to bide here awhile, drinking your uncle's fine spirits." He drains the glass. "I haven't had a good glass of port in too long."

"Cyrus…"

"Oh, all right." He unfolds the paper, and my heart lurches as I recognize Catherine's handwriting. "Seems your sister is in rather desperate circumstances. She sent me this letter."

I dig my fingers into the chair, waiting for him to finish drawing out the moment.

"Well, I won't bore you with the details. She just said that she knew we—that is, you and me," he says, gesturing between us, "had fallen out and that she had reason to think I might entertain the idea of another Montrose sister. She spells it all out quite clearly, said she wouldn't even try to pull the wool over my eyes, as it were. It seems she got herself..." he clears his throat delicately, as if this were somehow beneath him, and continued "...in a certain condition, and she needed my help to keep her respectable."

My insides are coiled ropes, tightening as he goes on. Oh, Catherine, what have you done?

"So, Lydia." Cyrus leans forward, drinking in the effects of his words with greedy eyes. "What will become of the baby? Catherine can hide out in the country for some time, her belly growing rounder and no one the wiser of her condition. But it can't be kept secret forever. Eventually people will wonder why she is never seen anymore. And what of a marriage?"

He goes on in that vein but I've stopped listening. He doesn't know. He doesn't know that the baby has already come and gone. And how could he? The only thing that proves that there ever might have been a baby rests in his hands.

"Are you paying attention? If I were in your place I would be listening very carefully, because, Lydia, I'm offering you a way out of this. Do you really want to bring more scandal crashing down on your family?" His sharp eyes settle on mine, softening just the slightest bit at the edges. "Let me help you."

"I would rather face a thousand scandals than accept whatever it is you would try to pass off as help." I stand up and move to the door. "We're done here."

But Cyrus doesn't move. He's staring at me so intently that I shift nervously despite myself.

"No," he says slowly, not breaking his gaze. "No, I don't think you would rather face a thousand scandals. There is a baby, the letter says as much. You might turn down my suit for your hand because a return to society isn't really such a prize for Lydia Montrose. But a baby, one conceived around the time the rumors of incest were spreading? Well, that's another matter entirely. Why, it would kill your mother! Catherine would be beyond ruined."

"You're not half so clever as you think," I manage to say. "You don't know anything about my family or what we've been through. I don't need you or whatever it is you would pass off as help."

"No? Am I missing something? Would you care to enlighten me?"

My face is burning and I'm trying so hard to look as cool and composed as he does. I must be failing miserably, because the smuggest, most delighted smile spreads over his face. "Your face always did give away everything, did you know that? You can't hide your true feelings to save your life. So, there is a baby, but you aren't worried about it being known. Now why would that be? Does your mother already know? Has she already put some scheme in place to pass the child off as hers? No, of course that's not it. She's much too old and fragile for anyone to believe it."

"We're going to pass it off as mine," I blurt out, desperate.

Cyrus just stares at me, and then breaks out in a fit of laughter, as if I said something genuinely funny.

"Oh, please," he says, gathering his breath. "What an idea. No one would believe it. First of all…you're chaste as a nun! And why even bother to pass it off from one sister to another? What would be the point?"

I bite my tongue. Cyrus is right: I'm not a good liar, and I don't know what to say that won't further tangle me up in the web he's spinning.

He's up now, pacing with his glass in hand, thoughtfully

swirling the liquid side to side. This is a puzzle, and he's enjoying solving it. I stand stupidly by the door, powerless to do anything but watch him prod and snake his way into my darkest secret.

"No one outside you and your sister know about it—well, and me obviously," he says with a little cock of his head. "I daresay even the father doesn't know, or…" Cyrus trails off, and for the first time since launching into this inquisition, his confidence fades, replaced by slow realization. He locks eyes with me, color slowly returning to his face. "No," he whispers. "Really? The rumors were all true then?" He's speechless for a moment. "My God," he says quietly, taking a long, slow drink. I close my eyes. I hate that he can read me like a book. I hate that after all this time he does know me so well.

"So," he starts with renewed energy. "The father must be nowhere to be found, or he would be back to take care of his little sister, the mother of his child." He pauses. "I say, Lyd, doesn't it make you sick?"

I can't take it any longer. "The baby died!" I hiss, "It's gone. I don't need your help or your…your offers to keep us respectable. I don't need you!"

He blinks, as if it had never occurred to him that he might not somehow fit into this equation. But then he tilts his head and gives me a pitying look. "There now. So the great mystery is solved. The baby has come, and the baby has died. But you're wrong about one thing, you do need me." He raises a brow and waves the letter again. "I still have proof of the baby's existence."

The air goes out of me. "You wouldn't," I whisper.

"Why, Lydia, do you need to sit down?" Trembling, I don't refuse his hand as he gently guides me back into my chair.

"You're delusional if you think you can blackmail your way into my family's money."

His brow darkens. "And you're delusional if you still think this is just about money."

I gloss over his meaning; Cyrus's feelings for me—or what he thinks he feels—are the least of my worries right now. "My family will deny the story if you decide to print it. We'll say the letter was a forgery."

He gives me another pitying smile, as if it pains him that I could actually be so naive. "Who would believe your family's word over mine? Everyone knows what went on between your brother and sister, and it doesn't take a great leap of the imagination to accept that there could have been a child. And me, I'm the son of a respected businessman, never mind one that is a bit down on his luck at the moment. Christ, I could say that you were a witch, practicing that same black art that got your ancestors hanged, and people would believe me over you."

How does he know about my ancestry? And why would he say such an awful thing? "Where did you hear that?" I ask in a choked whisper.

He gives a little shrug, but his gaze is piercing. "People say lots of things. Surely you are more than used to rumors. Of course in your family's case, the rumors often seem to hold more than a shade of truth."

Something deep inside me stirs. My heart beats fast and erratic, and it's hard to breathe. I push it back down, the slumbering thing that wants to awaken, wants to make itself known. Cyrus doesn't know what he's talking about, he's just trying to scare me. Nevertheless, my gaze flickers over to the book wrapped in brown paper on the table.

"I want you to leave, right now."

But Cyrus doesn't make any move, doesn't even give any indication of having heard me. He slants me a sidelong glance. "Say, did you know that I saw Tom Bishop recently? He still walks with a limp."

If I didn't know any better, I would say there was a hint of admiration in his tone. He drains another glass of port. "Do you remember that day? Tom does. In fact, lots of people do. It's funny the way people remember things like that, things that happened long ago but leave a stamp on the mind. Tell me, Lydia, should I be afraid of you too?"

My throat is so dry that I can hardly speak, and my words come out hoarse and choked. "What do you want?"

Coming around the chair, he crouches down in front of me, cupping my face with those fingers I once thought so elegant. I shrink back but he just presses his fingertips firmer against my cheeks. "Why, what I've always wanted, Lyd. Money. Fine things. You. That's all."

"And if I can't...?"

"A clever girl like you? I find it hard to believe you couldn't somehow get dear old Father to open his coffers for his favorite daughter, especially on the occasion of her wedding. But if you can't, then of course every newspaper in Boston, in New England, will have the story. Your sister will be ruined, and your poor mother will die of the shame. Is that really what you want?"

His finger is soft and gentle on my cheek, but it might as well be a reptilian claw. Why won't he just leave me—my family—alone? What do I have to do to make Catherine's mess disappear? It's not fair that Mother suffer because of Catherine's reckless behavior, and because Cyrus has a black, greedy heart. I squeeze my eyes shut. I just want it to end.

My body vibrates with fury, and pressure builds within me, as if a swarm of angry bees has been roused, and are looking for an escape.

"Lydia?" Cyrus's voice is far away.

My heart tears at its strings, rebelling against the confines of my ribs. Sweat slicks my palms and my ears burn. *It's not fair. It isn't right. Just leave! Go away and leave me alone!*

Cyrus must see something in my face because his hand falters, and he rocks back uncertainly on his heels.

I jerk away from his touch, and he pulls his hand back the rest of the way. He stares at me with a mixture of concern and bewilderment. "Lydia, what's happening? Are you all right?" I hardly know what I'm doing as my palm rises automatically out in front of me.

The pressure inside of me reaches its peak and I feel as if I'm being ripped opened and emptied out. The wind goes out of me, and with it, a bolt of something like invisible lightning. Cyrus gives a strangled yelp, and suddenly he's flying backward, slamming into the door with a great crack, as if a giant had lifted him up and carelessly tossed him.

I slump back into my chair, breathless and as fatigued as if I had just climbed a mountain. I close my eyes and when I open them again, he's still sitting dazed on the floor, his waistcoat flown open and hair disarranged. He blinks.

I'm trembling all over, from my hands to my knees, the pressure that felt like it was going to completely consume me, slowly evaporating.

Cyrus and I lock eyes, and I don't know who is more terrified of what just occurred. He braces his hand on the door behind him and slowly clambers to his feet. I can see his legs shaking from across the room.

"Lydia." His voice comes out in a crack, and he opens and closes his mouth several times. "You—"

But he doesn't have a chance to finish. He's just moved away from the door, a hand outstretched toward me as if looking for support, when suddenly the door swings open and Aunt Phillips comes in with Blake behind her, carrying a tray of tea.

She stops short, quickly taking in Cyrus's disheveled appearance and my white face. She raises a brow at me, her eyes warm with an amused question. If I weren't so terrified of what just happened, I would feel sick at her assumption.

"I'm sure I didn't mean to interrupt anything!" she says with twinkling eyes. "I'll come back later."

Cyrus, who has buttoned up his waistcoat and is making a valiant effort of composure, forces a shaky smile at Aunt Phillips. His urbane charm naturally takes over, and I can't but help being a little in awe, even grateful, that he's able to act as if nothing just happened.

"You'll do no such thing, Mrs. Phillips," Cyrus says, forcing a light smile as he reaches for his coat. "I was just leaving." Only I notice the slight tremor in his voice.

I sit heavily back in the chair, pressing my fingers against my eyelids until I see stars. My head is light and fuzzy, the alcohol dulling the edges of my senses. Maybe this is all just a bad dream. Maybe Cyrus didn't just go flying like a rag doll through the air. I've never been drunk before, is this what happens? But it's not a dream, and when I open my eyes again he's still standing there.

"Oh, and Lydia?" He turns from the doorway. I hold my breath, afraid that he'll divulge to Aunt Phillips what just happened. He pauses, as if weighing his words, trying to decide how much to say. But when he continues, his voice is light, as if nothing unusual had occurred. "I won't rush you into making a decision. Take a few days to think it over. This doesn't change anything, and I'm not going anywhere."

✿ *29* ✿

AUNT PHILLIPS HOBBLES in to breakfast the next morning, and before she's even in her seat she says, "Now I know better than to pry into the affairs of young folks, but if you want some advice, I'll tell you one thing—you'd do well to accept that young man."

"Yes, Aunt," I say mechanically, standing to help her push in her chair.

I can barely keep my eyes open. After the incident with Cyrus it was all I could do to lie in bed and try to calm my racing heart. When I did finally drift off to sleep, I dreamed that wolves were chasing me, wolves with neat white teeth that gleamed when they smiled, and dark eyes that saw right down into the deepest recesses of my soul. They pursued me through the narrow streets of Boston, never running, always just a slow, deliberate stalking until I was cornered and impotent to repel them.

I try to tell myself that I don't care, that Cyrus can't hurt me. I won't be cowed into doing what he wants. And as for his accusations, in the light of day I see how ludicrous they are. He knows my weaknesses, he knows just the right things to say to make me question myself. It was just another way for him to try to unnerve me. Of course it's not true, it can't be. But the little voice in my head says, *There's something different about you. You know what happened the other day wasn't normal. Didn't Mother tell you as much when you were younger?* I think of the book that I bought from Mr. Brown, tucked under the dresses in my trunk that I haven't dared to look at yet. Does it hold the answer to my questions? I would almost rather not know.

Aunt Phillips prattles on. "The family may be a bit down in the coffers, so to speak, but he comes with a good name, and after, well…everything—" she politely clears her throat "—you really can't expect to do much better. Besides," she says as she helps herself to a heaping plop of eggs and poached ham, "he's young and not too hard on the eyes, eh?"

I pick at my own food, doing my best to look like I'm listening to her, that I'm taking her seriously. I wish I could tell her that the young man in question is a weasel, a blackmailing scoundrel. I wish I could tell her that there's a man a thousand times better, handsomer, kinder, back in New Oldbury.

She's going on about some suitor she had back when she was a young woman, who had eyes "the color of morning dew and a smile that would melt the halo right off an angel," when Blake comes in bearing a tray with two letters on it.

My heart leaps. Mr. Barrett's written back. He understands why I went away, that it wasn't my choice and had nothing to do with him. But before I can reach for it, Aunt Phillips is plucking the letters from the tray and tearing one open.

"I wondered when that wicked husband of mine would write," she says, putting on her spectacles.

Just as fast my heart sinks. "And the other letter?"

She's in her own world, smiling to herself as she reads.

"Aunt Phillips," I say, trying to keep the exasperation from my voice, "who's the other letter from? Is it possibly for me?"

She looks surprised, but picks it up and squints at the envelope. "It's from Catherine, though it's addressed to me. Shall I read it?"

Of course it is. I give a half-hearted shrug as she starts reading. I wrote Mr. Barrett again last night. It took hours of crumpling up false starts and crossing out tear-stained passages before I squared my shoulders, took a deep breath and poured out six double-sided pages of everything that I've been holding inside me since the day I met him. Propriety and convention be damned. Before I could even look over what I wrote, I sprinkled the ink dry, folded up the envelope and in a moment of dramatic flourish, sealed it with wax. Now all I can do is wait.

"Wait, what did you say?" I sit up in my chair.

Aunt Phillips stops, and looks up from the letter. "Hmm?"

"You just said something about a Mr. Barrett, can you go back and reread that bit?"

Aunt Phillips furrows her brows, scanning back over the last few lines. "'Father's business partner, Mr. Barrett, has surprised us all by announcing his engagement to a young lady of the town. Of course we are all very glad for him, but Father is concerned that the wedding preparations and subsequent trip abroad will impact the upcoming construction of the new mill.'"

I swallow. "Can you... That is, does it say the name of the lady?"

"Let's see here... Abigail Tidewell." She looks up when I take in a sharp breath. "Do you know her?"

"Just in passing," I say faintly.

"Mr. Barrett," muses Aunt Phillips, leaning back in her chair. "The name is familiar. Though of course it would be if he's your father's business partner. Well, there will be a wedding in New Oldbury then. That must be something to look forward to, eh, my dear?"

My lips are numb but I think I agree, my voice faraway.

After sword fights and duels, succumbing to a broken heart is the most common way to die in all the novels. Ladies in towers languish and slip away from the affliction after refusing to marry their father's choice of suitors. Roguish highwaymen, taken by surprise for their feelings toward their virginal marks, find themselves stricken and helpless to go on without the pale face in the carriage that so captivated them. I always thought it terribly romantic, even though it's only a literary device and not an actual phenomenon.

But in this moment I know, I know it's real. My heart twists, a dull, tingling pain that pulses through my body leaving me choked for breath. It feels like the moment when I realized Emeline wasn't going to open her eyes again. It feels like death.

Aunt Phillips is still prattling on, blissfully unaware of the devastation she's just wrought. "Oh dear, and it seems your mother has come down with something. Nothing serious, Catherine assures us, but the doctor came and ordered that she stay in bed until she can get her strength back up, the poor thing."

I hardly hear her.

The days drag on, and with them comes the raw chill of winter that settles in my bones. Aunt Phillips continues to improve, though I don't think she ever really needed someone to help her so much as she was just lonely. I read to her in the evenings—always from the gazettes, never books as she doesn't have the patience for them—and she takes calls in the afternoon, staying abreast of every word of gossip that circulates Boston.

I exist in a liminal state of nothingness; New Oldbury is where Mr. Barrett is, and I don't think I could bear to be back so close to him, knowing that there is no future for us. If I must live without him than I would rather it be somewhere that I'm not constantly reminded of what might have been. And yet, in Boston I walk with my shoulders hunched forward, my eyes constantly darting about, afraid that Cyrus might spring out from the least likely places, demanding my answer or harassing me with fresh accusations.

My thoughts often turn to Emeline and her grave. Does anyone go to keep it cleared of weeds and place a flower there? Or is the stone buried in snow now, just another nameless, jutting marker in a field of forgotten souls? Does Emeline roam Willow Hall, looking for me only to find me gone? Oh, Emeline, I feel as restless and homeless as you must.

I'm sitting in the parlor, losing myself in *Ivanhoe* as the early December evening draws close around the city. I know that I'm supposed to want the lady Rowena to win Wilfred of Ivanhoe's heart, but I can't help but feel for Rebecca, who heals and cares for him after he's injured in the joust. As promised, I returned to buy the second volume from Mr. Brown, at once desperate to know what happens to Rebecca when she's put on trial for witchcraft, but also afraid to find out lest Ivanhoe isn't in time to save her from being put to the stake.

Putting down the book, I gaze out the window at the dusky winter street below. The witchcraft trial in the story draws my mind to that other book. I've been putting off opening it, hoping that if I ignore it long enough it might simply melt away into the shawl I wrapped around it. But I bought it for a reason, and I can either keep fretting about it, or face my fears. So I fetch it from my trunk and, taking a deep breath and closing my eyes, open it on my lap.

I read a few pages and put it down, half-relieved, half-disappointed. I don't know what I was expecting to find inside the covers, but it's not this. Instead of a history of witchcraft in New England, names of Salem families, or even accounts of the infamous trials, it's a collection of stories gathered from all corners of New England having to do with magic. The first story is the tale of a girl who takes spectral trips in the body of a yellow bird, and is one day captured by a farmer who makes her his wife. In return for her hand in marriage, the farmer must allow her to return to her bird form every full moon. It's fanciful, the kind of fairy story I would have told to Emeline years ago. Flipping ahead I see that another is about an old woman who lives in the woods and lures children to her cottage. Nothing good happens to the children. I flip ahead. My fingers stop as a page goes by, and I quickly thumb back to it.

There's an illustration, one of many sprinkled throughout the book. This one shows a young woman with a tangle of dark hair flying about her head. Her hands are outstretched in front of her, little lines of movement hastily drawn in emanating from them, as a man and woman cower in the corner. The man is, rather futilely, holding up a cross, and the woman buries her head on the man's shoulder in terror. But it's the young woman's hand that I can't tear my gaze from. Outstretched, vibrating, sending invisible power through the air. *Just like with Tommy Bishop. Just like with Cyrus.* There's a caption beneath it, but I don't read it.

I slam the cover shut, as if hoping to keep all the stories and pictures therein contained to the page, and not let them spill out into reality. Quickly, I slip the book under the cushion of the window seat and take up *Ivanhoe,* desperate to bury the image of the girl with outstretched hands with tamer stories of knights and chivalry.

But I'm soon jolted from my world of maidens in distress by a shrill laugh cutting the air. Aunt Phillips has a caller, one of the ladies from the Fragment Society, a fashionable group that makes and distributes clothes to the city's poor. If they distribute half as much clothing as they do gossip, then there shouldn't be a bare back in all of Boston. I've successfully ignored them for two hours, but now the woman is rising to leave.

"Well, I really must be going now. It looks like snow and I don't trust Jack once the streets turn slippery."

Aunt Phillips clasps her friend's hand from her seat. She has a habit of taking a turn for the worse whenever she has company, and takes to her chair as if she were an invalid so that her guests must kneel beside her to talk. "Oh, that's too bad," she says. "We're having company for dinner and it would have been *so* nice if you were able to join us."

I put down my book and wait for her friend to leave. After much cheek kissing and hollow promises of future engagements, we're finally alone together.

"I didn't know anyone else was coming over." I'm only just keeping my head above water with Aunt Phillips, and I don't know if I can play along with dinner guests now too. I'm so tired, and the book of magic stories has my head flying in a hundred different directions at once.

"Hmm? Oh, Mr. Thompson said you wanted to see him, so I invited him over for dinner first before you young people talk."

My book slips from my hand. "You…you invited Cyrus?"

"Yes, won't that be nice?" She glances over as if noticing me for the first time since speaking. "Is that what you're going to wear?"

Dazed, I look down at my striped cream dress. It's the one I wore the day I walked home with Mr. Barrett, the one that his body pressed against as he drew me close to him at the fork in the road. I've worn it for almost a week straight now.

The hem is stained brown from dragging through the muddy street on my walks, the puffed sleeves limp. "Yes, why?"

Aunt Phillips sighs and beckons me to her, pressing her lips together as if she has to deliver some distasteful news. "Sit down, my dear. I know your parents have taken a…lax approach when it comes to your upbringing, but you're in my home now and I'm determined to do everything I can to ensure that you have a bright future. Cyrus Thompson can give you that future. If you're worried that he's not going about it in the proper way by informing your parents, don't worry, I've already written to your father to let him know. Now, go upstairs, change into something decent and try to shake off whatever cloud you've been living in for the past few weeks." She pauses. "And why hasn't Mr. Thompson been back for so long? Did you two have a falling-out?"

I grumble something about having a disagreement, which I suppose is only half a lie.

She gives a dismissive wave of her hand. "Well, whatever it is, find a way to settle it. It won't do to let some silly little thing come between you two."

Yes, because blackmail is such a silly little detail.

Dinner is a blur of excruciatingly polite conversation from Cyrus, excited titters from Aunt Phillips and a steady flow of wine poured out for both of them by Blake. If I thought that what happened the other week in Aunt Phillips's parlor would deter him, I'm sorely mistaken. Cyrus acts as if nothing out of the ordinary took place at our last meeting. In fact, he is extra solicitous tonight, and more than once I catch him gazing at me as if I were a particularly fine pair of boots or aged bottle of Madeira—or whatever it is that someone like Cyrus covets—which he can't wait to get his hands on. I pick at my food in gloomy silence as Aunt Phillips and Cyrus discuss the establishment of the new Mercantile Library Association, to which Cyrus is desperate to gain membership. There's so many of these societies and associations cropping up in Boston every day that I can't keep them all straight.

"It would open up so many doors, and the connections would be invaluable for business," Cyrus says, before pausing. "Lydia." He puts his glass down and turns to me. "You're awfully quiet tonight. How are you finding Boston since your return?"

I glare at him.

"You'll have to excuse her," Aunt Phillips hurries to explain. "She's been a bit under the weather lately."

Cyrus gives a little wave. "That's quite all right. You know," he says around a mouthful of roast lamb, "Lydia and I were just talking the other week about the funny things that people remember after a long time. About Tom Bishop, isn't that right, Lydia?"

My fork wavers in my hand as I silently plead with him to stop, but he only winks at me, his eyes alive with delight.

He has Aunt Phillip's full attention. "Bishop..." She tilts her head in thought. "Wasn't that the boy down the street? You got into some sort of fight with him?"

"Cyrus, please—"

"That's right," Cyrus, says, beaming. "You have a sharp memory, Mrs. Phillips."

Aunt Phillips colors like a schoolgirl, tutting at his compliment.

"Oh yes, Lydia has quite a talent, it seems." He puts down his glass and furrows his brow. "I'm not sure I even know how to explain it, come to think of it. Something she does with her eyes, and her hands if I remember correctly." He gives a little laugh. "I even got to see something of a demonstration of it the other—"

"Cyrus!" My face is on fire. "Aunt Phillips doesn't want to hear about that," I choke out.

Aunt Phillips opens her mouth to protest, but Cyrus flashes a charming smile and says, "Well, I certainly don't want to bore your gracious aunt. Perhaps it's best left for another time."

I look down at my knuckles, white and shaking, and realize that I had been gripping the edge of the table. I let go now, twining my hands together in my lap.

"It does make me think though," Cyrus says, "about the things that happen when we're children. I can't for the life of me think what made me remember this, but I woke up this morning with a memory as fresh in my mind as if it happened yesterday. Would you like to hear it?"

"No," I say, draining the rest of my wine.

Aunt Phillips flushes scarlet. "Oh, I'm sure she doesn't mean that. In any case, I would love to hear it, Mr. Thompson."

"Mrs. Phillips," Cyrus says with an ingratiating smile, "you're too kind to indulge me." He flickers a self-satisfied glance in my direction.

He leans his elbows on the table, settling in like he's about to grace us all with gospel. "Well," he says, "when I was little, say nine or so, a ship from Macao put in at the docks. I was at the tavern on an errand for my father when some of the crew came in on their leave. I still remember those men, the leathery brown of their dark skin, the mellow scent of vanilla under the musk of ship-living. There was one man in particular who caught my young imagination. He couldn't have been anything more than a lieutenant, yet he wore a big gold earring, and when he ordered ale none of the other men would lift their glasses until he drank. And do you know what the best thing about him was? On his shoulder, he had the cleverest little monkey in a gold collar and chain. It cracked walnuts for him and did a little jig on the bar when the man whistled a tune. I'd never seen anything like it before and I knew right then that I had to have that monkey."

Cyrus pauses to take a dramatically long draft from his glass and dab at his lips with his napkin. I roll my eyes and he clears his throat.

"Well, I walked right up to the man and told him I wanted to buy his pet. I had a little money from my father that was meant for new shoes, and I showed him the coins in my hand. The man took a long slow drink, his black eyes watching me from over the rim of his tankard. When it was drained, he put it down and wiped his mouth. 'Odysseus isn't for sale, my little fellow. Save your coins for sweets and trifles.' And just like that, he took his monkey and left, the other sailors falling into line behind him, laughing at me over their shoulders."

Aunt Phillips looks puzzled but does her best to act like this is the most interesting story in the world. "A monkey!" she exclaims. "I can't imagine. What a curious thing to keep as a pet."

"Ah, but you see, Mrs. Phillips, it wasn't really the monkey I wanted. The creature probably had a whole host of diseases. No, it was the idea of possessing something that rare, something no one else had."

I'm pushing a pea around on my plate, trying to make it follow the snaking path of the ivy motif, but when Cyrus says this, I put my fork down and slowly meet his gaze. His piercing dark eyes bore into me, and an icy shiver grips me by the spine.

"Well," says Aunt Phillips, "did you ever get one?"

"You know, I never did. I heard that the ship went down a few months later under British guns." He looks up, flashing his neat, white teeth at me like the wolves in my dream.

"If the man had only sold it to me, the poor creature would have lived."

★ ★ ★

After the plates have been cleared away and Cyrus has exhausted the last of the wine, Aunt Phillips suggests that he and I retire to the parlor where we'll be more comfortable. All sense of correctness seems to have been abandoned in her desperate suit to get me engaged.

As soon as the door clicks behind her Cyrus gestures to a chair. I stay standing.

When he speaks, he doesn't meet my eye. "I was rather hoping it would be you who wrote to invite me over, not your aunt. A fellow doesn't like to always feel as if he's intruding in a lady's parlor, you know."

"And yet that's exactly what you're doing."

"Yes, well." He tugs at his cravat and looks like he wants to say something else, but just goes to the sideboard and pours himself a drink. I don't know how he can drink so much and still stand upright.

He downs the contents in one long gulp then wipes his mouth on the back of his sleeve. "Are you sure you won't sit down?"

When I don't make any move to sit, he takes a few steps toward me, then stops in his tracks a few feet away as if thinking better of it. "Well, Lyd, have you thought about it?" He is doggedly persistent, I will give him that.

For all his menacing accusations and threats the last time, he sounds like an earnest young suitor now, and when his eyes finally meet and hold mine, they're wide and unsure.

I stand up as tall as I can, determined not to be fooled by his act. "I'm not a trick monkey, something to be possessed."

"Of course you're not, I never meant to imply you were," he says quickly, taking my hand in his. It's damp, and tightens around mine as if he's afraid I might let go. "It's only that you are such a rare flower—I don't think you even understand yourself just how rare—and it saddens me to see you deny your true potential. How many other men do you think would say that after what happened the other day?" He's launching into his case again, this time rapidly telling me just how much I stand to gain by marrying him. "I would do anything for you, Lydia. I'd fight a duel for you if it came down to it. I'd protect you from all the gossip of Boston, setting you up in a fine house, making you the envy of all those who drove you out. You'll not want for anything."

"Because you'll be living off my father's money," I say sharply, pulling my hand back. "Money that you're extorting from me."

He looks hurt. "Only at first," he says softly. "I've a good mind for investing, and after the first year or so I'll have the business up and running again and bringing in all sorts of capital."

I stare at the repeating geometric pattern of the carpet, unable to focus my eyes. What is Mr. Barrett doing right now? Is he escorting Abby Tidewell to the tailor to have her measurements taken for her wedding dress? Is he tilting her chin up to him so that he can steal a kiss before he returns her back home to her mother? His silence in response to my letters all makes so much sickening sense now.

And what of my own mother? Catherine's letter mentioned that she was sick, but she said it wasn't anything serious. Even so, could Mother handle the shock of seeing Catherine's shameful secret in black and white in the papers?

Cyrus must read the battle going on in my face, because he moves closer to me, slipping his arms around my waist. "Say yes," he murmurs down into my hair, pulling me close. "We'll be so happy together."

My body goes rigid, but I don't pull away. "I'll marry you," I whisper. "But we'll never be happy."

❧ *30* ❧

THERE ARE ANY number of things I should be feeling that night as I slowly undress and get ready for bed. But as I slide between the sheets and blow out the lamp, I'm filled only with numb acceptance. It washes over me like a frigid wave, leaving me cold and cleansed. I won't have to worry about Mother ever finding out about what went on between Catherine and Charles, about the child that now rests at the bottom of the pond. I won't have to worry about whatever it is that's inside of me bubbling out because Cyrus has already seen it, and he simply doesn't care. If I give him what he wants, maybe he won't use it against me later. I won't have to worry about scandals or rumors or anything that could hurt Father's business ever again. Catherine and I won't have reason to be enemies; we won't even have reason to live in the same town for that matter. It's for the best. The only thing that gives me pause is Emeline. She will walk the woods of Willow Hall for eternity because I am too cowardly to come back and find a way to set her free.

But no matter how much sense my decision makes, a painful

tug of my heart drags my mind in the other direction. I idly trace a path with my fingers down my collarbone, between my breasts and to my navel, then up again. What would it have been like to lie naked beside John Barrett as his wife? What would it have been like to share not just my body, but my soul, my life with him? My fingers skitter lower. I imagine him embracing me, pulling my body tight against his, a refuge of love and passion. His mouth hot and urgent as it finds mine as my body rises to meet him. I can almost smell him, that clean, woodsy scent with the underlying musk of male sweat.

I stop my hand. Nothing good can come of thinking like this. What if Catherine and Cyrus are right, and there is something wrong with me, something that makes me different? Would Mr. Barrett have really wanted me, knowing that? Cyrus was right about one thing when he asked how many other men would be willing to accept me as I am. Maybe it's better this way. From now on I must cut free my silly hopes and impossible dreams. I must be an empty vessel. Even if I shatter completely, at least I will have nothing to lose. At least my family will be protected.

A letter arrives the next day from Catherine. I'm sitting, struggling to keep my eyes open after a night spent lying awake when Blake comes in with that silver tray I've learned to hate. This time the letter is for me. I sit up straighter, my eyes widening as I quickly take in the few hastily written lines. Mother has taken a turn for the worse, and I must come, right away. Apparently the illness is far graver than Catherine let on, and the doctor thinks Mother might not have much time.

Aunt Phillips hovers in the door, propped up on her crutch, worrying at her pearl necklace as she watches me throw things into my trunk. "But what about Mr. Thompson? He told me the good news before he left last night...you can't just up and leave now! What will I tell him?"

I press my fingers against my eyelids. I don't want to think about what's waiting for me at home, but if the worst happens and Mother is gone and Mr. Barrett is married, I'll be back here again soon.

"Tell him whatever you want," I say, slamming down the lid of my half-filled trunk. "He's waited this long, another few weeks won't kill him."

If Boston had been indifferent to my return, then Willow Hall has been waiting for me, holding its breath every moment that I was gone. My heart sinks as I step out of the carriage. The house glares at me accusingly from behind tight shutters and a mantle of snow. *Look what happens when you leave. You thought you could run away, that you could abandon your sorrows here, but there is no escaping the sorrow that I hold in my walls.*

I shut my ears against the house's taunts and race inside, nearly slipping on the ice, my heart in my throat. What if I'm too late?

Ada intercepts me in the hall. Before I can say anything, she throws her skinny arms around me, squeezing like her life depended on it. "Oh, thank goodness you've come, miss. You're in time, but she's been asking for you."

The air comes out of me in a whoosh of relief, and my knees sag under me. "Oh, thank God. What did the doctor say?"

Ada shakes her head and looks away, but her fingers fidget nervously at her cuffs. "It's a fever, and he's afraid it will move to her brain."

I slump against the wall. A fever is never something to be taken lightly, especially for someone who is already so diminished and frail. A few summers ago a fever swept over Boston, taking with it dozens of lives of elderly people and children. Our neighbor alone lost her three little boys.

"Can I do anything for you, miss?"

Ada looks at me expectantly, her small, freckled face etched with concern, and I find myself pulling her back into my embrace. "I don't know what we ever did to deserve you, Ada. Thank you, for everything."

She flushes and mumbles something, but I catch the fleeting smile as she runs off to the kitchen to make tea.

I find Father in his study, stacks of papers and ledgers towering above him, threatening to topple over and bury him completely. He's pale, his eyes dull and filmy. I have to knock on the doorframe three times before he looks up. "Oh, Lydia. You're back," he says, as if I had just stepped out for a walk and not gone to Boston for three weeks.

"Yes, Father."

He gives a heavy sigh, chin in hand. "All these papers, all these reports and contracts and meaningless numbers. How will I go on? How will I do it without my Martha?"

I've never seen my father like this, so helpless and drained. I put my frozen hand over his and squeeze. "I know, Father. It's all right. She'll be all right." But the truth is I don't know that she'll be all right, and I have to brace myself for what I'll find when I go upstairs.

"All these papers and numbers," he repeats listlessly, already lost in his own thoughts again.

Catherine's voice floats down the hall. "Ada, I asked about that broth over an hour ago, don't tell me it's still not ready. And have you checked the windows in Mother's rooms? They were letting in a draft before. I want them tight as a ship." I wince at the way she orders Ada around when Ada is already doing so much to help.

When she passes by the open door she stops and frowns at me. "Oh, you're here."

"You told me to come."

Her arms are full of stained linen, her eyes shadowed and bloodshot. "The doctor just left. Mother is resting now."

I nod, mute. What is there to say? Catherine gives me a curt nod in return and then disappears down the hall, already an expert in her new role as capable daughter and nurse.

I force my tired legs to take the stairs two at a time. When I get to the top of the landing, I stop, hand gripping the railing for support. Her door is closed, and maybe if I leave it closed it will keep all the bad things away, keep her safe. But whatever has my mother in its clutches is already here, and no amount of childish superstition will protect her. With a deep breath and a silent prayer, I slowly open the door and slip inside.

The embers of a dying fire cast the room in dim light, and before I go to her—or perhaps because I wish to postpone it just a little longer—I slowly take up the poker and cajole the lazy flames until they crackle and dance. I stare at the flickering pattern, mesmerized as my face prickles with heat. When my eyes start to water I finally turn away.

The bed swallows her up, she's so shrunken and fragile. When I take her hand in mine I can feel each bone, and the light, fluttery pulse of her heart. She looks like a paper doll, crumpled and used up.

For all that I tried to protect her, save her, it's been for nothing. First it was the rumors that shook her faith in her family, then it was Emeline's death that cracked her heart open. When I tried to take my own life it shattered the tender filaments that remained. Mother has been in a long, slow decline since then. It's all my fault. I should have tried harder.

"Lydia," she says, her voice so breathy and faint that I think I must have imagined it. "You came."

A chair is already by the bed, draped in a quilt, probably used by Catherine or Father as they kept vigil over the last few days. I lower myself down, still in my heavy wool traveling cloak. "Of course I did, as soon as I heard. Is…is there anything you need?"

She closes her eyes and gives an almost imperceptible shake of her head. "Ada and Catherine are taking good care of me."

There's something about a sickroom, a stillness, an absence of time, as if all the forces of nature bow their heads and hold their breath. No movement, no sound, the problems and troubles of the world all impossibly far away. Just a sick woman, fragile as a leaf, clinging to life.

"Oh, Mother," I say, unable to keep the sob in my throat from bubbling up. "I'm so sorry. I haven't been a good daughter. I've been a child, fighting with Catherine and spending too much time in my books instead of helping you around the house. If…if you… I'll never forgive myself," I blubber. Even now I can't help acting like a child, forcing my poor sick mother to comfort me when she should be resting.

"Lydia, listen to me." The weight of her voice slows my tears. "I'm the one who is sorry."

"Mother, you're perfect. You have nothing to be sorry for."

She's struggling to sit up, grasping at my arm to brace herself. Gently, I remove her hand and try to make her lie back down. Despite her frantic movements and the urgency of her words, her dark eyes are sharp and lucid. "I have to tell you something."

I hastily wipe away the last of my tears. "Please, try to rest. You can tell me as many things as you want later, once you're better, but now you need to rest."

"There won't be a later. I need to tell you now."

My heart wrenches, but she looks so desperate that I have no choice but to nod and let her speak.

Relief settles over her waxy features and she closes her eyes. Her dry tongue flickers over her lips in a vain attempt to wet them. I reach for the pitcher of water beside the bed and she takes a grateful sip before she goes on.

"I let you go through life, never knowing what you really are. I thought I could make it go away, that if you didn't know, maybe it would just disappear, and that by doing so I would protect you from the world. But instead I'm afraid it only caused you pain and confusion. I thought we could come here…" She lifts her hand and gives a weak wave around the room. "That this place could be a new start for all of us. But instead…"

I suck in my breath. The slumbering thing inside of me stirs again, Cyrus's and Catherine's words echo in my head. I'm afraid that I know what she's going to say even before she says it. My fingers curl around the arms of the chair.

"Instead it seems to have awoken it. It runs in the women of our family—my family. Even then, only some of us seem to carry it. My mother was one. I know the signs. I suspected it when you were very little, but it wasn't until that day that I knew for sure."

I don't need to ask her what day she's talking about.

The room spins. I take a deep, trembling breath and fight the growing wave of nausea in my stomach. My ears are ringing, Mother's words faraway.

"When Catherine was born I wondered if she would have it, but it didn't come down through her. It's been hard for her, I think. She knew that you were different and she wanted to be like you." She gives a wistful sigh. "I hope you two will find a way to be friends in the future."

I don't say anything because I don't want to crush Mother's hopes on that front. I swallow. "Does that mean that you are?"

She gives a little shake of her head. "It didn't come down

to me. Sometimes I wish it had so that I could have better guided you."

"And…Emeline?"

Mother closes her eyes, her lids as translucent and papery as the skin of an onion. Her answer comes out on the back of her breath. "Yes."

I should be as shocked at this revelation as I was at my own, but Emeline was always special, I knew that. The aching loss of her death folds itself around me all over again. Here is a journey we should have taken together, learning what we were, united in our secret. Instead I must feel my way forward in the dark with neither my mother nor my dearest sister.

"That night when the doors slammed…that was the first time I realized she might carry it too. You would have been too young to remember, but you used to do similar things when you were little. Whenever you got angry I had to whisk you away somewhere just in case something happened. Windows would fly open, candles would gutter and go out. One time a plate even flew up into the air."

"I…I don't remember any of that," I say in amazement. "But why only when I'm angry?" Surely I'm not such a dark creature as that? Is there nothing in me but anger and destruction?

"No, not only when you were angry. There were other times too, though not as often. Little things, like when your father brought home that cat. You were so happy, dancing about like a pixie child. When I looked at the ground, little flowers had sprung up in your wake. You didn't notice, and I daresay no one else did either. Perhaps it was those quieter moments that were more often overlooked." She reaches for my hand. "There is not one drop of evil in you, Lydia. Please do not think that."

Tears prick my eyes, and before I can blink them back they're streaming down my face, hot and fast. I bury my head in the blankets over my mother's frail body, sobbing like a little child. I don't want this, I don't want to be the thing that apparently I am, that I've always been. I can't even say the word. How am I supposed to go through life knowing this?

"You can't just tell me this and then leave me! What if other people find out? What will happen to me?" I think of the dour portrait of Mary Hale Preston downstairs, her shrewd eyes boring into me. Warning me. And then her visit to tell me as much. The last public hanging on Boston Common was only a couple of years ago, and though it was on a charge of larceny, I can't help but imagining myself as the swinging corpse.

"You're strong, Lydia. And is it any wonder? I haven't been any kind of mother to you. You don't need me. You've been strong this whole time."

But she doesn't know that I'm not strong. She doesn't know that I'm empty and weak, that I've taken the easy way out of our problems by giving Cyrus what he wants.

She lets me exhaust my tears against her chest, gently stroking my head. "There's something I want you to have." She nods toward the chest at the end of the bed. "In there, under the quilt. There should be a book."

My heart jumps. The book that Mary Preston told me about, the one that supposedly holds all the answers to my questions. The book that may well be the key to giving Emeline the peace she so badly needs. Perhaps I should be mad that Mother has kept it from me this long, but how can I be angry at her when all she wanted for me was the best?

I slowly scrape back the chair and make my way to the chest. The faint scent of dried lavender wafts up from the quilt as I lift it with trembling hands, and sure enough, underneath is a worn, leather-bound book. It fits snugly in the palm of my hand, the warm, mellowed cover speaking to years of use.

I close the chest and place the book in Mother's hands. A

wisp of a smile plays at the corner of her lips as she lovingly opens the little volume.

"What is it?"

She gingerly turns a page and I catch a glimpse of a black-and-white engraving. The image is crudely drawn, but the subject is unmistakable. A woman in Puritan dress hovers above a kitchen floor, a cat watching her from the corner. The margins are crawling with handwritten notes and marginalia in several different hands, no doubt the additions of generations of women in my family. The inscription under the engraving proclaims *VVITCH*.

She closes the cover but the word burns itself inside my eyelids and, no matter how hard I try to push it away, it taunts me, mocks me. *Didn't I always know, even that day with the Bishop boy? Didn't I know that I wasn't normal? How could I not?*

The darkness that has lurked at the edge of my mind since we came here, the dreams that have plagued me. Visits from Emeline, Moses and all the other spirits that sought me out. The way my herbs sprang up under my fingertips, growing and growing in their uncanny way. My scream that caused the trees to bend in the wind, the placid water in the pond to churn and swell. Even sending Cyrus flying back through the air. This place has brought to the surface what I've always had inside of me.

"This belonged to your great-great-grandmother, Mehitable Hale, Mary Preston's mother." She closes the book and gives it back to me. "You don't have to read it now, but someday. Someday soon. It will help explain everything that I can't."

"Mother, I—"

But before I can tell her that I would rather not know, a coughing fit seizes her. When it passes she's red and wheezing, a yellowish glaze settling over her eyes.

"Should I send for Father and Catherine?"

Her eyes close and her lips curl into that small wisp of a smile again. "No, not yet. I just need to rest. I promise."

The strange little book and what it means for me is quickly forgotten as I watch for the rise and fall of her chest, and I only exhale when I see she's done the same. When her breaths become slow and steady the knot in my stomach loosens a little.

Quietly, I gather up the book, brush my mother's feverish temple with a kiss and leave her to rest.

❧ *31* ❧

ADA BRINGS ME dinner in the parlor, but the broiled chicken and green beans grow cold as I stare at my hands in my lap. My nails are bitten and ragged, my knuckles still chapped from the journey. Is it possible that some latent power lies within these hands? If it were true, couldn't I run them over Mother's body, heal it and force her spirit to stay? Do some secret words rest deep inside me that I could call forth to recite? But I was unable to save Emeline, what makes me think that I could save Mother? If I truly am what Mother claims I am, then I must be the most useless specimen that ever existed; all I am good for is rages and storms, not healing.

My thoughts are interrupted by voices at the door. Snip yelps in delight, his boundless joy anathema to the dark veil that clings so tightly around our house. I run to the hall to scoop him up so that he won't wake Mother with his barking.

I stop short when Ada steps back from the door.

Mr. Barrett appears in front of me, stomping snow from his boots. He must hear my sharp intake of breath, because he looks up to find me staring at him, his lips turning down in not quite pleased surprise. I'll never grow used to the way my insides go all light and fluttery when he turns his intense sea green gaze on me, even now as I know his heart belongs to someone else.

Something in his face darkens, but he nods a polite greeting. "Miss Montrose," he says, as Ada relieves him of his coat. "I didn't realize you were back in New Oldbury."

There's an accusatory edge to his tone and I take a little step back, Snip squirming in my arms to be let down. "Only just today. My mother is ill."

His face softens and the darkness passes. He thanks Ada and moves farther into the hall, closing the distance between us, stopping just short of me. It takes every fiber of my being not to throw myself at him, wrapping my arms around his lean, muscled frame and pouring out all the sadness that has built up in me these past weeks. "Yes, of course. I'm so sorry. I... I just came to see your father, to see if there was anything I could do."

Just then Catherine comes trudging down the steps, a basin under her arm. Her face brightens when she sees him. "Mr. Barrett," she says as she hands the basin off to Ada. "It was so kind of you to come. I know how busy you must be with the new mill. Have you started construction yet?"

"Not until the spring when the ground can be worked." He carefully avoids my eyes as he speaks; I suppose this is just as awkward for him as it is for me.

"Of course," Catherine says. While Mr. Barrett and I tiptoe on eggshells, she blithely dances forward without a care in the world for our mutual discomfort.

Mr. Barrett clears his throat. "How is your mother? Is there anything I can do to help?"

Catherine puts her hand on his arm and lets it linger there. "How very kind of you. Father is finally sleeping in his study, and I wouldn't want to disturb him. It's been a hard few days for him. Will you come in and have some tea? This isn't an evening for standing about a drafty hall."

Wordlessly, he follows Catherine to the parlor and after a moment's hesitation I fall into step behind them, Snip trotting excitedly at my heels. All those sleepless nights and now he's right here in front of me, those same broad shoulders, the strong, sleek energy that thrums beneath the surface of his taut body. It's one thing to make a resolution in the safety of a bed miles and miles away, but quite another to see what I'm losing in the flesh.

Mr. Barrett stiffly seats himself in a chair, and I perch at the edge of the settee while Catherine chatters on. "It's so nice that we're all together again, isn't it? I'm dreadfully jealous of Lydia who's been on such a tear in Boston. I hear she's been quite popular there."

Even now, with Mother fighting for her life upstairs, Catherine can play her games as if it were any other day. I suppose the opportunity to make me miserable is too good for her to pass up. I'm burning up at her lies, but know better than to throw fuel on Catherine's fire, so I keep my mouth shut.

"I'm sure she has," Mr. Barrett says tonelessly.

"Well," Catherine says, rising. "I should go back upstairs. Someone needs to be with Mother." She gives me a pointed look and stands aside to let Ada pass with the tea tray. "Before I go, has Lydia told you her happy news?"

Mr. Barrett's gaze flickers to me and then back to Catherine, frowning. "I don't believe she has."

"Why, Lydia is engaged to be married." Catherine smiles warmly, though only I can see the malicious glimmer in her eyes. "Aunt Phillips wrote us earlier in the week. Isn't it wonderful?"

And with that, she leaves us alone, her words hanging in the air behind her.

Mr. Barrett's hand pauses midstroke on Snip's back. The muscle in his jaw clenches and I wish I knew what was going through his head, what he wants to say. I look down at my lap, unable to meet his penetrating gaze. When he finally speaks his voice is rough, and it's not so much of a question as a demand. "Who?"

Of course he would find out eventually, but I never thought I would have to sit in front of him and see the effect of my decision myself. I never thought he would actually care. My throat narrows to almost nothing. "Cyrus Thompson."

He nods, as if this confirms his worst suspicions about me. "The young man at Emeline's burial."

"Yes," I whisper.

"Well," he says shortly, "I wish you all the happiness in the world."

I thought I was numb, that nothing else could hurt me. But this hurts, more than I could have ever imagined. "And you, I hope you'll be happy too."

His brows draw together, puzzled, or maybe it's disgust. But he doesn't say anything in return, just stands up and puts down his untouched cup of tea. "I'm afraid I should be going. Please, do let your father know that I called. If he needs any-thing… Well, he knows where to find me."

I sit there, too stunned to move. His footsteps recede quickly down the hall, followed by the rustle of his coat as he slings it on, the door yanking open and then clicking shut behind him.

Before I know what I'm doing, I bolt out of the room after him. "Wait!"

I fling open the front door, and the cold air hits me like a wall. "John, wait."

Mr. Barrett turns on his heel, pausing in the midst of pulling on his gloves. He throws me a harried look and something hardens in my stomach. He's angry, at me.

"Yes, Miss Montrose?"

I wince at his formality. There's no warmth in his face, no encouragement. But if there is one benefit to being empty, to giving away everything you have, it is that there is nothing left to fear. What have I to lose?

"You never answered my letters."

He stops, glove halfway on, and raises a brow.

I plow on, determined to say my piece before I lose my nerve. "I understand you might have been offended by the first letter, that I didn't explain why I was going away or how very much it hurt to have to leave before you came to meet me as we planned. But the second one, I… I poured my heart out to you, and you couldn't even send me a word in response."

The ice cracks under his boots as he moves a step closer. He peers at me through the December dusk, slowly pulling his glove the rest of the way on. "You wrote me?"

"Twice!"

"I never received any letters. I came and Catherine told me that you'd gone back to Boston for the winter to visit friends."

I grit my teeth. Either the letters went missing in the post, or, more likely, Catherine is doing everything she can to live up to her promise of making my life miserable and somehow intercepted them. "I didn't want to go."

He nods, but doesn't look convinced. "Well," he says, his voice brisk and clipped in the cold. "I'm sorry that I didn't receive your letters. I daresay you were busy making wedding plans in any case."

My body flushes hot with indignation. "You certainly didn't waste any time after I left. What was it, two weeks?"

He parts his lips as if to say something, but for once his beautiful features and crystal gaze don't hold me in their sway.

"I never fooled myself about what I might mean to you, but I thought you would at least have the common courtesy not to treat me like some sort of diversion, getting my hopes up only to dash them again. You're a cad, just like your good friend Mr. Pierce."

Mr. Barrett weathers my accusations with that cool mask of emotion that I used to find so mesmerizing but is now only infuriating.

"You made me feel special. That kiss in the road... How many other girls in town have you seduced? Maybe it's not work that always keeps you so busy." How worldly and defiant I had felt that day, but now I see what a fool I was. This is exactly the reason young women don't go about unchaperoned with men like John Barrett.

I stop for a breath and he tries to speak. "I don't know what—"

"I was warned about you." Before I can stop myself the words slip out. "Moses came to me and tried to tell me that you weren't what you seemed and—"

His face goes white, and he takes a halting step toward me. "What did you say?"

I shrink back, wondering what could have possessed me to bring that up. I swallow. "N-nothing. I only meant that—"

But he doesn't let me finish. He's standing very close, the faint touch of his breath warm on my cheek. "Did you see something?"

His voice is soft but so icy that I shiver anew in the cold. Maybe there was something in Moses's warning about Mr. Barrett, something more than the fact he's a lying scoundrel. Maybe he's dangerous and even though it feels as if I'm being torn asunder, I've actually been spared some greater tragedy. My anger washes through me again and I remember that it's he that has something to answer for, not I. I take a step back, refusing to be intimidated.

"It…it doesn't matter. I begin to think I misjudged you."

He couldn't look more surprised if I had hit him. His expression shifts, from one of restrained anger to something like bewilderment.

"It's fine, Mr. Barrett. I'm sorry that we had a misunderstanding, but I need to be with my mother now. Goodbye."

Before he can say anything else, I turn on my heel and walk back to the house. I keep my pace measured and slow so that he won't know just how hard my knees are shaking, how fast and painful my heart is beating.

Urgent knocking at the door startles me from my dozing. I blink at my surroundings for a moment, trying to gain my bearings in the dark room. The haze lifts and I remember I'm in the library at home, that I'm engaged to Cyrus, that Mother is upstairs ill. I wish I hadn't woken up. The fire is dying, and when my eyes focus, the clock says it's two in the morning. Ada and Joe are probably asleep, and Catherine won't be able to hear anything from her makeshift bed beside Mother.

The knocking comes again and this time I have enough presence of mind to wrap the blanket around my shoulders and pad out to the front hall. Outside the wind howls and I shiver, loath to let the darkness into the house.

I press my ear to the door. News delivered in the middle of the night is never good, but what if it's something worse, like a thief, or a murderer? Neither of whom would knock first, I remind myself. "Who is it?"

The answer that comes back is muffled and impatient. "John Barrett."

I freeze, my sharp words from our last conversation still

fresh in my mind. What could we have to say to each other after that?

"For God's sake, Lydia, open the door."

My shivering fingers fumble to unbolt the lock. The door swings open to reveal Mr. Barrett standing hunched against the swirling snow, his eyes rising to meet mine like two lanterns in the storm.

"I... I hope I didn't wake your mother."

My head is still foggy and my eyes bleary. I might be imagining him in our drive, the sharp cut of his overcoat silhouetted against the snow, his marble complexion pink and polished from the cold.

The wind slices through the thin blanket around my shoulders, and it takes only a moment to notice the purple tint to his lips, his usually precise curl of hair, dark and bedraggled from the wet snow.

"It's the middle of the night. You didn't walk all the way from your house, did you?"

He blinks, as if this had not occurred to him. "I... What time is it?"

"It's nearly two in the morning."

"Oh, God. I shouldn't have come." He turns as if he's going to leave, to walk all the way back in the snow and wind to his house.

Without thinking I take him by the hand and pull him inside. His fingers are ice in mine. "You're here now. Come in before you freeze to death." He doesn't resist, following me as meekly and obediently as Snip would.

But we don't get any farther than the hall. He stops abruptly in his tracks, looking terribly wild and out of place. Despite the anger still curdling in my stomach, I want to cup his face in my hands, draw him to me until he's warm and safe.

It goes against all convention for him to be here in the middle of the night, alone, with me. I take a deep breath. "Well?"

"You said something when I was here earlier."

I swallow. Pale Moses and his cryptic warning seem far away and unreal now. A dream. How could I ever think Mr. Barrett was dangerous? "About your brother? I told you, it was nothing. I—"

He stops me with an impatient shake of his head. "You said something in the parlor, something about hoping that I would be happy too?"

My face flushes despite myself and I stammer out my words. "I meant…well, you wished me happiness in my engagement, and I thought it only right to return the sentiment to you on yours."

He stands stock-still. A clump of snow melts off his shoulder, landing with a *plop* on the carpet. When he speaks it's with restrained impatience, like one trying to explain something to a small child.

"I told you that I wasn't engaged, that you shouldn't put any stock into what a gossipy old hen like Mrs. Tidewell says."

"But Catherine wrote to me and said—" My hand flies to my mouth. In an instant it becomes so clear that I can't believe I didn't see it before. I let out a muffled groan.

Mr. Barrett surveys me from narrowed eyes. "Lydia," he says slowly, "I told you I would come for you. What did you think I meant?"

"I…" The hall is spinning, each tick of the clock echoing in my ears like a death knell. How could I have been so blind, so easily misled? My knees go weak and buckle as the realization of what I've done sweeps through me.

Mr. Barrett moves fast, catching me by the elbow.

"I've gone about this all wrong and upset you." He reaches out his hand to steady me, then he loops his other arm around my waist. "Come, let's get you into the parlor where you can sit down."

It's no use arguing, or telling him that he's the one with blue lips and looks like he could use a thawing out. But the room is still spinning and my legs ready to go out from under me again, as he walks me down the hall, his arm pulling me tight against him.

When we reach the library he guides me down into Father's overstuffed chair. His head is bent low, his cheek just grazing the top of my head as I sit. He's so close that I can smell his shaving soap. The sliver of air between us grows warm. I feel drunk, and I'm deliciously helpless to do anything but tilt my face up the last little bit to close the distance between our lips completely.

For a brief, blinding moment, everything else is forgotten. His skin is still cold from the snow, but his tongue is warm as he parts my lips, a gentle, probing kiss. I yield, my bones turning to jelly as I twine my arms up around his neck, reveling in the smoothness of his skin under my fingers. My body flushes with an aching longing. I want so badly to be as close to him as possible.

Breathless, I pull back. "We can't." Inside my head a little voice is yelling at me to hold my tongue, to pull him back down to me. Why can't I just have this moment? Why do I have to destroy every little droplet of happiness that rolls my way?

Mr. Barrett clears his throat, straightening up. I vaguely wonder if my lips look as swollen and beautiful as his do right now. "I know. Your mother is upstairs ill, but I couldn't—"

I shake my head, doubly miserable because I hadn't even been thinking about Mother when I pulled away. "No, I mean, yes…" I self-consciously tuck back a loosened strand of hair behind my ear. "You might not be engaged, but I still am."

His body stiffens and he blinks at me. "I see."

I can't look at him, instead I concentrate on my hands in my lap. "I'm so sorry, John."

He's quiet for a moment, the sound of Snip's even breathing, the crackling fire, my own thudding heart filling the silence. "Do you love him?"

"What?"

"You heard what I said." His voice is rough and holds a note of reproach. "Do you love him?"

I drop my gaze to my slippers, the pretty white ones with the little silk rosettes. There's a tuft of Snip's fur on the oriental carpet by my feet. The cleaning has grown lax now that Mother has taken to her bed. I can feel Mr. Barrett's gaze burning into me.

"No," I whisper. "Of course I don't. I love y—" I catch my breath, stopping myself just in time. It doesn't matter though. He takes a hesitant step toward me, then falls to his knees beside the chair, folding me back into his embrace.

"You don't love him," he murmurs against my neck, squeezing me so tightly that I think my ribs might crack. When he pulls back, he holds me at arm's length, surveying my face with unmasked delight. "You can call it off. Don't go back to Boston, stay here, with me."

"John…" My heart is fluttery and pounding, my body cold and burning up at the same time under his hands. "What are you saying?"

His voice is ragged, his gaze holding mine. How I could fall into those eyes and never come out. "I'm asking you to marry me."

I suck in my breath. Instantly the fire glows brighter in the grate, the lamps flicker happily. I don't know how it's possible, but he really does want me. My heart soars and then immediately plummets again. Which will make it all the harder to tell him what I must tell him now.

He looks at me with warm, expectant eyes, though there is a quiver of uncertainty around the corners of his lips. He drops his arms and gets to his feet. "Oh," he says quickly, his face coloring. "Forgive me, I thought—"

There's a sinking realization in his eyes that twists my heart. "You misunderstand me." I stumble to my feet, the blanket slipping away and with it all of his lingering warmth. "I—I want to be with you too. You have no idea how much." My cheeks are flaming and my tongue thick as I try to get my words out. "But I can't. I just can't."

"Yet you just said that you don't love him. If you think your father won't give his permission, I—"

"No, it's not that. I don't, I…" I can't stand the hurt in his face, even worse, knowing that I caused it. I can feel my resolve crumbling. Tears are bubbling up, my emotions already rubbed raw from a long day of travel and finding my mother on her deathbed.

He tilts my chin up in his hand so that I have no choice but to look into his questioning eyes. He couldn't be making this harder for me if he tried. "Lydia, you can tell me anything."

I'm so close. It would be so easy for it to all just well up and spill out of me. But if I tell him, that soft look that's melting my heart will harden in disgust. He would want nothing to do with me. So instead of words that come tumbling out, for the second time today, it's a deluge of tears.

⅜ 32 ⅜

"I'M SORRY." I wipe my eyes with the back of my sleeve, desperate to pull myself together. I can't help myself, I care what he thinks of me, and right now he must think I'm a madwoman. Forcing a smile, I take a step back from his arms and stand up straighter. "I'm fine, really. I don't know what came over me."

There's a dark patch on his vest where the brunt of my tears fell, and a stray hiccup escapes my lips. Mr. Barrett doesn't look so convinced. "Lydia, sit down."

"I told you, I'm fine. I just—"

But he's already installing me back in the chair, his movements brisk and brooking no argument. "Now. Will you be all right for a few minutes? I'm going to make you some tea."

I gracelessly snuffle back the last of my tears. "Tea?"

He gives me a long look, seems like he wants to say something and then changes his mind. "I'll be right back."

I let my head loll back against the chair, listening to the sounds of Mr. Barrett trying to find his way around the kitchen. What would Mother think if she knew I was downstairs alone with a man in the middle of the night? I laugh to myself. If only that were my biggest concern right now.

He returns a few minutes later with a wobbly tray of tea. The water is scalding, but I take a few polite sips under his apprehensive gaze before giving him back my cup.

"Now," he says, crouching down beside me, "do you want to tell me what that was all about?" His eyes are tired, his face ravished, but despite everything he offers me the hint of a weak smile.

Snip is lying in his basket beside the fire, snoring softly without a care in the world. Outside the wind wraps itself around the house in a crushing embrace.

I shake my head. "I... I can't tell you. I promised I wouldn't." Even if I hadn't promised Catherine, how could I tell him that those vile rumors he heard about us were true? He would be disgusted, walk away from me without a second look back. How do I tell him that Cyrus is exploiting us, that I have no choice but to marry him, lest he expose everything to the world? How do I tell him that I'm not even what I seem?

Mr. Barrett tents his fingers as he considers this. "Here's the short of it, Lydia. I love you. I have ever since that day I called to find you hiding behind your book. You glowed when I asked you what you were reading. I wanted you to go on forever. I... I think before that even. The first day I saw you, in the woods." He takes my hands in his, looking at me with heartbreaking earnestness. "Am I wrong in thinking that you might love me too?"

My fingers tighten around his. "No," I whisper. "You're not wrong."

He squeezes back, raising my hand to his lips, imparting a soft kiss on the tender skin of my wrist. "Then what?"

I think of Catherine upstairs, running herself ragged to take care of Mother. She may be my sister in name only, but there is still some primal part of me that grows protective when I think of her in trouble. Maybe I can still protect her where I failed to protect Emeline. "It's not my secret to tell."

"I see." He rocks back on his heels, pressing his lips in thought. "Whoever's secret you're keeping is very lucky to have you as a confidante and friend."

I don't say anything.

"I won't ask you to betray this person's trust, but you must see how it pains me to hear that you love me, but can't be with me." He reaches up from his position below me and grazes my cheek with his fingertips. "I wish you would let me help you."

Do I still owe Catherine some allegiance even after everything she's done? I squirm a little as it comes to me that I'm not keeping her secret because I care about her, so much as that I don't want Mr. Barrett to be disgusted with me by association. I was the one who carried her baby through the woods at night, the one who bundled it with stones and tossed it into the pond like a piece of rubbish. I'm the one who twisted Tommy Bishop's legs round 'til he couldn't stand, the one that put a mark on him with my mind so that his luck would run bad for the rest of his days. I might have forgotten about the way I saw his legs snap in my mind before it happened it front of my eyes, or the black cloud I envisioned circling him, if not for Catherine's and Cyrus's reminders that have brought everything back with sickening clarity.

"It's not just that it's a secret, it's..." I take a deep breath, choosing my words carefully. "I've done bad things. They were for good reasons—or so I thought—but I did them all the same. I'm afraid that if you knew who—what—I was, you wouldn't..." I look down at his concerned face, the high planes and Roman nose illuminated in the flickering candlelight. How can a man so beautiful, so kind, really feel that way about me?

He stands up and motions me to move over. It's a big chair but when he sits down the cushion dips, and my head falls against his chest. He wraps his arm around my shoulders, holding me. I close my eyes. A comfortable silence envelops us as I listen to the steady beating of his heart beneath my ear, and feel his warm breath against my hair. No matter how loud the wind whistles outside, no matter all the things that stand between us, as he pulls me closer to him, in this moment we are safe. We are together.

"Whatever it is you think you've done, I can assure you, you're not a bad person." I raise my head to object but he stops me with a gentle hand. "Listen to me. I've seen the goodness in you." He hesitates. "There are things about me, if you knew, might make you think differently of me. Perhaps if you can accept them, then you'll understand there's nothing you could tell me to make me change my feelings toward you."

The deep, sweet timbre of his voice reverberates against my ear, and even though I know there's nothing he can tell me that will fix everything, I'm content to let him talk as long and about whatever he wants. I give a little nod.

I feel him take a deep breath. "I had an older brother named Moses who died when I was a young boy. You saw his portrait with my mother when you were at my house, and, judging from what you said earlier, you've heard of him somehow already."

"Oh, I'm so sorry." Even though I've heard this story before secondhand from Mrs. Tidewell, hearing it from his own lips sends fresh waves of pity and sorrow through me. My words are inadequate to express how truly sorry I am, but Mr. Barrett brushes the top of my head with a kiss before going on.

"He was a cruel, vicious boy, though my mother doted on him all the same. He could do no wrong in her eye. She spoiled him, dressing him like a little prince, buying any trifle that might catch his fancy in a shop window. He expected to get anything he wanted, and if he didn't he would throw such tantrums. My mother would try to subdue him, often at the expense of injury to herself. I remember the livid bruises around her wrists that she used to try to hide with her sleeves."

"But... Your father. That is... I thought..."

I can feel Mr. Barrett look down at me, feel his surprise as his body tightens. "I would ask you where you heard that, but I have a feeling I already know." He takes a long, strengthening breath. "No, it wasn't my father. When Moses hurt her it wasn't intentional, it was always in the act of thrashing out during a tantrum. He loved her just as strongly as she loved him. But when he turned his sights on me, there was no mistaking his intentions. I was a small child—weak, my mother used to tell me—and there were many evenings I came home from playing with him in the woods with a black eye or bloody lip." The smallest of tremors runs through his voice. "God forgive me, but I hated my own brother."

I shiver. If he started this story as a distraction for me, it's veered into something else. His words come faster, more urgent, as if he must unburden himself of whatever it is he's been carrying with him.

"My father was a gentleman, in every sense of the word. He pleaded with my mother to send Moses away to a boarding school in Hartford. On the rare occasions when he disciplined Moses himself, my brother screamed and howled so wretchedly that my mother would collapse in fits of tears. I watched my father transform into a bitter, hollow man, driven to drink.

"One day Moses was in the nursery, even though he had long outgrown his room there. He had emptied out the chest where I kept all my prized wooden soldiers and was lining them up as target practice for his little rifle. It was thick and gray outside, and Moses had brought in a lamp to set on the floor for more light.

"I don't know what made that day different for me, but instead of slinking away, I went up to Moses and demanded that he stop. He pushed me, and though I was smaller, I pushed back. When he turned his rifle on me, I grabbed the lamp from the floor and threw it at him. It missed, and landed at the foot of the window, shattering. The drapes ignited and before I knew what was happening, flames were shooting up to the ceiling.

"My mother heard the commotion downstairs and came running. When she found us, Moses was red-faced and coughing on the floor. I was frozen. I must have looked guilty as sin. I never thought that the fire would spread so fast, that my brother would suffer a fit. My mother was kneeling beside him, trying to get him to his feet and escape from the fire. I..."

For the first time he falters, and instinctively I curl my fingers into his hair, wishing I could take away all his pain.

"I ran out of the room, slamming the door behind me. But you see, the nursery door locked from the outside. I never meant to... I never thought about what I was doing." His voice is flat, his eyes devoid of emotion.

"I didn't stop running until I was halfway down the road to town, where I met my father on his way home. I told him that a fire had started, that I didn't know how. He rushed off but by the time he got there it was too late. Half the house was in flames, the other half already collapsed. They found my mother's body where the nursery had been, but Moses's body was never recovered."

My skin prickles. Moses is still out there, wandering the woods. Lost and angry.

"Afterward, a rumor began going around town that my father had flown into a jealous rage against my mother, locking her and her favorite child in the house as he set it ablaze. My mother was a great beauty, and well loved in the town. Everyone turned against my father and he lost his business, his standing, everything. He had drunk himself to death by the time I was sixteen."

"Oh, John."

"You'll think me insane, but my brother haunts me still. I hear him laughing, laughing at me in my dreams. He...the day I met you, in the woods behind the mill, I was looking for him." He glances at me to gauge my reaction. When I don't say anything, he goes on. "Sometimes I fancy I see him, just a glimpse, in the woods. I chase him, hoping that if I can just catch up with him I can beg him to go, to let me be. But I never do. You must have thought me terribly rude when we first met, but I hope you'll understand why now I was so dismayed to learn your father had brought his family here. There's something about this place, something terrible and sad. It invites tragedy. I think it's always been that way, long before Moses and I came along."

I find his hand with mine. "You're not insane. I've seen him too. Spoken with him. I..." I stop myself, not sure how much I should tell him about what I've experienced. Moses is still here, his mortal remains forgotten and trapped beneath our house. The laughter, the footsteps, the endless watching, it's always been him. And the wailing in the night, the pale lady pacing the garden, that must have been his mother, her spirit somehow trapped, endlessly searching and mourning her beloved son.

Mr. Barrett studies me, his face unreadable. He's very still, only the slightly quicker pulse in his neck betraying that he's not in full possession of himself. He clears his throat. "Well," he says. "Now you know my darkest secret. I killed my own mother and brother, and I was responsible for the death of my father as well. I don't tell you this because I seek absolution or even because I'm haunted by guilt. I tell you because whatever it is you think you've done, whatever it is that you think can come between us, I guarantee that you're wrong. If you can take me as I am—secrets and all—then I can take you as well."

We've come to the fork in the road again. One path leads

to more secrets, more walls, more heartache and loneliness. The other path, once dark and closed, now opens before me in blinding illumination. I can put my hand in John's and we can walk together in love and truth. My resolve shrivels up to nothing, the last bastion of familial responsibility crumbling in the wake of his confession.

So I tell him everything. I pray he'll still want me when I'm finished. It pours out of me, everything from Catherine and Charles, to the baby and what became of it, the darkness that has plagued me since coming to Willow Hall, and even Cyrus and what he'll do if I don't marry him.

Mr. Barrett listens patiently, not once interjecting or flinching, even when I can't help but doing so. His steady, solid presence gives me the courage to go on. I unburden everything to him, everything except the book that lies wrapped in a shawl in my trunk upstairs and what my mother told me this afternoon.

For what man in his right mind would want a witch for a wife?

I'm not in John's arms the next morning when I awaken, but in my own bed, tucked up and warm with a well-stoked fire. I turn my head, almost expecting to see him sitting in the chair, watching me, like that day he came to visit me after the pond. But only the weak morning sun and crackling of the dying fire fill the room.

Catherine throws the door open, glaring at me. "So glad that you're getting so much sleep. It's your turn to sit with Mother. I'm going to bed."

"I told you I would sit with her last night but you insisted on staying with her."

But Catherine doesn't want to hear it. She gives a martyred sigh and disappears to her room. I close my eyes, desperate to cling to the dozy warmth of the bed, to the memory of my fingers twined through John's hair, of his promise that whatever must be faced we'll face together. If not for that I don't think I would have strength enough to swing my feet onto the cold floor and pad to Mother's room.

As soon as I enter, an overwhelming sense of wrongness hits me like a wave. The air is too cold, too fraught with vibration. Despite the sun outside, the shutters are closed, the curtains drawn and the room is as dark as if it were midnight. The fire alone gives off any light.

And that's when I see her. In the corner, beside Mother's bed, Mary Preston hovers like some dark angel of death.

I catch my breath, my hand on the door behind me. I want to flee, but I can't leave Mother alone with her. "What are you doing here?" My voice cracks. "What do you want from her?"

She turns her head slowly at my voice. The spirit is silent, but I can feel her hollow eyes trained on me. Mother is sleeping, vulnerable and small in her bed while Mary Preston's dark veil swirls about her like a greedy fog. Then she turns back, her awful veiled face just inches from Mother's prostrate head.

"Leave her alone!" Before I can think about what I'm doing, I charge at the dark lady, my hand outstretched just like with Cyrus.

But before I even get halfway across the room, I freeze in my tracks as if I'd hit a wall. Something cold grips me where I stand, preventing me from taking another step forward. My hand drops to my side.

Mary Preston rises to her full height, hovering above the floor. "Stand your ground, child," she says in her everywhere-voice.

"Don't touch her," I growl, as if there is anything I can do to stop her.

"You still think me foe and not friend, I see. I am not here to harm your mother. As I already told you, I was not inclined to evil in life, and death is no different."

Even for her horrid countenance, I reluctantly must believe her. After all, she did not harm me the last time she was here.

"So, she finally told you, did she? I wonder that she took so long."

I don't say anything. Mother twitches in her sleep and I struggle to release myself from my invisible bonds and go to her.

"I will release you when we have finished our talk. Do not be in such a hurry."

It is easy for her to say, someone who has nothing but eternity ahead of them. If these are to be my Mother's last moments, then I want to spend each one by her side.

My heart wrenches as Mother writhes and mutters something in her sleep. The fever is worse today. "Isn't there anything I can do for her? Can't I save her from this?" If I'm able to twist Tommy Bishop's leg around, or repel Cyrus through the air, surely I can cure my mother? "I want to be a healer, to help her. I don't want to only be someone who hurts people."

Mary Preston's shrug is in her voice. "There are always ways. But is that the kind of witch you would have yourself become? Are you willing to dabble in that dark end of the spectrum? It is one matter to be a healer, but another to pervert the laws of life and death. There are always consequences, as you have seen with Emeline. You brought her back, and you have witnessed for yourself the cost."

I catch my breath. "But...but how? I didn't mean to."

"Didn't you? You took something of hers with the intention of keeping her with you."

"The hair?" I ask in a whisper. When I took a lock of hers, and put mine in the coffin, it was an impulse, something I couldn't explain, but felt I must do to keep us connected.

How was I to know that my actions would have such profound consequences?

"Yes, the hair is part of it. It is a volatile sort of magic, fraught with risk." Her tone softens, so far as the hollow voice of a spirit is capable of softening. "Your mother is tired, child. She wants rest. Give her what succor you can with herbs, with the healing comfort of your hands, but understand that nothing is certain in this life, least of all dark magic. If she recovers, it will be because of nature's course, or her own will. Not through spells and talismans."

I think of Emeline, wandering that space between the living and the dead, herself and yet not herself. Would I condemn Mother to a similar fate?

"No," I whisper. "I wouldn't do that to her."

Mary Preston gives a small inclination of her head.

"Why are you here? Why now?"

"As I said, it is a hard thing for a witch not to have someone to teach them. No longer do witches congregate in covens for fear of apprehension. We learned that lesson soon enough in my day. No, they might not string us up or drown us with rocks as they used to, but it is still a dark time for women of our ilk. It is a shame that your mother is not a witch herself and so could not teach you as you ought to have been. More of a shame still that she did not give you the book sooner."

It takes me a moment to understand her meaning. "You... you're here to teach me?"

"I am here, child," she says, "to pay my respects to a Hale woman, though witch she is not. I am here, because it is where you are. Death, as you have seen, is not such a great divider, especially for our kind. You will not go through your journey alone. You will have generations of women behind you."

A lump forms in my throat, and I nod my understanding.

I will not be alone, and there is a chance, however small, that my mother may come back from this.

"Read the book, and add what you learn from your own trials. Never stop learning. A lifetime is not long enough to gather up all the knowledge of our kind. That is why we pass it down."

It seems an impossible task, but I realize that I'm thirsty for it. I don't want to waste my life hiding from myself. I want to heal, to love. I want to be close to Emeline, and I can do that by being true to what I am. But for right now, I just want to sit beside my mother.

"Will you release me now?"

In answer, I feel the cold bonds falls away from my legs. When I look up to thank Mary Preston, she has already vanished, a lingering chill the only trace that she was ever here.

I rush to Mother's side. She's twitching and fitful, her brow clouded with worry even in her sleep. When I take her hand and try to comfort her she jerks away and murmurs a jumble of nonsense. She calls for her childhood nurse. She insists that her mother is going to thrash her for making a mess of her embroidery sampler. She asks me who I am and what I've done with Emeline, her little pearl. Mary Preston was right; she wants rest.

I sit helplessly, dabbing at her brow when she's still enough to permit it, offering soothing words that I hope she can hear somewhere deep inside her mind. Eventually she exhausts herself, falling into a fitful sleep.

Outside the rest of the world is waking up. Joe crunches across the drive to fetch firewood, and a crow's rasping cry cuts the frigid stillness. I shift in my seat.

"Mother, I... I expect Father will have told you I agreed to marry Cyrus. That's changed now, everything has changed now."

I dab a wet cloth at her lips. Mother's eyes move rapidly under her lids, but she's stopped crying out. Talking is calming her so I go on.

"Mr. Barrett came last night. He asked after you, wanted to know if there was anything he could do. He wants so badly to help. He cares."

The cloth trembles in my hand. John told me that we would face Cyrus together, that he wouldn't let him publish Catherine's letter. In the safety of his arms it had been easy to believe him, but now with my mother lying fragile and dying in front of me, nothing seems certain.

"Mother, I made a horrible mistake in trying to handle everything, to protect our family. I don't know if I can undo it all without hurting you and everyone else. I know you told me I have nothing to be sorry for, but I am. I'm so very sorry."

I take her frail hand in mine, resting my head against her side. It might be my imagination, but as my eyes start to grow heavy I feel the tiniest pressure from her fingers. She hears me. And she forgives me.

When the door creaks open a couple of hours later I expect to see Ada with a bowl of broth for Mother and a cold sandwich for me, but instead it's Father's balding head peering in.

He looks lost, but when his gaze rests on me, he gives me a grim nod of his head. "That will do, Lydia. I'll sit with your mother now."

I rise to leave, and as I pass him, he puts a hesitant hand on my sleeve. "You're a good girl, Lydia," he says. He gives my arm a pat, and then gingerly perches himself on the edge of Mother's bed. His head is bent low to hers, murmuring secret words as I quietly slip out and close the door behind me.

❧ *33* ❧

EVEN MY ABILITIES cannot prevent the blanket of snow that has accumulated and covered my herb garden over the past weeks. I trudge outside, basket on my arm, but when all I can find are a few brown and withered stalks protruding from the snow, I return inside, deflated. I'm setting my basket down in the kitchen, wondering if herbs are something that can be gotten at a market, when I remember the small store I set aside for drying for Ada. They hang in the corner from bits of string, delicate and fragile filaments of hope. Closing my eyes, I let my fingers brush through the dried bundles. Just like the day the dark voice in my mind guided me to the rue, my hands work of their own accord. But unlike that day, the impulse that draws me to the right herbs is something deeper within me. Something light and pure.

Borage for fever. Chamomile for rest. Lavender and mint for comfort. Although Mary Preston said that if Mother recovers it will not be because of any magic, I can't help but focusing my thoughts as I prepare the tisane, pouring all my hope and wishes for Mother's health into the water along with the herbs.

I bring the cup upstairs, but Mother is too weak to drink it on her own. Tilting her head up in my hand, I pour the tisane in dribbles into her mouth. If nothing else, I hope it brings her comfort, a deeper rest.

"Should we call the minister?"

Catherine is standing by the window, watching the gathering clouds as she knots her hands together. Mother has lingered for two days on the cusp of death, showing no signs of improvement, though no signs of decline either. Every few hours I slip into her room with a cup of the tisane, making sure that she gets at least a few drops down her throat.

We stopped going to church around the time the rumors began back in Boston. All those disapproving faces watching us as we walked in became too much for Mother to bear. But even before that, we were never a family with much need of God. Father's business prospered, we were healthy, we were together. Now I wonder if we angered some divine force and are reaping our just rewards.

I don't think Catherine heard me and am about to ask again when she frowns and turns from the window. "I don't know. Father certainly doesn't care about ministers and that sort of thing."

"He might now," I say, thinking of the other day, of his head reverently bowed beside Mother, his hands clasped in supplication.

Catherine nods, for once mute, pulling a wrinkled shawl tighter around her shoulders. It's hard to believe this is the same person whose barbed words and bitter heart have made my life so miserable. Without all her makeup and bright smiles she looks worn and old. I take a step toward her, but then stop in my tracks, teetering. This is also the person who lied to me about John's engagement, who has systematically set out to ruin my life. It's too late for embraces, for gestures of reconciliation, so I just say, "I'll tell Joe to fetch the minister."

When Joe comes back an hour later it's not with the minister in tow, but John.

"Minister's at the Wheeler house," Joe explains. "Baby is breech, Mrs. Wheeler wants him there just in case."

John turns his hat in his hands, looking apprehensive, but when he catches my eye he relaxes. "I was on my way to town when I ran into Joe. He told me that your mother... I thought I would come." He glances at Catherine and then his gaze settles back on me, his expression full of our shared secrets. "I hope you don't mind."

I thread my fingers through his. "No. I'm glad."

Catherine's eyes widen as our hands link, but she doesn't say anything, instead turning on her heel and leading us upstairs with her back rigid and eyes straight ahead.

My legs are heavy, and if it weren't for John beside me I don't know that I could make it. Catherine cracks open the door, and we all peer inside, breaths held.

Father doesn't get up when we come in, his back to us, hunched over the bed. "It's a miracle," he whispers, tears choking his words. "My God, it's a miracle." Slowly, he turns to us. Dark bags line his eyes, his thinning black hair greasy and unkempt, but he's smiling. I've never seen my father smile so broadly, so honestly. "The fever is broken."

And that's when he moves to the side and we see her: Mother, propped up on her pillows, her eyes drowsy but open, her color pale but no longer splotchy with fever.

Everything else is forgotten. Catherine and I fly to either side of the bed, burying our heads in her neck, kissing her and smoothing her hair. All the little things I never thought

I'd do again. All the things that I feared would be robbed from me forever.

A smile curves her thin lips. "My darling girls," she murmurs.

Delirium washes through me, a sensation so alien that I hardly know what to do with myself. Mother's still here. She's still here and the fever has broken. Was it the herbs? The desperate pleas and wishes I cried into the tisane? Mother's quiet fortitude winning out over the illness? Or was it simple luck? It doesn't matter. I take up her hand in my own, pressing it against my cheek.

"Careful," Father warns, hovering over us. "She's still weak."

I've never seen Father so concerned, so…so present, and I find myself unable to do anything other than nod, and slowly get up with Catherine.

There will be time later, Mother's eyes seem to assure me.

Reluctantly, I throw one last glance over my shoulder as John gently guides me from the room. Oh, how I pray she is right.

Time slows down to nothing. A day passes, I think, maybe it's two. Catherine and I take turns sitting with Mother, making sure that she has everything she needs, watching out the sides of our eyes with cautious optimism as she continues to grow stronger and stronger. John comes and goes under the pretense of stopping on his way to town, but I see him bringing Ada baskets of food so that she won't have to brave the snow to go to the market, and in the early morning hours I hear him outside helping Joe bring in firewood.

I stand at the window, watching a scarlet cardinal and his drab mate as they flit among the naked winter branches. Every time that I hear a noise upstairs, I jump, ready to fly to Mother's bedside and find that she's relapsed into fever. Mary Preston said that if Mother somehow recovered it would be because of her will and nature's course. But how can I be certain that she won't relapse? What if Mother's will fades after all, or nature's course takes a cruel turn? We should bring her somewhere warmer, somewhere with better doctors and all the conveniences of a city that she might need.

"Lydia." John comes up behind me at the window where I'm chewing my nails ragged. He gently lowers my hands. "Whatever you're worrying about, stop it. If anything needs to be done, I'll take care of it."

My first reaction is to shrug him off, to insist that I can manage myself. But his warm hand hovering at my waist reminds me that I don't have to anymore. I give him a weak smile. "I don't know what we ever did to deserve you."

John pushes my hair behind my ear, then lets his hand linger along the line of my jaw. His gaze warms me to my core, temporarily banishing the dark clouds of the last few months. "Oh," he says with a glimmer in his eye, "you didn't think my services came free of charge, did you? My bill will be arriving at the end of the month. Cash would be preferable but I suppose I could make do with services rendered."

My smile spreads. "Oh? And what kind of services would be acceptable?"

He tilts his head to the side in consideration, then meets my eye with a wicked grin. "A gentleman doesn't like to say."

I can't stop the giggle that bubbles up in my throat, but just as fast I push it down again. Mother is upstairs, still ill. How can I laugh right now?

John catches my chin in his hand. "Did you know, you have the most charming little dimple when you smile?" He touches one finger to my cheek. "Right here."

"Mother used to say that's how she knew when I wanted

something. My dimple would come out." My voice catches on that tender word, and without saying anything, John pulls me into his embrace.

His arms tighten around me and I close my heavy eyelids. How good it feels to lean into him, to not have to say anything, to know that he shares the dizzying waves of concern and joy that crash over me in turn.

The door slams in the front hall, followed by raised voices. I stiffen in John's embrace, and a moment later I find out just how far and fast my heart can drop.

Cyrus stands in the doorway, Ada skidding to a halt behind him. "He wouldn't wait, miss! I tried to stop him—"

Cyrus's eyes are bloodshot and he sways on his feet as he barrels into the room, bumping into a table and nearly knocking off a vase. He stops dead in his tracks when he sees John and me. "Jesus have mercy."

I feel like a guilty child, caught sneaking sweets from the kitchen. But John's grip on my waist only tightens when I move to take a step back.

"Well this is a fine welcome for your betrothed," Cyrus slurs. "Made the bloody journey in the snow all the way from Boston to find you in the arms of... Who is this fellow anyway? Knowing the Montrose family it's probably some long lost brother." I shrink away from his leering face. He looks to Ada with a sloppy grin and she steps back.

"Cyrus—" I start, but John swiftly moves me behind him with a firm hand.

"Mr. Thompson," he says coolly. "I've heard so much about you."

"I'll ask again, who the hell are you?" He doesn't wait for an answer. Cyrus's unfocused gaze wanders about the room. "Damn, but I forgot what good style your family lives in. You must pass my compliments on to your mother on her very fine housekeeping."

My blood is boiling and I want to wipe that smirk off Cyrus's face. But John grips me by the arm, slanting me a warning look.

"Look, Lyd, you flew off from Boston in such a rush we didn't have time to settle any of the arrangements. The thing of it is, I've had some dreadful bad luck at the club, and owe a bit to some of the other fellows for cards."

I ignore Cyrus's lament. "Ada, go upstairs and make sure Catherine stays with Mother." I don't need Catherine to come down and get involved, giving Cyrus more fodder for his accusations. And I certainly don't need Mother knowing that he's in the house, agitating her and risking a relapse. Ada shoots me a grateful look and then flees.

I've never seen John angry before. Outwardly he's calm and composed as ever, but the slight quiver of his jaw belies the fury simmering just beneath the surface. His nostrils flare as he turns the full intensity of his gaze on Cyrus. Cyrus swallows, taking a wobbly step back.

"Miss Montrose has nothing to say to you." John's eyes are hard as they meet Cyrus's bloodshot gaze. "You can consider the engagement null, and if you find your eye even so much as landing on her in the street, I'll know about it. I have rich friends who would be most interested in a piece of your debts."

"Rich friends, oh my." He swaggers up to John. Side by side they're a study in contrast; one dark, the other light, one disheveled and clumsy, the other neat and cool. "I'm afraid you don't understand the particulars of the situation, my good fellow." Cyrus slaps him on the shoulder, leaning in conspiratorially. "You see, Lydia and I have so much more than just an ordinary engagement. We have an...understanding." He looks over John's shoulder at me and winks. "Isn't that right, Lyd?"

Oh God, please don't let him tell John about Tommy Bishop, or my ancestry. Don't let him tell John about what happened in Aunt Phillips's parlor. Those are my secrets, and I'll share them with John someday, but not today. Not like this.

John removes Cyrus's hand with a contemptuous curl of his lip. "I assure you, you're mistaken. There is no understanding, and she owes you nothing."

My temple is throbbing, John's and Cyrus's voices fuzzy and far away. Does it really matter anymore? Emeline is dead. Mother is clinging to life. Catherine and Father are shadows of their former selves. What's left to hold together? But they're still arguing, John's voice rising.

Let Cyrus spread whatever story he wants. Let him rant and rail over what he no doubt sees as an injustice in our broken engagement. I don't care. His words can't hurt me or my family anymore. Let him feed the flames of rumor, maybe it will assuage him enough from divulging my secrets.

"Please, John, you don't need to save us. Just send him away. Let him say what he wants back in Boston, only don't let him draw you into anything foolish." I just want this to be over, and for John not to have to be wound up in our family's sticky web of deceits and dramas.

Cyrus sneers, turning his attention back to me. There is little that I recognize anymore in his dark eyes. They are wild and mad. Hungry. But when he speaks is voice is cocky and imperturbable. "Are you sure that's what you want, Lyd? Don't forget, I have more than one Montrose story to peddle."

"You wouldn't," I whisper. John might forgive Catherine her sins, but he would never want me if he knew what was inside of me, what I'm truly capable of.

"I don't want to," Cyrus says like a petulant child, throwing himself down in a chair and crossing his arms. "But what choice do you leave me? You really are the most capricious of women. One moment you're in my arms, agreeing that you want nothing so much as to be my wife, and the next you're running off in a flutter back to New Oldbury. If it's a case of the nerves, then I assure you nothing will snap you out of it like a good dose of the truth."

My jaw is set so tight that it aches. "Cyrus..."

"Whatever it is, we don't want to hear it," John snaps. "Lydia," he says, turning to me, "go upstairs while I settle this."

"I will not!" He must be mad if he thinks I'm going to leave the two of them alone down here, snapping and snarling like a pair of dogs fighting over a bone, possible coming to blows.

With a fatigued sigh, John rakes his hair back, clearly vexed that I won't listen to him, but unwilling to try again. Cyrus looks on with unmasked amusement. He has John right where he wants him: flustered and roused.

"Oh yes," Cyrus says, picking up where he left off. "Lydia and I shared something quite unusual, quite...special, in her aunt's parlor when she was in Boston."

Misgiving flickers across John's face and he goes white. "What are you talking about?" he asks roughly. His gaze swings back to me, his voice lowering to a hoarse whisper. "Did he force himself on you? Because I'll kill him if he so much as laid a *finger* on—"

"What? No, but...what I mean is, it was nothing like that. I..." But I can't bring myself to tell John what I did, even if it means leaving him with the wrong impression.

Cyrus feigns surprise, sitting up in the chair and looking between John's bewildered face and my red one. "Oh, did she not tell you? Lydia has the most unique talent, and she was gracious enough to give me a demonstration. In fact, she—"

I close my eyes, bracing for the damning words to fall from his lips. But they don't come. Instead there's a crash and a scuffling, and I open my eyes to see John throwing himself at Cyrus, lifting him by the collar and slamming him up against the wall. I jump as a picture falls to the floor, the glass shattering.

"Goddamn you!" John's face is aflame, just inches from Cyrus's nose. Cyrus's eyes bulge as he gasps for air. "I won't listen to this slander for a moment longer!"

Cyrus struggles in vain to free himself, but his toes barely graze the floor, and his thrashing doesn't budge John. I hover behind them, wringing my hands uselessly. "John, stop it! Put him down!"

"My God, what is this?" All heads swing toward the door where Father has been standing for I don't know how long. Hands on hips he glares at us, taking in John's hands at Cyrus's neck and my useless efforts at pulling John away. Then he raises an accusing finger at Cyrus. "My wife is ill upstairs! How *dare* you come here with your threats and accusations?"

John abruptly lets go of Cyrus, who yanks away and straightens his collar. Cyrus doubles over, hands on knees as he struggles to catch his breath. "Is she, now?" he gasps. "You would never know by the way these two were carrying on when I came in."

That was the wrong thing to say. Although Cyrus is a full head taller, Father strides up to him, grabs him by his newly straightened collar and pulls him down to eye level. "Get out," he growls.

Cyrus's eyes flicker with uncertainty, but then he pulls back, laughing. As always it seems that nothing ruffles Cyrus; he is impervious to shame. "No need to get your trousers in a knot. I wouldn't dream of intruding on such a happy family gathering." He turns to me, executing an exaggerated, wobbly bow. "Lydia, the least you can do is do me the courtesy of sitting down and supping with me, especially after the monstrous way your friend here has treated me." He glares at John and makes a show of rubbing the back of his neck. "You owe me that much."

"She doesn't owe you a thing," John growls, stepping in between us.

Cyrus shrugs as if he hadn't actually expected this demand to be met. "I'm staying at The Black Mare the next town over if you change your mind. Or perhaps Mr....Barry, was it? You'd like to join me? We can engage in a more civilized discourse and see if we can't settle this like gentlemen."

"We have nothing to talk about," John says with venom. "You've shown yourself to be a slanderous meddler and nothing more."

Cyrus glances to me and then back to John. "Or we can talk in front of Lydia and her father, I'm sure they would be interested in what I have to say."

Father can't stand it anymore. "Get out!" he roars. "I don't care what you have to say. Make your dinner plans somewhere besides my parlor!"

"Oh, I was just going anyway," Cyrus says with an irritated hiccup. He turns back to me. "Lydia, I do hope you help your friend come to his senses and explain to him why he ought to keep out of this. If you don't, I will."

I keep my lips pressed tight, and watch in icy silence as Cyrus levels one last suspicious look at John before making his exit.

When the front door slams shut, John closes his eyes and takes a deep breath, rubbing the bridge of his nose. "I'm sorry you had to see that, both of you. I shouldn't have lost my composure. I'd better go," he says, gathering up his hat and overcoat.

Father slumps down in a chair, hand over his face. "You're a good fellow, Barrett. No need to apologize. If Martha were well, I'd ask you to stay, and she'd see a nice luncheon laid out for you."

John doesn't say anything, just gives him a short nod of his head that Father doesn't see, and then moves for the door.

"John, wait." There's something wild in his eye that makes my stomach uneasy. For all his faults and ugliness, Cyrus was always masterful at keeping his composure. Cold and calculating Cyrus scares me, but unpredictable and erratic Cyrus terrifies me. I put my hand on John's arm, and he looks down at me as if he'd forgotten I was here. "You won't go meet him, will you? Promise me you won't do anything rash." I can't bear the thought that a good man has been dragged into our family's mess, that our sins might be the ruin of him.

John drops a distracted kiss on my head. "You have no need to worry. I promise you Cyrus won't bother you again."

Before I can tell him that's not what I asked, he's out the door, leaving me alone with my roiling stomach.

My sleep that night is fitful and tortured. I dream that Willow Hall is ablaze, the smoke so thick in my room that I can't see my hand in front of my face. The laughter of a small boy echoes as beams and walls come crashing down around me. Just as my flaming bed is about to collapse in on itself, I awake drenched in sweat.

Unable to fall back asleep, my mind races, full of everything that has happened these past few days. My heart beats faster when I think about John, about all the bright promises the future holds with him, then plummets as I remember Cyrus's threats. John is a proud man, bound by honor, and though I admire this about him, I also fear his desire to protect me could blind him to reason.

Lighting a candle, I reach for the book Mother gave me and begin to read. I need something to distract me. It's not like the book that I bought from Mr. Brown, with its sensational stories of animal familiars and dark magic. This book describes a quieter kind of witchcraft. It speaks of spells whispered into cups of tea, herbs sprinkled on thresholds, protective sigils stitched into hems. Little rituals that exist outside the spheres of men and belong to women alone. It speaks of healing with plants, doing good. It's a revelation.

But the book also speaks to a well of energy inside every witch, a spark, that when harnessed can be a powerful force. I read every page, poring over the printed text and marginalia alike, ferociously hungry for information. The candle burns down to a nub and I fetch another. I want to understand what I am. I want to embrace the legacy my ancestors left me, as well as my mother even if she is not a witch herself.

In the yellowed pages I learn not only what I am capable of, but I begin to see patterns in my life. That day in the street with Tommy Bishop, when my eyes filled with red and my fingers trembled with energy like lightning, or when I sent Cyrus flying backward through the air, I didn't know what was happening; it was just my natural response to what I saw as terrible wrongs in the world. But the book explains and shows me how I can tame and channel my anger. And when I put a dark mark on Tommy Bishop with my mind, envisioned the ill luck that would plague him for the rest of his life, I can do that again too. I don't want to bring more pain, but a deep resolve builds inside me; if it means saving John from a terrible situation, then I would do everything in my power to save him. I don't know if there's anything I wouldn't do.

I read the other book again too. Fairy stories they might be, but every story starts from a seed of truth; if not, why would we be drawn to them as we are? I might not be able to turn myself into a bird, or make a plague of toads rain down, but perhaps there are lessons to be drawn from such lore. Knowledge is a powerful tool, as Mary Preston said, and I want to be as prepared as possible for what lies ahead.

Yet for the bounty of knowledge that rests between the books' covers, there is not so much as a clue as to what to do for Emeline. I had thought to find a spell, a ritual...something that would lay out the steps to reverse the terrible events I put in motion. Wait for a full moon and mumble some ancient words? Burn the hair? But there is nothing, and so after all my selfishness, I am no closer to helping her than I was before.

I must have dozed off at some point, because I awaken to a room so cold that I can see my breath. When a movement in the darkness catches my eye, I do not start in surprise. I am used to her suddenly appearing like this. Yet her presence still fills me with an intangible sort of dread.

I clutch the covers closer to my chin, darting my tongue over my dry lips. "What are you doing here?"

Mary Preston moves into the dim circle of the remaining candleflame, her flowing veil blacker even than the night.

"You've read the book," she says, ignoring my question. "Good. You will need it."

I have learned by now that there is no use trying to follow her roundabout way of speaking, that I need to be direct with her and hold my ground. "Emeline," I say. "The book didn't tell me what I need to do to help Emeline."

"So, you are ready then."

I bristle at her implication that I wouldn't help my own sister in her time of need. "I would not have her wander for eternity, not when I have the power to help her."

"And yet that was not always the case."

My cheeks burn and she doesn't give me the opportunity to respond before asking, "What went through your mind as you placed your hair in her coffin?"

"I... I suppose I was thinking that I never wanted to be

without her. That I wanted some way to be with her again, even if only for a moment." Her meaning dawns on me. "But...it was enough just to think it?"

The dark eye sockets dance. "Was it enough when you thought of Tommy Bishop's leg snapping?"

Surely it could not be so simple? What a terrible power, to be able to think something and have it be so. I open my mouth, but she stops me.

"You will learn to control such thoughts in time. For a witch to think something with intent is quite enough, though it takes skill to channel the necessary energy. The fact that you were able to with no training speaks to the power in you. You very nearly called up a storm over the pond in your grief after all," she says, a hint of admiration in her voice. "In Emeline's case, you added in a powerful talisman, binding the intent." She gives a bony shrug. "Though Willow Hall is a strange place, and Emeline had powers of her own."

"And you?" I ask. "Are you tethered to this world through some talisman also?" Will that be my fate as a witch, once I die? I shudder at the thought.

"I? Tethered?" Her skull tilts back and a rattling laugh comes from somewhere deep inside her. "I am old. I died old, and despite my demise, I died powerful. I come and go through the veil as I please. Emeline was but a child. Children are not meant for this in-between world."

I bite my lip, considering these revelations. "What about the others who roam the land here?"

"They are not your concern. They belong to Willow Hall now, bound to each other and the land by tragedy, unable to move on. You cannot help them. But you can help Emeline."

I touch the locket at my throat, Emeline's hair braided and coiled inside.

Mary Preston watches me as my thoughts race. "You already know what to do, Lydia. You've always known. Now you must simply do it."

I nod. It is one thing to know what to do, but another to find the strength and courage to do it. It is what Emeline wants though, and it is what's right. Perhaps with Mary Preston by my side it will not be so daunting. Perhaps she will leave me to my thoughts for now, and then reappear when the time comes to make certain that I am up to the task.

But still she hovers there. For the first time, Mary Preston lingers past the message she came to deliver. Her creaking jaw opens and closes as if she wants to tell me something more.

"What? What is it?"

She lets out a weary sigh. "Your young man," she says, her tone implying just what she thinks of young men, "is about to do something very rash, very foolish."

My heart stops in my chest as her words sink in, but in an instant I'm up, scrambling to find my boots. "John? Where he is? What is he doing?" But I don't need to ask to know what John has taken upon himself to do, and when I look up, Mary Preston is gone.

❧ 34 ❧

I POUND DOWN the stairs, right to the front door when I stop. Catherine is standing by the window in the parlor, bathed in the predawn light of a snowy day. Her shawl has fallen off, and she bites at her fingers as she gazes out into the palette of whites and grays.

"Catherine?"

She doesn't move and I catch my breath, wondering if perhaps she too is nothing more than a spirit. But when I say her name a second time, she slowly turns around. Even in the dim light her face is pale, her eyes bloodshot.

"When Cyrus was here yesterday I heard him say you and he had an agreement. What did he mean?"

"Oh," I say with a little breath of relief, "I thought something was wrong." There's no time for this, to explain everything. And even if there was, what does it matter? "I don't know. I suppose it was just drunken rambling."

She nods, but doesn't look convinced. "Lydia," she says, not meeting my eye, her fingers hovering near her lips, "I think that I...that is, I've been—"

"Can this wait?" I glance out the window where the first weak fingers of light are struggling over the trees. "I have to go."

She opens her mouth to say something, but there's no time. I might already be too late.

The first snowflakes are starting to fall as I plunge into the still December morning. I've barely gone as far as the front walk when a pale little form appears out of the frosty mist.

As soon as I see her all else is forgotten.

Emeline looks much the same as the last time I saw her; she has not decayed further, nor is she crawling with maggots, and thank God. But she is pale to the point of translucence, nearly as sheer as Mary Preston.

I run to close the distance between us, mindless of the ice and snow. "Oh, Emeline." I skid to a halt, falling to my knees in front of her. "Thank God you've come back. I... I know how to help you now," I tell her. "You need only say the word and I will make sure that you are free to rest."

She shakes her head. "Not yet," she says. "Not until it's over. I won't leave you until it's over."

A chill—heavier than the December cold—settles over me at her words. "Where are they, Emeline?" I ask in a whisper.

"You know where they are."

I close my eyes. Surely the pond is too deep in the woods for even tall men like Cyrus and John to be able to reach in the snow. I visualize John waking up, throwing on his greatcoat, and going to his desk to retrieve his pistol. Where does he go next? Where would he have told Cyrus to meet him? I take a deep breath, clearing my mind. And in an instant, I know.

I open my eyes, and Emeline is gone.

Joe cleared our drive of snow but one look at the road reveals that little carriage traffic has passed through in the last few days. I might be able to make it to town, but all the way to the old mill? My boots are a lady's boot, pretty and sturdy enough for a turn around the park, but not for trudging through ankle-high snowdrifts.

But there's nothing to be done about it, so I gather up my hem and start picking my way to the road, trying to ignore the icy bite of the wet snow through my stockings. Oh, why could John not have left well enough alone? What happened after they left the house yesterday? How could they have talked or argued or whatever it was they were doing right through the night until dawn and come to this conclusion?

I've hardly gone three steps when behind me the door slams. "Miss, wait!"

Ada is throwing on a shawl, hurrying toward me. "Where are you going? And without your good cloak. You'll catch your death!"

"Mr. Barrett's in trouble." I swallow. "I think… I think he and Cyrus are going to duel." It seems so ridiculous when I say it out loud. "I have to stop them."

There's silence for a beat, and then Ada's thin voice and determined step falls in behind me. "I'm coming with you."

"Oh, Ada, I can't ask that of you." I don't tell her that I'm afraid she'll slow me down, that I already don't know if I'll make it in time as it is.

She gives a stubborn lift of her chin. "I'll not let you go alone."

I'm already turning around, hands out at my sides for balance as I navigate over the icy gravel. "And I love you for it, but for God's sake then, hurry."

But when I glance back, Ada isn't there. She's running back to the house, door banging behind her. She must have seen the road and changed her mind. I can hardly blame her. I'm nearly to the bend in the road, lungs already aching from gasping in the cold air, when the sound of horse hooves crunching on the ice stops me.

Bundled up like a fur trapper and leading one of our carriage horses by the bridle, Joe trudges toward me. "It's no use trying to stop me, Joe. I have to go."

"Ada said you were determined to take a jaunt into town," he says with a crooked smile. "Ajax isn't much used to the saddle, but he's sure-footed, and so long as you give him his head, he'll take you as fast as you please."

Ajax bobs his head impatiently, surveying me out of the side of his dark, rolling eye. I swallow, sure that he would just as soon buck me and leave me with a cracked skull on the side of the road than take me to John.

Joe is already turning him about, looping the reins over the big bay's head. "What do you say, miss?"

It takes only one look down the winding, icy road to make up my mind. I hitch up my dress, the cold air greedily embracing my stockinged legs. "I say whatever Father pays you, it isn't enough."

Joe grins, helping my foot find the stirrup and swinging me up and astride the saddle as if I were a man. Ajax dances nervously, bucking his head up and down. My fingers curl around the reins and into his thick mane.

With a hearty smack to the horse's flank, Joe sends us off. "You be careful now, miss," he calls after me. "And you tell Mr. Barrett to leave off this foolishness and bring you home safe."

Oh, how I hope it's that simple.

Joe was right, I need only to give Ajax his head and he carries me swiftly across the icy road, plowing through the snowdrifts as if they were nothing more than tall grass. The wind stings my eyes, tears freezing on my face. I think of the book of magic stories, the one about the girl who could turn herself into a yellow bird at her whim and fly fast and undetected above the treetops. But if such magic is possible, it is still well beyond my meager abilities. It's all I can do to hunch into Ajax's neck and try to stay on. He must sense my urgency, because without asking my leave he extends his long legs, gobbling up the ground. We pass the fork in the road, veering into town and across the first bridge. The sleepy little village flies by in a blur of smoking chimneys and tightly shuttered houses.

We follow the path that I took that day with Catherine and Emeline in our pursuit of Snip. What an eternity that seems, another life. John was walking the first day we met him, caught by the summer rain, searching for Moses. And now I must find him in the swirling snow and gray mist.

My fingers are red, purple almost, and cracking at the knuckles. I should have heeded Ada's advice. It doesn't matter. I pass over the bridge, the water gurgling and at odds with the still, snowy landscape that surrounds it.

I can barely breathe, and my legs are rubbed raw from the saddle. I just have to go a little farther. The gaping windows and crumbling chimneys of the old mill are already visible ahead. I rein in Ajax, his breath coming as fast and labored as my own, and slide off him, falling hard onto the ground. Scrambling to my feet, I ignore the pain radiating from my sore hips and follow the two sets of footprints that lead around the mill to the river embankment behind it. My heart is in my throat, a silent plea running over and over through my head. *Please let me be in time. Please let him be all right.*

But it's too late. Just as I'm closing my eyes and gathering my strength, the first shot rings out.

❊ 35 ❊

THE COATING OF snow that moments ago I cursed I now thank God for, as I slide down the hill faster than I could ever run. My ankle twists under me as I tumble to the bottom, but I'm up in an instant, hobbling as fast as I can. The water runs swift and icy, pounding the mill wheel round and round in a deafening roar. That's when I see them.

They must have forgone a witness, because it's just the two men, their figures slashes of black against the white landscape. John stands on the embankment, coat flapping behind him, his shirt open, oblivious to the fast-falling snow. My breath comes out in a hiss of relief, my body slumping into itself. I follow his line of sight to where Cyrus is struggling to load his pistol. John must have had the first shot, and missed.

"John!" My legs are numb, my throat hoarse as I limp with outstretched hand. The wind carries away my words. "John, please! Stop!"

The snow comes faster. Cyrus raises his gun, pointing it into the dizzying whiteness.

My heart lurches to my throat. John might have shot wide

on purpose; a gentleman never shoots to kill. But Cyrus? Cyrus is no gentleman.

My ankle is on fire and I can barely do more than hop forward a few slow, painful steps at a time. Even if I could reach John, what good would it do now? But I have to try, so I hobble as fast as I can, trying to attract his attention.

Something is wrong with Cyrus's pistol—jammed, I think—and he struggles to cock it. All that I know about duels comes from my novels, highwaymen meeting at the break of dawn with their flintlock pistols to settle debts of honor. If those stories are in any way true, then Cyrus will have to count to ten once his pistol is primed and aimed. There is a little time yet.

"John!" I ignore the pain shooting up my leg as I stagger through the snow. My feet are numb and heavy. I'm so close now that I can see his hair dark and plastered to his temple.

It isn't fair. After everything John and I have been through, do I really have to watch as he throws it all away for the sake of honor? What if Cyrus misses and it goes to John again? Will John aim straight and true this time? He could be arrested for murder. He could hang.

Finally he looks up and sees me. With a quick glance at Cyrus struggling with his pistol and then back to me, he starts running to close the small distance between us. "Lydia, my God, what are you doing here?"

I collapse in his arms in a heap of relief. I made it. I didn't have to turn myself into a yellow bird, I didn't have to mutter some arcane spell. I made it here with only the help of Joe and Ajax and my own sheer force of will.

"John, please call it off. I don't care what he does. He can publish any story he wants. Please, just call it off."

But John isn't listening to me. He's taking my hands in his own and rubbing them. "You shouldn't be out here. Your hands are frozen. How did you get here? We need to get you back home."

He scoops me up before I can utter a word of protest. And oh, how wonderful it feels to be in his arms, to know that he is safe after so much heart-pounding anxiety. "Cyrus!" he cries out over my head. "Hold your fire!"

Cyrus looks up in surprise, his pistol fumbling in his hands before he regains control of it. "Lydia?" He gapes for a moment.

But instead of lowering his pistol, he raises it, training it on John. "Put her down, Barrett! We still have unfinished business."

John's fingers tighten around me. He mutters a curse. "Don't be a fool! Would you see her hurt?"

Through the snow I can see a ripple of uncertainty move through Cyrus's body, but his pistol doesn't waver from John. "Put her down and let her see who the real man is."

"John." My voice comes out in a whimper.

Gently, he places me down, and I wince as my weight lands on the twisted ankle. He takes me by the shoulders and squares me to look at him. There are dark smudges under his eyes and I wonder what happened last night. How did it go from talking sense to Cyrus to coming out here in a snowstorm to point pistols at each other?

"I want you to go back to the edge of the woods and wait for me there. If..." His words trail off and he shakes his head. "Just, wait for me there and don't move."

It's no use. With Cyrus's pistol still trained on him, both men watch me as I hobble back to the trees.

Tears sting my eyes as I brace myself against a pine tree. Anger roils my insides. *It's not fair, it's not right.* But I'm not helpless. I may not understand the breadth of my abilities, or even how to channel them quite yet, but I know enough. I have my memories and my natural instincts, as well as what I learned in my books and from Mary Preston. But, I promise myself, this will be the last time I use them in anger.

It doesn't matter if John sees what I am now, what I can do. If he is disgusted by me, at least he will be alive and capable of such thoughts, instead of dead in a box in the ground.

I'm not cold anymore, a warming calm wrapping itself around me. Tingles run down the length of my arms to my fingers. My body vibrates. Red tints everything around me from the porcelain snow to the gray sky above.

I feel alive, at one with every snowflake that melts on my skin, every lick of wind that raises my hair off my neck. My blood runs in time with the river. My ears roar. It's all so clear now.

The darkness that has hovered at the periphery of my vision since coming to Willow Hall—the same darkness that gave me strength when I fought Tommy Bishop, the same when I almost lost control with John after Emeline drowned—I can use that. I can grasp it and mold it, make it mine to use as I see fit. The book showed me how. I feel my blood run with the power of generations of women before me, feel Emeline as if she were standing right here beside me. Mary Preston was right, it's part of me. I see my mother's kind face, remember her gentle words. *There's not one drop of evil in you, Lydia.*

It seems an eternity, but when I look up again at Cyrus, he has only just called out eight of his count to ten. I slowly raise my hand. The air around my fingers is alive, taut, like dogs at the end of their leashes awaiting the command. The sensations that I've tried to ignore, to push down inside of me for years come alive. I never knew what to do with them before, but I know now. I will not hide anymore.

My eyes bore into Cyrus as I reach deep inside myself to use every power I possess. I envision his arm twisting around, snapping, the pistol falling as his fingers stiffen. The words from the pages of my book swim through my mind. *A witch has a third eye that she may use to see the world not as it is, but as it may be. See what you want to see, bend vision to your will.* Everything stills. I focus, hard, on his arm. Far away I hear John's voice, raised in alarm as he calls my name. Cyrus counts ten.

Three things happen at once.

Cyrus lets out a piercing cry. The crack of a shot rings out through the early morning. And a force slams against my body, searing me with heat and flinging me into the snow, just as my world goes black.

I'm so cold.

It's dark when I open my heavy eyes, the only light a hazy orange glow from the dying embers of a fire. Swallowing hurts, and there's something heavy pressing down on my chest. I try to sit up, but my arms are too achy, and whatever is on me won't budge. Something wet and cold prods my face.

"Snip," I manage.

His name prompts two happy thuds of his tail. I let him give me a sloppy kiss on the chin before he tilts his head up, ears pricked at the rustle of movement in the corner.

"You're awake." Catherine appears by the bed and Snip lowers his head back down, watching her with wary eyes.

"What...what happened?" My voice comes out in a raspy whisper.

Catherine raises a brow. "What happened? You ran off to play knight in shining armor and almost got yourself killed, that's what happened."

An image flashes across my mind of Cyrus standing with his pistol outstretched. My heart tightens, more painful than the ache in my shoulder. I can barely get the question out. "John?"

She gives an impatient sigh. "Mr. Barrett is wearing out the carpet downstairs waiting to see you."

I melt back into the pillows, hot tears of relief springing to my eyes. The details don't matter. John is alive, safe.

Catherine crosses her arms. "So, you and him."

It hurts to breathe but I take long breath. "Yes, me and him."

"I suppose I should be congratulating you."

I don't say anything.

Catherine moves to the window, restless, worrying at her shawl. "It's over now, all over, isn't it? You'll be married and I'll be the spinster sister, living with Mother and Father. Who would ever have thought? It's almost funny the way things turned out." But there's no hint of humor in her voice.

I could tell her that it's a light punishment for everything she put this family through, but what's the point? If Mother or Father had cared to they might have sent her away, far away, but they turned a blind eye and so her reckless behavior went unchecked. She's lucky that she's been afforded the chance to live any sort of normal life at all. But despite it all, I can't help but feel sorry for her. Maybe it's because I'm tired of losing those close to me, or I am finally realizing just how fragile and precious life is, but it brings me no joy to see her miserable and cast down.

"I'm sorry, Catherine."

She turns back to me, her brow raised in surprise. "Sorry?"

"For everything. That we aren't friends, that you're stuck here with me when you'd rather be with—"

"Stop it. I don't want your apologies and I certainly don't want your pity. You won the day, isn't that enough?"

"I don't feel as if I've won anything." Why doesn't she know it was never a competition? I never wished bad things for her. I close my eyes, wondering yet again what drives Catherine.

All my life I've tried to understand my sister and the restless spirit and meanness inside her. But now I know, there's no use trying to understand.

She presses her lips, studying me with naked disdain and a hint of curiosity. "Well, I hope you'll be very happy," she says tightly.

The edges of the room are fuzzy, my eyes heavy. "I don't know what you want me to say."

"I don't want you to say anything. I just want..." Catherine moves toward the door, her hand at her eyes, her voice shaky. "I want what you have."

By the time I register what she means she's already out the door, and I'm too tired to call out after her.

When I awaken again John is there, sitting beside the bed, his head leaned back, dozing. His eyes flutter open, a slow smile spreading over his face. "Good morning."

"John." It's the most delicious word, warming my mouth and running through my body like a flame.

"Catherine told me you were awake and talking last night, but I didn't want to keep you from your rest."

My conversation with Catherine is fuzzy and dark, and I almost wonder if I imagined it. It feels unfinished between us. I look around the room, taking in the chrysanthemum wallpaper bathed in late morning light, the snow sparkling on the sill outside.

"How...how long have I been here?"

"A day. No, don't try to get up," he says as I struggle to my elbows.

Pain sears through my shoulder and I wince, falling back into my pillows. Fragments of memories surface again. The barrel of Cyrus's pistol aiming straight for John's heart through the swirling snow. A sickening bang cutting the air like thunder. The red, the heat, the vibration, the light. Cyrus's arm jerking to the side as he cried out in surprise. Almost simultaneously a pain like I never felt before shredding into my shoulder. And then the darkness.

"Has anyone told my mother? She'll be worrying. You have to tell her that I'm all right."

"Would you like to tell her for yourself?"

I part my lips to tell him that if I can't sit up yet, then I certainly won't be able to make my way to Mother's room. But before I can say anything, he turns in his seat, and smiles over his shoulder. I follow his line of sight and give a little gasp.

Wrapped in a shawl and very pale, Mother hovers in the doorway. It's just like that day after the pond when her disappointment was etched on her face. But now she breaks into a slow, glowing smile.

John gets up and offers her his arm, which she leans on heavily as he guides her to the bed.

"My dear, dear girl." She perches herself on the edge of the bed, the roles reversed from just days ago when I feared she would never rise again. John melts into the background as Mother puts a warm hand against my cheek. "How do you feel?"

"I'll be fine," I tell her, barely able to feel the pain in my shoulder anymore now that joy and relief are warming me from the inside. "Truly. But what about you?"

"Tired," she says. "But much, much better. Better than I've felt in a long time." And she looks it. Her dark eyes are sparkling, and the heaviness, the weariness, that she has worn like a shroud not just these past months, but these past years, has lifted. "No sooner had I been granted a second chance at life than it looked as if I might lose you." Her voice quivers as she adds, "But here you are. Didn't I say you were strong?"

We sit in silence as she strokes my cheek; we both know

that there are years of secrets and questions that will need addressing, but that now is not the time. Not with her still so weak, and me injured. Not with John standing right there.

"I'll leave you to rest now, and I'd better do the same or your father will wear me out with worrying." She looks over her shoulder to where John is waiting by the door, trying not to intrude upon our reunion. "I suppose you'll want some time," she says, turning back to me with a raised brow. "But leave the door open."

I open my mouth to assure her that nothing untoward will happen between John and me, that nothing untoward *could* happen, not while I'm barely capable of sitting up. But then I see the glimmer of amusement in her eyes, and I smile. "You don't have to worry about me."

"But I do worry about you. It's a mother's job." She brushes my temple with a kiss, and gestures to John to let him know that she's ready. With his assistance she stands, and offers me one more warm smile.

After he's brought her back to her room, John hesitantly comes to stand by the bed. "I should probably let you rest now too."

"No!" The force of my voice startles me, and John stops. "I mean, not yet. You'll stay with me?"

John sits back down and takes my hand. "I won't leave you, not if you don't want me to."

I never want him to leave, so I just press a grateful kiss onto his hand before letting go.

"Oh," he says, reaching into his pocket. "I almost forgot. The doctor gave you something to keep you asleep while he removed this." John holds up a black metal ball. "Said if it had been even a hair to the left it would have shattered your shoulder completely."

I reach out and take the bullet, marveling at the tiny thing that was almost the instrument of John's death, and shudder. "And Cyrus?"

"Gone packing back to Boston to lick his wounds. He'll stay there this time," John says with finality.

"How do you know?"

"I told him if he ever tried to interfere again I would tell everyone he shot you, and I would press charges. Besides," he adds with grim humor, "I think he was more than a little unnerved by what happened."

We fall into silence as I process this and what it means for the future. No more Cyrus, no more threats, no more looking over my shoulder. If John is unnerved himself by what happened, he doesn't say so.

"You never told me that he loved you," John says quietly.

"I didn't think it mattered. Besides," I add, hesitant, "I'm not sure I would call it love."

"He called it that. Last night, he resorted to pleading, claiming that he loved you and wouldn't let me steal you away." John takes the bullet back, rolling it between his fingers. "A man driven by greed and money is one thing. A man driven by love is another. He's willing to risk anything."

For a moment I wonder if he's talking about Cyrus or himself. "Either way, it was a stupid thing to do. Do you really think I care about honor and justice so much that I would see you maimed or even killed? What happened after you left the other day?"

"It was stupid," John agrees. He rubs his jaw, which is bristled with golden stubble, not meeting my eye. "I met Cyrus at his inn, convinced that I could reason with him. He made outlandish claims about you and your family, and told me that unless I agreed to break it off with you he would publish them."

I suck in my breath, not even daring to ask what details Cyrus might have divulged.

"It became clear that he wasn't going to listen to reason, or even to accept money, and that's when he proclaimed his love for you and suggested a duel." John gives a humorless laugh. "Never in my dreams did I imagine that I would agree to a duel, but in that moment I thought that if I gave him that much, he might be satisfied. I just... I suppose the more I saw of him, spoke to him, the more I hated him and my reason abandoned me. He spoke as if you had shared some special bond. Whether it was true or not, I was jealous."

Stunned, I search for words. "John, all I want is you."

"I want you too," he says quietly. "But I know what you would do to protect your family, and it made me sick that a man like Cyrus could hold that against you, bending you to his will."

"You thought I would marry him after all that? I promised you that I wouldn't do anything without you."

"I suppose you wouldn't believe me if I told you I was still scared of losing you." He slants a sidelong glance at me from behind shy lashes, and I curse my shoulder that I can't get up and throw my arms around him, burying my head in his neck.

He clears his throat, as if determined to change the subject. "I brought you something." He reaches into his waistcoat pocket and produces a book. "I saw you reading the second volume, and thought you might like the next one."

He watches me with apprehensive eyes as I take the book. *"Ivanhoe!"*

"You don't have it, do you? I can send it back and exchange it for something else if you—"

"I don't have the third volume, and I've been dying to read it." I lean over, ignoring the pain, and kiss his cheek. Now I can finally learn Rebecca's fate, and if she is spared the stake, absolved of the charges of witchcraft. "Thank you."

We slip into silence again, me hungrily flipping through the crisp pages, John watching me and rubbing at his jaw. "Lydia," he finally says, "what happened yesterday?"

My fingers freeze on the page. I swallow back the urge to lightly ask him what he's talking about. I have to tell him at some point, it might as well be now. Putting aside the book, I sit up as straight as I can against the pillows. "There's...there's something I have to tell you."

He casually leans back, lacing his hands across his stomach, but the intensity of his gaze is anything but casual.

I swallow again, looking everywhere around the room but at his expectant eyes. "I... I should have told you along with everything else the night you came over, but I was scared. Scared that you'd change your mind."

"Maybe you don't know me so well if you think there's anything that could make me change my mind."

I don't point out that only moments ago he confessed his fear that I would change my mind. It goes both ways, the misgivings, the fear that what we each feel isn't shared by the other. That our story might not have a happy ending.

I look down at the book in my hands, studying the pattern embossed in gold on the cover. "Yes, well, the thing is I can hardly accept it myself."

"Maybe I can help you."

"I don't think so. You see... Well, you know those stories you read, the ones about the early days in Salem and all the women who were hanged? I always thought they were lore, myths. But it turns out they're real."

John looks surprised. "The witch trials? Of course those happened. I don't understand."

I shake my head, impatient. "No, I mean the reasons for the hangings."

I can tell from his expression that I'm not making any sense. I take a deep breath but there's no way to say it without sounding insane, so I just come out with it. "I'm a witch."

I shyly raise my eyes to gauge the effect of my words. John doesn't move a muscle, just continues watching me with unnerving blankness.

"A witch," he repeats tonelessly. "I see."

"But I never use my...my powers," I hurry to explain. "Well, except for when they seem to take over on their own. The other day, the duel, that was the first time I had any control over what I was doing. My mother gave me a book that explained what I'm capable of. It made certain...episodes in my life make sense. But there's something about this place that brings them out too, I think. Though, there was that time with Cyrus too in Boston and..." I'm running my tongue in circles, losing him again with each revelation. I swallow, nervously tracing my fingers along the edge of the book. "It doesn't matter. I wish you would say something."

John rakes his hand through his hair, leans forward like he wants to say something and then leans back again. "That evening at the pond, when you screamed it was almost as if the water...?"

I nod, relieved that he's at least asking questions and not bolting for the door. "That was me. I didn't know what was happening at the time, and I still don't know exactly what I did, but yes."

Silence, and then, "I didn't realize that witches existed outside of nursery rhymes and history books."

"I didn't either."

He considers this. "Sometimes it feels as if you put some

kind of spell on me. It was so sudden. One day you weren't in my life, and the next you were all that I could think about."

My fingers grip so tight around the book that they turn white. "I would never!" My voice hitches. "John, you have to believe me, I—"

But then I see the faint smile tugging at his lips, and I let out a little breath of relief.

"Do you still want me?" I ask in a small voice, my body bracing for the truth. "I wouldn't blame you if—"

He stands up and the air goes out of me as I wait for him to take up his hat and leave. But instead of turning toward the door, John gingerly perches on the bed beside me.

Careful not to graze my shoulder, he cups my face in his lean, strong hands. "Lydia Montrose," he says, his sea-storm eyes dancing with light, "you are an exquisite little mystery and I have never wanted anything or anyone so badly in my life."

He leans down and claims my lips in a long, hot kiss that scatters the last of my doubts and fears to the four winds.

The wedding was a small, simple affair with only Mother, Father, Ada and Joe standing as witnesses. We waited until spring, so that my shoulder would have a chance to heal, and the snow melted to make our upcoming journey to our new home in Vermont easier. Catherine had said she didn't feel well and wanted to stay in bed, but just as I was leaving she caught me by the door. "You aren't really going to wear that old rag on your wedding day, are you?" she asked, perhaps thinking of her own wedding gown holding her dark secret at the bottom of the pond. My dress was the most beautiful frock I'd ever seen, all creamy lace, nipped waist and embroidered leaves around the neck. I chose the same frothy pink silk that I'd chosen for my imagined wedding that day I went shopping with Catherine for her gown. John had looked so handsome in his black cutaway coat, standing at the altar in the dappled light of the stained glass, smiling with hand outstretched to greet me. When we left the church, I looked down to see little flowers springing up in our wake, just as my mother had said they did when I was little.

The next morning, we found a note from Catherine informing us that she'd left for New York. What she means to do there, or how she plans to survive, I have no idea. Perhaps she couldn't bear the thought of staying in New Oldbury, a spinster in her own eyes. Or maybe, belatedly, she thought it was for the best after all the pain she caused Mother—though she had to know that Mother would forgive her and would want her in her life. Knowing Catherine, whatever her reasons are, she has more than enough charm and ingenuity to make a success of it. I wish her luck.

Now as I stand next to my husband by the waiting carriage in the mellow April air, it's hard to see Willow Hall as anything other than a stately country home. Only the vacant corners of my heart stand as a reminder of all that I have lost in the brief chapter of my life spent in this house.

Ada puts a tentative hand on my arm, bringing me out of my thoughts. "Do you have everything you need, miss? There's the sandwiches I made, and if you get thirsty there's—"

"We'll be fine." I smile. "Thank you, Ada."

"I know you will. But...it just won't be the same without you." Ada dips her head, trying to hide the tears rimming her big brown eyes.

My heart tugs. Ada has been with us every step of the way since Boston, weathering the worst alongside of us. On an impulse, I take her by the hands. "Come with us. Come to Vermont. It's only twenty miles away." As soon as John had showed me the little farm nestled at the foothill of the mountains, I knew it was home. Mother and Father will move into Barrett House, and Willow Hall will be torn down. Whatever ghosts still call that unhappy place home will have to do so without the stark reminder of a house that has borne witness to so much tragedy.

"Oh, miss, I couldn't possibly. Your parents need me and—"

"I need you. Mother and Father will have Joe, and any number of servants if they so choose."

Ada glances uncomfortably at the waiting carriage. "I don't know…"

"Come as my sister."

Her gaze swings back to me, eyes widening. "What?"

"You're like a sister to me. I don't want to lose you. Please, Ada. Will you come?"

Ada bites her lip and looks up at me from under her mousy lashes. "Do you really mean that?"

"I do."

Her smile broadens and she throws her knobby arms around me. "I'll have to pack. I'll have to let your father know. Will you wait for me?"

"I'll tell Father. And of course we'll wait while you pack."

She scampers off back into the house. Father is clasping John by the shoulder, making a valiant attempt to blink back tears. Mother stands beside him, diminutive as ever, but rosy and smiling.

"It's a hard blow to lose one's daughter and business partner in one fell swoop," he says.

I come up to them, slipping my arm around Father's waist. "You're not losing us. We'll be a few hours away, and you can visit us anytime." I already promised Mother that we will visit her as often as we are able; after all that we have lost, our bond and our shared memories of Emeline are too precious to let slip away. And I have a lifetime's worth of questions to ask her about our family.

"I never thought I'd see my daughter choose to live the life of a farmer, but I suppose if that's what you want..." He trails off, looking behind us at Willow Hall. "I thought this house would be my legacy, a place for my children and grandchildren to build a life."

"I know, Father." I squeeze his shoulder. "But John and I have talked about it, and a quiet farm is just what we want." John won't have to work in mills anymore, and I'll have a home among nature, a place to raise my herbs. A place far away from society and all its ugly gossip and clucking tongues. I'll study the book Mother left me, learn who I am and how to handle my powers. And if we are blessed with a child—a daughter, perhaps—I'll teach her what I know, make sure that she grows up understanding and unashamed of what she is.

"I'll take good care of her, you have my word," John says, beaming down at me.

They clasp hands. "I know you will, Barrett. I can't say I'm sorry to have you as a son either."

"The best son we could ever ask for," Mother adds, with a wistful smile.

We have some time before Ada is ready so I twine my hand into the crook of John's arm. "Will you come with me for one last thing?"

John follows my line of sight up past the house to the woods. Darkness flickers across his brow. "Are you sure?"

My hand tightens around him. "I'm sure."

We set off up the little hill with Snip blazing the way, past the summerhouse and through the still woods. How many lifetimes ago it seems that Emeline, John and I followed this very path on an oppressive summer day. Then I had longed only for him to notice me and grace me with one of his rare, beautiful smiles. Now we walk as husband and wife, as two people who have bared their souls to each other, looking into them like mirrors.

The pond sits like an expectant blue jewel, impassive and cool. John gives my hand a squeeze. "I'll be here when you're ready."

I pick my way over the rocks to the loamy shore, the only sounds a gentle breeze rustling through the leaves and the long, content call of a mourning dove.

You took my sister, my secret and nearly my life, I think as I look out over the placid water. *But whatever you are, you also gave me a gift, whether you meant to or not. You gave me strength, the will to face what I am.*

A water bug skates across the surface, tiny rings rippling in his wake. Otherwise the water is still and silent. No shadow creeps at the edge of my mind today, no dark fingers worming their way into my deepest thoughts.

I reach behind my neck and fumble to remove my locket. The tiny braid of Emeline's auburn hair catches the late afternoon sunlight. How I would love to hold it every day, to never let this last memento go. But no trinket can replace the love I hold for her in my heart, and as long as Emeline is not at rest, neither can I be. I touch a kiss of farewell to the warm metal, focus my intentions and then toss it out in the water.

I linger a moment longer before turning to leave, when a movement out of the corner of my eye stops me.

Standing under the willow tree, just like that hot summer day looking for mermaids, Emeline watches me. Her dress is fresh and crisp, white as a snowdrop, her auburn hair glossy in the perfect ringlets I used to do for her. I raise my hand, half a wave, half a silent plea to reach out and make her stay. Raising her hand in turn, she hovers for a moment, like a hummingbird in flight, and then just as suddenly as she appeared, she's gone.

"Rest in peace, my love," I whisper into the sweet spring air, blinking back a tear.

The water shimmers in the evening sun, pollen hanging lazily in the low shafts of dappled light. John waits, hands in pockets looking out past me to the pond. He's as still as a statue, the wind tousling his golden hair, and my heart swells. I give him another minute to bid farewell to his own ghosts before rejoining him at his side.

"I'm ready."

Hand in hand we leave the dusky woods, walking back together to Willow Hall and the future that lies beyond.

★ ★ ★ ★ ★

Acknowledgments

MY HEARTFELT GRATITUDE to the amazing team at Graydon House, who worked so hard to make my story into a real book, complete with gorgeous cover and design. So much care and work went on behind the scenes, and I'm grateful to each and every person who was part of the process.

My editor extraordinaire, Brittany Lavery, who expertly and patiently guided me through a new process, and whose enthusiasm for my story and willingness to take a chance on me has meant everything.

The entire team at HQ for all their hard work and an equally stunning cover. Special thanks to Sarah Goodey for bringing my book to the UK and for her enthusiastic support.

I am incredibly humbled and fortunate to have such a strong advocate in Jane Dystel, who has believed in me and worked tirelessly on my behalf from the start. Miriam Goderich for her interest in my early manuscript and her continued support and work on my behalf. My thanks also go out to Amy Bishop and the rest of the team at DG&B.

Trish Knox, my outstanding critique partner and valued friend, who provided feedback and encouragement, without either of which this book certainly never would have been finished.

E. B. Wheeler, for her early reading and constructive feedback through Pitch Wars.

Jason Huebinger, for creating and running #PitDark, through which I connected with my agent.

In creating the fictional New Oldbury and Willow Hall, I relied heavily on the resources provided by Historic New England, both in print and from their historic properties. In particular, I am grateful to the wonderful guide who patiently answered my questions and led me through Barrett House, the historic home on which Willow Hall is modeled.

My friends, family, the Twitter writing community, and all my other cheerleaders. It's much appreciated.

Finally, Mike, for his unfailing support, enthusiasm and encouragement. And for all the latte runs.